I0694727

2023 Rude Jester Media Paperback Edition

ISBN 979-8-9883533-1-7
Ebook ISBN 979-8-9883533-0-0

Printed in the United States of America

SIGIL
A CYBERPUNK THRILLER

"Your leaders care more for a little piece of paper with a dead man's

head on it than your life."

~BLACKHAWK

C H A P T E R   Z E R O

Into The Storm

Death was an android, crouching in the dark, and its name was Athon.

It waited patiently, silently, and remorselessly for what was to come. *10:32, 37 seconds*, it recited in its artificial mind a time that had not yet passed. It looked human enough, although it was covered head to toe. Clad in all black carbon fiber and graphene-woven armor with a full face mask created solely for its wearer, Athon checked its watch—a timepiece that not only kept track of the seconds and milliseconds that passed, but housed the power of a star in its two inch wide framework—all strapped to the wrist of an instrument of war.

*10:29. 12, 13, 14…*Athon counted the seconds up as the watch's outer ring pulsated smoothly with a deep, sunny orange light. The ground shook, but Athon's stance did not waver. It stayed crouched, hidden in the blackness; a homicidal stowaway.

A Gulfstream 650, the private jetliner of Oklahoma billionaire oilman Grady Holtman, sliced through the night sky above a blanket of storm clouds that housed a furious concentration of lightning. The pilot had hoped to avoid turbulence by flying over the storm, but when flying so close, it was hard to avoid danger's cold touch.

"What the fuck is going on up there?" Grady, dressed in a three piece suit and tie, yelled up to the pilot. "I thought you said no fuckin' turbulence! Just spilled my goddamn drink!"

"Would you like another Manhattan, Mr. Holtman?" His personal assistant, the prettiest, sapphire-eyed blonde he could find, asked, as she bent over with straightened bare legs to pick up his martini glass and wipe up the whiskey and vermouth. The cherry was still inside the glass. She pulled it out, looked Grady in the eye, slid the cherry into her mouth, and slowly bit down, forcing it to crush and explode inside her mouth. It seemed Grady had hired as much of an escort as he had an assistant.

"Nah, I'm good. Maybe later." He replied, gawking at her legs that ran up and into a short miniskirt. She stood straight, holding the glass and turned away, poking her ass out. She knew what she was doing. It was exactly what Mr. Holtman liked.

"Yes sir." She strutted away toward the back of the cabin. Grady's business partner and fellow billionaire, Quasim Zaryab, a Saudi prince and ultimately, source of Grady's vast wealth, leaned over to him from across the aisle. "You should branch out, Grady. The world is not only blondes with blue eyes." He spoke in a sharp and expectable Middle Eastern accent. "Dua Lipa."

"Dua What?" Grady asked.

"Hah!" Quasim pointed a finger in the air. "Dua Lipa. I will meet her. Look." He pulled out his cell phone and typed into the search engine. He played a YouTube video for the pop sensation's single, *Don't Start Now*, and stuck his phone in Grady's face.

"She's blonde too." Grady remarked, as the video played.

"Ah, yes, but she recently changed her look. I am not sure why. She is perfect with her natural color."

Grady closed his eyes to signal his disinterest in the pop star. Quasim continued.

"She is from Albania. Albanian women are some of the most beautiful women in the world—"

"Quasim…" Grady interrupted. "I don't care. I got one type. Blonde. Blue eyes. Long legs. American. Does what she's told."

Quasim sat back in his seat. "Hmm. Perhaps you have only this type because you shut your mind away from the world, ah?"

"No, it's because blonde hair, blue eyes are the sexiest. Not your Albanian whatever the fuck."

Quasim allowed Grady to think incorrectly. "To each, their own. Is that the saying?"

Quasim routinely attempted to show Grady a way around his close-minded behavior. He may've been filthy rich, but he wasn't inherently bad. Regardless, he was about to become collateral damage, same as everyone else on the plane whose name wasn't Grady Holtman.

In the cockpit, a single pilot operated the yoke. It was a short flight, so there was no need for his usual co-pilot in the empty seat beside him. A thick leather curtain was pulled closed a couple feet behind him, giving him a little privacy as he chauffeured his boss through the night at over four hundred miles per hour. His comms headset didn't afford him the luxury of hearing what was happening on the floor behind him.

A white-hot metal blade slowly pierced through the black diamond plated aluminum and extended upward of about a foot. The aluminum may as well have been butter; it provided no resistance to the heated blade cutting through it. The blade began to make a large curve cut, and made its way around to form a circle. The cut out section dropped away slowly.

The masked, android assassin slowly stood until erect. It had been hiding in the wheel well directly under the cockpit. The katana it had used to slice into the plane's cabin was so hot it warmed the cockpit and illuminated it enough for the pilot to notice. He turned toward the source of the heat, and before he could react, the blade cleaved his head off above the mouth.

Blood and brain matter peppered the window and instrument panel, sizzling as the heat from the sword dissipated.

Grady's blonde-haired assistant scrunched her nose and sniffed. Something was burning. She was on the other side of the curtain and quickly opened it to see if there was any danger. There was indeed danger.

She was snatched inside before she saw what was sprawled all over the cockpit. It was the end for her as well.

Grady had two armed guards with him. He'd made enough enemies through his ruthless business strategies that he felt he needed them, although no one had ever made an attempt on his life. One guard was reading a motorcycle magazine. The other had been eating a bit of falafel he'd grabbed when they'd picked Quasim up at the UAB. He was the one who noticed Grady's assistant pulled into the cockpit. *Could have been the pilot*, he thought, *but should check anyway*.

He stood and made his way up to the curtain. When he got close, the cream-colored carpet slowly staining blood red told him this was a very bad situation.

He pulled his pistol from inside his suit jacket. He'd been trained by the military but had perfected his skills as a mercenary in Afghanistan, which led him to becoming a personal bodyguard. None of that mattered now. He'd spent his life transforming himself into a man of reserved violence just to come to this moment.

Athon sliced its katana down into the guard's wrist, severing his hand. His finger hitched, and still pulled the trigger. The single shot got the attention of everyone else.

Athon burst out from behind the curtain and sprinted toward the next threat: the magazine reading guard. He was cut right through the belly and up to his shoulder before he could get up straight. Blood sprayed all over the cabin as he twirled around, following the android as it never lost its stride.

Athon launched into the air with one leg, straight toward the remaining gunmen: Quasim's royal guard.

Athon disappeared into thin air and before anyone could react, the android reappeared right in front of them, still in mid jump; Its katana chopped off one of their heads. Athon landed, light on its feet and spun around. The guard beside that one jumped back in an attempted escape, and fired his pistol toward Athon. He tripped over his own feet and missed. Athon warped over beside him before he could hit the ground and cut his gun hand off, immediately following with a stab down into his face. The thrust was so hard the blade lodged into the flooring. His head slid down the blade slowly.

Athon looked to the final guard, who was firing as fast as he could, emptying his magazine into the assassin's direction.

With another reality bending warp in and out of sight, Athon was behind the guard. It brought a knee up to his back at wind-ripping speed. The sound of bones crunching into spinal tissue was the least of his worry. His neck was broken just after by a lightning-fast elbow. He crumpled to the floor—bones cracking the whole way down.

Grady and Quasim were the only ones left. Every muscle they both had was tensed up and locked; their bodies frozen in shock as this cybernetic ninja had just cut down the most highly trained men they could find.

Athon stepped back over to the previous guard, jerked its sword from the floor and corpse's head, and looked to Grady—then to the orange pulsing watch device on its wrist. *10:32, 34, 35…*

Grady had been so surprised he had forgotten he had a gun himself.

He plunged a hand into his briefcase and pulled a huge chrome bull revolver out and started firing before he got the pistol up to Athon's direction. One round exploded the seat in front of him. Foam and leather strips peppered the air. He got off a good shot; one bullet that screamed directly to his attacker's head.

Athon spun to its left and with an impossibly graceful flick of its sword, caught the speeding .454 round on the tip of the blade, twirled its body, rotated the sword and redirected the bullet right back at the oilman almost at the same speed it was fired. His head popped like a cantaloupe, showering Quasim in crimson viscera. He had nothing to say. He hadn't let out a breath since that first gun shot. Shock was a hell of a thing.

Athon snatched its hand into a fist. The watch on its wrist's hue changed from orange to blue and a portal blasted open behind it, creating a crack of thunder inside the plane along with a reversed gravity pulse that knocked back the bodies and debris around it. Athon jumped backward into the ring of blue flame and sparks as the force emanating from it began to tear into the hull of the plane.

***

Athon dropped through the other side of the portal and landed on a grated metal platform. It stood straight, brandishing the katana and mocking Quasim on the other side of the fiery window, who still hadn't accepted his fate. He hadn't even processed what *was* happening, let alone what *had* happened.

The portal ripped the plane in half and it all fell out of the sky in formation, down into the lightning filled clouds below. The portal closed. The job was done. Athon pressed a small switch on the katana just above the handle, and it spewed steam all around its wielder as it rapidly cooled off, shedding the residual blood as well.

Athon turned and left the cloud of steam where the portal had been and walked off the platform that supported an arch with energy capacitors every two feet—around 20 of them in total—that all pulsed with the same blue aura as Athon's watch. The capacitors' light slowly faded but never completely went dark. This was the portal gate that allowed Athon to travel through space and time at an instant; and it was directly linked to the pulsating watch on the android's wrist.

Athon slowly walked toward its creator: a massive machine the size of a large SUV, suspended from the ceiling of the chamber they were in. It was enclosed in thick plating—possibly armor—that separated at the middle to open. Thick tubing containing data transfer wirings that were so large one could walk inside them, cascaded down from the ceiling and into the machine on four corners. When the plating pulled away, Athon could see the familiar workings inside.

An intricate and chaotic mixture of red, blue and white wires, circuitry, and gold wrapped around each other, structured by thick copper rods that resembled a brain. The massive spherical shaped "head" of the machine descended and came to a rest around ten feet in front of Athon.

This was the world's very first quantum computer, and it had a singular purpose: protect the masters.

"NEXT TARGET: HAZUKIRO OKADA." The machine spoke through loudspeakers in a deep and digitized, booming voice.

Athon nodded as the image of Okada displayed on the interior of its visor.

"EXIT LOOP: 01:27:12. COORDINATES: 35.68945° NORTH, 139.68693° EAST." The arch behind Athon whirred as it powered back up and the capacitors' blue glow brightened. The android's watch turned from blue to orange again, indicating an open time gateway. Another portal began to open in the center of the circle and extended until it almost touched the inside ring of the gate itself. On the other side: Tokyo. A large, red neon sign in Japanese lettering sat at the end of the rooftop the portal just opened on. Athon, equipped with a language decoder chip, could read the sign, but that was unimportant.

It stepped through and the portal closed with a shrill hiss, as if air was squeezed through a tiny opening. A section of the floor directly under the massive machine lifted and opened. Super-cooled air crawled out into the warmth of the chamber. A small vial of a thick, black liquid rose up from the freezing, open hole in the ground, held in place by a rubbery clamp. A hefty, snake-like arm composed of pneumatic muscles wormed its way down to the vial.

BOOM! A deafening explosion came from across the room. Concrete and dust peppered the walls of the chamber and the machine as fire enveloped a large portion of the room but dissipated quickly. The machine closed its armored plating to protect itself and began to lower the vial of liquid into the ground, but the mechanism was quite slow.

Armed gunmen and women—maybe a dozen or so—poured through a smoldering hole that had been blown into the chamber. One went straight for the liquid, while the others cleared the room, aiming high and low with rifles and pistols.

Behind them, as the smoke and dust settled, stepped in Blackhawk, dressed in a leather trench coat and cowboy hat with aviator sunglasses. It was too dark in the room for those, but he didn't care. He had a steel revolver holstered at his side that rubbed on his leg, chafing his jeans so much that his metallic, cybernetic thigh showed through.

"Now, when we told you to do your thing..." Blackhawk spoke in a Southern accent. "We did not mean *try your hardest to cause the end of the world.*"

One of his henchmen grabbed the vial of black liquid just before the floor could close it off.

"*TO PROTECT, I MUST DESTROY.*" The machine replied.

"Destroy what?" A new voice rang out from behind Blackhawk. His friend, Ramsay. He stepped in wearing a motorcycle jacket and boots, but was unarmed. "Destroying the world isn't protecting us, dude!"

"*DESTROY THE SINS OF THE PAST.*"

"Ramsay, I'm ready to blow this bucket o' bolts the fuck up." Blackhawk looked to his friend.

Ramsay was shaking his head in disagreement. "No, we need it to run the infrastructure for the city. I'll shut it down. Mostly."

Blackhawk looked at the arch gate.

"Is this it?" He asked the machine. "Wormhole generator? Where's that android you been sending through it?" Blackhawk narrowed his eyes and surveyed each dark corner of the chamber he could find.

The machine had no choice but to reply. *"TOKYO. 1998."*

"Oh, *shit*! What is that, over 25 years? And it'll just come back through this, huh?"

Blackhawk signaled all his platoon to train their weapons on the wormhole generator.

"Well I guess we're waiting for that to happen now."

He didn't have to wait long. A portal burst open at the gate, knocking some of the men back a step. Athon came through, leaving a sea of sliced up and mangled bodies of Yakuza gangsters behind.

Every soldier opened fire on Athon, but they hadn't expected the android to warp out of harm's way. No one ever did.

Athon jumped left and right, up and down, in and out of view as it gutted and disarmed—literally—every threat in the room through a hail of gunfire and muzzle flashes that brightened the room enough that Backhawk's aviators actually served a purpose. Within seconds, Athon had obliterated the entire platoon. It warped over to Blackhawk, who was drawing his pistol, but neither would get the chance to attack.

The machine burst open another portal at the wormhole generator, wrapped its snake-arm around Athon's leg, and hurled it into the portal, which immediately closed.

Blackhawk had his pistol out and trained on the archway, but lowered his weapon when he realized Athon was gone again.

"Where'd you send it!?" Blackhawk yelled at the machine.

"I DO NOT KNOW."

The machine wasn't lying. It was not allowed to lie to the masters. Ramsay had been hiding behind the concrete wall. He wasn't stupid enough to take on a cyborg, time-hopping ninja. He walked along the newly formed carpet of bone, flesh, blood and entrails, courtesy of Athon, searching for the black vial, which was what they'd come for.

"There we go." He jumped in excitement and bent over to pick up the bloodied glass tube of liquid. Grimacing at the thick blood spattered across the cylinder, he held it up to eye level and pointed it toward the machine.

"So…" Ramsay looked past the vial and directly to the sentient computer. "What's this black goop for?"

***

Athon erupted through the portal as normal as ever, but when it thought there would be ground, it was mistaken. Its feet caught nothing but air. It looked down only to see the ground below speeding upward. It must have been a few hundred feet by the time the android noticed it was falling toward the Earth, completely oblivious to its whereabouts. There was a city nearby; a few tall buildings but nothing it considered to be a skyscraper. Regardless, it did not have time to form a plan; not that one would have helped anyway.

It could have used the wrist mounted device to warp, but that wouldn't change the fact that it was still rocketing toward the Earth. A warp didn't affect inertia. It would still crash.

Athon slammed into the dusty Earth with the force of a high speed train wreck, and was never heard of again.

CHAPTER ONE

Abduction

"How much money did you make playing that thing?" Deli, an African-American woman in her 50s, dressed in dingy sweatpants, torn at both knees, rubber rain boots and 2 jackets, trudged along the sidewalk with a bad left knee that caused a slight limp.

"Uh, hold on." Leyla, a young woman in her mid-20s, opened up the faded velvet Crown Royal bag she kept cash and change in and pulled out the crumpled, hastily folded one dollar bills inside. She counted quickly. "Seven dollars. With the change, maybe nine."

Leyla had a discarded off-brand acoustic guitar slung over her back with a strap made out of shoestring. There was a hole punched into the wood on the side, but it still sounded decent, even if it was missing the high E string. That was Leyla's favorite string. It broke the week before. The bigger issue was the fretboard being so old it had cracked in several places, which affected the sound the most. But she'd still been able to panhandle a few dollars a day playing it on the corner of Walnut and Sixth streets. She wasn't very good, she thought. In her mind, every cent she'd made was a "pity" penny.

She was also wrapped in similar ragged clothing to Deli, except she had a bleach spotted brown hoodie on. She'd pulled the hood down and off her head. It was May now and in Cincinnati it was quite a nice temperature but the nights could still be brutal with the right conditions. That's just the way of the Midwest.

Deli scoffed at the dollar amount Leyla had guessed. "That ain't even enough for two slices at Sal's. I'm hungry, shit. And I ain't eatin' outta no damn dumpster today. It's my birthday."

"It was your birthday last month."

"Baby girl, when you get to my age, your birthday is whenever the hell you want it to be, and ain't nobody gonna tell you different."

Leyla thought for a second, following half a step behind Deli. "We could do Heart or Dick."

"Oh, okay girl, see I like the way you think." Deli turned back to Leyla, smiling as wide as she could.

Heart or dick worked most of the time, but they could only try it once in a while and never at the same place twice.

"But you doin' dick. I don't feel like crawlin' all over the damn sidewalk today. It's hot. And it's my birthday."

"Dick didn't even work last time!"

"That's cause you tried it at the one Stop & Go in Cincinnati that had a gay man behind the register, with yo oblivious ass!"

"Oh! Oh ok that explains the tight pants."

"Straight men can wear tight pants too. And shit I be lookin' like a mother fucker. I don't give a damn if he gay or not. Boy got a nice booty."

Leyla laughed. Deli never gave a shit about tradition or norms. It was endearing and oftentimes hilarious.

"He did give me the food though." Leyla replied.

"That's cause gay men are nice as fuck! But I ain't walkin' all the way uptown to get a slice of gas station pizza from Petey. We gettin Sal's today."

"Ok, since it's your birthday. Do I look good enough today to do dick?"

Leyla had dark brown, wavy hair that always looked as if it was sprayed with sea salt and eternally honey tanned skin. Her lips were puffy enough to show her youth and her front teeth would show if she opened her mouth slightly. She didn't like her teeth but Deli said it was cute. Her most striking feature was her eyes: brown until the sunlight hit them. One could then appreciate the light green-hazel shine they emitted.

Leyla knew when she had to play "Dick" she needed to turn toward the sunlight to use her eyes as much as possible.

Heart or Dick, by the way, was a clever ruse she and Deli would pull off when they didn't have enough cash for something. They were homeless, but they weren't stupid. They'd take turns in roles. Leyla was the younger and traditionally pretty girl, so she played dick. This meant she would try her best to seduce their mark and distract them while Deli snuck some items into her jacket. Heart was Deli's job, if called for. She would feign a heart attack and gain the attention of damn near everyone with her theatrics. She knew how to do it well; she'd actually had one before.

Deli stopped walking and turned to Leyla. "Here lemme fix ya hair." Deli pulled Leyla's hair back and up into a bun and left a few strands on each side hanging just over her eyes. She used a twist tie she'd saved to keep Leyla's hair up.

"You're pretty enough for it every day." Deli assured her. "Take ya jacket off. Show them little boobies."

"It's a hoodie." Leyla replied, pulling the hoodie over her head and handing it over to Del.

"Same thing. And baby girl, don't do the sexy eyes. That shit don't work. You look like a drunk fish."

"I know, cuz I'm a sexy shark." Leyla replied, baring her teeth and making claws with her hands.

"And now you look like a bear gettin' tazed by a cop. Get yo little ass in there and distract that man. I'll be waitin'. If it ain't workin', you know what to do."

***

Leyla rested her guitar against the outside wall and entered the pizza place Del stopped at. They'd never been to this one. The good thing was, there was a man leaning behind the counter, maybe 40, wearing a red polo and unkempt scruff for facial hair. Most likely not gay, Leyla hoped. He'd probably be better groomed if so.

"Welcome to Sal's. Whatcha want?" The man greeted her in a strikingly monotone voice that could only mean he'd said that phrase twenty thousand times that week.

Leyla slinked toward the counter and locked eyes with the middle aged man, who stood upright upon realizing a much younger minx was walking up to him like Catwoman.

"Mmmm I think there's plenty in here to want." Leyla slid up to the counter and bowed forward, puffing her chest out.

Of course, the man stared right where she wanted him to, and then back up to her. She cocked her head slowly to the right and her eyes found that sunlight pouring in from the window. Deli entered the restaurant but the man didn't even notice.

"Um, we got uh, fresh cheese coming in…"

"Mmmm coming…" Leyla interrupted and grinned.

Deli realized the man was falling for the "dick" play, and dropped her head a little to sneak around the tables and to the other end of the counter. She looked over to Leyla, who was undoubtedly about to do sexy eyes.

"Don't you fuckin' do sexy eyes. I told you don't do sexy eyes." Deli mumbled to herself.

The man leaned in closer to Leyla. She could have had him jump off a cliff at that moment. What a weakling. Leyla tucked her chin in and let her eyelids draw down, half covering her eyes.

"Goddammit woman, you doin' sexy eyes." Deli mumbled to herself again, but she was screaming inside. Sexy eyes never worked.

The man drew back a little. "Do you want pizza or what?"

"I'll go for the *what*." Leyla replied, and locked in those damn sexy eyes. Drunken fish, all the way. At least she committed to it. Deli backed out from behind the counter. This has happened before.

"Are you okay, ma'am?" The man asked Leyla. "Your eyes are twitching."

Leyla didn't reply. Her eyes really were twitching. Deli had told her she had absence seizures. She would zone out and come back to reality in a few seconds. For some reason, the sexy eyes triggered it this time. Either that, or the anxiety of having to seduce some ugly, pathetic dumbass.

"Ma'am?" the man straightened up, sensing something was wrong.

Deli did the only thing she could do.

"Oh!" She yelled and grabbed her chest, acting out in pain. "My chest! My heart!"

The man finally broke his attention on Leyla to see who was yelling.

"I'm having a heart attack!" Deli yelled. She was even changing her dialect to a U.K. accent. She may or may not have done theater when she was younger. "Young man! Help me!" She beckoned to the man and walked backward over behind a table and dropped to a knee.

The man left the counter and got to Deli as fast as he could. Leyla finally came back from her seizure and noticed the man was gone.

"Ah shit." She said to herself. Now it was her job to sneak some pizza out of there.

"Don't call 911 yet! I'm scared of paramedics!" Deli told the man. "And I may perish before they arrive!"

Leyla laughed at the show Deli was putting on. That man was definitely occupied now. She rolled over the counter and got to the pizza boxes that had been pre-assembled. She grabbed the smaller one because it would fit under her hoodie. Except, she'd removed her hoodie. Now she'd have to just grab and run. Deli would be smart enough to find her later.

In that case, why not grab the big box? She asked herself.

She slid a large box off the top of a stack and opened the back of the display where the warm pizza was, catching that all too perfect aroma of sauce, cheese, and garlic bread immediately. It almost distracted her. But it was go time. It was pizza time. She stuffed as many slices as she could into the box; more than a single pizza. She may have fit two entire pies inside the flimsy cardboard.

Deli was doing her job very well. "Young man!" Deli grabbed the man's shoulder. "If I die today, just know…" She grasped her chest and gritted her teeth. "Know that…" Deli didn't know what point she was trying to make. She was out of ideas. But Leyla had filled up a box with pizza and was making her way past the fridge that stored all the sodas and bottled water for purchase.

The man turned to look back to the counter, but Deli grabbed his cheeks and pulled him back to her.

"You dare look away when a dying woman is telling you her last wish?" Deli growled at him. Damn, she was good.

Leyla knew she couldn't carry more than she had. But a cold Coke and a Sprite for Deli would just be too perfect. She awkwardly opened the fridge door, still holding the pizza box, which was now beginning to buckle under the weight of the pies inside. She managed to get it open and pulled out as many bottles of soda as she could. The Coke went to her left pants pocket. Sprite went to the right.

She still had an open armpit, so she stuffed a Coke in there and grabbed a bottle of water. She finally let the fridge door close and made her way to the door, being careful to not drop anything.

"My last wish is that…" Deli told the man, but he looked away again, this time catching Leyla stealing half his stock - and halfway out the door.

"Hey! What the fuck are you doing?" The man leapt up away from Deli and sprinted toward Leyla. She almost turned to run but she would drop everything. She pulled the Coke from her left pocket and vigorously shook it and slammed it against the wall. Fizzy soda sprayed *everywhere*. She threw it at the man like a carbonated grenade. Coke made its way into both of his eyes. Temporarily blinded, he ran right into a chair; the back corner of it nearly crushing his manhood. He yelped and collapsed to the floor, clutching what he believed to be the worst pain imaginable.

Deli couldn't help but be amused. *A Coke grenade? Damn Leyla, you crazy*, she thought. Leyla had already made it out of the door to safety.

The man attempted to get to his feet but he could feel a devastating rush of nausea coming. Deli walked up and patted him on the back.

"Least it ain't a heart attack." she scoffed, and walked out the door as well, picking up Leyla's guitar and leaving the man confused, broken, and with around forty bucks in lost product.

***

Deli and Leyla made their way over to their home a few blocks away. They'd chowed down on pizza along the way, and Deli had gulped down her Sprite before even taking a bite.

Their home was a village of tents and makeshift shacks under a freeway bridge. They had separate tents but they were right beside each other.

Deli had occupied a space beside a light pole that luxuriously had an outlet attached, so Leyla could charge the cell phone she'd found a while back; although it wasn't much use when they were there. There was no WiFi.

Deli and Leyla slumped down into their folding chairs outside their tents, exhausted but with full bellies.

"You know, this is the 16th winter I've survived out here. Ever since 2019." Deli said, reaching into her thick jacket and pulling out a well used zip-lock bag full of various items like a half used toothpaste tube and a toothbrush that's missing bristles and broken in half. There was a very old wallet sized picture tucked inside as well, but the faces are too scratched, faded, and abraded to distinguish.

"I don't know if that's sad or triumphant." Deli pointed up to the concrete freeway sprawling over her head. "Thousand people a day drive over us. Shit. Probably ten thousand. They don't give a shit if we're alive or dead or ghosts or werewolves. Damn zombie apocalypse could start right here under Fort Washington Way and the city officials would bring out a fire hose and shoo us away. Know why they keep us here? It ain't cuz they can't get rid of us. It's cuz it makes them feel better. Makes them feel better cuz they up there, and we down here. They got a home. We got a tent. They got heaters. We got one fire barrel. ONE. And they made that shit illegal too! Can't light a fire on city property. Aight, fine then. Take us to jail! Give us some food! Give us a bed! Won't even do that. Had a cop come through one night and just straight up pour flour on the fire and walk away without a word. Damn sociopaths."

"And damn, babe..." Deli finally looked over at Leyla, who was still munching on a cooled slice of pizza. "How long you been here again?"

"Uh, I think three years. Maybe. Little fuzzy."

"Yeah, least three. I remember you showed up here after all that COVID shit. They had nurses come through in vans and hand out masks. MASKS! Hey, we know you don't even have a home, or a bed, or food, but here honey *here's a mask*. Don't spread corona! K thank you bye."

Deli immediately burst out in laughter straight from the belly, loud enough to startle Jesus two tents down. Jesus wasn't the son of God. Jesus wasn't even Jewish or Hispanic.

Jesus was a skinny, balding Korean man in a yellow pleather jacket with black stripes on the arms. Yes, like Bruce Lee's famous costume, as stereotypical as it was. Jesus was always wearing wired headphones that were never plugged in to anything except his left pants pocket, but Jesus was always listening to music in his head—and nothing could distract Jesus from his head music—except Deli's laugh; because as much as he liked Deli, he could not *stand* Deli's gutteral laugh.

"DELI! Shut the fuck up Deli! Loud ass laugh!" Jesus immediately followed up with a mocking *HO HO HO HO.*

"Man shut the fuck up Jesus!" Deli paused, then laughed even harder, grabbing Leyla's shoulder. "Shit..." Deli did a Catholic crucifix motion over her chest. "I just told Jesus to shut the fuck up."

And then Deli laughed *even* harder, enough to cease emitting sound, and could only gasp for air here and there.

Leyla, laughing as well, jumped into the newly started conversation. "Why do they call you Jesus anyway?"

"Fuck if I know." Jesus shrugged and held his palms up to the air. "I'm Korean I keep telling you fuckers my name is Ken."

On that, Deli's laugh evolved into a snot-nosed cackle. "Ken!!! Where the fuck Barbie at?!"

Leyla absolutely lost it, rolling to her back in side splitting laughter. Jesus had no comeback.

He just nodded in acceptance of defeat. "Okay that's a good one."

Deli fought through the laughter and helped pull Leyla back up. "Leyla, girl, I been meaning to ask you. Why you here?"

"What do you mean?"

"Like, *here*." Deli motioned to the tents and other denizens of the homeless village. "You still got your youth. Hell you still got your looks. You ain't aged one damn day since you been here. Still lookin' like a baby."

Leyla had drifted off, staring into space. Deli waved her hand and snapped her fingers in Leyla's face, but got no response, so she politely waited. Another absence seizure.

Close to 10 seconds passed and Leyla automatically responded.

"I don't know. I like it here."

"Oh, you back?" Deli said.

"Back from where?"

"Absence seizure. You had one again." Deli explained.

"Oh damn. Getting those more lately. Sorry, Del." Leyla said, as she pulled another slice of pepperoni pizza from the box.

"You *still* hungry after all that? Yo skinny ass ate a whole pie already."

"Iths good!" Leyla replied with a mouth full of bread and cheese. "Bethides, a had tha thoo dthick. I thetherve thith."

Deli broke into laughter. "What in the fuck are you *thaying*? Mike Tyson ass."

"Who's Mike Thython?" Leyla slurred again, prompting a harder laugh from Del.

Leyla chewed and washed down the pizza with the last swig of Coke in the bottle. "I had to work my ass and tits for this! I deserve it. I'm eating it."

"It's OK baby girl, you do deserve it. You deserve a lot more. Get the fuck outta here. You mean to tell me you like it here with Korean Jesus and Mayor Coleman?"

Coleman got his nickname from his Coleman four man tent. It had no holes and was the largest tent in the village, and he declared himself Mayor the previous Spring.

"You know nobody tried to run for Mayor against him yet? Deli pointed to Coleman.

"Well yeah, he used to be a cage fighter, right?" Leyla responded. "No one wants to take him on."

"Shit I could probably fell that boy with one good fart."

Leyla, again, fell back to her back, cackling at Deli's remark, and was interrupted by Korean Jesus's voice from two tents down.

"Why they call you Deli?" Jesus had a half-baked comeback, albeit a late one.

"Fuck if I know! I keep telling y'all my name is Aladdin!" Jesus began to respond, but left his mouth agape. He had no retort again, outsmarted as always by Deli.

Leyla and Deli both ring out with a laughter speckled melody of *A Whole New World* in unison.

"Okay, okay okay okay. Shit..." Deli heaved out some words through her laughs, tears running from her eyes. "We gotta stop; my sides hurt. We gotta stop, baby girl." Deli inhaled and slowly exhaled as much as she could but the laughter took over again. "Dammit!" Deli yelled, making Leyla laugh even more, gasping for air as well.

It was a good five minutes before they were both able to breathe normally. "Ahhhh that was a good one. Good laugh." Leyla remarked, lying on her back and catching her breath.

She and Deli laid in silence for a moment, gaining their composure.

"No really though." Deli continued her previous inquiry. "Do you really like this? You like this life?"

"Don't have much of a choice."

"I suppose you right. You going back to the subway again today? You know they ain't shit there for you." Deli asked, leaning on one arm toward Leyla. Leyla's brow curled slightly, echoing the turmoil in her mind at response to the question. There was nothing. No memories floating around. No pictures. No dreams. Just a dark abyss, that she'd stumbled through and out the abandoned subway a couple miles down the road a few years earlier.

"I'll find something eventually."

"Mmmhmmm. You gon' find a damn serial killer or somethin; you keep pokin' your head around that place."

"Well what do you expect? I've been here three years and that's the first thing I remember. Then I ended up here. If I'm ever going to figure out who I am, I'll find something there."

"You hit your head in an abandoned subway and wake up, and walk to a homeless village in Cincinnati? That's a little cray cray. How'd you know your name if you didn't remember nothin'?"

Leyla shrugs. "Honestly, it was the first name that popped in my head so I figured that was it."

"Girl lemme tell you somethin'. This ain't a life people just 'go with'. Things happen in life that lead you to this. Drugs, husbands, shitty family, abuse. Like me, you know? All that all at once. Get fuckin' cancer, can't pay bills, lose ya business, hooked on drugs, lose ya family, lose ya house, live under a bridge. I'm a troll. I'm Shrek."

"What's a Shrek?" Leyla, clueless, is seriously asking.

"How you be on that phone for an hour a day and not know what Shrek is?" Del was referring to the old smartphone with a cracked screen that Leyla had found in a garbage can. It still worked, and she would connect the wifi to hotspots and watch Youtube sometimes.

Leyla stared back at Deli, thought for a moment, and shrugged negatively.

"No, I'm serious girl. I think you got animesia. And it's why you got them seizures."

"Hold on, did you say *animesia*?"

"Yeah, animesia."

"Amnesia."

"You knew what I meant." Deli laughs.

"Yeah I did." Leyla was laughing as well, but was perturbed by the fact that she couldn't remember her life before 2032. Her eyes darted back and forth, searching for memories forgotten.

***

Leyla walked alone along the Central Parkway later in the day. It wasn't too far a walk from the tent village she'd lived in for almost three years to get to her destination: the now legendary entrance to the abandoned Cincinnati subway. Leyla spotted the distinct block of concrete jutting out from a matching concrete tunnel covered in weeds and dirt.

From what Leyla had researched online, it was originally intended to be an exit for the railcar to the surface, but construction of the entire system was halted in 1928, and left to rot ever since. For 100 years, many of the city's residents hadn't realized there was a multitude of dark tunnels hidden beneath their everyday lives. Many urban explorers and dark tourists had made the trek into the mysterious tunnels with cameras and cell phones to capture a glimpse of the past. Some had even produced full length documentaries on the cryptic labyrinth under Cincinnati. Despite the multitude of folks that had been down in the forbidden tunnels, some agreed that there seemed to be more down there; but it was just a rumor to drum up dreams. Or nightmares.

Above all else, it seemed that everyone could agree this was a terribly uninviting area for humanity. Even as the homeless population of the city refused to call it home, this was the very location of what Leyla believed to be her first memory.

***

2032. April. Almost Spring, but the morning frost could still bite. She remembered the cold more than anything, because she'd happened to awaken wearing clothes, yes, but they were so full of holes and tears that they provided no protection at all to the upper Midwestern chill.

She'd thought she was blind at first, but after walking some way without bumping into something, she was able to make out a light at the end of the tunnel she was in. The subway entrance was open, ever so slightly, providing enough sunlight to guide her out of the dark.

***

Leyla stood at the entrance now, three years later, in 2035. It'd been shut and bolted closed yet again. Someone would eventually come along and pry it open for some thrills.

"I know I'm in there somewhere." Leyla said aloud, perhaps declaring to the universe that she was onto its ruse.

She squeezed a couple fingers into the crack on the overlapping door and tried to jostle it loose but it was pointless.

These doors must have weighed a ton each. Leyla, letting out a sigh that could only mean *of course*, backed away a couple steps. That's when she noticed them. Tire tracks. One or two different sets at least, leading in and out of the doors.

"Ok so, trucks?" Leyla mumbled to herself. Her eyes widened as a brilliant idea formed in her mind.

***

Back at the tent city, it was almost the end of the day. It was still a little chilly outside so the nights could still be dangerously frigid. Deli sat in front of her tent and pulled a blanket over her shoulders and stuffed some newspapers into her zipped up jacket. Crumpled newspapers could be an amazing insulator.

It was a trick many street dwelling citizens had adopted for the winter. Deli had just the right spot in the village and she could see the sun setting over the city skyline almost every night. It was her favorite thing in the world. She waited as the sun slowly descended from the sky.

"DEL!" Leyla spoke a little too loudly for how close she was to Deli, having essentially snuck up to her. Deli jumped, startled, and almost fell out of her old and worn camping chair.

"Motherfucker WHY YOU YELLIN' LIKE THAT oh hey Leyla damn where the fuck you come from? I missed you!"

"Remember I told you where I remember waking up?" Leyla didn't bother acknowledging Del's reaction.

"The old subway. Door's closed now. I guess that's normal, but I found footprints and they lead to big truck tracks."

"Okay Miss Navajo what's that mean?"

"What's a Navajo?"

"What's a—girl never mind I keep forgettin' you got the animesia. Go on ahead with your story."

"That's it. There's tracks. People are uh, getting a truck there and I don't know–they're going inside. Maybe it's supplies or something, I don't know." Leyla could barely contain herself in a mix of excitement and confusion. Deli, however, was still recovering from the near coronary she just had.

"Well you do know it could just be construction workers or something."

"Del, construction stopped on the subway like a hundred years ago."

"Well yeah but people gotta check it every once in a while to make sure it doesn't collapse and, you know, kill downtown."

"I think we should stake it out." Leyla said, stone faced.

"Stake it out? What are you, a detective? You Little Miss Hard-boiled now? Stake it out. Shit only 'stake' I need is medium well, A-1 sauce, with mashed potatoes and a jar o' gravy. You ain't getting' another stake out of me. And girl, it's *cold outside*. We ain't gon' be nowhere except in our tents, bundled up, waitin' for Spring to sprang."

Leyla had already walked off.

"Leyla! Did you not just hear me?"

"I did." Leyla turned to face Deli, but continued to walk backwards. She did the 'finger guns' gesture toward Deli. "But I'm gonna stake it out."

"Finger guns? Really?" Deli remarked under her breath. "Leyla, hold on! Dammit girl you gon' be the death of me. I'm a help you! Hold on! Jesus!"

Korean Jesus poked his head through his tent door as Deli passed by.

"Not you. I'm talkin' bout Jesus Jesus. But shit, watch my tent. Leyla doing some dumb shit and I gotta help her."

"Watch your tent? The fuck I look like? Security camera?"

"Motherfucker you Jesus you see everythang don't ya? Watch my shit please. Thank you."

Jesus sneered at Deli but decided she was worth helping. "Okay I will. But you gonna owe me! Keun sigan!" Jesus snarled.

"Aight, cool!" Deli agreed, having no idea what Jesus just said in Korean.

Deli caught up to Leyla. "Okay baby girl, so what's your plan here?"

"Get my stuff, and hike back there, and watch and see what happens tonight."

"What if nothing happens? You not think of that?"

Leyla stopped walking and turned to Deli. "And what if something does happen? What if there are people there that can explain why I woke up with rotted clothes inside an abandoned subway *where people don't go?* Del, it's been almost three years. I didn't even think about who I was or why I'm here I just *exist*. You don't think that's weird? I had no ID, no memories no *nothing*. Maybe I got hit on the head, but I didn't have a scar that I remember. I know this is a long shot but it's all I've got. If I find nothing, oh well, I tried, back to living in tent city and laughing at Korean Jesus, but for now...I'm staking out the entrance to a scary abandoned subway tunnel."

Leyla turned and continued to her tent, followed closely by Deli. "We." Deli speaks up. "*We* staking out the creepy tunnel. Better not be no ghosts and shit."

Leyla and Deli quickly tore down the small tent and packed the blankets and a small bit of food and belongings and headed off. "How far is this walk?" Deli asked.

"Not too bad. Maybe an hour."

"An hour?! Girl what I look like? A marathon runner?"

***

Leyla strutted up a hill, nearing the entrance while Deli heaved and dragged her feet. She was too old for this shit.

"See?" Leyla asked Deli. "Not too bad a walk."

She looked over to Del, who was following a couple paces behind, giving her a death stare with her oxygen-starved face.

"Okay okay I know. It's further than normal." Leyla said.

"This ain't normal. This is some Army hike shit."

"Coulda stayed behind and entertained Jesus some more." Leyla laughed.

"So you walked all the way here this morning, and then back to me, and now you walkin' back again?"

"Yeah..."

"And you not tired?"

"I guess not."

"Damn superhuman ass. Captain Hobo. That's what I'm a call you. Captain Hobo. That's your superhero name from now on."

Leyla cracked a grin. "Well, we're almost there. Right over this next hill."

Leyla and Deli huffed it the last few hundred feet over the hill and Leyla stopped at the crest. She surveyed the land a bit and decided they needed a good spot where they could camp and not be seen; at least not immediately. She found a spot that seemed good enough.

She could see the sealed entrance to the subway as well as the spot where she believed people meet with the trucks. "Right here. I think." She said as she basically dragged Deli along. "Should be able to see most of everything when it goes down."

"When it goes down..." Deli said out loud, chuckling. "Sound like a dick if I ever heard one."

"A dick? What did I do?"

"No a dick like a detective, it's like slang. Damn girl I need to show you some old TV shows on that cell phone you got. Your pop culture knowledge is b-a-d *bad*."

The two pitched their worn down tent and rolled out their blankets inside. Not much else to do but wait. So that's what they did.

"Damn, look at that." Deli tapped Leyla on the arm. Leyla looked up to see Deli looking in the opposite direction. The sun was resting on the horizon perfectly. "Looks like a big ol" egg yolk don't it? Sunny side up." She chuckled at her small joke.

"Yeah it does look like an egg." Leyla agreed, then looked back to the subway entrance. Nothing yet. Still sealed. No vehicle. No mystery men. "Come on." Leyla impatiently sighed.

The sun took its time rolling off the edge of the Earth, guarded the entire time by Del's hypnotized eyes. She'd never miss a sunrise or sunset if she could help it.

As the daylight died and the moon began its shift in the night sky, Deli retired into the tent.

"Wake me up if you need some sleep, I'll watch for you." She assured Leyla.

"Sure thing, Del."

But Leyla wouldn't need it. She somehow stayed wide awake through the entire night, like a sentinel charged with guarding an emperor. The hours crept by slower than usual. Eventually, the sun was rising again.

Leyla reached inside the tent and grabbed Deli's foot from outside the blanket and shook it.

"Hmmmm? Oh...." Del mumbled, waking up at about the same pace she always does.

"Sunrise." Leyla reminded Deli, pointing at the sun. "Eggs." She could hear Deli laugh inside her blanket at her joke.

"Yep, eggs." Deli replied, muffled by the blanket. She coughed. It was a heavy and heaving cough. Always worse in the mornings.

Del pushed herself up to watch the sun and controlled her breathing to keep from coughing more.

"So...see anything?" Del asked.

"Nothing. All night. Nothing."

"Maybe they get their truck on Tuesdays."

"Do we even know what day it is?" Leyla laughed.

"Nope. Might be Tuesday now, shit. Could be Moosday."

"Or Fraturday."

"Girl you need sleep. Let's go."

Leyla and Del packed up the tent and blankets and started back to the homeless tent village.

"Could use a bite to eat, too." Deli reminded Leyla.

"Yep. Be nice if we had some cash."

"Don't worry I'll get somethin' whipped up when we get back. If Jesus actually watched my shit like I asked, that is."

"I'm sure he did, Del." Leyla stopped walking, suddenly overcome with an overwhelming sense of dread mixed with what felt like vertigo and a strong sense of familiarity.

Deli stopped and held her shoulder. "You aight?" She asked, worried.

"Damn, deja vu. Just had it. And again about saying I had it..."

"Deja vu my ass, you look like you about to fall over–"

Thunder rang out from what seemed to be right behind Del. Red hot sparks showered her back, pushing her into Leyla. Leyla slipped on a rock and dropped hard onto her back.

Leyla could almost see the sound waves crawl across Del as she caught herself with one step. As the sparks and rush of wind passed over Deli's back, Leyla squinted her eyes to try and make out what's happening. She could make out what seemed to be a window hovering in mid-air. A circular window, encased in writhing blue ropes of energy that dissipated into hot sparks. A window that led to somewhere that wasn't the same world they were in now.

A darkened figure, dressed in some very futuristic matte black leather and carbon fiber, dropped down from it and landed with such light feet it barely disturbed the dew-dropped grass below.

Leyla felt like she was seeing everything in slow motion. She could practically feel the weight of the air around her, as if she were in water.

The armored person wrapped its arms around Del before she was able to turn around to see what all the fuss was about behind her, and before Del could release a gasp of shock, she was jerked backward into the window to another world. A terrified scream slowly escaped Del's mouth as she and the other person fell backward through the portal, which closed in on itself in a split second and fizzled out.

Del was gone. Just like that.

The air seemed to lighten around Leyla. That feeling of being underwater went away. Hyperventilating and scrambling to her feet, she tried to call for Del. But shock is a hell of a thing, and her voice was non-existent. Barely a whisper escaped. No one was going to hear her plea.

No one was going to save her friend. No one was going to care. To make things worse, Leyla spaced out and fell over into the grass. Another absence seizure.

Leyla was awoken a few moments later by a jetliner flying relatively low overhead. She sprang off the ground to wave them down–hoping with every fiber of her being that the pilot or a passenger or *someone* would see her and report that they've seen someone asking for help. Stumbling over rocks and tufts of grass and trying to follow the plane, she felt the hope bleed from her heart as it got smaller and smaller, exiting her view into the clouds.

She turned to the freeway a few hundred yards away and tried again, waving wildly to passing cars. Not a single driver paid attention to her, so she gave up and ran back to where Del was taken.

But Leyla noticed it now: the wormhole where the kidnapper came through had not fully closed just yet. There seemed to be a small, quarter sized hole still open with sparks jumping off and floating through the air until they fizzled out a few moments later. Leyla cautiously made her way over to the tear in reality.

A low rumble began to emanate from the closing rift. A tiny black dot appeared as the tiny window closed. Leyla's clothing pulled toward it, and then she felt her entire body fall toward the little black dot. She tried to resist, but her feet dragged.

"The fuck?!" She screeched, as she dropped to all fours and turned, digging her fingers into the ground. Pebbles and mud rolled past her toward the dot. The air around her felt heavy and water-like again. Her body lifted off the ground and she was raised into the air. She felt her back pull into the spot where Del had vanished, and it felt like a hot needle going into her skin as it touched her.

And then, everything stopped. She dropped to the ground, free of the magnetic force. The rocks and pebbles remained in the air for a moment longer, and then dropped to the ground as well.

Committed

"Leyla...Doe?"

Leyla looked over her shoulder to find the face to match the uber-masculine voice she's just heard. There he was. A clean cut, athletic, movie star looking police officer holding two cups of coffee, making his way around her and to his desk, which was where she'd been sitting for over 30 minutes.

"Do you drink coffee?" He asked, holding the cup in his left hand out toward her slightly. Leyla had never really had coffee—not hot anyway—but she nodded yes and took the cup. The officer opened a drawer and pulled out some red creamer singles and his own personal sugar container. "Creamer and sugar?" Leyla smiled this time and nodded. "That's Coldstone Sweet Cream, and it's the best. Gotta order 'em on Amazon. They don't sell those in stores much. Gotta buy the big thing of it and I don't have a fridge in here, so I get those." The officer noticed an especially confused stare from Leyla. "Have you never seen these?"

"Nope. The only coffee I've ever had was cold and gross."

"Oh, alright then. We're gonna do this slowly then." The officer pulled her cup to his side of the desk and poured in one creamer single, then opened the sugar and swirled it four times over the cup, counting each swirl, all closely watched by Leyla. The officer laughed, noticing Leyla's stare.

"I gotta count the swirls. I don't like too much or too little. Four is perfect. We'll see how you like it. Here you go." Leyla took the cup and sipped. Her eyes lit up. It had to be the single most perfectly amazing thing she'd ever tasted. She looked up at the officer, who'd not yet taken his seat, and he knew what she was feeling.

"Yep. I know. Good right?"

"Mmm hmm." Leyla mumbled as she took another sip.

"Sergeant Donnie Wells." He finally pulled his chair out and took a seat. His chair was set higher than hers, so she still had to look up at him. He noticed this as well and pulled the lever on his chair, releasing air with a hiss, and lowered it to meet her. He stretched his legs out straight as it lowered, possibly an attempt to show that he's a laid back guy. Leyla cracked a smile.

"I'm not here to put you in jail, if you've been thinking that. I'm here to make sense of what you told Officer Harrison a little earlier. Leyla looked over to Officer Harrison, who was filling out paperwork a few desks down. Harrison was the officer that responded to the initial report of Deli's disappearance, detailed by Leyla herself.

"Harrison can be a little blunt and cold...just doing her job though."

"No, she was fine." Leyla said, attempting to be courteous.

"Hmm...Okay, good then. Anyways..." Officer Wells took a sip of coffee. "So...This is a lot. You reported that you and your friend were down near the subway entrance, you'd seen some tracks that go in and out, you spent the night there waiting for something to happen, and then...a…portal…opened, a person dressed in all black with no face jumped out, and grabbed your friend, and disappeared into another portal, never speaking a word to you—have you drank that whole cup?"

Leyla looked down at the cup of coffee, now empty. "I guess I did."

"What were you doing at the subway entrance? Wanna tell me what you were waiting for? Harrison says you wouldn't tell her."

"I said there were truck tracks. We were waiting on trucks."

"What's special about trucks?" Wells noticed Leyla's hesitation, and waited for an answer anyway.

"Honestly? I'm not sure. It was something to do other than sleep on the street another night." Leyla lied, looking down at her empty cup.

"Okay, well, when you decide to tell me the full truth, you can get back to me. But, since you have no ID either, things are a little complicated. Due to the report you gave and the nature of these events, I *have* to submit you for an IVC. " Wells said, shuffling some things through his desk drawer.

"What's that?"

"Involuntary commitment order."

"Still don't know what that means."

"Well, there is an upside and downside. It's a forced psychological evaluation. Upside is—" He stopped talking as Leyla began shifting in her chair. "Now, don't run. That'll make it worse and I guarantee you, you won't make it far with all these officers in here. You want Harrison tackling you? She's a former soccer player. She is rough. I've seen it."

Leyla settled, although getting a little fidgety due to the rush of caffeine she'd never had before. Coffee was a different monster than the Coke she normally liked. Wells continued.

"Upside is, you won't be on the streets. You'll have a bed. You'll have food. You'll even have TV and books. Downside, you can't leave until the psychiatrist clears you. But it ain't so bad. Just cooperate. You're not a prisoner. Just making sure you're okay. I'll come check on you there later. Personally."

Officer Harrison, wielding handcuffs, had been standing behind Leyla during Officer Wells's not-so-convincing speech, and she tapped Leyla on her left shoulder with one open cuff.

"Unfortunately per procedure we have to put those on." Wells remarked, barely easing Leyla's newfound anxiety.

Leyla was cuffed and escorted out of the office, looking over her shoulder at Wells as if he'd betrayed her very soul. She had no words to toss at the situation. Wells pushed Leyla's paperwork into a thick plastic folder, closed it, and shoved it into a hidden drawer in his desk.

***

Officer Harrison unlocked Leyla's handcuffs outside the deliveries and receiving dock behind Glenwood Behavioral Health Center. The cuffs had dug themselves into Leyla's wrists, reddening them. Two male orderlies exited double doors and made their way down the stairs from the dock toward the car.

"Normally we don't remove these until you're fully in their custody." Harrison told Leyla, referring to the cuffs. "But Sergeant Wells insisted you're treated with special care. Whatever that means."

Yeah, what does that mean? Leyla wondered.

Harrison removed the cuffs. "Don't try anything stupid with me or them. You can still go to jail."

The orderlies extended their hands to Leyla and helped her walk away from Harrison, who was already getting into her squad car and preparing to make the drive back to the precinct.

Leyla and the orderlies made their way toward the dock stairs and a middle-aged woman with uncomfortably perfect blonde hair exited the double doors to meet them. She was wearing a gray pantsuit and a white collared shirt, with a badge clipped over her left breast. Leyla thought of the Imperial officers in Star Wars. That's what the lady looked like to her.

Before Leyla could make out the name on the badge, the woman spoke in a matter of factly tone with a seemingly *very* rehearsed script.

"Hello, I am Doctor Ava Jensen, welcome to Glenwood Behavioral Center. You are in good hands here. I will be your primary evaluation specialist and prescribing doctor. An officer at the office you came from has detailed your experience to me and I assure you, you have nothing to worry about from now on."

"I'm pretty effin' worried." Leyla snapped at Dr. Jensen, who replied with another unassuring line.

"As I said, the officer filled me in on your experience. For now, you're going to be processed."

Processed? Leyla thought. *What am I? Meat?*

Up until then, the orderlies had been semi-polite and tender. This time, they jerked Leyla toward the double doors as Dr. Jensen side shifted and let them pass. Through the doors was a long white hallway with worn paint on the walls and another set of brownish red double doors at the end. No one said a word for the entire walk down the hall.

They went through more doors. Down more hallways. The entire hospital seemed to have been made like a maze just for her so she couldn't find her way out. Finally, the four came to a door with a thick glass window, the kind with steel wire inside so nothing can break through.

Who do they think I am? The Hulk? Leyla thought to herself, desperately hoping this was simply normal procedure. On that, Dr. Jensen chimed in in the worst way possible.

"We've had a number of patients claim to have seen things down at the abandoned subway. The hospital director has instructed me to personally see to anyone with these sort of claims due to the rather unusual nature of said claims. Rest assured you will be taken care of."

Rest assured. Leyla thought. *Getting tired of being assured.*

The orderlies shoved Leyla into a final door at the end of the hall, almost knocking her off her feet, but she was able to stay upright by stumbling into the wall on the opposite end.

"Someone will be along shortly." Dr. Jensen claimed, and then shut the thick steel door. It automatically locked. Leyla didn't try to resist or make a commotion; she'd deemed it pointless already.

"Fuck." She sighed.

***

Hours passed—which to Leyla seemed like weeks. Empty beige concrete walls and a single door with no windows in a tiny little cell truly stretched time out to a ridiculous extent. The hard concrete floor wasn't doing her butt any favors either. There was a bed, but it looked just as uncomfortable as the floor.

"I thought they put crazy people in padded rooms." She murmured aloud.

"They do." Officer Wells's voice emanated, muffled, from the thick door, surprising Leyla. The door's lock mechanism clicked as an electronic beep released it and the good looking officer stepped through, pushing past the orderly putting away his key card. He wasn't in uniform now, so Leyla guessed he was off duty, walking around in jeans, a plain black t-shirt and a nice, wool pea coat that stopped at his thighs.

"But, I don't think you're crazy." he said.

"Can you go back out there?" Leyla motioned to the door. "And tell them that?"

Wells looked around the scant room. "I do apologize. I thought this place would be nicer than this. This is Russian gulag shit. I'll say something to them outside. Look, I signed the IVC. Now it's up to the doctors to release you, not me. But I need to talk to you. This whole thing…" Wells paused, thinking over his intended next words. "The subway thing."

Leyla sat a little straighter. Wells had something interesting to say. Something he wouldn't say back at the office.

"You are the *only* person I have spoken to about things that have happened there. Ever." he said.

"So this is the first time you've heard about this, I'm sure." Leyla replied.

"No no. You're the first live person I've spoken to." Wells whisked up the large, thick folder from his precinct desk's hidden compartment and dropped it at Leyla's feet. "That is seventeen testimonies from witnesses that mention that subway. Every one of them for someone who went missing near there. And the weirdest thing?"

Leyla's eyebrows twitched up a little—even more interested.

"Each person they report missing? Doesn't exist. No records. No socials. No driver license. No family. Friends. Nothing. Ghosts. One or two reports like this can be a possible prank or false report but seventeen? That's weird. And then, eventually, the folks that report the missing people seem to forget everything. And you're the only one who saw something actually happen, that I can talk to before you somehow forget too. So either something weird is going on in that subway, or you've kidnapped and erased seventeen other humans from existence. Eighteen, counting your friend."

Leyla slid herself a little further from Officer Wells at the apparent accusation. And Wells hadn't bothered to sit down or even lean against the wall yet.

"Relax. That last part was a bad joke. Your side of the story seems pretty accurate. But I really need to know if you saw or even heard anything else. There's a good bit of missing folks floating around out there. Maybe you can help."

"Promise you won't think I'm crazy?" Leyla asked.

"Hey, we're way past crazy at this point. Doesn't matter if you are. I just wanna get a grip on what's happening."

"Why doesn't a detective or something have that folder? Why just some normal cop?"

Wells smirked again. "You are definitely smarter than you look. No offense." Leyla didn't reply. She gave Wells a stern *answer me* face. Wells stared back, clearly bothered by the inquiry. "Look, I just have a personal stake in this too, alright?"

Leyla scoffed. "Bunch of people going missing at a subway entrance and the whole police department just lets you keep the file? Sounds fishy."

"I'll give you that one." Wells replied, laughing.

"You want me to be open?" Leyla asked. "Then you be open."

Wells sighed, slightly annoyed but understanding of Leyla's request. He looked down at the floor and moved to the wall beside Leyla, but not too close to her, and let out yet another sigh. He squatted down and eyed her very seriously.

"The precinct investigated the first two of these disappearances. Only two. It was a big thing. People were just disappearing. That doesn't happen. People go missing but these folks' entire existence was just...gone. Thought it was a prank. Then a third went missing. And a fourth. Spaced out over time, usually a few months in between. Had, I think, 4 detectives working on it, including me."

"Wait, you were a detective? I thought that was like a higher rank or somethi—"

"It is. I'm getting to that. Seventh person goes missing. Same as before. Last seen near the subway."

"And you knew this one." Leyla said. Wells gave her a *smart cookie* grin.

"Best friend. Officer Greene. Played baseball in high school together, went to BLET together, gained rank together, but he wanted to stay on the street and I wanted to *detect*. One day Greene pulls a guy over for rolling through a stop sign, guy ran, he chased him. Right into the subway entrance. He's calling for backup on the radio over and over. Nobody got to him in time. That's the last anybody heard of him or saw him." Wells's voice started to crack.

Leyla chimed in. "So a cop went missing? Wouldn't that be a big deal?"

"Yeah, no shit." Wells snapped back. "But, after him, nothing. Precinct dropped the case. I pushed, got demoted. Gained some rank back but they won't give me detective again. Weirdest thing? The whole department won't even acknowledge Officer Greene even existed. I searched his records. Not even deleted—they're just gone. Like they didn't exist. He never worked for the CPD. He never went to Mariemont High School. His own *mother* denies his existence. Ran me out of her house like she didn't know me."

"Okay, that is a little weird..."

"And that was over three years ago. Since then, the total went up to 17. Every time someone reports it, it gets swept under the rug. But you're the first one to actually see something, and come back. I sent you here, so you can be away from the PD, because I don't trust them, and I want to find my best friend."

"Same here." Leyla said. "We went there because Del asked me where I was from and I realized the earliest thing I remember is walking out of there three years ago."

"Wait, walking out of the subway?" Wells straightened up. "And three years ago, just like Greene?" Wells stood, shook his head, and mumbled to himself. "No, that's just coincidence. Perp he chased in was male."

Three heavy knocks come from the door of the room; one of the orderlies, probably. Wells turns and looks at the door with an irritated expression. He knelt back down to Leyla.

"I'll be back." Wells assured Leyla. "We got a lot to talk about." Wells stood and walked toward the door, giving it his own three knocks, with the knuckle of his finger—not as heavy as the orderly's. The door opened and Wells exited, giving Leyla one final glance and a small, almost unnoticeable nod. But Leyla did notice, and gave him a nod of her own, albeit an awkward one as she didn't know what the nod was for.

As the door closed and locked, Leyla nodded to herself with a confused face, still working out what that even meant. She sucked in a huge breath and heaved an equally large sigh out through closed lips, making a bpbpbpbpbpbp sound.

"I'm hungry!" Leyla said loudly enough that she thought the orderly could hear, and then lowered her volume mid-sentence when she realized just how loud she was. She then spoke to herself with a normal volume. "Food would be great. Sandwich or something."

***

Leyla wasn't sure how much time passed. There was no clock in the room. She was the only thing in there that wasn't beige and even that was pushing it; she'd never gotten a tan in her life—that she knew of. Finally, she heard a beep at the door, and it opened. There were three different orderlies this time. Bigger ones. They walked straight at Leyla, dead-eyed and almost sociopathic.

One grabbed her left forearm in his immense hands and tugged, pulling her across the floor for a few inches before a second orderly latched onto her right arm and they both used their free hands to push her shoulders to the floor. The third orderly got ahold of both feet before she could even think to start kicking.

"What are you doing? What'd I do?" She asked, knowing she wouldn't get a response.

Doctor Jensen walked in through the door so fast her hair kicked up behind her. She was holding a needle that had to be at least six inches long; so large it should be used on a bear.

Leyla's face grew pale and her frenzied breathing paused. She'd never actually seen a needle. She had no memory of doctors or their tools. This silver spiked monstrosity in Dr. Jensen's right hand was a nuclear level threat, and Leyla did the only thing she knew to do: try to run.

Her legs moved so fast the orderly at her feet lost his clutch. Leyla's right foot found his chin just by chance. He lost three front teeth, a splat of blood and consciousness. He dropped on his right side so loosely that Leyla thought he was dead.

Jensen tried to hurry over to Leyla's side since she was still pinned down but Leyla wasn't having it. The men on her shoulders were at least 200 pounds each, but she pulled her left shoulder as hard as she could away from Jensen and her needle. The orderly didn't lose grip, so Leyla brought him along with her arm, dragging him across the floor a good two feet as she rolled to her right side. Jensen stepped back, trying to avoid stabbing the orderly with whatever sort of wild animal tranquilizer she'd pumped into the vial.

The orderly on Leyla's right side tried to pin her down, but she pulled her right hand free and raked her fingers across his eyes. Leyla wasn't sure how much she injured the hulk of a man, but she felt skin, hair, and possibly eyeball get caught under her worn down fingernails. The orderly let go of her completely, recoiling and screaming hysterically, and brought his hands up to cover his face. He rolled away from Leyla like he was trying to avoid being eaten by a mountain lion, screaming and writhing.

Jensen backed away from the remaining and struggling orderly until she hit the wall behind her.

Leyla forms a fist and, with all her might, whipped it into the orderly's temple so fast a crack rings through the air. The orderly dropped on top of her as if he'd just been executed.

Doctor Jensen was frozen in place, still brandishing the needle upright in her right hand as Leyla stood, almost in slow motion, like a dragon rising from the flames it beset on a village, never taking her gaze off Jensen.

It could've been the adrenaline, but there was a fire in Leyla's eyes. A primal hunger for violence. Leyla may as well have been a wolf, foaming at the mouth, closing in on her prey for a final, life-destroying bite.

Leyla felt the hair on the back of her neck stand up. She could feel every single fiber of muscle in her body awaiting her orders. She and Jensen's eyes were locked in a predator and prey stare for a fleeting eternity.

The inevitable alarm for the ward sounded off, loud enough to break Leyla's blood-thirsty trance—likely saving Doctor Jensen's hide. Leyla turned away and bolted to the open door. Jensen slid down the wall and to the floor, still holding the needle up and unable to let out the breath she'd been holding in for over a minute. The face-raked orderly's agonizing cries had become raspy and forced.

Leyla careened down the hallway, never giving a thought to which hallways went where. She didn't remember how they got to the room she'd just escaped from. She was on auto-pilot at that point. Her legs were taking her wherever they wanted her to go. Red lights painted the hallways on and off, timed to the siren's incessantly loud screech. Leyla rounded a corner and barreled toward two more large orderlies carefully planting their feet to the floor as if they had a chance at stopping the coming train wreck.

Leyla hit the men so hard she felt their ribs crunch and their bodies seized like they'd been hit by lightning.

They smacked the floor; the backs of their heads bounced off the linoleum—sending both of the men into convulsing piles of future vegetables.

Leyla barely lost momentum. She turned another corner and hit a door, expecting to burst through it, but it didn't budge, and it knocked her to the ground. She quickly recovered and jumped back up. She looked back down the hall. Security guards were coming this time. With weapons. They were coming with *guns*.

"Don't move or we *will* fire!" One of the guards shouted as he raised a pistol at Leyla, closely followed by the other three guards.

Through sheer, damn near perfect timing, the door behind her opened, and a single security guard rammed through it, not expecting to be met with Leyla grabbing his arm and wrapping it around the edge of the door. His bones crunched like a bag of Doritos. The guards on the other end of the hall didn't fire, lest they hit their newly crippled co-worker. Leyla slid through the door and she finally saw them: the red double doors leading to the dock.

There was no one between her and the doors. She just needed to make it to them before the guards chasing her could catch up and take her out. Her legs were a blur, carrying her seemingly all on their own with no input from her brain, speeding down the empty hallway. She heard the guards burst through the door behind her but she didn't bother to look back.

A hot, beating, and biting sting pulsated through her right shoulder and lower back out of nowhere. Her legs stopped working and buckled. She slammed to the ground at full speed, sliding into the red double doors so hard her body circled back around to see that a guard had bulls-eyed her with his taser.

Leyla clutched one of the barbs from the weapon—the one buried in her shoulder—and whipped it toward the guard in defiance of the white-hot pain running up her back.

The guard ducked, but he didn't have a chance to dodge the incoming second barb from Leyla's back. That one hit his collar bone with enough force to burrow into his skin, resulting in the man tasting an electrified helping of his own malice.

The remaining guards, coming in at full speed, tripped and rolled over the convulsing idiot like clones of the Three Stooges. Leyla was back up to her feet and out the double doors before any of them can recover.

Now outside and still not safe, Leyla started to run for the treeline, but in a moment of survivalist brilliance, stopped to grab a long steel bar used to pull the dock plates up for trailer shipments and forced it into the steel handles of the doors, effectively locking them shut.

Several heavy thuds and slams soon followed as the guards rammed into the unexpectedly immovable objects. One of the guards could be heard yelling to his colleagues "Who the fuck is this bitch?"

Leyla stopped and turned once again to the doors with an offended look on her face. She reached up above the right door, grabbed hold of an insulated electric line and ripped it out of the housing, exposing the live wires inside. She wedged the wires into the crack above that door, and was quickly greeted with barely comprehensible swear words and pain ridden cries of disbelief from the other side.

She turned and finally bolted for the tree line, hoping to eventually get a lay of the land and figure out where she should go. It was after dark and the only light was from the moon so she should at least be concealed. The only thing crazier than what just happened was that she'd not had an absence seizure during the escape. They usually happened when she was excited.

Luckily, the hospital was on somewhat of a hill North of the city. Making her way out into a small clearing, Leyla could see downtown Cincinnati a few miles away, which was simultaneously a good thing since she now knew where she was and a bad thing because that was one long ass run home. Yet, she started running again and kept running until the alarm from the hospital was masked by sirens of police cars and ambulances.

***

Leyla made some surprisingly good time, running from the hospital to Fort Washington Way's tent city in just under an hour. She was afraid to take a break with the constant hovering sound of police car sirens in the distance.

She caught a glimpse of the blue lights more than a few times on the way. She rounded a corner, almost home, and was smacked with the sudden realization that going home was a terrible idea. Police had blocked off half of the road. There were blue lights everywhere. Cops brandishing large flashlights, some even with lights mounted to their weapons, were scouring the tent city like militarized ants, tossing the belongings of the citizens and tossing the citizens themselves aside in a search for the one that just massacred a psych ward up North. Korean Jesus was *not* pleased, letting the police know exactly how he felt.

"Hey Porky! You all b-b-b-b-big and bad, huh?" Korean Jesus yelled at an officer a couple tents down. "Quit jerkin' each other off, we don't like bacon wrapped wieners around here!"

Leyla couldn't contain her laughter at the comment and let a snarling giggle through her nostrils, immediately covering her mouth and deciding what to do next. She slinked back into the darker street she came from.

***

Leyla carefully navigated the blanket of police presence downtown to cross the freeway and around to the berm beside it. Back to where the fiasco began: The abandoned subway entrance.

There were no signs anyone even attempted to look for Del. Leyla could see the scuffles she'd made trying to back away from Deli's attacker.

She approached slowly, fully expecting the same carbon-clad monster to emerge from the void again and take her out and tie up a loose end. A sharp gust of wind blew by Leyla, spiking her blood pressure. She whipped around to see nothing. No threat. She paused and listened, hearing nothing but the rolling traffic passing by.

She shuffled over to the still sealed entrance. No change at all. Even the tracks from whatever vehicle was there were the same as well as the footprints she and Deli saw. Nothing or no one has come through the entrance since.

"I knew I'd find you here."

Leyla jolted at the voice cutting in the dark, familiar as it may be. It was Officer Wells. He'd drawn a Glock 40 with his right hand but he kept it pointed to the ground and finger off the trigger, ready to defend himself if need be.

"Oh, sorry, didn't mean to—" he said.

"FUCK! Scared the shit out of me!", Leyla exclaimed, quickly eyeing the weapon at Wells's side.

"Again, I am sorry." Wells pleaded, holding his left hand up, palm open toward Leyla. "So uh...you have become very interesting."

Leyla, as always, prepared to run.

"Hold on, hold on." Wells, still with his hand up, made his case. "I'm not in uniform. Off duty."

"So what's that for?" Leyla pointed to the pistol at Wells's side.

"Self defense. You just steamrolled ten guys twice your size like the damn Juggernaut."

"What's a Juggernaut?"

"Nothing, point is, I want the same thing you want. I don't trust the PD to help me out, so I'm hoping you can. Can I trust you to not put me in the ICU too?"

"Are you gonna poke me with one of those long, sticky thingies?" Leyla asked, unsure of how to describe the needle she'd evaded.

Wells, rightfully confused, dropped his weapon more to the side. "Sticky thingy? What? What are you talking about a sticky thingy? I don't have any sticky thingies."

"It was like a..." Leyla attempted to describe the needle with hand motions. She held her right hand's index and middle fingers up and pushed her thumb toward them, mimicking using a needle. She brought her left hand up to her right, still making the squeezing motion, and pointed up to the sky, and just gave up outright and blurted aloud what she's thinking.

"It was a big pokey stick and water came out the end of it, and they held me down so they could do whatever they wanted to do with it, and I just fought back and ran."

Wells immediately understood what she was talking about and let out a huge sigh that morphed into laughter. "A needle? You hulked out on those guys over a needle?"

"I don't know what that's for! Or what it does! What do you expect?!"

"Okay, okay, I get it." Wells holstered his pistol. "Have you never had a shot? You've never seen a needle?"

"Nope."

Wells held his mouth agape, trying to figure out how anyone alive wouldn't at least know what a simple needle was. But he didn't pry.

"I don't like needles either. Doc shoulda explained what it was to you, I guess. So, can I trust you? You're not gonna pancake my skinny ass on the pavement?"

Mister, Leyla thought, *you are not skinny. I can see your pecs from a mile away, but whatever.* "Long as you don't pull out a needle. And you're not skinny, you're...athletic."

"You know what the word 'athletic' is but you don't know what a nee—okay you know what? Let's get in that subway there."

Leyla relaxed, only slightly, prepared to run if need be, curious to what plan Wells had.

"You said three years ago, you walked out of that entrance, and that's the first thing you remember?" Wells inquired, pointing to the sealed subway.

"Yeah..."

"And that's not weird to you?"

"It's weird."

Wells sighed, relieved at Leyla's honesty as well as frustrated at what she may be holding back. "I'm gonna pull that wall down." He assured Leyla, gesturing at the entrance.

Wells waltzed confidently around the corner. Leyla heard the cranking of an engine and heavy exhaust.

A full size pickup truck, a big Dodge Ram, rolled into her view, equipped with mud tires, lifted high, an extended cab, and most importantly, a winch. It was enormous.

Of course that's what this guy drives, Leyla thought to herself.

Wells drove the pickup forward a bit, then whipped it around until it faced the subway entrance and moved up to around another truck length from it. He exited the truck and walked to its front end, grabbed the winch and pulled the hook toward the wall of the subway, which had always been suspiciously flimsy. After searching for a good spot for the hook for a moment, he shrugged his shoulders and nonchalantly slammed the hook into a seam in the middle of the wall.

"Nice truck." Leyla said, half sarcastically.

"Yep." Wells agreed, entering his truck and closing the door. He moved the gear to reverse and slammed the pedal hard. The 4X4 lurched backward hard. An audible crack was heard as the steel winch tightened. Leyla looked to the subway entrance. It was giving. Wells released the accelerator, put the truck in drive and moved up a few feet, releasing the tension on the winch.

He then dropped it to reverse again and jammed the accelerator, jerking back against the wall again. Another crack, louder that time. Wells repeated the process two more times. Leyla moved a few feet away, expecting the doorway to explode. One last time, Wells moved up more than before, slipped the truck into reverse, and backed up hard.

The growl of his V-8 almost covered the cracks of splintering wood. The doorway finally failed and split open. The entire structure fell outward and to the ground. Wells kept pulling backward to clear the way a little more, but he'd done the job. The subway was open. It was nothing special; just dark inside.

Leyla moved closer to the entrance, peering inside the best she could. She saw nothing but blackness. Wells exited his truck, removed the winch from the debris, and entered the cab again. The winch wound up until the wire was fully retracted to the front of the bumper.

"Hold on, I'm coming." Wells called out to Leyla as he pulled his pickup a little closer to her. Once he was beside her, he pointed over at the passenger side. "Come on, get in."

Leyla reservedly stared at the passenger seat of the large pickup.

"Hey, I care more about what's down there..." Wells pointed into the dark tunnel. "...than what you did up there..." He pointed north toward the hospital.

Leyla walked around the front of the truck and entered the truck's passenger seat, closing the door softly. The interior light stayed on.

"You gotta, you gotta close it a little harder, it's not shut all the way." Wells patiently told Leyla. She opened the door and closed it a little more firmly. The light went out.

"Alright then. Door is ajar no more." Wells said in a slightly over the top country accent, whilst pushing the accelerator and moving the truck into the dark tunnel. Even with the bright LED headlamps burning, the tunnel seemed impossibly dark and stretched on infinitely. Wells looked over to Leyla.

"You remember anything? Bout being down here?"

"No, not really. Have you been down here before?"

"Yeah, a couple times. First time we had a missing person case. Whole squad of us came down here and searched for hours and hours and came up empty handed. Went all the way to end of the tunnel. Nothin' but rock there."

"And your friend?" Leyla asked.

"Yeah that was the second time I came down; but by then the PD was actin' fuckin' weird. Told me to lay off and drop it. Didn't make any sense. Came down on my own then. Got nothin' out of it. Folks come down here, and they just, poof, disappear. That's when it got sealed up. Cut the whole entrance off to the world."

"What about us?"

"I guess we'll see." Wells said, ominously.

Ten minutes of driving straight into the dark abyss and the only things either Wells or Leyla had seen were the occasional graffiti on the wall or some bits of garbage possibly left by squatters. Wells let off the accelerator to slow the already creeping pickup. They'd come to the large stone wall he mentioned before. The end of the line. It looked like it was attacked by a beast of immense size, clawing at it and searching for something or someone to devour.

"The hell did that?" Leyla asked Wells, hoping it wasn't actually a towering demon.

"Mining drill. It's how they dug out the tunnels." Wells replied, no longer taken aback by Leyla's oblivious nature.

"Oh, good. Good. Not a giant monster, then."

"That we know of." Wells poked fun at Leyla.

"Nope. No we're not doing that. We aren't playing the scare Leyla game. We are deep down in a dark tunnel where people vanish for good. Not cool, man."

Wells laughed. "Sorry. It is creepy as hell down here. I gotta smile somehow." He opened his door and got out, walking slowly to the front of the truck. Leyla followed suit, quickly rounding the front end and nearing Wells. Perhaps if there was a monster down there, it would choose to slaughter the larger, meatier muscle man and not her.

Stepping near the wall, Leyla felt a bit of a tingle on her spine. Almost like a chill but more subdued. Wells's cell phone rang from his pickup. Wells instinctually smacked his back left pocket where he normally kept his cell phone only to find that it was, in fact, in his truck.

"I'll be back." He said to Leyla and half-jogged to the door. Leyla barely paid him any mind at all. The fine hair on her arms stood up. The closer she got to the wall, the stronger the sensation. She could hear Wells answer his phone and speak to someone on the other end but that didn't matter. The wall was very strange; irresistibly gravitational. She stretched her fingers out to touch it, and felt a tingle in her fingers the closer she got.

Wells finished up his phone call and closed out the screen. "Alright sorry about that."

Leyla drew her finger away from the wall and turned to Wells as he walked back up toward her.

"So, supercop…" Leyla said to Wells. "What are we looking for now?"

Leyla tried to be smooth and cool and crossed her arms and leaned to the wall. But her shoulder hit nothing. She went right through as if there was no barrier. She was so surprised she could only let out half a horrified yelp before the wall swallowed her completely.

Wells ran to the wall after seeing that and hit solid rock.

"What the fuck?" Wells backed away and kicked the wall. Indeed, it was solid. "Leyla?" Wells yelled.

No response.

Leyla was gone.

CHAPTER THREE

SubCity

Leyla fell into complete darkness, slamming shoulder-first into what felt like a metal platform; maybe a grated floor. It was still dark. The kind of dark where one starts to *feel* sounds and see the blood pumping through your own eye. But monsters don't have steel grating for stomachs. At least Leyla didn't *think* they did.

Shit, I just fuckin' died, she thought to herself. *The creepy tunnel monster just ate me. I'm falling down its throat and—* suddenly, she was nearly blinded by a rush of rich, blue light. Her eyes hadn't adjusted to the darkness and now they had to be shocked by this. Neon bars had illuminated her surroundings. The ground she'd felt was indeed a gigantic, grated metal platform;as large as a small parking lot. It looked like a huge *elevator.*

Just as she felt an incoming panic, the ground beneath her lurched downward. She jumped to her feet and tried to go back to the wall she'd fallen through but she was dropping away from it too quickly. The whir of gears and cables surrounded her and confirmed she was in an enormous elevator. *Probably to transport humongous man-eating monsters*, she thought.

Descending into the Earth at a fairly rapid pace, she caught a glimpse of where she was going through a small window, but it passed upward too quickly to get a good look.

She moved closer to the edge of the elevator, hoping another window was coming. She got her wish. Another window, only a foot high yet several feet across, passed by. She was able to get a second peek.

A sea of lights. *That looks like a city,* she thought. *Underground?*

The window had passed. She moved ever closer to the opposite wall as it rushed upward, letting her know she was going further and further underground, all the while illuminated by the blue light.

Another window passed but this time it was immediately followed by another. And then another, and another. She saw *buildings,* albeit obscured by the steam passing in front of her.

Why is there steam? She asked herself. Not important, really. She'd just seen *buildings* inside a cave.

The elevator slowed rapidly and stopped as immense locking mechanisms snapped into place with an intense metallic clang that echoed its way back up the shaft she'd just descended. The air was warmer, convincing the goosebumps she had to go away. Leyla couldn't help but notice the air even felt more crisp and less polluted than the city above.

The wall in front of her separated down the middle, revealing itself to be a massive door. Each side slid away from each other as the steam from outside poured into the elevator, taking Leyla over before she could see outside. She heard some machines kick on overhead. Leyla ducked, not realizing nothing was going to harm her. The steam was sucked into rather large ventilation fans that had been attached to the elevator for just this purpose. Then, Leyla looked forward, and saw it.

Buildings, coated in lights, stretching upwards of at least a few hundred feet. They were *skyscrapers*, beneath the city of Cincinnati. A web of monorails and walkways connected the buildings, which were painted in neon light with hues of blue, purple, pink, and gorgeous white. Leyla stepped out of the elevator and onto the street level of this impossible location. The buildings may've been interesting, but the actual flying cars that were drifting in and out of view just couldn't be real, she thought.

Leyla finally noticed the *people*. They traversed the city at every square foot, looking like an ant colony hard at work, if ants wore clothes that glowed and had robot parts.

Wait…that's even more weird, Leyla thought, noticing that seemingly every person she could see had some sort of metallic or cybernetic body part of some kind. They were all moving across the walkways, through the street, in and out of buildings, and some simply sat and stood outside, resting at cafes and street diners exactly like any normal city except…they had robot parts.

The only place Leyla had seen anything like this was in a discarded comic book she'd found during a day of rummaging through a dumpster next to an apartment building. In it, there was a guy that was nearly all robot parts called Cyborg. He was friends with Superman.

Is Superman down here too? That would be nice, Leyla let the image of a shirtless Man of Steel run over her mind.

FOOD! Leyla sniffed, realizing she was finally near a meal for the first time in hours. Her mind was consumed by the thought of whatever the hell this place had to eat and she just ran toward the first place she saw people chowing down. Then she smelled what simply must be actual heaven. But it was coming from another direction than she was headed. She broke left, toward the familiar smell.

It was from a small street vendor with a rolling cart that had an oven attached, with at least a dozen people standing in line waiting. She didn't bother to notice the several patrons that had metallic limbs in place of flesh and bone. This was about the food, not the people in the way.

The street vendor bent over to pull whatever was in the oven out and was met with Leyla's voracious energy upon standing, holding her creation on a large, wooden spatula: a classic pepperoni pizza with minced garlic and Italian seasoning. Virtually every person Leyla skipped to get to the front was yelling obscenities at her, but her mind was focused on one thing.

"I'll pay you back!", Leyla yelled at the surprised vendor.

She looked at Leyla for a second like she was crazy, then down at the simple pepperoni and cheese pizza she'd just baked, then to Leyla.

"Pay me back for what?" The lady asked in a Brooklyn accent.

"I don't have any money, I'm so sorry, but I haven't had food for at least a day. I can pay you back somehow, if you can just give me a bite of it or something! It smells amazing!" Leyla pleaded with the vendor, who recoiled when she heard the word *money*.

"Okay…" The vendor replied. "SubCity don't use money. Oh shit—are you—your chips are fried, huh?" The vendor asked, only half sarcastically.

"Fried chips? What? Like potato chips?"

"No. Your head. Implants? Your ch...ok are you here for pizza or not?"

"Yeah, pizza; I'm here for pizza. Always here for pizza." Leyla couldn't take her eyes off the gorgeous, steaming pie.

"Might wanna head to Cross-Eyes to have your chips checked. Those old implants are always fuckin' failin'. Let me scan your SD and you can have however many slices you need."

Leyla had no idea what an SD was, and her facial expression said as much.

"They fried that bad? On your wrist, airhead. Your wrist." The lady pointed to Leyla's left arm.

Leyla looked at her wrist and back to the lady, still confused. Someone behind Leyla yelled.

"Get out o' the fuckin' way, you're holding everybody up!"

The vendor reiterated about the SD again.

"Your wrist. Your SubDermal? Come on. Pie's gettin' cold and I got hungry folks."

Leyla shook her head in confusion. The vendor reached over to grab Leyla's left hand, but Leyla pulled away from her.

"Ah Hell." The vendor explained, then pulled back from Leyla and held her left hand up, pointing to her wrist. "There's a chip under your skin, right here. I need to scan it. You get food. And then you take your skinny little ass to Cross-Eyes to get re-coded."

Leyla reluctantly gave the pizza vendor her hand. The vendor held a small digital scanner over Leyla's wrist. Nothing happened. She waved the reader over the wrist a few times. Nothing. The vendor then waved the reader over her own left wrist. A blue light blipped on from under her skin, and the digital scanner beeped in a higher pitch than before.

"I don't think I have one." Leyla said, referring to the most likely absent SD.

"You do. Everybody's got one. Your biochips are all out of wack. Probably what's causing the memory loss."

Whatever you say, lady, Leyla thought, and shook her head in agreement with a new confusion as the vendor sliced the pizza into eight pieces with a cutter.

"I scanned my own damn SD so it's accounted for. Here you go. 2 slices of Pepp."

"Thank you, you're amazing!" Leyla snatched the pizza from the vendor and bit straight into the crust first, letting out an audible *mmmmmmmmmm* that could easily be mistaken for an adult film sound bite.

The vendor almost said something about the sin of biting into pizza crust-first but decided it didn't matter.

"Cross-Eyes is down the street, just past Fritzy Joe's, the loud ass bar with all the string lights." The vendor said, as Leyla had already turned to walk off, stuffing her face with pizza.

She gave the vendor a thumbs up, smeared with marinara, and then quickly retracted the thumb to suck off the pizza sauce. She turned back to the vendor with the most satisfied face in history, with emotional, puppy dog eyes, and with a mouthful of pizza, said "Thank you!"

The vendor waved back at Leyla, still processing the odd encounter she'd just had. The customer behind Leyla stepped up, grimacing.

"She ain't got the right to be skippin' all us! Shoulda told her ass to go."

"HEY! You damn well know that was probably one of Blackhawk's girls. Now gimme ya wrist! And don't mention even seeing her here. I don't even wanna deal with that shit storm."

***

Leyla made her way down the main street; a singular stretch of concrete-asphalt that ran for maybe a quarter mile straight ahead. It was absolutely teaming with shops on both sides, each one glazing the road with its own unique shade of neon. There were actually a few older motorcycles and cars; normal ones with wheels, but they were all modified at least a little. That deja vu feeling crept in again, and crawled its way up Leyla's spine and into her brain.

This place was a little too familiar, but she thought it was likely due to the similarity of the big street festival in Kentucky a couple years ago. It was right across the river from the city. Leyla and Deli had made their way there to try and score some sympathy food from the tourists. It had worked a little too well.

By the time they were crossing the river to get back to the tent city they were both so bloated and over-fed they puked over the railing and into the water. It was a good day. One of the best memories Leyla had of Del. Hopefully, this is where Leyla can find her.

"HEY! Watch it! Are you five?!" Leyla bumped into one of the citizens on the street, hard enough to cause them to drop their plate of noodles and chicken and fire back in anger.

"Sorry! Oh, that smelled good. Sorry." Leyla sniffed at the food she just caused the man to drop and then looked up at him. The sight of him was enough to make her take a step back.

The man was bald, but when he was yelling, the skin on his head *peeled up* like flaps. Kind of like the pet chicken Korean Jesus used to have; it would flare its feathers up when it got pissed off. And now Leyla'd found a new chicken. But the guy didn't appreciate Leyla's stare.

"What?! Do I got a dick on my face? What you staring at?" He said.

"Your head. It looks like chicken feathers." Leyla replied, cocking her hand up to head and springing her fingers to the air to imitate the man's weird head flaps.

"Really? That's mature." The guy said, and walked over back to the line where he got his food, shaking his head.

This was when Leyla really looked at *everyone*. It was a little tough to see back at the pizza vendor; it was darker there. But now the lights brought out all the details of the people of this sprawling underground city. In the line with Chicken Head Man were at least seven or eight other men and women with prosthetic arms. Another ten with metallic legs. Some of the legs were partially covered in skin; some were just bare metal and wire circuitry. Every single person had some sort of body modification. The more Leyla studied the crowd, the more extreme the body mods got.

One woman in the line was bobbing her head to music from what looked like headphones jutting out from behind her ears. When she got to the vendor to order, the headphones automatically retracted *into her head* to allow her to hear the ambient world again.

"Oh that's so cool!" Leyla remarked to herself, forgetting that this was definitely strange enough for her to be worried. The thing was, she didn't remember enough of the world before to understand that this was not normal. For all she knew, this was just where all the weirdos lived, and that was that.

Not to mention, she thought the city just looked amazing. Never before had she seen such a shiny and fantastic vista as this city. It was grimey, but it was gorgeous. It was mesmerizing and it was loud and it was chock full of delicious smelling food. Neon tubing crawled its way up the buildings like vines on trees and cast everything in a rainbow of color.

There was a wide selection of plants as well, from bushes to palm trees, flowers to ferns, most of which seemed to have been infused with vibrant fiber optics that pulsated to nearby sounds, hinting that the flora could react to their environment in ways Leyla had never seen.

Each shop was playing its own music. Some of it she'd heard before as cars would pass by or when she'd use the free WiFi outside the McDonald's near the village on the cell phone she'd found; she learned to play her guitar on YouTube that way. Other music, though, sounded completely different. Almost futuristic; crunchy and grungy. Kind of like sci-fi techno from the 80s but more aggressive.

Leyla heard a pounding and heavy synthwave beat overhead and looked up to find the source. Stretched between two of the walkways above that connect the buildings, there was a billboard, much like the ones up on the city above, except the advertisement on it scrolled across in a holographic 3D fashion and it had huge speaker boxes on either side. That was where the music was coming from. It read 'Don't miss The DigiDevils at Fritzy Joe's! Friday At MIDNIGHT! Free E-Spaz for all WOMEN!"

"Fritzy Joe's..." Leyla read the billboard to herself through squinted eyes. *Oh! Fritzy Joe's! I'm supposed to go there. Also what day is it?* Leyla turned to find the nearest person, which happened to be a woman passing by that didn't have a shirt on, exposing what was left of her chest—mostly a cavity protected by clear material shaped like breasts, which also bounced exactly like normal and had nipples. The clear chest piece had a keyhole, and the lady was wearing a necklace with a key to match. Strange.

Leyla could see the woman's very real heart beating inside, although it was supplemented with carbon fiber and titanium tubes and vents. Her chest even had accent lighting that cycles color from red to green to blue to white, illuminating her organs like a macabre and strangely hot Christmas tree. The woman noticed Leyla's eyes trained on her chest, but she seemed unbothered by it. She cupped her translucent breasts and lifted them up sarcastically. The bare chested woman walked right on by, winked, and ran her tongue across her top lip at Leyla, who finally began to understand how off kilter this place was.

"What day is it?" Leyla asked the woman.

"Friday." Christmas Tree Boob Lady remarked nonchalantly, and strode on past.

"Thanks! I like your chest!" Leyla attempted to compliment the lady but recoiled in embarrassment.

"Oh that didn't come out right. Not like your uh your chest like, your, inside the, okay. But your chest is nice too! I"m just gonna walk *that* way now."

Leyla pointed toward Fritzy Joe's and shrank herself down a bit to stave off her mouth from blurting out any more awkward nonsense. Twiddling her fingers, she noticed some string lights down the street a bit more, at least a thousand big bulbs spouting out enough light to ensure that whoever they belonged to was noticed from anywhere on the entire street. *Must be Fritzy Joe's,* she thought to herself.

***

Fritzy Joe's was as much a music venue as it was a bar. It was also as much a strip club as it was a restaurant. Nestled in the legion of bright, slightly yellow string lights was a sign made of large Edison bulbs attached to a black backboard, much like the marquee staple of 1920s America. It read 'GET FRITZY'.

Once inside, Leyla noticed the staff, composed of men and women—unanimously drop-dead gorgeous—were all shirtless. They were serving drinks and dancing with patrons and some just sat and casually talked with everyone.

More nipples, Leyla thought. *This place has freed the fuck out of the nipple.*

To compliment the loud decor, an equally loud sound danced its way into the street where Leyla approached. Intense, crunching guitars. Pounding, hypnotic bass and snares. Electronic synths akin to the 8-bit melodies of a Super Nintendo game score with a shot of industrial metal.

It was the same song that was playing on the billboard outside.

At the forefront of that song was a voice that soared into the very being of anyone that heard it; grungy, raspy, and torn, yet fantastic, embracing, and with ridiculous range. It was the vocal cord mastery of the one and only Vox Vermin, who had some flashy cyber-ware over his vocal cords, giving him a musical edge like none other. There weren't many celebrities in this metropolis but Vox was an absolute rockstar, and he was blowing everyone away on stage right now.

Leyla was quickly bewitched by this figure, stomping to the drum beat and slinging his vintage, blue 1958 Gibson Explorer guitar at his waist, strumming his rhythmic pattern only to belt out more vocals, and the hypnotized crowd joined in.

"Hey!" Vox growled into the mic. "HEY!"

The crowd replied. *"Hey!",*

"HEY! *You fuckin' BREAK ME!*" Vox screamed the chorus to the absolutely electrified patrons.

The drummer behind him was particularly interesting to Leyla, who held two drumsticks in each hand for some odd reason. To Vox's left was another musician wielding a bright orange Yamaha keyboard guitar to top off the song with its iconic synthesizers. He seemed to have no body modifications to speak off, at least on the surface. It seemed everyone down here had something unique going on.

Mist and lasers erupted around the members of the band, shrouding them in a cacophony of smoked out badassery.

Aside from the small folk bands at the street fair with Del a while back, Leyla had never seen or heard anything that came close to this live performance, let alone experienced the entrancing sound of heavy guitars and electronica banging on her eardrums. Before long, Leyla had joined in with the other concert goers closer to the band, bobbing and weaving her head, tossing her hair around, eyes closed, grinning as wide as possible.

Suddenly, there was nary a care in the world. For a moment, she'd forgotten about the tent city life. She'd forgotten about Del and the asylum and its crazy orderlies and doctor no longer existed in her mind.

This was the first live rock show experience she'd had. The world was simply the moment, and the music. Euphoria.

Suddenly, the lights all cut out and the band went completely silent. The only thing heard were the whispers of an anxious crowd. A high pitched guitar tone faded in, growing louder and louder until one beastly riff interrupted and then immediately stopped after two muted strums.

The lights, lasers, and mist erupted all at once with the guitars and drums punishing the crowd's eardrums with a bridge/solo as epic as anyone there has ever seen, at least since the likes of Ozzy Osbourne and Metallica were dominating stages in the mid-80s.

Vox was silent, but he was head banging and swinging his long hair all over the place in tandem with the drums and his perfected guitar licks. The madness on stage took a turn for the extreme as the drummer's arms each split into two. The now quad-armed master of rhythm laid into the drums at double his original speed just as Vox and his keyboardist mate doubled their efforts as well. Leyla couldn't help but imitate Vox's headbanging, allowing her hair to wildly flail around. The song had entranced everyone in the club from the music-loving crowd to even the bar-back, bobbing his head as he scooped dirty glasses from the polished wood-grain bar.

The music stopped. The lights went dim yet again. But this time, the crowd exploded in cheers and whistles and a few cries of 'I love you, Vox!' were peppered throughout.

"And we love you." Vox replied through the microphone, shrouded in darkness. This prompted an even louder reaction from the countless patrons. After a few moments, the lights came back, but the band had left the stage and some people scurried onto the stage to remove their instruments and gear. This was a band with the clout to neglect proper goodbyes to their fan base.

Leyla was grabbed by a fan walking by. "EFFIN' AMAZING!", the fan screamed into Leyla's face. She had no reply available, so she just smiled and nodded *yes*. The owner of the establishment, Fritzy Joe himself took to the stage.

"HEY!", Joe exclaimed to the crowd, many of which were migrating to the bar to re-order drinks. He didn't expect a reply, and was interrupted by fans of the band, still under the last song's spell. "HEY!", more than half of them yelled back, mimicking Vox's chant earlier.

"Yeah ok, I gotcha!" Joe yelled back but quickly continued. "So my man Vox and the DigiDevils just informed me that they are gonna be back in here a little later to hang out upstairs in the E-lounge. Everybody is. "

Joe's speech began to skip like a scratched compact disc. "Every-Everybbbbb...Everybody-Every. "

Leyla had been making her way to the bar nearby. A 40-something athletically fit woman with dirty blonde hair at the bar, sipping on a whiskey sour and smudging the glass with her pink lipstick, noticed the new face.

"Hey, haven't seen you in here before!" The woman said to Leyla. "But you obviously liked the music."

"Is he okay?" Leyla asked the woman about Joe.

"Oh yeah, Joe's fine he's just on the fritz. Get it? HA!" The woman clearly loved the joke, even if it seems she's told it a hundred times before.

"Oh." Leyla let out a nervous laugh. "So what's that mean?"

"Well he used to play here too. Had a few high quality reactor implants in his cortex. One night he plugged his gear into a faulty electric line and...zap. Implants shorted out."

"Oh, wow."

"Yeah. Caused that thing. The stutter."

Joe slapped the top of his head fairly hard, but it allowed him to continue. "Everybbbbbody is welcome up there! Remember free E-Spaz for you ladies! Guys gotta pay and sign the waiver cuz remember those things give you a boner for like seven hours. Not doctor recommendddded."

The woman continued with Leyla. "But, as you can see, he is okay. He tried to get Cross-Eyes to repair his brain but you know, changing out deep cortex implants is dicey. So, he changed the name of his bar from Uncle Joe's to Fritzy Joe's. People took to that even more and the place has been packed every night since."

Leyla nodded, unsure of what to say in return. Thankfully, the woman took the lead again.

"I'm Mari." The woman said, holding out her hand to shake. For once, the socially awkward Leyla knew what to do, and reached back to shake in return.

"Now *that's* a grip!" Mari replied to the unexpected firmness from Leyla.

"Did you say Cross-Eyes? I think I'm supposed to see Cross-Eyes." Leyla replied. "Oh and, I'm Leyla! Leyla is my name."

"Yes, Leyla, nice to meet you. Think that's the name of the main character in a show I like! Cross-Eyes is the next shop down. Leave here and turn right. But uh, he ain't open 'til morning. Maybe 9. Maybe Noon. He does what he wants. You just gotta kind of hope you catch him."

"So I can't see him til the morning?"

"Most likely not. What's going on?"

"I don't know, the pizza lady said I have potato chips in my brain or something."

"Potato chips? Ok you know what, I'm gonna stop being nosy. Sorry. Personality trait. Or programming. Shit, I don't know the difference in this place anymore. You'll have to wait 'til morning for Cross-Eyes either way."

"Oh. Well, I don't remember where uh, I live." Leyla slowly let a lie roll off her tongue. She wasn't very good at it.

"Mmmm. Guess the pizza lady was talking about your biochips. Makes sense. Memory loss is normal when they fail. Either that or you were one of Blackhawk's girls. Either way, you can crash at my place for the night if you need."

Blackhawk's girls? What's that mean? Leyla asked herself. She was unsure of trusting this Mari character. Perhaps she was just extremely friendly. So far, everyone else down here seemed helpful at best and rude at worst. She decided to take the chance.

"Sure." Leyla replied to Mari, who'd just gulped down the last bit of her drink.

"Don't worry. I promise I'm not a serial killer." Mari laughed.

Leyla almost asked Mari what she meant by Blackhawk's girls, but kept the question for later, if ever.

"But, promise me one thing." Mari asked, holding up her index finger to Leyla. "You don't tell anybody I let you stay either."

"Ok, yeah. Sure." *She is 100% a serial killer*, Leyla thought. *But it's either chance staying at her place for the night or sleeping on the street in a crazy robot-people-city.*

"Ok, good. Now let's go meet Vox before we hit the sack." Mari quipped, and Leyla's eyes widened. "Vox?" Leyla replied. "The singer?!"

Mari reached behind her bar and nabbed two high gravity beers. She popped off the caps with her thumbs.

That's a cool fuckin' party trick, Leyla thought.

Mari smiled and held the beers head high. "They don't trust sober people. Hope you like barleywine."

CHAPTER FOUR

Cross - Eyes

The sun peeked through bamboo blinds, tickling Leyla's eyelids just enough to wake her. She opened her eyes slightly, but the sting of bad sleep forced her to close them and stretch her legs instead. She was under some intensely smooth fabric, certainly more luxurious than the old sleeping bag she was used to. Opening her eyes again and blinking the burning sensation away, she could now get her bearings on where she was.

I thought it was dark down here, Leyla wondered. *Now daylight? Am I back on the surface? Was I dreaming?*

First, she noticed the fine material of the sheets wrapped around her bare legs. Definitely silk. Matching pillow case, wrapped snugly around a down-stuffed cushion. Across from her was an aged white dresser with an ultra wide television perched on top. It powered itself on.

"Hello, Good Morning Ms. [IDENTITY UNKNOWN], would you prefer the blinds open or closed?", the TV AI spoke to Leyla.

Robot TV, okay, not dreaming. Leyla told herself.

"Uh, closed?" Leyla replied, knowing her eyes could barely take the amount of light already clawing at her corneas.

"Very well. Mari is preparing breakfast for you. I will alert her that you are awake. Have a nice day, Ms. [IDENTITY UNKNOWN]."

"Leyla." Leyla mumbled, burying her face in the pillow.

"Leia?"

"No, LEYLA. Leyla is my name."

"Very well, pleased to meet you, Leera."

Leyla didn't bother correcting the TV that time; she raised a thumb up, unsure of whether the TV could see her as much as it could hear her.

She pulled herself out of bed. She was dressed only in panties—not hers—and no top. Her skin felt smoother than normal; less gritty and greasy.

This feels nice, she thought. *Did I take a shower?*

"I have cleaned your attire, Ms. Leera, it is currently in the dryer awaiting removal," the AI spoke through the TV again.

"Stop talking."

"Yes ma'am." The AI went silent.

Leyla slid out of the luxurious bed and headed for what seemed like the bathroom door. Fortunately she was correct.

After taking care of business there, she heard Mari calling for her from another room, so she investigated, catching a whiff of bacon in the air. She was covering her breasts with an arm and entered a small kitchen/dining room where Mari was cooking. The frying bacon almost distracted her from the apartment itself. It was all concrete walls under flat yellow and white paint that began to fade away a long time before.

The entire apartment was very minimalist. There was only furniture where there should be furniture, and even that furniture was plain. It was weird but damn, it was also relaxing.

"Figured you'd like some breakfast." Mari said, standing over some sizzling bacon and a pot of southern grits. "Grits and bacon. Sorry, out of eggs til the next shipment comes down."

"Grits?"

"Southern food. I'm from the Carolinas. Y'all don't eat this much up here, but it's good for you. How's your head?"

"I'm fine. Don't remember much though."

"Really? After that many drinks? No hangover? Damn girl you're a beast. You out drank Vox last night. Blacked out. Tracer brought you up."

"Tracer?"

"The drummer. Here, eat up. It's Saturday, but Cross-Eyes is usually in for a while on weekends.."

"Do you have a shirt? Did Tracer see me…with no shirt?" Leyla asked.

"You challenged Vox to a game of strip pong. He won. You refused to put a shirt back on. Yelled *free the nipple* for an hour straight. So yes. Tracer saw the girls. Everyone did." Mari laughed. "But I left a shirt for you on the end of the bed, you didn't see it?"

"Oh, no!" Leyla rushed back to the bed and, yes, there was a loose fitting t-shirt lying on the foot end. She put it on and went back to the kitchen. Mari had set the table for her.

Leyla flushed red and pulled a chair from the small dining table. "Did they laugh?"

"Laugh at what?"

Leyla motioned a circle around her chest.

"Oh, girl, don't worry. We are as free as we want to be here. No one's freaking out over your chest. Eat up."

Leyla tried the grits, not exactly thrilled. But she scarfed down a strip of bacon easily.

"It's okay if you don't like the grits. I got cereal too."

"No, it's okay, it's good!" Leyla forced down spoonfuls out of politeness. *Too salty. Too gritty. Too buttery. Nope. Hate it.*

"Your clothes are cleaned but, girl, you're dressed like you live under a bridge. No offense."

"Really?" Leyla almost told Mari she was right.

"Let's pick you an outfit from my closet. Unless dirty hobo is your style. I'm not asking a bunch of questions."

"You'll give me clothes?"

"Yeah, come on." Mari walked Leyla into a large, well organized closet. Pants and shoes on one side, shirts and jackets and hats on the other with a mirror at the wall opposite the door.

"Whoah!" Leyla gawked at the lavish closet."

"Yeah, one of the best closets in SubCity." Take your pick. Got mostly loud, flashy stuff, being the club owner but, you'll look good in whatever."

"Wait, you own a club?"

"Yeah Fritzy's."

"I thought Joe was..."

"Joe used to own it. Once he had his accident he gave control to his book keeper." Mari explained, pointing at herself. "Now come on, pick an outfit. I'll be in the other room.

***

Mari organized some business files on a PC in her living room, next to a large window with a view of the city outside. A few succulent plants rested on the shelf in front of the window. Sunlight poured in, drowning the room in natural light.

On the desk with the PC lay a book titled *Throw Your Shit Away:The Art of Japanese Minimalism*. Leyla walked in wearing a horribly mismatched set of clothes, also eyeing the book.

Well, that explains the bare ass apartment, she thought.

"How is it so bright out there?" Leyla asked, pointing to the window.

Mari looked up. "Oh, solar simulators. Just like daylight. Keeps the plants healthy too." She looked at Leyla and held back a laugh.

Leyla had picked a form fitting baseball tee, white with yellow sleeves that stopped just below the elbows, dark blue leather-type pants with a metallic sheen, and a pair of bright red Converse Chuck Taylors, which were the first thing Mari noticed in this monstrosity of a mismatched outfit.

"I see you went with the vintage Chucks! Everything else is uh, well, you've certainly got an outfit. Alright, come on I'll take you down."

"Is it bad? Are these clothes okay?"

"You look like you fit in more here. No one down here gives a shit what anyone else thinks."

Well that's not much of an answer, Leyla thought. *Fancy way of telling me I look like an idiot. They're your damn clothes, lady.*

Mari led Leyla to a small entryway with an elevator. Pressing the button to call the elevator, Mari turned to Leyla.

"Now remember, you weren't here. Just have Cross-Eyes check you out and get back to Blackhawk once he's got you up and running. Don't tell anyone I let you chill here."

"Ok, you mentioned this Blackhawk thing before, what's that?"

"He. Blackhawk is our uh, I'm not gonna say *leader*. He's just, like, a dad that wants the best for everyone but sometimes he can be a little too strict. Don't tell him I said that. Actually, you weren't here."

The elevator dinged and opened up.

***

At the bottom floor, Mari and Leyla exited the elevator into Fritzy Joe's, all locked up and darkened after the wild night before. All the chairs were turned upside down and placed on their tables.

"Oh you live above the club?" Leyla asked.

"Yeah, it's kinda nice."

Instead of going for the front door, Mari turned and led Leyla around the cleaned bar, to a back entrance. She was serious about hiding Leyla—or at least the fact she had let her stay the night. Mari exited into a small alleyway beside the club with Leyla just behind.

"Now, again, you were not here." Mari stopped Leyla, who then nodded in agreement. "Leave here, turn right. Cross-Eyes is the next building down. Big red cross on the wall. Well, an X actually."

"Okay, thank you for the food and clothes. And bed. And last night, whatever happened."

"Feel free to sneak off again sometime, I got you. Long as you don't say anything to anyone." Mari waved Leyla off.

Who the fuck is this Blackhawk guy? Why do I have to keep secrets now? Leyla wondered. *This is too much damn work. Need to find Del. Everyone keeps saying Cross-Eyes is important. So, he's next up. Maybe he knows something.*

***

Sure enough, the building next door to Fritzy's was adorned with a mammoth Red Cross sign turned on its side to resemble an X. The graphic was so large that the entrance to the establishment had no choice but to jut itself into the intersection of the X.

Leyla wondered why Cross-Eyes would have gone with an X instead of a normal medical symbol, but she didn't dwell long. A bearded man stormed out of the doorway, yelling obscenities back inside. He was carrying his own detached left arm—a skeletal and metallic limb that was twitching like a snake with its head freshly cleaved off.

"Have fun." The man snarked at Leyla as he passed. The twitchy arm grabbed Leyla's as the man passed, so she jerked her arm out of its grip and instinctively brushed off her arm in the same manner as if it were just touched by a nasty insect.

Keep your robot hands to yourself, douchebag, she thought.

She heard someone inside the clinic yell back at the man just before the door swung closed.

"I told you 'iss the micron servos! See ye next week!" The disembodied voice called out in a sharp Cockney accent. Whoever it was kept talking, but the door had closed now and it was only an inaudible jumble to Leyla, who turned to look back at the angry man walking away, and then back to the clinic door. Nothing else to do but go in.

***

Cross-Eyes, muttering and cursing the man who'd just left, made his way around a heavily modified dentist's chair to clean the previously used medical instruments. The items strewn about the table beside the chair looked like more of a mix of surgical tools and overly-complicated auto repair gear. The man himself was dressed in cargo jeans and a black t-shirt, with a sleeveless doctor's jacket. Calling the jacket white would have been too generous. It was full of stains and more of the cream color one would end up with if they left fabric in a damp cellar for ten years. He had replaced his eyes with some very advanced goggles. They had two lenses rotated and switched places from time to time, much like an old 8 millimeter camera, as Cross-Eyes focused his vision through them.

Damn man has a camera for a face. Leyla made herself laugh at that thought, but she hid it well.

The room itself was mostly clean and organized but it had the vibe of an old and musty motel rather than a medical clinic— complete with a short circuiting light bulb in the back corner and an audible water drip coming from somewhere. And why did it smell like vinegar?

"No more patients today!" Cross-Eyes abruptly stopped walking, noticing Leyla stepping into the door. "Detrich there, that bloody lump of wet bread, just fried my re-core board. He finks he's smart'ah dan a doctor! Smart'ah dan me! Who da 'ell are you?"

"I'm, uh–"

"Well spit it right out, then. Do ye not know ye own name?"

"Leyla. I was told to have you check for potato chips."

"Potat'o chips? What you on about?"

"Oh wait, uh, chips. Brain chips? Brain chips. I don't know, the pizza lady said check my head out. I don't remember things sometimes, I'm sorry!"

"Oh!" Cross-Eyes finally catches on. "Your neural transponders, likely. So what's goin' on? Memory problems? Increased sexual appetite? Ye suddenly cravin' spinach and red meat?"

"Why would I crave spinach?"

"The transponders start actin' up, it decreases the iron in ye body, so your body wants more iron. Is 'at it? You goin' Popeye on me?"

"No, I don't think so..."

"Well, actually, your iron doesn't decrease. Fault'y transponders juss make ye brain fink it did. So what's goin' on?"

Cross-Eyes raised a brow at Leyla, polishing one of the medical instruments. "You smellin' it?"

"What?" Leyla asked.

"Vinegar." Cross-Eyes said.

"Yeah."

"Aye. Madness stench. Could be schizophrenia. Could be psychosis. Who knows. I would know. You wouldn't. Just imagine iss apple pie."

"Okay..." Leyla prepped to run if needed.

"So, what's ye problem? Chips actin' up?"

"Um, yeah. I can't remember anything from before three years ago."

"Free years ago, eh? Das odd. Normally iss more short term loss."

"And, I have these seizures. My friend Del called them absence seizures. Maybe that's why I can't remember stuff?"

"Oh yeh, fault'y neural circuitry can have a similar effect if you got them Pantheon versions. You're prett'y fancy if you got those implants. Only people that got those are..."

Cross-Eyes stopped moving around again and stared at Leyla like she'd suddenly become a werewolf. Leyla knew exactly what he was about to say.

"Blackhawk's girls." He said, proving Leyla's intuition correct. "Oh, you poor girl. He's gone and done it again."

"Done what? Who's this Blackhawk guy?"

"Sit. Here." Cross-Eyes pointed to the dentist chair. Directly above the chair was a rather large orb connected to the ceiling that was outfitted with a dozen other medical apparatuses, including a bright LED light for working on patients. It looked like a freaky spider-monster, and it was basically telling Leyla to get the fuck out of there. *If he touches that thing*, Leyla decided, *I am bolting.*

"Look, if you're not rememberin', it's likely because you *chose* to have your memory wiped. Sometimes it doesn't take. And that's no good. It initiates an adverse reaction with the nano machinery in your gray matt'ah, and it concludes with cellular breakdown of da tissues."

"What's that mean? I had my memories taken?"

"Not taken. Wiped. But if I don't fix dis, you're dead. And I'll not have one of his circle die on my hands."

"Who's Blackhawk?"

"Blackhawk is the man that's goin' to save the bloody effed world, he is. And you girls are da key to it."

"Girls? What girls? And what if Cross-Eyes is wrong? What if my memory isn't erased? What's a nano thingie? What if—"

Leyla's thoughts slowed to a stop and her head went numb.

Her eyes twitched back and forth and everything went black. Yet another anxiety induced seizure. Cross-Eyes was quick to catch her as she collapsed, out of consciousness. The ordeal only lasted a few more seconds and she came to, picking up right where her mind had left off.

"What if I'm not one of his girls?!" Leyla yelled out, before realizing she was now in Cross-Eyes's arms and on her knees on the floor.

She swung and smacked Cross-Eyes with an open palm, putting him on his ass and gifting him a nice sting.

"How did you move so fast?" She asked him.

"I didn't. You just had one of ye seizures. Bloody 'ell dat hurt."

"Oh, sorry about that, then."

"It's fine, I been hit 'ard'ah." Cross-Eyes rubbed his cheek. "That was bloody stiff, though. You got to be with the Pantheon with a hook like that."

"Pantheon?"

"Blackhawk's girls."

"I'm not sure I want to meet this Blackhawk dude."

"Oh you do." Cross-Eyes got to his feet and helped Leyla up. "Look, he's not scary or bad, like some of these folks down here make it seem. Matt'ah fact, everyone down here looks up to the man. He's saved every one of our arses at least once."

"So, if it's so good, why would I want my memory wiped?"

"Oh, everyone's got their reasons. You got yours, I don't ask why. Which I suppose means I also done said way too much. Let this be the end of it. So how about we take a gander at your *potato chips* now?" Cross-Eyes asked through a slight smile.

Leyla finally let a laugh out, even if it had to push through anxiety and fear.

"All I gott'a do is scan your SD, it should give me da codes for whatev'ah could be wrong." Cross-Eyes ran another type of scanner across Leyla's arm, same as the pizza lady had done. This scanner was larger, though, and had a screen attached.

As before, nothing happened.

"Yeah pizza lady had an issue with that too..." Leyla remarked, prompting a giggle from Cross-Eyes.

"If you're talkin' about the pizza cart down the street, her name is Carol."

"Oh, okay. Carol couldn't scan the thing either."

"Hmmm. Alright then." Cross-Eyes suspiciously got a little quiet as he tried another scan and nothing happened. His eye lenses rotated, effectively zooming his vision in. They now glowed with a slight shade of red. He lifted Leyla's arm a bit and stared at her wrist for a moment. He then moved Leyla's hair away from her neck and stared at both sides, under her ears. Leyla didn't question what was happening, despite still having justified trust issues with the doctor.

"All...good..." Cross-Eyes forced himself to speak. He walked around to the front of Leyla.

"I need ye to undress."

"What?" Now Leyla was back to defensive mode. "Why?"

"Would you like me to ensure that you are okay or are ye afraid of letting a doct'ah look at ye legs and arms? I don't need ye to be naked. Just off with the shirt and trousers. I'm ruling out any issues that could arise."

Leyla very reluctantly complied, moving to remove her shoes first.

"If you're braless today, you can keep the shirt on and I assume you're wearin' some knickers."

"Knickers?"

"Underwear." Cross-Eyes said.

"Oh, uh, am I?" Leyla pulled her pants out at the waist and luckily, she'd taken a pair of bright green panties from Mari's closet as well. "Ok, yeah I gots on the knickers!" Leyla imitated Cross-Eyes' accent as a coping mechanism.

"You makin' fun o me?"

"No! Sorry. Anxiety."

"Ah, all good 'den. I'm just scanning for those transponders or any other mods that might be actin' off the trolley."

Leyla removed the Converse sneakers and then her pants. She almost removed the shirt but remembered that Cross-Eyes offered for her to keep it on. She did not opt for a bra from Mari. Bras were evil.

Cross-Eyes got quiet yet again, forcing Leyla into another ridiculous thought sprint. *Did he find something weird? Do I have robot parts somewhere? Am I an alien? Why would I be an alien? No, has to be robot parts. I hope it's robot parts. If I'm an alien, where am I going to find a spaceship?*

He orbited her as she awkwardly stood there. He finally came to a stop at her side with his head cocked, sporting a confused expression.

"You've got nuffin'." he said.

"Nothing what?" Leyla's heart rate picked up. Her leg muscles tightened. She was ready to book it.

"No transponders or even nanites up here." Cross-Eyes tapped his head. "No mods. No mods nowhere."

"Isn't that good? I won't die?"

"Oh no, you won't die."

"So why are you acting so weird now?" Leyla shifted her weight toward the door.

"Because you're not supposed to be here."

Leyla decided that was enough of the creepy doctor and bolted for the door, leaving the clothes behind. She made it halfway to the door before she blacked out again, crumpling and smacking her head on the concrete floor.

***

Leyla jolted awake, immediately reeling back into a fetal position upon feeling the piercing headache she was now cursed with. The world was black—an abyss accompanied only by a faint, buzzing hum of sorts and the occasional drop of water into a puddle not far away. Even those low decibel sounds were enough to make her head pound even worse. And now, she couldn't see. She was sure her eyes were open, but she blinked a couple times, which magnified the pain in her head, but she had to check. Yep, eyes are open, she thought.

Can't see shit. Hopefully it's just really really dark.

She forced herself up onto her knees and crawled forward slowly, using her left hand every couple inches to feel in front of her until it eventually smacked cold steel. She ran her hand up the thick, vertical bar she'd found and then to the side, discovering another bar. And another, followed by another. This was a fucking cage.

Before that revelation had time to fester in her brain, her vision thankfully began to brighten up, although everything was a blur. Blinking her eyes more, she was able to get the ailment under control and, eventually, her vision was back. That was weird. It was like an old computer booting up one program at a time.

It was still dark, but she could make out her surroundings now.

She confirmed she was in a makeshift prison cell, unfortunately, and the rest of the room was all concrete with a large steel door on the opposite end. The room wasn't very large—maybe as big as a studio apartment. An audible click could be heard from the steel door, and it opened shortly after with a high pitched creak from its rusted hinges. Cross-Eyes popped his face in through the partially opened door and immediately made eye contact with Leyla. He stepped all the way into the room.

"How's your noggin'?" he asked.

Leyla stared at him, expressionless. *This is your fault, you creepy weirdo*, she thought.

"You fell. Smacked it pretty good on my floor. I called Blackhawk to collect you."

Shit. Tried to avoid him for now, Leyla thought to herself. "Why would you call Blackhawk? That's like, the worst idea ever. What's he going to do?"

"He'll tell you 'imself. Now, how's your head?"

"Hurts."

Cross-Eyes moved in closer, just inches away from the bars restraining Leyla.

"He ain't your enemy. But he's gonna want some answers. And he ain't stupid."

Leyla refrained from replying yet again. Cross-Eyes gave her a moment to say something, then politely bowed his head and turned to leave. Leyla spoke up.

"What do I say?"

"Trust me, you'll want to tell him the truth. All he wants to do is help."

Cross-Eyes exited through the steel door and locked it, leaving Leyla alone.

Why lock that door? I'm already locked in the cage way over here. You people are so extra. She thought to herself.

She wasted no time. She stood and pulled each bar of the cell, hoping one was loose. That's how they sometimes got out in movies. Of course, this was a fruitless endeavor. They were all as sturdy as they could possibly be. There was nothing else to try that she could think of. There wasn't a dog with a key in its mouth like in that pirate movie.

She grabbed one bar with both hands and pulled and shook. She tried to pull two bars apart as if she was in a strongman competition. Nothing. The bars were spaced too closely to get more than her forearm through. Certainly, if she tried to push out to her elbow she would get stuck, so she didn't attempt it. There was nothing else in the room save for a mop and broom, a trash can and some cardboard boxes.

The steel door was unlocked again. Leyla backed away from the bars, feigning innocence, and awaited whoever was coming.

The first thing she heard after the door opened was boots on concrete; an unmistakable thud as each hefty heel made contact with the floor, coupled with the sound of leather rubbing on itself, and a vague clacking of metal on metal. Maybe a jacket with big buckles? The mystery figure came in, but it stopped just shy of the light in the room like it knew it was scarier in the shadows. It had something on its shoulder; it looked like a bird.

Leyla heard the fluttering of wings, and a large hawk flapped down from the figure's shoulder and landed on the ground right in front of the shadowy figure, bouncing to a stop. The hawk had *blue* eyes.

That's new, never seen a bird with blue eyes before, Leyla thought.

The figure lurched forward and stepped around the door and into the room, now bathed in the same dim light as Leyla. It was a tall man that commanded attention.

Who the fuck? Is this the Grim Reaper?

The hawk jumped from the ground and back up to the figure's shoulder. It let out a raspy, digitized chirp and turned its head sideways a little.

Please don't be Blackhawk, please don't be Blackhawk, please don't be—The man interrupted her thoughts.

"I'm just gonna guess you know who I am." the man said with a deep and raspy radio announcer voice.

Leyla allowed her immediate thought to bleed out through her lips. "Blackhawk?"

The man nodded. "That's right, Miss. I'm Blackhawk."

Leyla's heart sank. *Fuck.*

CHAPTER FIVE

The Tour

Blackhawk was wearing a long sleeved, brown leather duster jacket with the sleeves bunched up to his elbows, and a black button up shirt underneath. The top few buttons were undone so Leyla could see a little chest hair. Dark blue vintage jeans and sturdy, black military-style boots that had straps running around to cinch them down on his ankles just screamed former military.

He had a huge, old school revolver dragging along his jeans that made a metallic clink every time it struck his steel thigh underneath, and it sent a chill up Leyla's back. He made his way over to Leyla, grabbing a chair and dragging it along the way. The hawk perched to his shoulder as he moved, sometimes spreading its wings to keep balance.

In terms of looks, he wasn't a bad looking guy to Leyla. Bad meaning ugly. But he wasn't the best looking, either. Possibly in his mid to late 40s, he had a thick, dark brown, mid-length beard that enveloped his face and accentuated the frowny lips that chewed on an already burnt out cigar.

His hair was long and black, but most was up in a bun with two strands braided from each temple to hold the rest that ran down to his shoulders in place.

Maybe he's a Viking, Leyla thought. *Like a robot Viking. That would be pretty cool. No, wait, he's scary. He's not supposed to be cool.*

Once he was close enough, Leyla could make out his light blue eyes. These were eyes that had seen the worst the world had to offer. Eyes that hadn't known a good night's sleep in ages, as evidenced by the bags he had. He stopped about a foot away from the cell, staring into Leyla's very soul. He studied her for a few seconds, sizing her up.

Is he a mind reader? Is he reading my mind? She thought. *Quick, think about something that he would be scared of. Big spider!*

"So, who are you?" He spoke again with that gravelly, southern accent.

Dammit. Big spider didn't work. "Leyla." She answered, annoyed that her big spider mind trick failed.

"Leyla who?"

"I don't know."

"How'd you get here?"

Leyla cleared her throat the same way all bad liars do. "There was, uh, a wall. And, I just walked through."

"So you walked through, huh?" Blackhawk nodded and raised his eyebrows.

He knows you're full of shit, Leyla thought. She didn't know what to say now.

Blackhawk took his time replying. He crossed his arms. "No one just walks through that wall. Who were you with?"

"No one." *Hopefully he doesn't know about Del or Officer Wells...*

"Uh huh." Blackhawk replied, openly hinting he sensed a lie.

Shit. Yeah, he knows about Del and Wells. "Can I have some water?" Leyla changed the subject, although she was genuinely thirsty.

"I've got some food and drink coming up in a few minutes. Now..." Blackhawk stepped closer to Leyla and knelt down to her level, somehow seeming even more towering and intimidating doing so. "Why are you here?"

Leyla eyed the big revolver hanging off his hip. *He is going to kill me with that thing*, she thought, feeling her heart race. Before she could answer, another voice rang out from the doorway, distracting Blackhawk.

"Yoohoo! Lunch time!" The voice, definitely more inviting and warm than Blackhawk's, signaled that the aforementioned food and drink had arrived. Leyla gazed past Blackhawk to catch a glimpse of whoever the other person was. It was none other than Blackhawk's right-hand man: Ramsay, wearing a light brown motorcycle jacket and well fitting dark jeans with some old, beat up work boots.

He was a classically handsome young guy, maybe late 20s or early 30s, and he had brown, wavy hair—kind of wild and unkempt but it worked for him—and dark brown eyes.

He looks like he could be a character in an older movie or TV show, Leyla thought. *And he's definitely prettier than Blackhawk.*

He was carrying a brown paper bag and a glass bottle of water for Leyla to drink.

If he's feeding me, I already like him, Leyla thought. *Whatever the food is, it smells great; maybe French fries?* she guessed.

He strolled up beside Blackhawk and made eye contact with Leyla.

"Got you some Peyton's. Hope you like burgers. If you don't, you'll like 'em after this." Ramsay assured Leyla.

Leyla couldn't place his accent. It was very American, but it sounded a little old school. Like a classic movie star accent.

"If I open this cell door, you gonna behave?", Blackhawk asked. Leyla nodded in compliance.

He moved to the cell door a few feet down and punched a code into an older looking keypad. Leyla heard six beeps. Each had its own tone like a phone. For some reason, the six beep melody stuck in her head.

Beep, boop boop, beep beep boop! She replayed it in her mind and bopped her head side to side along with it.

The door unlocked. Ramsay walked over to it, pushed it in and handed the bag of food to Leyla. He sat the canteen on a chair next to the door, but didn't exit the cell as expected. Instead, he leaned his back against the wall and propped one foot up to it.

"Well come on. It's not poisoned!" Ramsay motioned to the bag of food.

"You saw our lovely city out there, yeah?" Blackhawk interjected. Leyla nodded.

"Everyone out there has mods. Replaced arms or legs. Sometimes a heart needs help or a sickness needs to be gotten rid of but everyone here is a modder. And we absolutely do not, under any circumstance, communicate with the surface. Because humanity is shit, and won't allow anyone living a good life on their own terms to keep living that life. Down here we do what we want, when we want, how we want. We don't worry about when we're going to eat or what bills need paying. We have spent a long, long time building SubCity up and setting up an infrastructure that allows our little society true freedom. And I will be goddamned if I'm letting someone come along and fuck that all up. Got it?" Blackhawk explained to Leyla, almost bragging. "We need to seriously take a look at our security systems." He was glaring at Ramsay, who reeled at the indication that his system was faulty.

"I checked it out! No malfunctions or flubs in the capacitors or anything. Doesn't matter how fancy your tech is, it can never be 100% reliable. I'll run some diagnostics on it."

Blackhawk looked at Leyla for a second, who still hadn't opened the bag of food to eat.

"Well for one, I can't know everyone down here. There's a lot of us. So, I'll take a risk and say you're in the right place and get you set up." He said to Leyla. She finally spoke up.

"That doctor said I'm…one of your girls."

Blackhawk laughed. "Nope. You are not."

Why's that funny? Leyla thought. *Am I not good enough? I could be one of your girls, asshole. Why am I even thinking that? Blackhawk's girls sound like hookers. Never mind. Ask the scary man about memory wipes.*

"That doctor said the girls want their memory wiped sometimes and then they don't remember anything after."

Blackhawk studied Leyla for a bit. The cogs in his mind were clearly turning. He looked at Ramsay. Then back to Leyla.

"Ramsay, get her set up at the Arches."

"Oh, the Arches?" Ramsay replied, seemingly surprised at Blackhawk's response. Ramsay looked at Leyla and grinned. "The Arches are *nice*."

Blackhawk pulled Ramsay further away from Leyla and spoke in a low enough tone to keep Leyla from hearing. "We keep an eye on her. She's holding info from us. Be nice. Get her to trust you. She ain't here on accident. I don't wanna wipe her just yet."

Blackhawk patted Ramsay's shoulder as a goodbye and turned to exit the room, leaving Ramsay alone with the still very reserved Leyla.

"That's a wagyu beef burger." Ramsay pointed. "Up on the surface that thing costs like 65 bucks. Worth every penny. Come on, it's still warm." Ramsay coaxed Leyla with a warm smile. She finally opened the bag and was hit with a waft of charred beef and cheese aromas. She dug into the bag, past the fries she had correctly guessed, and opened a white paper that contained a cheeseburger that looked so scrumptious her pupils dilated. One bite and she was hooked. She scarfed it down in huge bites, prompting Ramsay to clap and rejoice.

"She likes! Ok so, when you're done let's get you to your new home."

"Justh like that?" Leyla asked with a mouthful of cheeseburger. "I live here now?"

"Let's just say that when people come down here, they don't leave. In a good way! That sounded much better in my head. We love it here. That's what I'm saying."

"You had to put me in jail just so you could give me a house?"

"Apartment, not house. And this isn't a jail; this was actually a security room left over from about a hundred years ago. Police station for the subway, I think. And yes, we restrained you because we don't know what you could do. Lucky for you, you uh, stayed calm. You like the burger?"

"Yeah, it's pretty great." Leyla wiped her mouth with a napkin from the bag and then stood. Ramsay straightened up and pushed off the wall as well, stunned.

"A wagyu burger…is just, just great? Okay, I refuse to be offended by that. Come on, I'll try and explain this crazy place to you on the way."

***

Ramsay led Leyla out of the room, into a hallway, and back out into the open city. Now they were at least ten stories up off street level, giving Leyla a new perspective on the city. From up there she had an even better view of the vehicles sailing through the air, the bright and colorful advertisements of various products scrolling across holographic displays, and the hundreds of modded pedestrians weaving in and out of view.

"Okay, so Welcome to SubCity…" Ramsay turned back to Leyla as he walked and did a semi-bow. "First off, I don't understand how you got out of here and then back in without knowing what was going on in the first place, but that's okay. Blackhawk just wants to help folks. "So, really, what were you up to before you ended up down here?"

Leyla didn't want to mention Del to Ramsay; not yet. *Can't trust him.* "I uh, can't remember much. Well, anything, past three years ago. Woke up in the tunnel leading here and made it outside."

"Ok. I'll hand it to you, that warrants finding a way here for answers."

"And then I just walked. Ended up down under Fort Washington Way with the homeless folks. Stayed there ever since."

"So three years ago you woke up and you just stayed in that tent city? You didn't try to figure anything else out?"

"Well, when you're homeless and you look homeless, people don't help you until something really crazy happens."

"And what was that?"

Leyla declined to mention Del and the portal hopping assailant that took her.

Ramsay placed his hand on her shoulder to slow her down and pointed to the right when they came to an intersection on the walkway they're on, prompting her to follow him in that direction, toward a tram that can take them to the Arches.

Leyla decided to give Ramsay a little info. "I came to the entrance a few times. And um, found my way through the tunnel, and fell through that big fake wall." She hesitated to say anything else.

"Ah, yes, the re-force wall. Its solid "rock" unless your specific nanites are encoded to react with it. Cross-Eyes said you didn't have any of those so, how you just fell through is a *dad gum mystery*." Ramsay explained through a veil of sarcasm, letting Leyla know he suspected something was off with her story.

Dad gum? What a weird thing to say, Leyla thought. but she noticed Ramsay's insinuating remark. "Well I—"

"Don't worry. You're here now. Unless you come in here guns blazing, we welcome you. We're not North Korea. People come down here for a better life." Ramsay interrupted.

He thinks I sound suspicious, but Blackhawk must have sensed something too. Leyla decided to choose her words more carefully from there on if she could help it.

The tram, which on the surface would have been suspended on a cable, floated up to the platform Leyla and Ramsay just got to. The bottom of it glowed blue, almost like flame, but it didn't give off any heat that Leyla could feel. A couple women exited—one of which had lime green and electric blue neon glowing hair.

Oh, cotton candy hair! Leyla thought while staring at the woman. Ramsay laughed at her remark as the women passed, staring at Leyla.

Ramsay ushered Leyla in. There was no operator; all automatic. It began its descent to the street at a calm pace while Ramsay and Leyla steadied themselves by grabbing some stability bars.

It was a lot smoother of a ride than she expected.

"So, you don't need money here." Ramsay said. "Everything you need you can get. Food, furniture, clothes, entertainment, everything. But to have it all accounted for in our inventory shipments, you need a SubDermal implant. Cross-Eyes said you don't have one. Or any mods. That's the weird part."

"Why's it weird?"

"Well, like Blackhawk said, every single person here has some kind of cybernetics. Most folks that found their way here were recruited but someone else that lives here. Usually war vets, or traumatic injury survivors. People with cancer or other bad diseases. We fix it."

"You…fix it?"

"Long story short: you need a new leg? We've got legs. New heart? Got it. Need sickness out of your body? It's out."

"So, you're like a big, creepy, secret robot hospital?"

Ramsay laughed. "Little more complicated than that but, yeah. Although, some folks don't have injuries or sickness. Some just want to live the modder life."

Leyla thought of Del. Had she known about this place, she'd never gone into financial ruin and drug addiction thanks to cancer treatments.

"So why don't you just do this everywhere else?" Leyla asked.

"That was my thought years ago. Blackhawk's too. We actually contacted a pharmaceutical company. Showed them what we'd come up with. Know what they did?"

"What?"

"They laughed at us. Never gave us a chance to show them how it really worked. That company nets about seventy billion dollars a year selling chemicals to cancer patients that just makes them sicker and die slower. Humans are cattle to these companies. Money farms. Pills sell better than cybernetics and nano tech. So, Blackhawk said you know what? Screw 'em. We build up our own society on our own terms and keep to ourselves. Live good lives. We've been working on a way to get the surface to be a better place but we haven't figured it out yet. People are Grade-A shit, pretty much."

"Why go through a company? You can just help people without a bunch of rich folks approving it."

"We do. They come down here, join us, we treat them."

"No, I mean you have all this technology already. Just go to the surface and do it anyway."

"Valiant idea, but on such a massive scale we would need more resources than we have or a technology we don't have. Yet. Hence, us asking billion dollar big wigs for help. At least we tried. Not to mention, have you *seen* America?

If we come crawling out of a hole in the ground with metal arms and world altering tech, we would be shot by some Buckeye rednecks in ten seconds, calling us "illegal aliens."

"Fucking rich parasites and the poor people that follow them." Leyla said, echoing Del's exact thoughts on corporate America.

"That's exactly right!" Ramsay said.

"So, how do I get a sub...thingie?"

"We'll get you an SD right now actually. Gotta stop by Gusto's. He repairs them or replaces them for us all."

The tram stopped and the door slid open. The sounds and smells of the street rushed in. People chattered as they walked by. Various styles of music were the usual notes on street level; a cacophonic assault on the senses. Ramsay sniffed and closed his eyes.

"Ah, I love that. The way all the sounds just slap you in the face. And that smell there is Peyton's, where I got that burger. It's right there, don't forget! You'll want to try everything on the menu." Ramsay pointed at a diner across the street, adorned in chrome and pink neon lights like it was transported from the 1950s.

"But first, Gusto's."

Conveniently enough, Gusto's CyberWare was almost directly across from Peyton's Diner.

Ramsay led Leyla in, and they were immediately greeted by a heavy set, bald man with a thick, curled mustache. This was Gusto, assumedly, surrounded by loose circuits and cybernetics scattered on various tables.

"Ramsay! Moy drug!" Gusto spoke in Russian.

"Oh you're Russian today?" Ramsay asked.

"Oh! Izvinite, derzhites..." Gusto pulled his sleeve up to expose his left forearm, which had a touchpad and a few buttons embedded in it. He punched in a few notes and...

"There! Sorry, Mila was in here earlier for a repair. I keep telling her to just get a Babel-Chip but you know her. So proud of the Motherland." Gusto now had an average American accent. "What do you need?"

"Leyla here needs a SubDermal."

"What's up with the old one?" Gusto asked.

"This is the first one. I think."

"Oh! New arrival! Welcome!" Gusto waved at Leyla.

"Yeah, something like that." Ramsay turned to Leyla. "So, it's gonna be a needle. SD is teeny tiny. Like microscopic. Feels like a...mosquito bite. Without the annoying itching after."

Leyla's eyes widened as soon as she saw Gusto pull a needle from his kit, ready to run just like in the psychiatric ward. Ramsay noticed.

"Ok, you don't like needles. Hey uh, Gus, can we do it the other way?"

"That'll take longer."

"See her face? She's either about to run or whoop your ass over that thing."

Gusto looked at Leyla. "Okay, I see it. No needle, then."

Gusto put a cap on the needle and put it away. He then pulled out a small container that looked like a fancy cigarette case and clicked it open. Inside were single dose, clear capsules that contained SubDermals.

"I'd be more opposed to this if she had one already but, since this is the first one, this is fine." Gusto removed one pill and handed it to Leyla. "Take this, with a big ass glass of Coke or a beer or something. The carbonation helps it go down."

"Can I take it later?" Leyla asked.

"You can, but it takes about one or two hours to find its way under your flexor muscle, right here." Gusto pointed to the meaty part of his right forearm. "You don't feel anything. No needles. The unimportant parts dissolve in your belly and you just...poop it out later."

"Okay okay." Ramsay avoided talking about poop, and pulled Leyla out of the shop.

"Have a good one, Gus!"

"Yep. Hey, if you see Teejay tell him get his ass in here! He keeps calling and setting up appointments but forgets to show up!""

"Will do, buddy."

When Leyla and Ramsay exited the shop, he stopped at a soda vending machine; an older, vintage style Coca-Cola machine. He scanned his forearm under a window on the side and out dropped a glass bottled Coke that read *Hecho En Mexico*. He picked up the perfectly chilled drink, used the bottle opener attached to the machine to open it and gave it to Leyla.

"That's the Mexican kind, it's the best one. I don't know why; it just is."

"Thanks." Leyla replied.

"It's for the pill."

"Oh, I'll take it later. Can I do that?."

Ramsay almost pushed, but remembered Blackhawk's words. Be nice. Gain her trust. "That's fine. Hey, we're almost there." Ramsay rounded a street corner where another shop was that smelled like sage and a few other interesting aromas.

Leyla racked her brain to think of a question.

"Does that SD thingie work through your jacket?" Leyla asked, gesturing to Ramsay's covered arms. She hadn't seen many people wearing a jacket there, so Ramsay stood out.

"Oh, it would. But I don't have one. My bio-sigs are hard-coded to the city itself."

Leyla was momentarily distracted though, by a shop she was passing with crystal beads acting as a door. Nestled inside was a black-haired woman in her early 30s sitting in a chair with a bowl of what looked like actual clouds swirling inside. Her forehead had some kind of runic symbol glowing in red neon just under the skin. *Floating* candles surrounded the woman as she raised her right hand, palm up and undulating. The crystals she'd carefully placed around the bowl began to levitate and encircle her, then started glowing.

Leyla's eyes widened and she realized she'd stopped mid-stride to glare at the woman inside the shop. The woman looked up and her eyes met Leyla's. She winked back through the floating crystals.

"That's Clara." Ramsay interjected., glaring at her, almost hiding behind the curtain. "She's the local cyber-witch. Honestly, I'm not sure if that's some electromagnetics or if she's actually doing that. I'm not asking. She's scary. Come on. Arches are right over here."

Ramsay led Leyla up the stairs of a structure with stone columns carved into the wall like old Greek temples. The ancient aesthetic was broken by huge blue neon lettering that read *ARCHES* above the columns.

The large wooden doors automatically opened for Ramsay as he neared them. An electronic, yet soothing male voice chimed in and said "Welcome, Mr. Ramsay, to the Arches Condominiums." Ramsay looked up in surprise.

"Oh, they added a greeter."

The large, cavernous lobby had a floor made of a mixture of bamboo and marble texturing. Quite an odd combination but for some reason it was very pleasing to the eyes. There was a line of real palm trees on either side of the room, creating a tropical path to the elevator in the middle of the room, which Ramsay and Leyla were headed toward. More solar sim lights sat atop the room from the vaulted ceiling a good thirty feet above, drowning the area in a natural light equal to what was outside, which was useful for the various large, tropical-looking plants that dotted the room. It all reminded Leyla of videos of the luxury hotels of Dubai that she'd seen online a few times.

"Are you sure I'm supposed to be here?" Leyla asked, feeling like the building was much too luxe for her.

"Everyone here is equal. You have to stop thinking you're homeless, because as of right now, you are not. It's quite different down here. It's better. Hakuna matata."

"Haka what?"

"Lion King. Great movie." Ramsay motioned for Leyla to enter the appropriately nice elevator before him.

"Anyways, the building is mostly empty for now. Don't have to worry about loud neighbors."

"I kind of like having neighbors. I'm used to it."

"Yeah, maybe, but the quiet is a nice luxury down here that a lot appreciate."

The elevator door closed and the same electronic voice from earlier chimed in. "Where to, Mr. Ramsay?"

"Uh…" Ramsay turned to Leyla. "Do you want a low floor or high? I'd go with high."

"Ok, yeah, high, I guess?"

Ramsay smiled and looked up to the speaker in the elevator.

"Floor 45, and can you load in Miss Leyla's SD profile? It's code uh…A-2081514. She's gonna be a resident. SD isn't loc'd yet but it's in Gusto's system."

A holographic laser beamed out from under the speaker and scanned Leyla's eyes.

"Hello, I did not get your last name." the voice addressed Leyla,

"I, uh, don't know my last name. Maybe I'm like Elvis!"

"Assuming you're speaking of the pioneering rock star from the 1950s, Elvis Presley had a last name. It was Presley." The AI corrected Leyla.

"Oh." *Smart ass*, Leyla thought.

"Would you prefer I call you Leyla, then?"

"Yup."

"Very well, Leyla. I believe you would find Suite 453 to your liking. It can provide the best view of our lovely city at any time, and is equipped with a version 3 Auto-Chef."

"What's an Auto-Chef?" Leyla looked to Ramsay.

"Just know you're going to be eating better than those billionaire idiots on the surface soon. Still no substitute for real cooking, though." Ramsay told her, and then winked.

The elevator slowed and with a nice *ding*, the doors opened to the 45th floor and Ramsay placed his hand on the small of Leyla's back to guide her out. She wasn't comfortable having him touch her but maybe it was chivalrous, so she didn't say anything.

"453 is to the left, should be. Oh, it's a corner suite too. Groovy."

Groovy? *What*? Leyla scrunched her face upon hearing his extremely outdated dialect again, then she anxiously smiled as Ramsay tenderly grabbed her hand and moved her forearm closer to the scanner on the door. There he goes touching again.

"You only have to scan once; After this, you're encoded to the suite and it's yours. New system we're working on. No need for keys."

The door beeped but didn't open. Ramsay remembered Leyla opted for the slower option of an oral SD implant.

"Oh, right. You can't scan til tomorrow at least. Ok, I can get you in. Don't forget the pill."

He pulled a small smartphone sized device from a cargo pocket and typed in a few codes, then held it near the locking mechanism on the door. Ramsay then gently pressed Leyla's thumb on the scanner. The door beeped and clicked the lock open.

Ramsay pulled a small chip from his device, handing it to Leyla. "This chip is a temp SD. You can use it just like a normal SD 'til yours settles."

The entire door slid away from Leyla as she put the chip in Mari's pants pocket, enough to clear the wall it was flush with, and then slid smoothly to the left to reveal her new home.

It was a corner apartment, so the two outside walls were actually windows from floor to ceiling, allowing as much natural light as possible, even though the light was simulated there. The entire layout of SubCity could be viewed from her apartment, like the world's greatest desktop screensaver.

There was a different texture seemingly every few feet. A lightly stained hardwood floor with a very pleasant and plush runner carpet led from the door. The runner was even flush with the floor to avoid tripping or bunching.

Each wall was a different material. To the left, patterned bamboo tiles created a sense of Japanese homeliness. On the right, a more futuristic white wall with fiber optic glass covering it had faint, flowing waves of pink and blue. The light inside the glass sometimes formed into shapes and figures. A koi fish. Clouds. Sunset. A panda.

Oh! I love pandas! Leyla thought to herself.

"These are the newest homes in SubCity." Ramsay explained. "We wanted to go a little more upscale for those that wanted it. But most of us like the whole "low life" thing more. Seems like you got the "tradition meets the future" theme. I hope you like a Japanese aesthetic."

"Oh, it's nice. *Really* nice." *Too nice*, she thought. *Too nice to be true. Feels like a spider web and I'm the fly.*

The room opened up on both sides after a few feet with a curved wall and, to the right, stood a single slate of polished marble as the backdrop for an open kitchen equipped with what looked like an absurdly expensive stove, oven, microwave, prep table and, well, everything. There was even a coffee station that would make a barista faint.

From behind the prep table, which doubled as an island with barstools, an android arose. Stainless steel from head to toe, it was very human-like aside from having no facial features other than the large black screen that projected a digital face. It was only *slightly* unnerving. It turned to Leyla and greeted her.

"Kon'nichiwa!"

Ramsay laughed. "Even the auto-chef is Japanese. Luckily, they all speak 45 languages."

"English." He told the android.

"Greetings, Master Leyla, I am R1-C76, your personal Auto-Chef, Version 3 OS. Please let me know your personal preferences on the holotab at your earliest convenience." The android spoke in a lovely British accent.

"British? Well, that *is* English, I'll give you that." Ramsay remarked.

"Oh what?! Do I have a butler now?" Leyla had no idea what to think. Yesterday she was homeless. Now she was in an apartment that millionaires dreamt of with a personal chef. The android continued.

"Not a butler, but a chef. I am bound to this area only; your kitchen. You may customize my name if you like, Master Leyla. So, will it be R1-C76 or a new name?"

Ramsay leaned in close to Leyla and whispered into her ear. "Say Texas Chainsaw Massacre."

"Texas Chainsaw Massacre?!" Leyla looked at Ramsay, only repeating what he said out of how ridiculous it sounded. The android heard, of course.

"Very well, Master Leyla, my name is Texas Chainsaw Massacre. What a lovely name!"

Ramsay's eyes lit up like he'd won the lottery and he didn't bother trying to hide his jubilance and surprise.

"Haha! TEXAS CHAINSAW MASSACRE! Brilliant. I love these things!"

"Wait, his name is—"

"Yes, his name is now Texas Chainsaw Massacre, the greatest horror movie ever made." Ramsay may have been tasked with keeping an eye on Leyla, but he wasn't going to forego his brand of humor.

"Oh my God you are horrible. I would have named him Princess Paddywinks. Or, Robotthew McConaughey." Leyla said, rolling her eyes. Ramsay's smile went nowhere.

"You can change his name anytime you want." He tapped her shoulder to get her moving.

"Well I can't change it *now*, poor guy'll have an identity crisis!"

"Come on, let's look at the rest of the apartment."

As the two walked away from the prep table, Leyla noticed a sliding bamboo door that was half open; the entrance to what must be the bedroom. She could hear running water on the other side. But there was more to the room she was already in. A study area on the wall next to the window with that gorgeous view was equipped with a desk built into the wall but had no chair.

"It's a little empty now, but on the holotab, you can order furniture and other amenities. Would you like to see something neat?"

"Uh, everything *is* neat." Leyla replied. *Neat? Who the Hell says neat nowadays?*

"Fair point, but, look at this."

Ramsay flicked a switch on the wall next to him and a section of the ceiling opened up. A hefty, white orb descended, suspended by a piece of tubing colored to match, with wires spiraling up and into the open section of the ceiling. The orb then split open and extended; spreading out into a table that rested about a foot and a half off the floor. Once it was settled, the suspension tube rotated to give a clear view of the window wall. Ramsay was grinning the entire time.

"All the Arch suites have these; coolest coffee tables on the planet. But that's not even the best part."

Ramsay walked over and pressed down on the right corner of the table and yet another small section opened up to reveal some buttons and a touchpad. He pressed a button and slid a finger down the touchpad. The entire window wall tinted itself to make the room darker, while the very center section of the window darkened completely and revealed itself to be an immense electronic screen. The screen powered on and a dragon swooped across it, flying over an icy landscape while soldiers fought beneath it.

"Oh boy! Game of Thrones! What a classic! Terrible ending, though. Two thumbs down."

Oh boy? What planet is this dude from? The only time anyone had ever said "oh *boy*" was in those super old black and white cartoons Leyla had seen on the internet.

"This is a great show. Just remember, shitty ending. But you got plenty to watch. The world up there streams everything. We have it all installed on qubits so it's instant, and all Ultra HD. If it's been uploaded to a network anywhere in the world, you have access to it."

"Ok. Cool." Leyla replied, now wondering what a qubit was. "What's that mean?"

"Well, the rest of the world has Netflix and other streaming services; we combine all of them into one platform and then some. If digital media is on any network in the world, you have access to it, right here, on this entertainment console."

Leyla failed to stop a smile from coming through.

"What?" Ramsay asked.

"You sound like a guy trying to sell something at Best Buy."

Ramsay laughed. "Best Buy *wishes* they had our quantum fiber entertainment tech."

"Cool. So, what's in there?" Leyla pointed to the sliding door she saw before.

"Bedroom and bathroom. You don't care about the two hundred inch theater system?"

"Well yeah it's cool but I haven't slept in a real bed in, like, ever."

"Oh, I see your point. There should be a guest fold out somewhere in the wall here…somewhere…" Ramsay looked around the apartment. Once he found the proper section of wall, which happened to be beside the desk, he pressed a slyly hidden button that folded out a full size mattress on a low sitting bed.

Another section of wall beside that folded down to act as a nightstand.

"Okay, *that's* cool." Leyla said, eyes widened.

"Cooler than the two hundred inch TV wall? Really?"

"Well no it's…I can't sleep on the TV."

Ramsay stared back at Leyla a bit. "Once again, fair point. Anyway, feel free to explore your bedroom and bathroom. I have to head out and take care of a couple things. You can get food, clothes, whatever on Rail Street."

"Rail street?"

"Yeah that's the big main street on the "ground" level with all the shops and cafes and diners and such."

"Oh ok. Is that where the pizza is?"

"Yes. That is where the pizza is." Ramsay cracked a smile. "Alright, I'm out. Oh, if you head down there, pay a visit to BlueTooth before dark-fall. She's easy to find, just ask someone. She can get you set up with a comlink implant."

Leyla gave Ramsay the "ok what's that" stare and shook her head.

"And, you're wondering what that is. Well, itty bitty cell phone that fits in your ear." He explained.

"Oh ok like those BlueTooth ear things. Oh! I get it. Bluetooth. Store."

"Yep. You figured out the mystery of the shop name." Ramsay sarcastically affirmed.

"And what's dark-fall?"

"It's when the solar simulators get…dark. It'll be like night time. But get the comlink. You can call me if you need something. Or anyone, you can call anyone but, just, throwing my name in the hat." Ramsay explained, while opening the door to leave. He stopped and turned back.

"Don't forget the pill."

"I won't l, I won't." *Geez, you and that damn pill. Not taking that pill*, she thought, as Ramsay closed the door and left.

Leyla moved over to the bedroom/bathroom door as Ramsay exited. Sliding the bamboo door to the side, she noticed the empty, spacious bedroom with adjustable windows similar to the large ones in the common area that control the light in the room from outside. There was nothing particularly interesting in there just yet. The door to the bathroom was a frosted glass one that automatically opened for Leyla when she got near.

Looking inside, it was almost as if she'd stepped outside into a rainforest. The bathroom was as large as the bedroom, but it was markedly more interesting. The walls were all dark granite and rough like you'd find on the side of a real cave. A small tree jutted from the floor in the left corner. Leyla believed it to be a fake, at first. But upon closer inspection and feeling the bark and leaves, it was most definitely real. A few other tropical looking plants populated the room.

There was a toilet, obviously, but it was a lot fancier than the ones she'd used in the public restrooms at gas stations and such. A table ran along one wall of the room with a sink on the far end and a mirror covered the same length above the table. There were a few cabinets that match the dark gray of the granite walls.

The true draws of the room were the bath and shower; the source of the running water sound she'd been hearing the entire time.

The bath was a couple feet deep that doubled as a jacuzzi. There was no water in it at the moment, but it was catching the actual *waterfall* coming from a few openings in the wall above and allowing it to drain through.

"A waterfall shower?! Are you kidding me?" Leyla blurted out to herself. "What is this place? I'm dead. I died. I am dead." She was interrupted by a female voice.

"I can detect a resting heart rate of 31 beats per minute and a body temperature of 97.2 degrees, fahrenheit. You do not appear to be dead."

Leyla jumped back, almost far enough to exit the room, and scanned the walls for another person. She found no one.

"My apologies, I have startled you. I am your version 3 bath assistant. Do you prefer a bath or shower today?"

"Uh…bath?"

"Of course. Most prefer a water temperature of 100 degrees. Would you like it cooler or warmer than this?"

"Hold on, hold on, what all do you do here?"

"I am an artificial intelligence equipped to give you the perfect shower or bath every time along with aromatics, fragrances, and mineral supplements as needed for optimal conditioning for skin, hair, mind, and spirit."

"Spirit?" Leyla asked, noticing the odd addition.

"I can play whatever music you like."

"Ok. We're friends now."

"I am happy to hear that. But, before you bathe, I have not gotten a data entry from any of our atelier's shops. If you bathe now, you would have to allow time to wash and dry your current clothing, as well."

"Where's the washer and dryer? And what's an at—ateller-yay?"

A section of wall slid away near Leyla to reveal a black machine with a single door. The AI described it, as asked.

"Here is your version 5 personal washer and dryer combination. You only need to put clothing in. I control everything else; the washing, drying, and pressing. And, our ateliers are the finest collection of artists and designers in the world. You will find them on the holo-tab in your common area at your desk. You may feel free to order clothing, furniture, entertainment, art, and narcotics or alcohol at your leisure."

"Drugs? There's drugs? What kinda drugs? Never did drugs."

"As long as they are nano-compliant and natural substances."

"Not even gonna ask. Ok, so, can you see me? Or do I finally have privacy?"

"I do not have visual access to anywhere aside from thermal imagery through 17 sensors throughout the room. Your entire apartment is a privacy haven. The windows are one way nano-resin."

"Okay okay, I'll take your word for it. Honestly I don't care at this point, I just want that bath."

"Yes ma'am. Place your clothing into the wash and I will warm the bath for you. If you like, I can add a lavender and sea salt supplement to aid in relaxation and soothing of the muscle."

"Yep. Do that. Don't know what it means but it sounds nice." Leyla replied as she undressed and tossed articles of clothing into the washer one by one.

"And what music do you, uh, suggest?"

"The most preferred with the sea salt and lavender is a Japanese ambience with rain and thunder background."

"Rain and thunder? Okay. I can do that. Sounds like it costs a lot but, whatever."

"Members of SubCity are provided for under the Code of The Modders. You never have to pay for anything. Your water is ready."

Leyla, now naked, moved over to the bath just as the waterfall stopped pouring and revealed a salted and steamy bath with lavender petals floating throughout. Sure enough, some cultural Japanese stringed instruments and light percussion permeated the atmosphere, softened by the steam in the air. She dipped one foot into the water to test it out. It was perfect. The saline and flowery air caressed her lungs. She slid into the water completely.

"Oooooohhhhh that's nice. My *word* this is perfect water. So…what's the Code of The Modders?"

"*Libertatem Ascensionis.* Freedom Through Ascension."

"So what's that mean?"

The AI played an old recording of Blackhawk speaking to the people of SubCity, audibly dated 9-03-1998. "A society cannot progress if they are crushed under the weight of tradition and complacency. SubCity is a place where the downtrodden and misfortunate find new purpose, new life, and new value, free from the confines of the echoes of pseudo-Roman ruled society that balances its future in the hands of the greedy, the wealthy, the meek, and the corrupt."

"Ok, that was way more complicated than I expected." Leyla scoffed.

"In layman's terms…" The AI replied. "Everyone down here is free to do whatever they want or need without worry of financial, societal, or familial issue. So long as they are not being harmful to each other, of course. The Modders are not only surviving, but thriving. And growing."

"Oh…so it's…

"True freedom." The AI affirmed.

"Well, I'm a fan of your liber-tater ass-a-whatchacalit." Leyla no longer bothered pronouncing new words.

"Libertatum ascensionis."

"Mmmhmm. That." Leyla closed her eyes and enjoyed what could be the first bath she can remember. *Del would fucking love this place*, Leyla thought. *Soon as I find her, we can live together in the Arches, maybe.*

"Your heart rate has dropped by one beat per minute. It would seem the bath has already taken the desired effect."

"Yeah."

Leyla sat in silence, enjoying the extremely relaxing Japanese instrumentals and the rain and thunder effects. Even living mostly in the elements for the last couple of years, the storms always relaxed her more. Luckily, the tent city had always been uphill and never had a flood during heavy rain. This bathroom and apartment, though, was something she'd never imagined she'd have. If this was a dream, she wasn't going to bother pinching herself to wake up.

Leyla remembered Deli again, in her layers of clothing sitting on her bench that looked out at the river during every sunset. It was almost as if Leyla was sitting with her once again, running the memory through her mind.

***

Deli had her eyes closed. Leyla was beside her, munching on a granola bar she'd stolen from a convenience store a couple blocks away. Deli spoke up, breaking the long silence they'd just shared.

"What would you do? If you weren't here?"

"Hmmm?" Leyla asked with a mouthful of Nutri-Grain.

"If you weren't here. Homeless. Living in a tent. What would you be doing?"

Leyla stopped chewing, combing her mind for a quick answer, for which she didn't have.

"Well..." She quickly chewed and swallowed. "I don't know."

"Oh come on, girl. You gotta have a dream other than sleeping in old dirty rags in a tent full of holes covered in duct tape."

"I don't know! I don't even know what I did before all this."

"Yeah...I guess I can understand that. Kinda hard to have goals and dreams if you don't know who you are." Deli said. This cut deep into Leyla, who shrunk back a bit and looked down.

"Oh, sorry, baby I didn't mean anything bad by that!" Deli noticed her comment hurt Leyla a bit.

"No it's...you're right."

"Shit. I just be speaking my mind not thinking. I didn't mean to hurt your feelings, baby girl."

"What would you do, Del?"

"Me?"

"Yeah."

Del straightened up a bit and took a deep breath. She let out a huge sigh.

"I'd be the President."

Leyla laughed. But Del kept a straight face. She was dead serious.

"I'm for real. I'd change shit. I'd hire people that would change shit. You got people like us sleeping on the dirt. Sure some of us deserve this life but...most of us just had some bad luck. Most of us...life just wanted to kick us in the nuts for no good reason."

Leyla looked back at Del and nodded in agreement. Del continued.

"You know what a government is supposed to be for? It's supposed to take care of its citizens. Who's taking care of us? Us. And only us. Government is useless. We go to apply for a job. No, get out. You got no home address, you can't work. You got no cell phone, you can't work. You got no references, no family, no friends, no work. It's always no, no, no. No matter how hard we try, it's always against us. Once you're down, you can't get up. And then some asshole with a rich daddy is given everything for free and suddenly he's better than us. He's better because he has a suit. And a nice car and a big house. But you know what he ain't got?"

"Hmm?"

"He ain't got a heart. We need somebody that's got a heart. The world needs somebody that's got a heart. I'd be the President. I'd be important. I'd fix shit. Wouldn't be no homeless motherfuckers in this country, shit, on this planet, if I was the President."

"Important sounds nice." Leyla finally had something to say.

"Damn right it does. Important. To be seen. To be noticed. To have influence to change things for good. How many people walk by you every day and won't even look you in the eye?"

"I quit paying attention."

"Yeah. They did too. They did too…"

Del watched the sunset with melancholic eyes until the sun disappeared over the hill across the water. Leyla never finished the rest of her granola bar.

***

The memory was broken up by the female AI voice.

"Your clothes are washed, dried, softened and folded. If you spend more time in the salt bath, your skin may over saturate. You have reached an optimal—"

"Okay okay okay just…I'm getting out."

"You do not own any towels yet."

"Guess I'm air drying, then. Libertater ass and boobies!"

"Libertatum Ascensionis."

"I know that. I made a funny. You're supposed to laugh."

She walked out of the bedroom and into the common room with the giant window. The TV had been playing the entire time. Texas Chainsaw Massacre, upon seeing Leyla naked, turned away and retreated into the cabinet, giving her full privacy.

Leyla located the corner of the coffee table that controlled the TV and tried a couple buttons until the TV faded itself off. She didn't bother trying to get the table itself to retract back to the ceiling. That seemed too complicated. The window brightened itself to the "natural" brightness again. Hoping the AI was correct about the one-way viewing comment, she strolled right up to the window in the nude, finally taking a breather and soaking in a gorgeous view of an impossible underground city that she may be calling home now.

And that was the damndest thing. *Home.* Yesterday she was homeless. It was dawning on her that all of this was truly *insane.*

This apartment? How? This city. These people. Blackhawk. What's his deal? And Ramsay. Mister touches too much. Everything is free? Bullshit, nothing is free. How do they have all this crazy technology and no one knows about it? Doesn't make any sense; this place is way too big to hide.

It could take a while to find Del in a place so big. Might need help.

CHAPTER SIX

Down to Business

Leyla didn't bother relaxing. There was still some "daylight" left in SubCity, so there was still some time to ask around for Del's possible location—if she was even down there. Maybe Mari from Fritzy Joe's would have some pointers. So far she'd seemed the most trustworthy.

***

Mari was hanging out in front of Fritzy's, smoking a clove cigarette when Leyla shuffled up to her, devouring a slice of pizza from the same stand as the previous night.

"Well, hello. Bringing my clothes back?" Mari joked with Leyla.

"Oh, I still have to order some. Tonight. I'll do that tonight. That smells good." Leyla referred to the sweet and smoky smell of the burning clove cig.

"Relax, I'm kidding. Told you you could keep 'em. And thanks. Beats a Marlboro any day."

Leyla paused, still hesitant to ask about her friend. Asking the wrong person could be bad; she could lose Del forever, but she had to start somewhere.

"Hey, so, I'm looking for my friend."

"Ok, so Cross-Eyes *did* jog your memory. That's good."

"Well no, he…ok yeah he did." Leyla didn't bother explaining what had happened at Cross-Eyes. Didn't matter. "She's a little older, 50s I think. Black lady; likes to talk. Super sweet. Her name is Deli."

"Mmmm don't know a Deli."

"She's not from, uh, here; she's new."

"Whatever you're trying to say just spit it out, I'm not an FBI agent." Mari laughed.

Leyla breathed in deep and sighed, looking away. She was just going to have to tell the truth. Mostly.

"We were outside. On the surface, outside the entrance to the subway."

Mari puffed her cigarette. "Ok, interesting start."

"She was taken. Like, snatched. Right in front of me. By um, this is crazy but, it was a portal, or something. Like, all blue fire and sparks. Almost knocked me down. And it opened up, and this person all dressed up like a ninja jumps out, grabs Del, and then disappears the same way. Gone. Just like that."

Mari's expression switched sharply from peaked interest to grave concern. "Not crazy."

Mari put the cig out on the wall and grabbed Leyla's arm. "Come inside. People don't need to hear this."

Leyla allowed Mari to pull her inside. *Did I just fuck up?* She thought. Mari locked the door. *Yeah, I fucked up.*

***

Mari fired a question off right away. "Did you tell anyone else?"

"No, just you."

"You sure?"

"Yeah, no one, why?"

Mari walked further into the closed bar and looked around to ensure no one else could be listening. "Been almost ten years since I heard of anything like that."

"So you've seen it before?"

"Nah, never saw it in person. Just heard about it. They called it Athon. Real Angel of Death type. Some sort of assassin, I guess. Was hiding somewhere here in the city."

"Well, shit…"

"Yeah. I'm a little dark on details but, at some point, Athon just vanished. Most likely, Blackhawk killed it."

"Why do you keep calling Athon an *it*? Isn't it a person?"

Mari laughed—the kind of laugh someone does when they're about to tell you something ridiculous but true.

"From what I've heard, no way that thing was human. Not the way it moved. Took out a whole platoon of men here in seconds. Warping all over the place, slicing people up. Had to be a new type of android. No human being can move like that, modded or not."

"Oh…" Leyla's heart sank. Deli was definitely in some deep shit.

"Blackhawk found that thing one night and took some men down there to catch it. Haven't heard about it since."

"Down where?" Leyla asked, feeling the dread creeping up her back. If Del was taken by that monstrosity, she was either dead or didn't have much time left.

"Yeah, down in The Fridge. Big cold room they keep SIGIL in? Blackhawk tried to make his own Athon after that. For some reason, he only uses women. Real advanced tech and gear, more than we all have on the street here."

SIGIL? Another new word. Leyla thought. *Whatever. Ask about Blackhawk's girls.*

Leyla perked up. "Make his own Athon? Is that what everyone means when they talk about Blackhawk's girls?"

"You catch on quick. The Pantheon. Group of volunteer women. Experiments. Normal folk like you and me. Wanna be part of something bigger, I guess. But when Blackhawk is done with them or they 'don't work', memories get wiped and they're tossed back into SubCity to start all over again. Just like how you showed up." Mari seemingly froze with a pensive stare into nothing; the kind of aimless gaze one gets when their past trauma floods in and takes over their mind.

Leyla narrowed her eyes. "You were one of them."

"Mmm I didn't say that." Mari changed the subject as quickly as she could. "I'm just your friendly neighborhood bar manager."

Leyla knew Mari was avoiding the insinuation, but she let it go.

"How do I get to them?" Leyla asked.

"To who?"

"The Pantheon. How do I get to them?"

"Oh, girl, I have no clue. They're hidden. Hanging out wherever Blackhawk is calling home now."

"I'll ask Ramsay."

"Slow down, you forget Ramsay is Blackhawk's right hand man. Best friend. Been here since the beginning, for fifty years. I'd be a little more cautious about this shit."

"Fifty years? That doesn't make sense. He's no older than I am…"

"You really *aren't* from here are you?" Mari laughed.

"Im just, new...But how does he look so young?"

Mari smiled. "All of our cybernetics? Arms, organs, implants, whatever—are foreign bodies. And the human body naturally rejects anything like that. In the beginning we had to take injections and pills constantly to fight sickness. But being sick was better than being paralyzed. But After they got that big computer down here, our tech got way better. No more medicine. Now nanobots take care of it all. Best side effect? Slows the aging process. By a *lot*. Hell, it even took years *off* some of us."

"Damn. How old are you?"

Mari laughed. "A lady never reveals her age."

"Fair enough. So, you mentioned a big computer. Iis that what SIGIL is? What's that do?"

"Don't even try to quiz me on specifics, kid. I just know it works and I'm not in a wheelchair anymore."

Outside, a commotion could be heard. The street crowd was agitated. Mari rose from the seat and looked outside to see some people run-walking past the window and all of them were looking up.

"The Hell?" Mari slid out of the seat and got outside, followed closely by Leyla.

As soon as the two women stepped outside, a loud crackling could be heard further down the street. The sound reverberated off the walls of the parlors and shops so much it was hard to tell where it's coming from.

The crackling was immediately followed by a loud and inconsistent whirring noise, and what sounded like backfiring exhaust.

"Please don't let that be what I think it is…" Mari remarked, now speed walking out into the street to get a bearing on the situation.

"Shit…"

Mari froze as she looked up high toward the top of the buildings of the city, which was essentially inside an immense cavern, hollowed out to make space for the towering structures. Nestled under the bedrock that hung above every inch of SubCity, were those glowing objects that were shaped like hourglasses, around the size of small cars, that emitted blue energy waves from top and bottom—the same glow as the tram Leyla rode earlier. They were everywhere along the rocky ceiling, forming a grid over the city. One of them was shaking and sputtering. Mari looked to Leyla.

"Fucking GravGen is going out, fuck!"

"GravGen? What's happening now?"

"Gravity generator. Holds everything above it up. If those fail...Cincinnati comes down on our heads."

Before Leyla could reply, a new sound could be heard overhead, almost like a small fighter jet. She looked up to locate it. Maybe it was another GravGen going down?

A few hundred feet overhead, a human figure soared through the air, dressed in all black, similar to Del's kidnapper. It was outfitted with an exo-suit with mechanical wings. Small jet boosters spat blue fire—again the same color as the GravGen's glow—to propel the person wearing it through the air, granting them the ability to fly with ease. Del had told Leyla stories of things like that from a book she'd read. She called them angels, except they were less robot and more bird.

The 'angel' was quickly joined by another, sporting similar flight tech. These two were then greeted by one more flying figure, forming a trio of angelic cyborgs. Leyla thought she could make out long hair. Were they women?

They flew in unison to the malfunctioning GravGen, which had lost enough power to force the nearby GravGens to also be overworked and begin sputtering. They all had to work in unison or the entire grid failed. And that was a catastrophically bad thing.

The first generator abruptly shut down. It dropped from the sky, prompting cries of horror from hundreds of people in the city, all of whom were locked in suspense, hoping this wasn't the end.

One of the cybernetic angels swooped down and grabbed it with its arms in a spectacular display of strength. The boosters on the wings kicked into overdrive to support the extra weight.

The rock bed where the generator failed gave way. Another angel flew up and slammed into the rockbed, then blasted their jets at full force, saving SubCity from an immediate cave-in. The third cyborg angel helped pull the failed generator back up into position.

Finally a *fourth* angel appeared, hauling some equipment. It delivered the equipment to the two holding the dead GravGen, and then flew up to assist the one that was single-handedly holding up the ceiling. Within the minute, they had the GravGen repaired, back in place, and disaster avoided. All four angels floated in place long enough for the entire city to erupt in applause, almost as if they expected the gratitude, then flew off to who knows where. Leyla's mouth was wide open.

"That…was The Pantheon." Mari said, and stepped away, making her way back to where she was originally smoking her cigarette. Leyla followed her back, stunned and mouth still wide open.

"You used to do *that*?"

"I told you, I never said that." Mari snapped back at Leyla, this time irritated.

Okay lady, chill, Leyla drew back. *Touchy subject, I guess.*

Mari cooled down quickly and rested her back on the wall and lit a new cigarette.

"Look, I wouldn't know where to find your friend. But if she was taken, it had to be by one of The Pantheon. The only way you're finding out more is through Blackhawk or Ramsay. Maybe they got that warp tech running like Athon had. I don't know."

"Is there a way I can ask Ramsay or Blackhawk about all this without getting in trouble? I just want to get my friend back safely."

"Hold on, slow down. I'll check on some things first. I got a few strings I can pull. Take the night and see the city, get your mind relaxed. Get a new wardrobe, find food, you know? Check back with me later."

Leyla didn't like the idea, but she didn't have much of a choice, either.

"And run by Bluetooth's right down the way and get a comlink so we can keep up."

"Oh, right, Ramsay said to do that."

"You've met Ramsay?"

"Yeah, and Blackhawk."

Mari leaned in closer to Leyla. "Be careful, okay? I want to help you. But don't go around telling everyone how you got here and what you're doing. Get your friend. Get out. Now go on. Get dolled up. At least try to look like you belong here."

Get out? This place is awesome, lady. I'm finding Del and staying right here. Fuck living under a bridge. I have a chef now.

CHAPTER SEVEN

Shopping Around

Leyla cautiously walked down the street, passing all the neon drenched shops. *This place is gorgeous*, she thought. *What a shame to hide it from the world.*

She noticed one shop with eight foot tall yellow and green signs that were shaped in Japanese kanji. The door to the place was clear, and the word *ink* rested overhead and between the kanji letters. Leyla peeped inside. It was a tattoo shop not unlike the ones she'd seen on the surface once or twice, but here, the tattoos were *glowing* bright neon. Some pulsated to the menacingly loud music in the shop, which happened to sound a lot like Vox's band from that concert. She couldn't remember the band name.

"Well, that's cool...but, no." Leyla decided against getting a likely radioactive tattoo. At least for now. She exited the shop.

The next spot down was what she was looking for, judging by the illuminated mannequins with carefully picked outfits: a clothing store named *Til Death*. Odd name, Leyla thought to herself. But that was nothing new here. Everything and everyone had an odd name in SubCity.

As soon as her face peeked inside the store, she was greeted by an android that looked similar to Texas Chainsaw Massacre, albeit with vastly different styling and personality. And this one had legs.

"Look at *this* bad bitch!" The bot moved toward Leyla, wearing slim jorts and a pink mesh collared shirt with no sleeves. Leyla was taken aback by the insult.

"Me? Wh—why am I a bitch? What did I do?"

"Oh, girl, nothing! Except walking in the perfect shop to wrap some threads around that perfect little booty of yours!" The android complimented her.

Leya looked around at her own butt. Mari's pants were pretty flattering in that regard. Leyla agreed with the bot with a nod. The bot turned and motioned for Leyla to follow it.

"Come on, girl. I am your hype bot. If it makes that ass roar like a fucking lion, I will let you know. If it compliments your perfect, electrifying eyes, I will make it known. I am all you need. Whatchu lookin' for?"

"Uh…I think, everything?" Leyla said.

"Ok, we got you. You gonna slay…til death."

Leyla laughed. "Ha! I see what you did there. Til Death. Got it."

***

Leyla spent a solid hour inside *Til Death,* and as she was exiting the shop, the hype bot reminded her of a couple things.

"Now, Bluetooth is two shops down and don't forget to stop by Kirosaki's for that haircut we talked about, okay? Trust me it'll look fucking perfect on you."

"Okay!" Leyla waved back at the bot, smiling and walking with a new outfit and an entire wardrobe being delivered to her apartment soon. Mari's clothes were in a bag, but now Leyla was rocking some dark red, low rise leather jean style pants that had pores added so they weren't too hot. A white low cut tank top exposed more of her chest than she'd ever allowed but that hype bot was damn good at its job; she actually felt comfortable and sexy with it.

The only thing that'd take some getting used to were the black leather, silver studded boots with chunky heels. They were a bit awkward, seeing as she'd never worn heels, but not too bad. Better than the ugly mismatched and torn shoes she'd been stealing from dumpsters for years.

Next up, she needed to visit Bluetooth's once and for all. She found the shop pretty easily, which had the universal symbol for "Bluetooth" over the door. In she went.

At the counter was a woman with long, braided hair and shaved sides. She had a few Nordic runes tattooed on her face. She did *not* look friendly. Hopping across the counter a few feet away was a raven that looked over to Leyla and croaked, as if it was saying *hello*.

"What do you want?" The woman said.

Nope. Not friendly at all.

"I'm uh, looking for a, com…thing?" Leyla had trouble remembering what the device was called yet again. "Sorry, my memory is an asshole lately."

"I don't have com things, I have com links."

"Ok, a com link. That's it. Everyone says Bluetooth has them."

"You want internal or external?"

"What?"

"Odin's fucking beard, is it your memory or do you have a brain at all? Do you want it inside you or outside you?"

Leyla recoiled, scared of conflict as always. "Uhhh outside?"

The woman squatted down and dug through some cabinets.

"Are you…Bluet—"

"Yes." Bluetooth replied. Leyla shrank, trying her hardest to not annoy Bluetooth, but she couldn't help but notice a picture of Clara, the cyber-witch Ramsay mentioned before. Leyla wasn't going to forget that face.

"Is that a picture of Cl—"

"Yes."

"Ok." Leyla stared down at her new boots, wiggling her toes inside.

Bluetooth continued to rummage through the cabinet. She cursed a couple times in annoyance, likely due to not finding what she was looking for fast enough. The raven hobbled over to Bluetooth to check on her.

Leyla failed again at keeping her mouth shut and being patient.

"Are you guys a couple?"

"YES! Fuck!" Bluetooth snapped and stood straight up, glaring at Leyla, who froze and stared back. The raven squawked and flapped back a little, also startled. "What are you? Five? Sorry Hug." She apologized to the bird, but not to Leyla.

Leyla didn't know how to respond to such hostility. "Hug? Is that the bird's name?"

Bluetooth reeled herself in a bit. "Yes. And he's a raven. Smartest thing down here. Look, it's a shitty day. Anytime those fucking GravGens fail, I'm the one that gets yelled at for the next *three* days for all the comms being screwy. I don't know why it happens. I don't know how to fix it. It will be fine in a few days. I just want to go home to my wife, and eat some fucking ramen, and watch TV, and not talk to people. Here's your com link. Sorry I yelled," Bluetooth explained, still using an aggressive tone.

"It's okay." Leyla replied, taking the com link from her. "Sounds like a good night. Don't you need to scan my SD chip?"

"Nope. My scanner is shit today too! Just take it. Link code is on the left side. And hey…"

Leyla stopped walking out and turned back.

"Name's Lana. Bluetooth is just the shop name. Judging by that old ass SD chip, you're new. You should give Clara a visit soon. She's helpful. She'll clear your head."

"Ok, thanks. I'll put Clara on the ol' to-do list. Well not, like to do like, you know, sex, but…"

"I know what you meant."

"And I like your hair." Leyla waved as she exited the shop.

Well, she's not bad at all, Leyla thought to herself. She figured now was the time for some food, then a haircut. Aside from the mysteries of who Blackhawk was and what exactly his plans may be, SubCity was a much better alternative to living under an overpass. Hopefully, Mari would have some information on Del soon. SubCity could be a great place to be if Del was safe.

Leyla kept pushing down the thought that something terrible could have happened. She couldn't fathom losing Del.

She would check with Mari after the haircut. That should be the end of a long day.

CHAPTER EIGHT

Watchful Eyes

Officer Wells had spent the entire day running through his precinct as discreetly as possible, combing every inch of files that could be linked to the disappearances he told Leyla about. And now, she was gone too. It had only been one day since Leyla fell through that rock wall but it felt like a week. It was like everyone except him was in on a seriously fucked up prank.

He made his way back to the Subway entrance again, ducking the watchful eyes and ears of the precinct. The door was already repaired, but not bolted shut like before. But he remembered something Leyla mentioned. Truck tire tracks that led into the Subway. They'd already driven inside and he never thought to look where those tracks went. So, this time he drove his truck down the subway tunnel, all the way down to that impossible wall Leyla disappeared through.

Sure enough, there were heavy duty tire tracks that ran directly into the wall on the ground. Leyla wasn't the only one able to get through. So it was time for Wells to put his detective hat back on. He reversed all the way back out of the tunnel and whipped his truck around, hoping he hadn't stirred up the ground enough to deter whoever was driving the trucks down the tunnel. He pushed the doors closed as much as he could and moved his truck about a half mile down the road, and parked it in a lot near the Stop N Go gas station.

He ran inside, grabbed a couple beers and bottles of water, dropped them in his small cooler and pulled his personal firearm from behind the seat: a custom, smoke-black Kimber .45 with gold lettering engraved with the words "Love Or Die", a gift from his friend that went missing at the subway. Wells had a custom leather shoulder belt holster made for it with the same words stitched on the strap, which the pistol rested in. He put the holstered pistol on, grabbed his jacket and walked briskly back toward the subway, hoping he would get lucky.

It was close enough to evening that the sun would begin to set soon. Wells positioned himself on top of the entrance, overlooking the door. That should provide an easy view and access to a truck if it shows up, he thought.

He cracked open a beer and relaxed; waiting as the sun began to burn orange and light the sky on fire, inching slowly toward the horizon.

***

Down in SubCity, Leyla had a full belly and a fresh new haircut. She'd tried to describe the cut to the stylist just as the hype bot described. She got it pretty close. Leave the top and back of the hair, but trim a quarter inch to rid her head of the split ends, cut the sides a little shorter, and tease the long hair that's left with sea salt and StaticGel. So, now she had that exact hairdo: a wild and wavy mix of a mullet and surfer locks, and looked like she belonged in a Vox Vermin music video.

Is that a thing? She wondered.

"I could be in a music video." She said out loud as she passed the mirrored wall exiting the stylist shop.

She made her way back to Fritzy Joe's just as the staff was preparing to open for the night, and she still had Mari's clothes in the bag from *Til Death*, intent on returning them as thanks for the kind gesture.

Mari wasn't there. She stopped one of the waitresses that had just arrived there. "Hey, is Mari around? I have something for her." Leyla asked, brandishing the shopping bag.

"Dunno, just got here." The waitress said, then kept walking. Leyla spotted Joe behind the bar inside.

"Jen, don't fuckin' punch anyone tonight o…kkkkkkkkkkay?" Joe stuttered, pointing at another waitress as she pulled her top off, revealing pierced nipples.

"Oh, you mean the grabby goober with the "magnetic" hands!?" She replied. "My piercings are silver! Not magnetic!"

"Okay, you can punch that guy again, he was an asshole, but no one else, okay?"

Leyla walked up to the bar and before she could get a word out, Joe noticed her and pointed directly at her.

"You the new girl? You're late. Get that top off and help Jen fill the dddddddamn beer canon. We open in ten."

Leyla looked down at her chest, realizing he was telling her to get half naked. "Oh, no! No, I'm Leyla, just looking for Mari."

"You and me both. Mari ain't here. Ain't here. Here. Ain't here. She's MIA."

"Seriously? Any clue where she could b—"

"If I had a clue I wouldn't be ttttttellin' you she's ggggggone, now would I?"

"Did you check her apartment upstairs?"

"Did I check her ap…you think I'm stttttttupid?" He snapped back. Seemed he went on the fritz more when he was stressed out. Leyla could relate. Her head still kind of hurt from falling at Cross-Eyes. Those damn absence seizures came a lot more when she was too excited.

"Ok, sorry. These are hers. I'm gonna leave them here. You're in charge. I'll come back later. Thanks! Bye!" Leyla dropped the bag on the bar in front of Joe. He almost got pissed but he was more impressed that Leyla just told him what to do. No one does that around here.

"Damn right I'm in charge." He mumbled. "I'm always in charge."

***

Ramsay knocked on Leyla's door at the Arches, but there was no answer. He waited for a second, then knocked again. Nothing. Guess she's out and about, he thought.

He turned to see Leyla gawking at him down the hall, having just exited the elevator.

"Hey! Are all these yours?" Ramsay motioned to all the delivery packages from shops that sat at her door. "Wait…new threads, new makeup, new *hair*? You look amazing!"

"Thank you." Leyla said, standoffish.

"Welcome…something wrong?" Ramsay expected a smile. She was more friendly before.

"No, just tired. Been a long day." Leyla walked toward Ramsay, trying to figure out when to ask about Del and how to do so. For now, it may've been a better idea to just be nice and get him trusting her. *Be careful. It's what Mari said,* she thought. "You can come in if you want. I need help with that holo-tab thing."

"Oh! Yeah, yeah I got time. I came to see if you were settled in anyway."

Leyla scanned her SD chip and opened the door. Ramsay grabbed all the boxes he could and moved them inside.

"Hello Master Leyla. And Mister Ramsay, nice to see you both! Texas Chainsaw Massacre greeted them. "There are no preferences set in the holo-tab. Would you prefer I…"

"Not hungry, sorry!" Leyla interrupts.

"Very well."

"Do you check on all the girls to see if they're settled?" Leyla asks Ramsay.

"I'm just being nice."

"Sure."

"I'm serious."

Leyla leaned against the prep island in her kitchen. "So…holo-tab?"

He picked up the holo-tab and brought up the menu. He sat on the guest bed he'd extended before. Leyla moved over to sit close and faced him.

Make him think he's got a chance, she thought to herself. It was something Del had told her a long time ago to manipulate men into doing anything. She put on her best sexy eyes. Ramsay looked at her. She didn't realize she'd made herself simply look like a drunken moron. He burst out laughing.

"What is that face?" He said.

"What face?" She replied, laying into the expression even more, to a comical extent.

"Is that a sexy eyes? Are you doing sexy eyes right now?"

"No!" Leyla straightened up and whipped her eyes back to normal, and Ramsay bellowed laughing.

"Ok, so first we set your auto-chef preferences so you can have some home cooked meals."

"Can he make pizza?"

"Yes, he can, but please try some other food. I programmed these guys with an absolutely insane amount of culinary arts algorithms, they can make any damn thing in the world."

"You made that thing and you don't have one?"

"I didn't make the bot, I just programmed it. Plus, I like to cook for myself. Now, let's go through the list. If you like an ingredient, check yes. If not, check no. If you don't know what it is, I can explain it."

"Okay. Go."

"Anise."

"Nope, don't know what that is."

"Spice. It's like…licorice almost."

"That black candy? Ew. Nope."

"Ok. No, then." Ramsay seemed offended. "Asafoetida."

"Ass of what?"

"Checking No. You know what? What do you know you don't like?"

"The black candy, um…sushi…"

"SUSHI?!" Ramsay yelled.

"It's not even cooked!"

"Have you had California rolls? Eel? Tempura?"

"Nope."

"It's cooked sushi. Try it."

"Ok, I can do cooked."

"So let me guess. No rare steak?"

"Nope."

"Okay, *you* are gonna do the holo-tab foods checklist later with Texas Chainsaw Massacre, before I have a heart attack. Let's order some furniture. You can't kill me with your preferences there, I don't think."

Wells had finished his two beers and night had fallen. It had gotten a little chilly, so he pulled on a light jean jacket.

Four pairs of headlights made their way around the bend heading toward the subway entrance, but they stopped a couple hundred yards out and powered down. The headlights turned off but the parking lights were still on. They looked like they belonged to 18 wheelers. Wells moved to the edge of the entrance, just over the doors, and heard a voice that sounded like it was coming from inside the dark tunnel. Wells listened in until he could make out what the voice was saying as it drew closer.

"Just a sec. Gotta run a scan out here real quick, you know how it is. I'll ring you back when it's done." A male voice crawled out of the subway and through the cracked door. "Fuck, did we forget to seal it up last week?" The voice said, now directly under Wells.

Wells heard something drop. *Maybe a bag of tools*. Two thick sounding clicks were heard. *Nope, maybe a pelican case or something*. Something started whirring. Wells peeked down at the doors, one of which was opened slightly. A small drone flew out and went straight into the air around 50 feet. It stopped, and began spinning. Wells remembered the man said he was about to run a scan. *Could be looking for people that aren't supposed to see this*, Wells thought. He dropped down behind an old piece of machinery and peeked through a small hole. He'd picked out the spot earlier just in case he needed to hide. It seemed to work; the drone dropped back down to the door.

"All clear. Move in." The man said, communicating with the trucks stopped two football fields away.

Their lights powered up and they moved forward, forming a single file. The doors under Wells opened up.

Jump on the last one, Wells told himself. *Jump on any others and the driver behind will see you.* Wells waited and made his profile as low as possible as the first truck passed under him. They were only going around fifteen miles per hour. *Should be easy to drop down on without killing myself*, Wells assured himself. The second and third truck passed under. They were all carrying shipping containers. *What the fuck is down there that needs four shipping trucks?* Wells readied himself as the last truck passed under. *This is it.*

The last container was passing under him and into the subway. Wells pushed himself up and dropped straight down. He landed well; he used to be quite an athlete, but he was knocked off his feet hard by something from behind him. It was the top of the doorway. He'd thought of everything except that. It hurt like Hell and knocked the breath out of his chest. He grit his teeth, trying hard to not cry out in pain and alert the driver.

"FUCK. Idiot…" Wells let out a quiet growl at himself. But his plan so far had worked. He was on the truck's container. Either he was lucky or he was fucked, and there was only one way he was finding out.

Let's see if that magic wall lets me in now.

The trucks all followed each other down the subway tunnel. Wells couldn't see past the container in front of him. The tunnel was just wide enough to fit the trucks, let alone a view around them. Eventually, they slowed down and stopped, but only for a moment and began moving again. Wells figured they had to be near the wall by then. It was near the section that opened up wider. The truck lurched right. They were at the end of the tunnel. His truck pulled up next to the one in front of it, as the four trucks had all formed up beside each other, all still moving at a crawl. Wells ducked down more and looked ahead. It was where the wall was, but it was no longer there. The trucks drove right through and into the gargantuan freight elevator Leyla had passed through a few days earlier.

The elevator lurched down and sped up.

"Are you fuckin' kidding me?" Wells spoke out loud in disbelief. The elevator stopped. The mammoth doors opened. And then he saw it.

The sprawling, hidden, absolutely impossible network of buildings connected by walkways and trams, occupied by *hundreds* of people. He counted at least a dozen vehicles that soared through the air. Cars that were taken right out of sci-fi movies and games and placed in the real world under the city he'd worked in for fifteen years. It was as crazy as it was gorgeous.

He was so stunned by the realization of a hidden city under Cincinnati that he almost didn't notice the truck he was on had pulled out of the elevator and out into the street in front of them.

"Oh shit!" Wells grunted as he saw what a vulnerable spot he was in.. *Gotta get off here now*, he reminded himself. The truck was moving slow. Easy peasy. He rolled his leg over the edge and slid down the side, hanging from his fingers. He let go and dropped only a few feet to the ground level. Frantically and awkwardly, he scattered toward cover. The closest thing was a big cylinder that had a few glowing lights on it. *It'll do*. He dropped down behind it, hoping someone hadn't seen him so far.

All four trucks parked in line with each other and released their air brakes with a fairly loud *pssshhhhhhhh*. The drivers all got out and walked back to the rear of their containers, carrying bolt cutters.

They each snapped the bolt lock on the doors and pulled them open. Wells couldn't see inside the containers from the angle he was at, but he heard a loud buzz from his right, toward the city.

A few dozen robots floated down from somewhere, each sporting two metal blades in front. They were forklifts. *Flying forklifts*. They glowed underneath with the same blue gravitational energy as the GravGen grid protecting SubCity from a cave-in.

The bots went to work, unloading pallet after pallet of supplies from the trucks. In and out of the containers they went, working so fast that Wells could visibly see the trailers lifting up from the ground as weight was reduced.

Each pallet removed soared off to a different area of the city. Wells was smart enough to put it all together: *supply trucks*; *Supporting an entire hidden city. Leyla was right.* The drivers conversed with one another for a few minutes while the bots unloaded their shipments. Once empty, they closed the doors, jumped in the tractors and all made U-turns to get back on the freight elevator. The door closed and sent them back up to the surface.

Wells cautiously left his hiding spot and headed into the city, finally on the hunt for either Leyla or his missing friend. With any luck, he would find both and get the Hell out. *This was what the precinct was trying to bury,* he realized. *Someone on the force is being paid to keep this all hush hush. That has to be the case.*

***

Ramsay had already left Leyla's apartment. She knew how to use the holotab to order things for her apartment now and felt pretty comfortable doing so. *He can't be a bad guy,* she thought of Ramsay. *He was way too nice.* Unless he was being nice to throw her off. She hoped not. He was a pretty cute guy. Maybe he took a liking to her. She let her thoughts go wild but drew her mind back to the reason she was there in SubCity in the first place: *Del. Where is Del? And how do I find her?* She asked herself. No one knew anything or at least, no one would say anything. But if Del was there, she would make her presence known eventually. Unless she'd been taken hostage…

Leyla stopped pacing in front of the large window overlooking the city. Shit. What if Del is locked up somewhere? Where would that be?

Leyla started pacing again and looked out the window. She could see those bright lights from Fritzy Joe's from up there. Mari had said something about a computer and avoided talking about it earlier. And now, it seemed like she was gone too. Wells had also pushed about people going missing near the subway. *Shit! I forgot about Wells*, she remembered.

She started pacing even faster, racking her brain. *How do I get back to Wells? He has to be looking for me too.*

A nice little chime reverberated throughout the apartment; a custom doorbell jingle that Ramsay showed her how to make on the holotab. Someone was at the door.

Leyla opened the door and saw no one, but she looked down to find more packages—a *lot* of packages, big and small. Looking down the hallway she saw a small cargo bot floating back toward her, carrying even more packages. It was painted white and light blue, had two big eyes, and had a little itty bitty antenna on its head. It spoke out in a cute little robot voice.

"Hello Miss Leyla, your orders from the holonet are here!"

"That was fast. And you are so stinking cute!" Leyla replied, almost squealing.

"Thank you! I can move the packages in and assemble them if you like."

Leyla looked into her near empty apartment and it didn't take long for her to make her decision.

"Yes. I am not putting all the shit Ramsay ordered together."

Leyla stepped back out of the way and let the bot carry the boxes in. Some of them were pretty large. Texas Chainsaw Massacre looked over to the bot as it entered and greeted it just like anyone else.

"Greetings, ship bot!"

"Greetings, Texas Chainsaw Massacre!" The bot replied, which surprised Leyla. How did it know her auto-chef already?

"How do you know his name?" She asked the bot.

Texas Chainsaw Massacre answered for the bot. "All androids in SubCity are connected to our secure intranet, same as your holotab. We are what you would say, a hive mind."

"Oh. Well damn. Means I can't tell you which droids I hate around here."

"You can. We would just all know what you said."

"I know, that's the point, I can't gossip if you…ok never mind. It was a joke. I gotta remember you guys don't have humor installed."

"Would you like me to download the comedian protocol?"

Leyla blinked her eyes the same way Del used to when someone said something unexpected. "What the Hell is a comedian protocol?"

"Humor." Chainsaw Massacre replied dryly.

"You've been able to be funny this whole time?"

"With the availability of comedian protocol, yes."

"And you didn't say anything?"

"You did not ask."

"Download that shit. I wanna hear some jokes."

Leyla turned to check on the cute little ship bot. She stopped abruptly.

Her eyes widened, and she didn't realize her mouth was hanging open. That cute little bastard had assembled *everything* already. The couch. The shelves - stocked with books. The nice, fluffy rug. Art on the walls. A shiny, new Martin acoustic guitar was mounted on the wall beside the desk. Everything she and Ramsay had ordered was there.

"How the fuck? What? How did you…what?" Leyla blurted out at the ship bot. It floated for a second, as if processing a reply, and then its backside opened up and a dozen little slender, pneumatic arms snaked out.

"I have twelve appendages." It explained, and then retracted the snake-like arms.

"Ok now you're creepy. Get out."

The bot didn't have an expression to make, but it tilted forward a bit as if it was sad and floated toward the door. Leyla couldn't help herself. She rushed over to the bot and put her hands where it should have cheeks.

"Oh no no no, I'm so sorry! You're too cute to be mean to. I didn't mean it."

"Of *course* she meant it! She's a horrible person! Just last week she murdered a baby and threw it at an elderly person!" Texas Chainsaw Massacre told the bot, except now he had more of a light hearted Chicago accent. Leyla jered her head around to look at Chainsaw Massacre, surprised by the offhand remark.

"No I didn't! What are you talki…"

"Just joking!" The android interrupted. "Comedian protocol has been downloaded and activated. You're fucked now, missy!"

"*That* is your funny mode? Dead babies are funny to you?"

"It is if you're not a dead baby."

"No no, we're changing that. Are there other funny styles?"

"You gonna let that ship bot go or are you gonna keep holding its head 'til it dies?

Leyla realized she was still holding the cute little bot and let go. "Oops, sorry! Thank you for your hard work!"

"You are welcome Miss Leyla! I'll just take this. Have a nice night!" The bot replied, and picked up a cardboard box that it had neatly compressed all the other package boxes into, and floated away. Leyla closed the door and turned to Texas Chainsaw Massacre: the baby hating android.

"We're not doing dead baby jokes. What else ya got?"

"You want kid friendly or you want raunchy?"

"Oh! Raunchy! Wait…how raunchy?"

"HBO wouldn't air my jokes."

"Ok go."

"So there's this woman on a business trip in New Orleans right? She's single cuz men are trash. Anyway she's out shopping and having fun in the French quarter the night before she flies back to New York. She finds this little shop there, called Voodoo Dicks. Ok, that's interesting, she thinks. She goes in and sees it's a freaky little sex shop, right?"

"Oh shit." Leyla replied, interested in the story.

"Yeah so, the guy behind the counter greets her and says we got one thing and one thing only. Voodoo dicks. She's like what's a voodoo dick? Guy says it's a dildo infused with voodoo magic. You say its name, and then tell it where you want it to go, and it goes there and doesn't stop until you say voodoo dick, stop."

"Is that a real thing?" Leyla asks.

"Hell if I know, but the lady doesn't believe this guy. She wants a demonstration. Guy says okay. Voodoo dick! And this huge dildo just rises up and floats, awaiting orders, right?"

Leyla leans in closer to Texas Chainsaw Massacre. "And?"

"Guy says *table!* And the voodoo dick shoots down to the table and it's just going to town like the world was about to end. This lady is like whoah what the fuck?! Guy says voodoo dick, stop. The dildo drops down and it's lifeless. This lady throws money at the guy and takes the dick and leaves."

Leyla laughed, but the joke wasn't over.

"So that night she almost tries the dildo out, but she's like nah, I'm gonna wait til I'm home. She goes to sleep and wakes up and she boards the plane the next morning. They get up to 30,000 feet right? She gets to thinking. Mile high club. Magic dick. I'm doing this."

"Oh noooooo!" Leyla put her hand over her mouth. "This is a bad idea!"

"Lady reaches in her bag and grabs the super dick and hides it under her shirt and damn near runs to the little airplane bathroom. Luckily no one's there. She locks that bitch and pulls down her pants and sits down on the toilet, legs wide the fuck open."

"No no no no." Leyla felt second hand embarrassment coming in a big way, but damn this was too interesting.

"She spits on the dick and slicks it up and says, Voodoo dick? She lets go. It's just floating there, waiting for a command. My *pussy*. It shoots down there and goes inside so hard it almost lifts her ass off the seat and it's a monster; it's going to town. It's beating so fast she could feel the fucking heat coming off it."

"Oh my god!" Leyla kept her hand over mouth.

"And she knows she's about cum, so she puts her hand over her mouth but there ain't no holding this in. This is one of those transcendental orgasms, and she lets loose a scream that could wake a fucking cemetery.

She's thrashing all over the place. Shaking, sweating, convulsing, eyes rolled back all that shit."

"I need to find one of those…"

"No you don't, because here's the thing: she was so fucked up from the greatest orgasm known to humanity that she couldn't speak. She couldn't tell it to stop."

"Oh, not good."

"Good is a matter of opinion. It's fuckin' her actual brains out. She's screaming, crying, kicking."

"Ok, I don't like where this is going."

"She kicks the door open and another damn orgasm hits. She's all over the place. She's thinking ok, maybe I don't need the dildo to stop."

"I'll allow it. Keep going." Leyla grinned.

"But yeah, now the door is open and some crazy lady is screaming like she's being murdered in the bathroom. Fuckin' air marshall runs back there to see what the commotion is. He sees this lady all in a puddle and eyeliner all fucking melted on her face. He's like what the fuck is happening here?"

"Voodoo dick!" Leyla interjected.

"Yeah! She's so caught up in paradise she forgot to even tell the thing to stop but she's like, THERE'S A VOODOO DICK IN MY PUSSY!

Air marshall takes a look at her all sprawled out and clawing at the walls, but her long skirt has since dropped down, so he can't see what's really happening so he doesn't believe her. He goes: VOODOO DICK, MY ASS!'"

Leyla waited for the next bit but realized that was the story and, *oh! Oh no! His ass*! She fell out of her chair laughing.

"Oh nooooooo!" She cry-laughed on the ground, struggling to catch her breath.

"Mile high club got eeeeemmm!" Texas Chainsaw Massacre added.

Leyla got to her feet. "Man, okay, that one. That's the comedian I need. Oh shit. I can't breathe."

"Do you have a voodoo dick in your pussy? That could be why."

Leyla dropped to her knee in laughter. "No, no no no stop, please! Can't breathe!"

"Yes ma'am"

Leyla pulled herself up to her feet and put her hands on her knees to catch her breath.

"Oh man, Del is gonna love you."

***

Leyla's conversation with the now comedic android played through a low-fi speaker mechanism coming from an older android in a different part of SubCity; in a room that wasn't as nice as Leyla's apartment.

This room was a little more grunge; not dirty, just older. Lived in.

With a hive mind, like Texas Chainsaw Massacre said, every android knew what the other was up to. That included Leyla's auto-chef's transponder unit, which was relaying their conversation across the city.

Blackhawk sat beside the older droid, smoking a cigar and listening in; he was spying on SubCity's newest guest.

"What the fuck are you hiding?" He rhetorically asked the audio recording. No way Leyla just walked through the wall. She couldn't be there on accident. No way.

"Nothing." Ramsay, a few feet away and listening as well, put in his two cents. "She really doesn't remember anything. Whoever she was, she doesn't know. But, she's from here. No doubt. Wouldn't have gotten through the wall any other way."

Blackhawk stood and walked over to his own window that looked over all of SubCity. He was in what he called "The Bullpen", his private lounge/apartment he'd converted from a room that had once been the control station for the abandoned subway.

"Check on her in the morning. You're doing good, man. I think she's starting to trust you. But be careful. We can't lose everything we worked for."

"I know." Ramsay added. "It's like she had a memory wipe, but she didn't." Ramsay tried to push down the feeling that Leyla was simply a cute and bubbly, innocent young woman that he quickly took a liking to.

Who knew what she was capable of?

"No mods either. That's the weird thing. She's somethin' else. But she's here for a reason. I know it." Blackhawk said.

Leyla's voice played through the droid's speaker.

"I'm going to take a shower. And then, bed. I am so, *so* tired. And I want pancakes tomorrow morning!" She said to Texas Chainsaw Massacre.

Blackhawk looked over to Ramsay. "You're thinking the same thing I am."

"She's not. Wouldn't make sense; completely illogical. No way." Ramsay replied.

"You sure?"

Ramsay stood as well and walked up beside his old friend. "If she was, we'd be dead already."

CHAPTER NINE

The Detective

Wells knew not to just start asking for his friend or Leyla willy nilly. He'd been spending the last hour or so scouting the streets and soaking in what kind of place he was in. But Leyla and Greene were both down in this city, no doubt. He couldn't believe this was kept such a secret. It had to be there for decades to be that built up. And all the cybernetics, flying vehicles, and *robots*? How had this tech not made it to the surface somehow? *This place is light years ahead of the rest of the world*, he thought.

It was pretty late, maybe 1AM by that point. He was tired. The thought of a hotel crossed his mind, but this didn't seem like the kind of place that would allow simple guests from out of town.

One way in, one way out? This seems more like a prison, he thought. *Just smells better. Damn, what is that smell?*

Sure enough, it was Carol, the New York pizza lady with the cart that had greeted Leyla when she arrived. She was further into the city from where she had been the previous night; this time beside Fairfax's Virtua-Cade, a big VR gaming joint with a mural of famous video game characters painted on the walls. It looked fun, but Carol's pizza wasn't letting Wells think of anything else.

"Hey, how much for a slice?" He asked, not assuming money was any different from the surface.

Carol looked up at Wells, perplexed, but she remembered Leyla from before.

"Okay, that's two of you in a row, but you make less sense."

"Huh? Lady, I just want a slice of pizza. No need to get rude off the bat."

"Yeah yeah. Well I'm too tired to explain to you the same thing as the last moron that had a shifty memory."

"My memory is fine, what are you talking ab—"

Wells remembered Leyla's memory issues.

"Young lady? Mid twenties? Brown hair and eyes? Real pretty and innocent?" He spouted out Leyla's description in the most "cop" way imaginable.

"Yeah, dingbat skipped my whole line."

"Where did she go?"

"What's it to you? I don't know you. I don't know her either but I ain't sending some random guy after her."

"She's my uh, girl. My girlfriend." Wells lied. "She doesn't remember things sometimes. Just trying to make sure she's good."

"Hmmm. Shoddy story but you seem ok. She probably went down to Cross-Eyes."

"What's that?"

"Oh, my, *God*. Seriously? What am I? The fuckin' encyclopedia? Am I Google now?"

Wells didn't know how to reply so he just reeled back and held his hands out, questioning why Carol was being so hostile.

"Clinic down the street, way back toward the riser. No more questions. You want pizza or not?"

"Yeah, just one slice. You got Hawaiian?" Wells replied, pulling his wallet out and refraining from asking what the riser was. Maybe she was talking about the big elevator.

"Got pineapple, ran outta bacon."

"That's fine with me." Wells handed over a five dollar bill. Carol looked at the bill and then to Wells.

"You cosplayers are somethin' else." She said, and took the money from Wells without furthering the annoying conversation.

"Keep the change."

"Uh huh."

Wells walked off from Carol as she shook her head and bit into the pizza. His eyes widened and he looked down at the cheesy, pineapple topped slice. It was so good he turned to look back at Carol to see who created such a masterpiece.

"Thanks for the pizza! Fuckin' amazing!"

Carol waved back at Wells, hoping he would just go away.

Wells headed back toward the freight elevator. He remembered passing a spot that had a big Red Cross turned over like an X. That could be the clinic. But it was getting later and later, and Wells's eyes were stinging and heavy. He thought maybe he'd stop at that shop he smelled coffee at on the way.

***

When he got to what he suspected to be Cross-Eyes' clinic, it was all locked up; no one there. *Well shit*, he thought. *What now?* Maybe there was another way in. It was a clinic, and clinics kept records. At least they did everywhere else in the world.

Wells walked around the corner of the closed up building and almost stepped on a rat. A real rat—as far as he could tell. Rodents and pests could show up anywhere that had a hole to squeeze through. The rat squeaked; it didn't expect a hard-boiled detective to almost flatten it that night, so it scurried off and into some rubbish laid out for the cleaner bots to pick up later.

Wells stepped lightly. Not because of the rat; more because he didn't want anyone to catch him breaking and entering. The alley he'd stepped into got darker the further it went. He thought about pulling his cell phone to use the flashlight function but that could draw more attention than walking loudly, so that was a stupid idea.

Just like he hoped, there was a back door. It had some shipping pallets stacked up beside it high enough to block the view from the street. The top pallet was unopened. Must have come from the trucks he'd snuck in with, Wells figured.

He got up to the door and realized it didn't have a door knob or a latch. In fact, it didn't have a way to open from the outside at all.

"Ah, come on." Wells remarked to himself in a low growl. He pushed on the door out of frustration, but it moved in about a half inch and then came back to place; but it was opened further than before.

Wells luckily noticed this, and flicked out his pocket knife. He slid the blade in the crack of the door and twisted it. The door didn't move. Either it wouldn't open or the knife blade was at a bad angle. He pulled the knife out of the crack and positioned it so the tip of it could jab into the door while the side of the blade was resting on the door frame like a fulcrum. He slowly pushed the knife toward the wall.

The door actually moved out this time; enough for Wells to put a finger on the side and hold it to reposition his blade to pull it further out. He did this twice until the door was open enough to get a grip on it. It opened right up. It had some weight to it; it must have been held closed by a hydraulic spring like most industrial doors. Wells slid inside before someone could see him.

***

The following morning, Leyla's window de-tinted itself to let the simulated sunrise in. Those light simulators were truly a magnificent creation; they cast the entire city in a warm and sharp blanket of light. And that light made its way right over to Leyla's eyelids, just as it had the previous morning at Mari's. She'd fallen asleep on the couch instead of the lavish bed she'd just gotten. But this time, the light didn't wake her. Something else did.

A piece of eggshell landed on her forehead. She didn't budge. A larger piece plopped onto her nose. Then another hit her right in the eye. That one got her. She jolted awake and shook her head and smacked her own face so hard it stung.

"The heck!?" Leyla sat up straight, clawing at whatever was on her face.

"Hey! Sleeping fuckin' beauty! Good morning!" Texas Chainsaw Massacre greets her. He was the egg tossing culprit.

"Why are you throwing eggs at my face?"

"One: you don't have an alarm clock. Two: I am literally bolted to the floor over here and I couldn't go over there and shake you. Three: I am making you some fucking amazing French toast and sausage for breakfast. Texas Chainsaw Massacre style."

"Oh. I forgot to order an alarm clock. I'll do that."

The huge window/TV was playing. Apparently Leyla did not go to bed. She instead had begun binge watching "Roommates", a sitcom produced, shot, and distributed only in SubCity. It felt a lot like a show from the surface Leyla had heard about but this one was great in its own right, she thought. On screen, a bubbly, brown hair and brown eyed woman entered a room where two of her other roommates, both males, were sitting on couches. She was carrying a pizza box, but she'd already taken a slice out and just hadn't started eating it before she got to the apartment.

One of the character's friends, a male, looked at her and said "Hey! You can't open the pizza box before box opening time!" An invisible crowd could be heard cackling and laughing at the remark.

"What do you mean, box opening time?"

"There's a time you open the box!" The invisible crown laughed again.

"Well I was hungry. I opened it to—"

The male character flailed his hands and leapt out of his chair. "No! Box opening time is when you're here, with everyone salivating! And we're all ready for box opening time! You wait! It's a rule!"

"Who made up that rule? That doesn't make any sense."

"I don't know! But now it's box opening time, and *you already opened the box*!" The TV audience roared with laughter.

"So what's that mean? The pizza is still good." The female character bites into her slice *crust first*, prompting a horrified reaction from both male characters as well as the TV audience.

"That's it! You're out of the gang!" The other male leaps up, repulsed at the sin of biting into pizza crust first. The crowd laughed harder than before. Leyla held her hand up at the TV.

"What's wrong with crust first? I do crust first!" Leyla agreed with the woman on TV.

The woman on the show looked at both the men and, with an evil grin, bit the *side* of the pizza. Both male characters freak out. One put his hands over his eyes and called out to the female character.

"Leyla! You can't do that! It's like, bad luck or somethin'!" He said with a strong Brooklyn accent.

Leyla? That's creepy, Leyla thought. *She has the same name as I do? And eats pizza crust first?*

Leyla wondered if this TV show character shared any of her other traits, but Texas Chainsaw Massacre called out to her.

"Miss Leyla! Pain perdu parfait!" The android said.

"Dunno what that means but I smell food!" Leyla rolled out of the couch. "Was that French?"

"Well yeah, I speak like, all the languages."

"Mmmm. I like it. Say some more." Leyla requested, as she sat at the prep island where the android had placed her breakfast.

Texas Chainsaw Massacre allowed her to take a bite first. "J'ai mis un cafard dans la nourriture!"

"Mmmm damn man, this is amazing! Seriously! And what did you just say?"

"I put a cockroach in the food."

Leyla spat out the delicious food she was devouring.

"Just joking!"

"You ruined it. You ruined the whole thing you had going there."

"Hey, missy?" Chainsaw Massacre pointed a finger at the food. "You don't tighten up and eat that food that I slaved over? Pancakes are gettin' 86'd from the menu."

"No! Not the pancakes! I'll eat this! I'm eating it! Is there really a cockroach?"

"No! Seriously? You think I would ruin a masterpiece with a bug?"

"Okay okay, I love it. Hey, weren't you supposed to make me pancakes? I asked for pancakes last night."

"Outta flour. Shipment was last night, I think. Just ordered more. We had brioche, eggs, cinnamon and sugar, so I figured French toast was a viable option."

"You were correct, sir."

"Sir? How dare you misuse the improper pronoun for me! I identify as an android! Not a sir!"

Leyla froze. *Oops.*

"You will not address me as a sir, or a ma'am! Not she nor he nor they or them, not even it. I shall be addressed as bbbrrrppttttt." Chainsaw Massacre made a raspberry fart sound.

Leyla had no idea how to respond. Texas Chainsaw Massacre bent over in laughter with its non-existent face.

"I'm just yankin' yer chain! Pronouns don't mean shit to me. I'm a fuckin' robot!"

"Oh good. Had me scared." Leyla sighed. "I don't want to offend my friends."

The android stopped laughing.

"Do you…you see me as a friend?"

"Well I…I guess. Yeah. You're pretty cool."

Texas Chainsaw Massacre seemed legitimately touched—if an android could feel such a thing. But before it could reply, a *very* heavy knock could be heard from Leyla's door.

"What the fuck?" Chainsaw Massacre jerked its gaze to the entrance. "Must be a pig! Everyone hide the booze!" The bot grabbed a bottle of sherry it preferred to cook with and retracted into the floor, completely hiding its body.

Leyla slowly got up and walked to the door. "Yeah?!" She yelled. "Who is it?"

"Leyla?"

She knew the muffled voice, but she couldn't believe what she'd just heard. No fucking way, she thought, as she lunged for the doorknob, turned it and yanked the door open as fast as she could. Her ears hadn't betrayed her. There he was.

Sergeant Donnie Fucking Wells.

Leyla screamed in Wells's face.

"AAAAHHHH!" She jumped forward and wrapped her arms around him. It hadn't even been two days since they were separated but he was finally the familiar face she needed. He instinctively hugged back, smiling.

"How did you find me? How did you even get here?"

"I was a detective. I did some detecting. You got a haircut? And new clothes? Wow, you look good!" Wells said, as Leyla pulled away from him and retreated back into her apartment. She pulled him in by his arm.

"Yeah, you like it?" Leyla ran her fingers through the poofed, 80's punk rocker mullet.

Texas Chainsaw Massacre sprouted up from the floor holding a knife. "I knew it was a pig! So you've come for me huh, *copper*?!"

Wells stepped back and went for his pistol. Leyla did not expect to see a gun.

"Hey whoah whoah whoah what is *that* for?!" She put her hands up, pleading with Wells to calm down. They still hadn't shut the apartment door.

"What's up with the killer robot?" Wells asked.

"Killer robot? I'm a fuckin' chef, I don't know what you're talking about." Texas Chainsaw Massacre picked up a tomato, tossed it up, and sliced it several times mid-air. The slices landed rather neatly on a cutting board in front of it. "And I'm damn good at what I do. How do you take your omelette?"

Wells stared back at the bot. "Wh…chef?" He looked to Leyla.

"Yes, auto-chef. He cooks. And he *jokes too much*!" Leyla glared at the android.

"Hey, there is no such thing as "jokes too much"."

"I almost shot you!" It hadn't quite registered to Wells that he was talking to a robot. He'd seen them on the street before he got to the apartment, but he hadn't interacted with them.

"If you strike me down, I shall become more powerful than you can possibly imagine." Chainsaw Massacre replied.

"Was that a Star Wars reference? Did he just make an Obi-Wan quote?" Wells asked Leyla as he relaxed a little and pulled the door shut, finally.

"I don't know, haven't seen Star Wars."

Both Wells and Texas Chainsaw Massacre jerked their gazes to Leyla and reacted simultaneously:

"What?!" They both yelled.

"We're fixing that when we get out of here." Wells told Leyla.

"Yeah, and that C-3PO has got a hot ass." Chainsaw Massacre added.

"Can you both just kind of, I don't know, shut up for a second!?" Leyla yelled back. "Wells, I haven't found Del yet. And this place is so, like, *weird*. And also, it's awesome! I can't make up my mind."

"Yeah, no shit! Robots, cybernetics, holographics, flying cars. How has Cincinnati not caved in on this place? We have to be directly under the city."

"Oh! I actually have an answer for that!" Leyla perked up and pointed at Wells. "There's these things way up high, a bunch of 'em, and they glow blue, called GravGens. They're like, gravity generators, uh huh!" This was the first chance she'd gotten to explain something to someone else for a change. It felt great, and she had a huge and proud grin across her face.

"Holding up the city from a collapse." Wells replied, working out the rest.

"Yeah! One almost fell yesterday and…oh…"

"What?"

"If they fail, that thing you don't wanna happen happens."

"Well then we got to warn Cincinnati! But no, first thing I'm doing is finding Greene, and we're finding your friend too. And then we're getting the fuck out of here." Wells walked into the apartment, finally taking a look.

"Well damn. They certainly set you up nice. What did you do to convince them to give you this?"

"Nothing. They just gave it to me."

"Yeah." Wells didn't trust that. *They* must have an agenda. "And uh, who is they?"

"Um, I think the leader of this place is named Blackhawk, and he has a friend named Ramsay. Ramsay seems really nice. Super smart too. Little bit weird."

"Okay. Did you ask either of them about Del?"

"No, I don't really know how to. Like, what if they don't want Del found? What would they do to me? What would they do to Del?"

"Yeah, good point, actually. What's this Blackhawk like?"

"Think about like, a dad, but scary, and you just punched his kid in a playground cuz that little prick stole your hairbow."

"He's got a kid?"

"No, he—"

"You punched his kid? Why would you do that?"

"NO! It was a comparison!"

"Oh, scary dad type. Got it."

"Yes!" Leyla smiled, finally getting her point across.

"*Are* there kids here?" Wells asked. Texas Chainsaw Massacre entered the conversation.

"To date, no kids down here in SubCity. We androids ate them all."

"I said no dead baby jokes!"

"Oh right, just dick jokes."

"Exactly!"

"Does he want an omelette or you two gonna leave me hangin'?" The android pointed to Wells.

Wells stared at the bot and then Leyla. She'd been up to a lot since falling through that wall. "You've just made friends with everything down here haven't you?"

"It's what I do!"

Wells looked back to the bot. "Two eggs, dash of cream, whipped hard, salt and paprika. Cheese, tomato and spinach. Can you do that?"

"Ah right. Pigs don't eat ham."

"I love porkchops, wait, cop joke, I get it. Hardy har har."

"Hey, when's the last time you slept?" Leyla tapped Wells's shoulder.

"Not since the night before you showed up at my desk." Wells's eyes were bloodshot and droopy. A few more hours and people would mistake him for a vampire.

"Criminy crackers, Batman! You need rest!"

"Batman never gets any rest." Chainsaw Massacre interjected, but was ignored.

"Yeah, but I got down here didn't I? You got a bathroom in this little slice of Heaven? Gotta piss like a race horse."

"Yeah it's right over here." Leyla walked to the sliding door. "You should get a shower, too. It's a, well, the shower talks. So, don't freak out. It'll wash your clothes really fast too."

"Trying to get me naked already? We just met."

"I would like to see the hot cop naked!" Chainsaw Massacre yelled from across the room. Wells actually laughed at that remark.

Leyla flushed red. "No! I mean, you're um, you look good but, I was just—"

"Relax, it was a joke. That creepy ass bot isn't the only one allowed to do that."

"I was not joking." The bot replied.

"Look, take a shower, mister. And a nap." Leyla stamped her foot and pointed to the bedroom.

"Okay, okay mom. Don't ground me."

"Oh look, he's into role play too." Chainsaw Massacre just wouldn't stop. "Oh wait, are incest jokes on or off the table?"

"Off." Both Leyla and Wells responded.

"Right-O, cheerio." The android finally took a break and went back to prepping Wells's breakfast.

Wells walked into the bathroom, where the AI greeted him and gave him the same introduction it had given Leyla before.

"Is that a rainforest shower?" He asked out loud.

"Yes!" Leyla replied from the other room.

"Shit. If Greene has this I'm gonna whoop his ass."

Leyla approached Texas Chainsaw Massacre as it warmed up the flat top grill.

"Hey, last night, you said androids have a hive mind. What's that mean exactly?"

"Oh, well basically, we all know what each other is doing or did."

"Like, can you tell me what another droid saw or heard?"

"If it saw or heard something, sure. Only problem is, you need core access to that. Privacy is still a thing in SubCity, little missy."

"How do I get core access?"

"You don't. Only the big wigs around here get that kind of power."

"Blackhawk and Ramsay."

"Yep."

"Screw it I'll try anyway. Have any other droids heard about or seen Del? Older black lady–likes to curse. Got pulled down here by a super ninja."

Chainsaw Massacre paused cooking for a few seconds and froze. Its face screen blanked out. It came to again and looked over to Leyla.

"Nothing about a Del, no."

"Wait!" Leyla pointed at the bot and bounced on her feet a little. "You said I can't ask unless I have core access!"

"Well either I was wrong or you have core access."

A knock came from the door. A rhythmic rapping; the same pattern she'd caught Ramsay doing the previous night.

"Oh shit!" Leyla blurted out, looking at the door and then to the bedroom where Wells had undoubtedly stripped and was in the shower.

"Oh shit oh shit oh shit!"

"Leyla? I hear you. Any reason you're not answering?" Ramsay called from the other side.

"Um, hold on!" Leyla yelled. "I'm uh, getting dressed!" Leyla mimed putting clothes on.

"You know he can't see you?" Chainsaw Massacre added.

"Shut up!" Leyla snapped, and ran over to her bedroom door, poked her head in and whispered as loud as she could. "Don't come out, wait here!"

"What?" Wells turned to Leyla's hushed voice. Falling water drowned out what she said.

She slammed the door, startling Wells, then ran to her apartment door and readied herself. She opened it as calmly as she could.

"Hi!" She leaned her head on the door well and smiled.

"Sorry to interrupt your morning, just checking on you." Ramsay smiled back, then he looked toward the shower. Leyla's heart sped up immediately.

"Is your shower on?"

"Uh, yeah…" Leyla began to panic instantly. *Shit. Fuck. Shit.*

"Why would you leave the shower on if you're getting dressed already?"

"Why are you so nosy?" She attempted to get him to back off.

"I didn't mean to—" Ramsay stopped, gazing toward the bedroom. *Fuck.* Leyla knew exactly why. She dreadfully turned her head.

Wells was of course standing outside the door, dripping wet and cut like a Roman God, wrapped in the very towel Ramsay had picked out for Leyla's apartment.

"Oh, shit." Leyla's heart shrank into her gut.

Wells waved nervously to Ramsay and retreated back into the room.

Leyla looked to Ramsay like a puppy that had just been caught eating a pair of Italian leather shoes.

Ramsay cleared his throat. His confidence melted away and he stepped back out of the apartment. "I see you're doing fine." He feigned half a smile and shuffled sideways, scratching his head, and then awkwardly gave Leyla a thumbs up.

He isn't mad, his feelings are hurt, Leyla thought.

"Hey, no! This isn't what it looks like!" She attempted to remedy the situation.

Never thought I'd be the one saying that cliche bullshit, she thought.

"It's okay." Ramsay replied and walked down the hall.

"Well, shit. Now I feel like I'm a character in *Roommates*." Leyla said.

An invisible crowd burst into laughter. Leyla ducked and looked around. She was pretty sure she wasn't a guest on a talk show tonight.

Texas Chainsaw Massacre was the culprit, playing the sound bite through his vocal unit.

"Oh, you asshole!" Leyla flipped the android the middle finger, then quickly retracted it, realizing that was a little extreme.

"Hey! I can see I'm growin' on ya!"

"Yeah whatever, back to this whole core access business—"

"Who was that?" Wells interrupted, now dressed in his cleaned pants and shirt.

"No!" Leyla pointed at Wells. "You wait!"

Wells shook his head and held his arms out. Leyla looked back to Texas Chainsaw Massacre.

"How do I have core access?"

"I said you might, lady, chill."

"How do I know if I do?"

"What's core access?" Wells asked.

"I said wait!" Leyla yelled.

Texas Chainsaw Massacre decided to end the bickering by playing a loud foghorn through his vocal unit that deafened Leyla and Wells. They both jumped back and covered their ears.

"Texas Chainsaw Massacre?! What the Hell man?" Leyla yelled.

"Texas Chainsaw Massacre? Is that its name?" Wells tried to get an answer again.

"Oh, here we go again with the useless pronouns. I am a *robot*, you sexy piece of bacon."

"Yes, Ramsay named him Texas Chainsaw Massacre." Leyla answered.

"Ramsay was here?"

"Yeah, that was him earlier."

"The friend of the leader of a giant hidden city with robots and flying cars and a ton of missing people was just here and you're not freaking out?"

"Well not until you said it like that…"

Wells shoved his still damp feet into his shoes and headed toward the door. "I have to follow him, that's how I find Greene."

"Whoa wait, what are you going to do?"

"Nothing, just follow him." Wells dashed out the door, leaving Leyla bewildered and alone with her chef.

"Wanna come with me? Wanna go be my sidekick?" Leyla questioned the empty room. "Wanna find our friends *together*? No, you can't, because I'm grumpy Batman, and *I work alone*!"

"Are you talkin' to yourself or me?" Texas Chainsaw Massacre asked.

"I'm talking to Wells."

"Wells just left."

"I know that!" *Fine*, she thought. *I'll go find my friend myself.*

CHAPTER TEN

Greene on the Other Side

Wells rushed out of the elevator he'd taken down from Leyla's apartment and out into the street, hoping he would see Ramsay. Looking left, then right, he caught a glimpse of that motorcycle jacket round a corner, so he dashed toward it. He slowed almost to a stop at the corner and peeked around it. Ramsay was hurling his leg over a classic Indian Scout motorcycle—maybe an 80s or 90s model—completely unmodified.

Nice, Wells thought. *Haven't seen one of those in a while, even on the surface.*

Ramsay powered up the bike and pushed off toward Wells, who jerked his head away from the corner just as he heard the throaty bike engine and exhaust rev up. Ramsay was coming his way.

Shit, how am I going to follow this guy on foot? Wells asked himself. *Gotta find an option fast.*

He had to scramble behind a soda vending machine as Ramsay rode past, then he saw what looked like an electric bicycle leaning against a wall on the opposite side of the street. Ramsay turned right and Wells ran across to the bike. Thankfully, it wasn't chained down. Theft never was an issue in SubCity—until that moment. He hopped on the bike and pressed what he assumed to be the power button. Nothing. Ramsay was getting further away. *Shit*, Wells thought, as he knew he didn't have time to figure out the mechanics of powering the bike on. He set his foot to the pedals and pumped away, in not-so-hot pursuit of his ticket to his missing friend.

***

Leyla tried calling Mari on the comlink as she neared the bar, but got no answer. Where are you? She wondered. Joe said she was MIA. Maybe she will be there when I get to there, just been busy.

Leyla approached the bar but it was shut down completely, just as it was the previous morning. All the lights were off and the chairs were on the tables.

She remembered the side door that Mari had sent her out after she'd stayed the night, so she went around the corner into the alley to try it.

The door had an SD reader just like her apartment door. Well dammit, she thought. Wonder if mine will work?

She pulled her temporary SD chip from a pocket and moved it under the reader and the locking mechanism beeped and sure enough, unlocked the door.

"Really? No way!" That was a long shot, but things down in SubCity just kept going her way. That never happened on the surface. "Core access, bitches…" she said to herself, as she slipped inside the darkened bar.

She rounded the bar and tables and made it to the elevator, never letting her thoughts leave her.

Why does everything keep going so right for me here? I'm never lucky. Have to fight for everything. Here it's like I'm a queen. What if I am the Queen? Cyber-Queen! Ruler of SubCity! All bow to the majest—

The elevator dinged and opened into Mari's apartment.

"Hello?" Leyla called into the home. "Mari?"

No answer.

The home was just as bathed in light as it had been the previous day, but it was lacking in the delicious bacon in the pan smell department.

"I don't do well with creepy silence, so, if you're here, don't jump out at me mmkay?"

Still no sound aside from Leyla's own light footsteps.

When she got into the common area, she saw that Mari had left her PC on. Glancing at the screen, there weren't any programs open, but there was a notification on the bottom, pulsing with a red blip. Leyla leaned over and tapped the blinking red dot and up popped a messaging program.

It was a conversation between Mari and someone named Artemis. It was fairly short, but read:

Mari: Hey, been a long time. Are you free anytime today?

Artemis: So, the wipe did not take.

Mari: No. I'm fine with it.

Artemis: What did you need?

Mari: We have a problem.

Artemis: Such as?

Mari: Athon is back.

Artemis: How? That's not possible.

Mari: Girl here earlier, said her friend got kidnapped through a portal by, guess what, a black armored badass.

Artemis: When?

Mari: Couple nights ago. Up on the surface.

Artemis: I am free now. Meet at the ventilators.

Artemis: Delete this thread.

Leyla stood straight. *Mari must have not seen the last message about deleting the thread. And the ventilators? Where and what is that?*

These messages were from one day ago, when Joe said Mari had gone MIA. That's another missing person, this time from inside the city. Have to get back to Wells and figure something out fast. Maybe he'll come back to the apartment when he finds something out.

***

Wells's legs felt like he'd dipped them inside a volcano. He'd been pumping and pedaling as hard as he could to keep up with Ramsay, who seemed to be nonchalantly cruising around the city on a joyride. *Goddammit, you asshole,* he thought. *Will you just do something important!? Legs are about to fuckin' fall off.*

Ramsay finally slowed his cruiser down a little, stopped, kicked the stand out and parked it outside a Peyton's Diner, which he'd already passed three times.

Seriously!? Fuck you! Wells screamed inside his head as he forced his noodled legs to pedal into an alley nearby. *Fuck leg day. Gonna feel this for a week!*

Wells stopped and struggled to pull his leg over the seat while the other trembled. He'd passed muscle failure a mile back, thanks to Ramsay's Sunday Funday ride. Was it even Sunday? Wells couldn't remember. Didn't matter.

Ramsay strolled into the chrome and pink neon relic of an establishment, immediately greeting the attendant behind the bar.

Wells wiped the sweat from his brow and tried to pull his hair back into some sort of style that didn't say "I just followed a man on a motorcycle whilst on a bicycle like a total idiot." He entered the diner, keeping his eyes trained on Ramsay, who'd taken a seat at one of the bar stools. Wells opted to take a booth seat not too far away so he could eavesdrop when the time came.

"You got that new brioche French toast right?" He asked the server, who wore a white collared shirt and a 50s style soda jerker hat that had neon fibers pulsing through it.

"Oh yeah, brother, with the truffle syrup injected inside?"

"My God, yes, gimme an order o' that and a Mexican coke please."

"Comin right up, brother."

The server pulled a bottled coke out of a cooler hidden behind the bar. He grabbed a bartender's bottle opener and popped the cap off, flicking it into a garbage bin a few feet away in one fluid motion, then sat the Coke down in front of Ramsay.

Fuck, that's a good lookin' Coke, Wells thought, as he watched Ramsay down a huge gulp from the perfectly near-frozen and dew kissed bottle. He hadn't had anything to drink besides the beer earlier. Hadn't even thought to bring a bottle of water when the trucks showed up. Ramsay let out an audible *aahhhh*, and put the bottle down. He turned to Wells's direction.

Wells snatched a menu off the table and covered his face in the most suspicious way possible. Luckily it worked. Ramsay suspected nothing.

"Hey there! Can I get you a drink to start?" An android waitress appeared beside Wells, startling him. It had a mid-length blonde wig and a red checkered sundress.

"Uh, same Coke that guy's having, please. Don't bother him, just look at the bottle."

"Coming right up, [IDENTITY UNKNOWN]!" The android waitress buzzed loudly, as if announcing his mysterious presence to the entire restaurant. Wells recoiled at the abrupt tone change. Ramsay, hearing the waitress, looked over his shoulder to Wells, who'd let the menu drift away from his face, and now Ramsay was staring him down.

Well, shit.

Ramsay slid off his bar stool and made his way over to Wells, half sitting into the booth seat on the other side of the table.

"Hi." Ramsay said, smirking.

"Hello." Wells tried his best to hide his discomfort by playing cool, leaning back and placing an arm on the back of his seat. He found there wasn't enough room to hang an arm so it slipped off. Wells awkwardly placed his hand on the table. *Good job, slick,* he chastised himself.

"Haven't seen you here before. First time?" Ramsay said.

"Yeah. Yep."

"You followed me here. On that bicycle. That's why I rode around the city three times."

Wells didn't have an answer other than a dumbfounded expression. Maybe his hard boiled detective skills truly *had* waned.

"You did pretty good, though. Bet your legs feel great."

Fuck you! Wells screamed at Ramsay, silently, through a forming smile. "Yeah, yeah I used to run cross country in college."

"Really? So did I! MIT! You?"

"Uh, Cincinnati."

"Hey! Go Bearcats!"

"No, the community college." Wells, mumbled.

"Oh okay. So, you Leyla's new squeeze?"

"Squeeze?" Wells had never heard that expression. Sounded like something from an old Hollywood flick.

"Boyfriend." Ramsay corrected. He sometimes forgot that not everyone understood his older slang.

Wells reflexively cleared his throat. "Oh! No, no. That's why I, uh, followed you." *Damn*, he thought, *I'm doing fucking terrible at this detective thing right now.*

"Why would she send you after me?"

"To tell you I'm not her boyfriend."

"She has my number. She can do that."

"Oh, well I will let her know that."

The android waitress returned to the table with Wells's Coke.

"Hello, Ramsay!"

"Hi!" Ramsay replied to the bot.

"Here's your Mexican Coke, [INDENTITY UNKNOWN]."

"Thanks…" Wells took the Coke and gestured at the bot while looking at Ramsay, trying to play off the missing name as a glitch.

"I don't know what's up with that thing." He said.

"Nothing. Might be your SD."

This was the first Wells had heard of an SD and, subsequently, had no idea what Ramsay was talking about, but he could smell the suspicion melting off his face.

"Really?" Wells replied. "I'll have to get it fixed today. It was fine earlier." *Please let that lie work, please let that lie work,* Wells pleaded to the universe.

"Yeah, might want to."

"Yo brother!" The soda jerker hat-wearing bartender waved Ramsay down. "French toast is up!"

Ramsay swung his head toward the bar. "Gotcha, Johnny!" He then looked to Wells. "Well I am not going to let *that* get cold." Ramsay stood and leaned over to Wells. "Don't follow me again. Not a fan of that. Thanks."

"You got it." Wells said as Ramsay walked off.

Then he caught something from the corner of his eye. Through the window behind the bar, past the soda jerker hatted bartender and into the open kitchen. Orange-tinged, wavy hair. A bit longer than he'd remembered, but the color was unmistakable as it dropped over the porcelain skin of his neck. The wide, football player shoulders. The toned triceps—and a tattoo of an eagle on his left arm, just above the elbow. *No way that's him,* Wells thought. *No fucking way.*

Without another delay, Wells got up and walked away from the android waitress, who was waiting for him to place an order, and made a beeline for the swinging kitchen door.

Opening it and stepping half in, he saw his face. Bushy, orange eyebrows that matched his hair that sat over sea green eyes. Eyes that coincidentally matched his name. He was the reason Wells had come down there.

It was his long lost friend, Officer Greene. More than a friend. A partner. Both in the force and off.

Wells rushed over to his long lost friend and softly gripped his elbow, pulling him to the side, interrupting his duties at the prep table. Green locked eyes with Wells, but something was off. Something was horribly wrong. Greene's stare didn't match Wells's in the same way as it had three years earlier. It was instead more of a confused and half-angry glare instead. A glare that asked why the fuck some random guy was interrupting him at work. Wells's smile faded quickly.

Wells gulped a dry heave of air down his throat. "Greene?"

"Yeah, that's me. Who the fuck are you?"

"I…" Wells's heart dropped, and it dropped right through his stomach and into Hell itself. "I'm…"

He couldn't figure out how to answer. *This wasn't supposed to happen,* he thought. This wasn't the happy reunion he'd imagined.

Greene winced. "Can you take your hand off my arm, dude?"

Wells pulled away. *Dude?* Somehow being called *dude* made it hurt more.

"I'm Donnie, we, you don't remember me?"

Greene laughed. "Nah, and I got a good memory. You got me confused with someone else."

Greene wasn't lying. The man had the memory of an elephant. He never forgot. Wells looked down to Greene's ring finger. It was bare.

But Wells was still wearing the tungsten ring that Greene gave him when he asked Wells to marry him.

Outside, a loud buzz alarm sounded in three short bursts. Some folks rushed off the street, others activated translucent, holographic field generator umbrellas.

Wells could feel his chest tightening more and more. His throat closed. His eyes fought back the tears that signaled the terrible realization forming in his mind.

Greene had no idea who his own fiancé was.

Rain drops began to pelt the windows outside. Wells pulled away from Greene, who coldly went back to cutting vegetables at the table.

Wells made his way back out to the diner. Ramsay paid him no mind this time; he was chowing down on that brioche French toast. Wells shuffled to the exit–the glass windowed door where simulated rain water trickled down like small tadpoles in a vertical river—mocking him.

He doesn't recognize me. How does he not remember me?

Wells turned, glaring at Ramsay. That motherfucker had the answers Wells needed, and he knew it, sitting there chomping on his fucking toast.

Maybe not right now, you asshole, but I'll get you alone somewhere and I'll beat those answers out of you.

CHAPTER ELEVEN

The Gun Show

Leyla had stopped at the DingaBing Ice Cream parlor on the way back to her place. She couldn't resist the huge holographic ice cream cone advertisement as she'd walked past. Plus, she'd had to get out of the random rainfall that had started.

She'd opted for a double scoop of strawberry cheesecake explosion in a freshly made cinnamon waffle cone. She was so voraciously demolishing the scoop that she had to periodically take a break to wipe her face clean with the napkin the android attendant had thankfully given her. Hopefully I find Del soon, she thought. She's gotta try this stuff.

She rode the elevator up to her apartment hall. Stepping out, she saw Wells, slumped onto the floor, leaning against the wall across from her door. He hadn't been able to get inside without an SD, and had passed out from lack of sleep. Poor thing. And he was soaked; dripping wet.

Leyla had almost finished the cone as she approached Wells's still body, and she noticed the ring resting around the end of his index finger, threatening to fall off and onto the floor. She instinctively crouched down and pushed the ring up onto his finger to safety, and then placed an ice cream soaked hand on his shoulder to wake him. She shook his shoulder lightly but he didn't stir. He's *out* out, she thought.

"Wells!" She yelled in his face and gave his shoulder one good lurch. He jolted and his eyes opened, bloodshot, like he'd been crying.

"I'm up." He mumbled.

"How long have you been here?"

"Don't know." Wells pushed himself to his feet and noticed his engagement ring on the wrong finger. He pulled it off his index and put it on the correct digit.

"So…did you find anything?" Leyla stood up.

Wells allowed his back to fall against the wall.

"Yeah." He pushed off and shuffled toward Leyla's door. "Found Greene."

"Oh shit! Seriously!? What are you doing back here then?"

"Can we go in, please?"

Leyla rushed over and scanned her SD chip to unlock the door. Wells pushed it open and sulked inside.

"Wells! What's up, why isn't he with you?"

"Greetings, Miami Vice!" Texas Chainsaw Massacre sprung up, the energetic asshole that he was. "Greetings Master Leyla!"

Wells walked past the bot without a reply. Leyla waved at her auto-chef.

"Hey!" Leyla grabbed Wells's shoulder again and pulled him to a stop. "What's going on?"

Wells stared out the window wall into the city. Another crying stretch of glass. Another mirror to his own torment.

"He doesn't remember me."

"Wh–" Leyla stopped herself. She immediately remembered Cross-Eyes mentioning memory wipes. Mari had also talked about them. She looked to Wells, who was frozen in place, framed by SubCity's "skyline"; The raindrops sliding down the window disappearing into Wells's stout figure. A strong and confident man who'd just been broken. Snapped like a dry twig. Maybe now was the time to let words stay unsaid. Even Texas Chainsaw Massacre sensed the dripping sadness in the room.

Leyla thought back to the day that she'd woken up inside the dark tunnel. The way she'd made her way into the city. Confused, lost, and scared. Del wasn't the first to see her walking down the street, but she was the first to offer help.

"Here, baby, take my soup, just warmed it up."

Del had given her the only food she had for the day, warmed on an electric stove she'd either scavenged or stolen. Warm inside the can. A can of chicken noodle soup.

"It's gonna be okay, baby girl, I got you." Del had said. She'd pulled Leyla into her breast. A motherly embrace to a lost child. Leyla had clung to her ever since.

It was this memory that brought Leyla's arms up around Wells, pulling him in tight, his back to her cheek. His hand found hers, and squeezed in return.

"Didn't remember his own fiancé." Wells muttered. "He forgot me."

"No, he didn't." Leyla pulled her face away from Wells's back and spun him around to face her.

"They can wipe memories here. Make you forget." Leyla said.

"So he chose to forget me?" Wells asked through a pained expression.

"Maybe not. Might have not had a choice."

"What's that mean?" Wells pulled away from Leyla. Anger was creeping its way into Wells's body. He stamped as he walked. His brow drew low. His breath drew heavy.

"You said he chased someone down here. Maybe he got in here, on accident, like I did. I don't know. But for whatever reason, they wiped his memory. Maybe." Leyla said. She turned to Texas Chainsaw Massacre.

"Hey! Hive mind!"

"Yes, your royal highness?" The bot acknowledged her.

"His friend! What do you know?"

"Need more than "his friend", I don't know what the fuck that means, missy."

"Uh, Greene! His name is Greene. Right?" She looked to Wells.

"Nate Greene." Wells replied. A glint of hope crossed his eye. "Working at Peyton's Diner now."

Texas Chainsaw Massacre froze for a bit. When its screen-face fluttered back from blackness, it looked to Leyla.

"Redacted."

"Redacted? What's that?" Leyla shook her head.

"Means deleted. It's a secret." Wells said. He turned and strode toward the bot at the prep table. "You got any beer? Whiskey?"

"Beer, no, but there's a 25 Year Macallan Sherry Oak in the climate compartment." The bot explained.

"Don't know what that means."

"Very nice Scotch."

"Good enough. Give it to me."

Chainsaw Massacre dropped down and reached into a compartment under the prep table, and pulled a bottle of unopened scotch whiskey out. It placed it on the table and turned to the cabinet to grab the appropriate glass. Wells snatched the bottle by the neck and saw it had a cork, not a cap.

The auto-chef slowly pried the bottle from Wells and wound a corkscrew in and popped it out. THOONK.

Texas Chainsaw Massacre poured a round of the ridiculously expensive, aged drink into the glass and slid it to Wells.

"I know that look, partner." The bot took on a classic, Western movie, John Wayne–ish accent. "That look needs a drink."

Wells gulped down the double shot. It didn't taste much different from the normal Jim Beam he was used to. Maybe smoother.

Leyla stepped over to the bar as Texas Chainsaw Massacre poured another round for Wells.

"Maybe there's a way to fix it. Maybe we can fix Greene. Get his memories back."

"Uh huh. I'm all ears." Wells said, as he kicked back a second double shot.

Leyla wasn't sure that was the best idea, but it was all she had. She had to help Wells. He could help her find Del.

"I'll call Ramsay. I'll get him here. We can team up. Ask him how to fix things. He has to have answers."

Wells slammed the empty whiskey glass down and motioned to the android for another shot. He leaned over, resting in the prep table that was now his makeshift bar.

His loose hand felt the Kimber .45 pistol hidden under his jacket. He felt his anger transform to malice.

"Yeah. Call Ramsay."

***

Ramsay was in his own apartment. It was less a living space and more a garage converted into an electronics lab. There were loose wires and half constructed machine parts strewn in every crevice. Heavy drummed synth music droned through a set of old, wood grain speaker boxes. He bobbed his head to the melody as he tinkered with a small, fist sized object; poking it with a sharp tool in one hand and securing wiring with tweezers in the other.

The room was absolute mechanical chaos, save for one section: the kitchen. It was spick and span. A carbon fiber table sheened over by a clear coat of graphene acted as an immense prep/cut table above a dual oven. Four burners on a stove were covered and cooled. On the wall, a set of steel Japanese Santoku knives clung to a magnetic strip. Coated, non-stick cookware and a few differently sized cast iron pans hung just above those. Cook books were neatly organized in a shelf nearby.

If he wasn't cooking, he was tinkering. Food occupied his mind as much as electronics did.

His apartment was a wide open garage of sorts. Multiple classic motorcycles and cars populated the space that wasn't the kitchen and entertainment center. A World War 2 Harley Davidson. An '87 Buick Grand National. A 1980 Lamborghini Athon concept car. That one took some fenangling to acquire. A 1993 Mitsubishi 3000GT. A green and white dirt bike. That one was special. Jackie Chan had jumped onto a train in the movie *Supercop* with that one. He had an old, gray tarp draped over a project bike he was working on. A big, fat tire peeked out from under the tarp, reminding him that he was procrastinating.

He also had a huge corner of just musical instruments. A double layered keyboard. A cello. A couple violins. Drums. Trumpets, tubas, guitars. He had enough to form an orchestra.

His comlink rang out.

"Ramsay…" he answered.

"Hey!" Leyla was on the other end. "Um, sorry about earlier today."

"Yeah. It's fine." He replied as he jerked away from sparks that shot up from whatever he was working on.

"Okay…well um, do you wanna hang out?"

"You sure your boyfriend would be okay with that?" He toyed with her.

"He's not a boyfriend!"

"Relax. I'm kidding. I'd like to hang out, sure. Your place or mine? Or public. You pick."

"Mine."

Of course, yours, he thought. This stunk of trickery. But maybe not. "Alright. When?"

"Uh, now?"

What are you planning? He thought. "Okay, sure. I can push back my projects a little. I'll be over in a bit."

***

"Well he agreed to that pretty quick. What voodoo magic did you put on that poor man?" Wells grilled Leyla, jokingly.

"I didn't do anything! Guess I just got the *stuff*!"

"Sure. When he walks in, I'll take him down. Hold him in place. You just stay calm til I'm able to subdue him, okay? No one gets hurt."

"Yeah, okay." Leyla put on a facade of confidence. Inside, her very heart and muscles were fucking screaming that this wasn't going to work. This was a bad idea. They would get caught. They would have a memory wipe and forever be stuck in a prison of bare-existence. At least the food was good.

"I like the hair, by the way." He told Leyla.

"Oh thanks! Makes me feel like a rockstar."

"Look the part too. Just need some tattoos."

"Slow down there bud, needles are the Devil."

Wells laughed and pointed at the acoustic guitar hanging on the wall. "Can you play that thing or is it just decoration?"

"I'm okay. Taught myself with a broken one we'd found outside an apartment building. Used it to try and make some money some days."

"Oh yeah? Can I get a sample?" Wells didn't particularly care to see if Leyla had any skill; he just wanted his mind off his fiancé for a moment.

"You want me to play something?"

"Yeah let's see what you got." Wells stood from the bar stool at the prep table and walked over to the couch.

Leyla took hold of the guitar from its mount and sat on the suspended coffee table in front of Wells, positioning the guitar on her hip.

"Now, I'm not super good, so don't laugh."

Wells held up three fingers and touched his pinky and thumb together. "Scout's honor. Won't laugh."

Using her thumb, Leyla plucked each string to ensure they were in tune.

"Hmm, came to me already tuned, neat."

She began to pluck a melody mostly with her thumb, index, and middle fingers. She gracefully switched cords with her left hand on the frets. She'd really practiced. A lot. Wells sat straighter and leaned forward.

He'd heard the tune before. Nothing Else Matters, by Metallica. It had a pleasant warmth coming from Leyla's Martin classical guitar as she plucked through the intricate harmonics and finger work. She was good. Really good. She watched her own fingers do the work, not confident enough to look away from them yet. When she did look up to Wells, she missed a note and flushed red.

"Oop! See? Not that great."

"Are you fucking kidding me you're amazing!" Wells laughed and brought his hands up to his head. "You just taught yourself to play that well?"

"Oh stop."

"I'm serious. 100% that was beautiful. Can you sing too?"

"Yeah, I'm not gonna be singing in front of *anyone* for my entire life. No. That is terrifying."

"Alright alright, fine. But damn! Wow! Give yourself more credit. That sounded so good!"

"But can she play Bethoven?" Texas Chainsaw Massacre rang out from across the room.

"That's not even guitars!" Wells yelled back.

Leyla stood and placed the guitar on the wall. "Thank you! But, we should get ready. Ramsay might be close."

Ramsay had gotten off the elevator to Leyla's hall and stopped at her door. This time, he didn't simply knock. He put his ear close, wondering if Leyla was up to something. Seeing Wells at the diner after being followed was too coincidental for his liking. He didn't hear anything; and he wasn't sure if that was a good or bad sign.

He knocked—same pattern as he always did. The door *immediately* opened.

"Were you just standing there?" He asked Leyla, who had that look that a toddler has when they were trying to hide something obvious. She was *really* bad at lying.

"No! Uh, just, talking to my chef."

"Your boyfriend here?"

"He's not my boyfriend!"

"He said you sent him to follow me to tell me that."

"He *what*!? I did not send him after you!"

"Bro, the pig is gay." Texas Chainsaw Massacre said. Leyla turned and glared at the bot. Great, Leyla thought, just tell Ramsay that Wells is a *fucking cop.*

"Pig is gay? What is that code for something?" Ramsay asked.

"No. Inside joke." Leyla explained. Finally, a decent and smooth lie. "Come in, I wanna show you my guitar skills!"

"Yeah, okay." Ramsay could smell trouble. That was the thing about former military intelligence officers. They had a sixth sense. But he entered the apartment anyway. Leyla stepped to the side and backed up—expecting something. Her moves were rehearsed. Whatever was about to happen was going to come from behind.

Ramsay saw an arm slip around his collar through his peripheral, from the right side. He felt that arm tighten around his throat. Another hand slapped down on top of his head and squeezed. A choke hold. *Alright. We're doing things that way, then.*

Ramsay snatched both his arms up and dug his fingers around Wells's and kicked backward into the wall. He hunched forward as hard as he could and pulled Wells off his back and tossed him like a ragdoll toward the open kitchen.

Wells managed to grab hold of Ramsay's jacket as he flew over, stripping it off and exposing Ramsay's cybernetic arms. The pneumatic muscles on them rippled and pulsed with the strength of a maddened ape.

Wells slammed to the ground a few feet in front of Ramsay. It hurt, but not bad enough to keep him from fighting. He hadn't expected those arms, either. Time to step it up a notch.

As he stood, as quickly as he could since Ramsay was making his way to him, he drew his Kimber .45 and flung it up toward Ramsay.

Leyla screamed and ducked out of the way, even though Wells was a good shot and careful to miss her. Ramsay also ducked the first shot. Wells wasn't trying to kill him. He'd aimed at his arm.

Ramsay was a fast fucker, and he used his hand to keep his balance and thrust toward Wells like a panther, ending up behind him. Wells spun and tried to get another shot off, but Ramsay grabbed the muzzle of the pistol as it fired.

That round went straight into Texas Chainsaw Massacre's head. Metal and wires blasted out the back and sparks showered the stove behind as the bullet itself struck an iron pan. DING!!!

Ramsay crumpled the steel gun in his palm and brought his other hand into Wells's armpit, lifting him up and slamming him down onto the prep table, just missing a razor sharp chef's knife. He held Wells down by the throat with one arm and brought the other up, ready to pound the man's brains out—literally.

When he brought his fist down as hard as he could, something stopped it. He first gave Wells the confused look, almost as if asking him why he couldn't bring a hammer fist down between his eyes. Wells looked past Ramsay, choking, and eyes red and watering. He was turning purple.

Ramsay tried again to pull his arm down, but the servo motors at his joints whirred and ground. He finally decided to look back and see what the Hell was going on.

Leyla had taken hold of his cybernetic wrist with only one arm, and she had the look of a wild fucking animal in her eyes. Why he hadn't effortlessly picked up her small frame and tossed her across the room on accident, he didn't know. But he felt something hard crack the back of his head, and the room went white. He crumpled to the floor.

***

Ramsay came to with blurred vision—almost black. He could see Wells limping away. Everything was sideways. He tried to move but he was tied down to the coffee table. He looked down. Duct tape. They used duct tape.

"Where the Hell did you have duct tape?" He didn't realize he'd said that aloud.

"You ordered it! *Every home needs duct tape.*" Leyla said from out of view, mocking him.

He looked around. His arms had been *detached* and were on the floor a few feet away. His head pounded and stung like hornet venom at the back. He saw Wells pick a frying pan off the floor and put it on the prep table.

Really? Ramsay thought. *He hit me with a frying pan*? He felt himself blacking out again. It wasn't long before he closed his eyes. He heard Leyla.

"Isn't it bad if you fall asleep with a concussion?"

"Not if he just tried to kill me." Wells replied.

A few minutes later, Wells hung a dampened washcloth under Ramsay's nose. He twitched violently, opening his eyes— revolted at the smell.

"The fuck is that? Smells like piss!" He yelled.

"Ammonia. Basically it is piss. Found it in the cleaning supplies."

Ramsay squinted hard, trying to ignore the dull sting from where Wells had cracked him on the head. "The fuck do you want?"

"Answers. About everything."

"We're just trying to find our friends." Leyla stepped into view.

Ramsay laughed. "Good luck. Won't get shit outta me."

"Oh, you'll squeal, buddy." Texas Chainsaw Massacre said from across the room, now with a distorted voice.

All three of them snapped their gazes to the android. They thought he was a goner for sure.

"What? Something in my teeth?" Chainsaw Massacre held its hands up.

"You got shot in the head!" Leyla yelled.

"Central processor is inside the body." Ramsay said. "Head's there for show, mostly. And the vocal processor."

"What do you mean, he'll squeal?" Wells approached the bot.

"Truth serum."

"Sodium Pentothal is some movie magic. Doesn't work."

"Oh no, I'm talkin' nano-compliant psychedelics." Chainsaw Massacre confidently explained. "Synthetic transponder narcotics."

Ramsay let his head drop down. "Ah, shit."

Wells crossed his arms. "What? Mushrooms? Acid? You can't depend on psychoactive drugs for truth. Dude's gonna be stoned out of his mind. Truth to him is gonna be pink elephants and flying cars." Wells looked out the window. An AV floated past. "Well, okay the flying cars are real now, but still."

"Oh, you precious, innocent little, sexy man." Chainsaw Massacre replied. "Drugs in SubCity are a lot more fun than your boring surface bullshit. Down here, we got something called Brain Drain."

"Ah *shit.*" Ramsay huffed again.

"And Brain Drain is taken, usually on dates, to connect with each other on a spiritual level, through raw and unfiltered truth. But yeah, he *will* be high as giraffe pussy."

"I fucking *hate* Brain Drain." Ramsay said, almost like a toddler complaining about doing chores.

Wells looked to Ramsay, duct taped to a coffee table, armless and annoyed. Leyla turned toward her auto-chef.

"Order that shit." She had a half grin on her face.

"On the way now!" Chainsaw Massacre replied, and then it looked at Ramsay's detached arms lying on the floor. Using a creepily accurate Forrest Gump voice, it couldn't resist a joke.

"You ain't got no arms, Lieutenant Dan!"

Wells tried to hold it in, but a hard and cackling laugh escaped his throat. "Fuck, that's good!" He slapped his knees as Leyla joined in, not understanding the reference. Wells stood straight and looked at Ramsay's writhing, duct-taped body.

"Lieutenant Dan, I got you some ice cream!" Wells took on a Gump accent as well, and laughed harder.

"Fuck you." Ramsay said, almost under his breath.

Wells stiffened and killed his laughter. "I ought to break your legs off too, you little piece of sh–"

"Hey!" Leyla intervened. "He's our info guy! Chill, okay?"

Texas Chainsaw Massacre couldn't resist once more lightening the mood.

"Maybe I should order some butterfly wings to replace those arms. You could be the cutest little giant fairy in SubCity!"

Leyla held her mouth open, loving the idea.

Ramsay closed his eyes, and sighed heavily, letting it turn into a groan. "Oh, I really fuckin' hate Brain Drain."

CHAPTER TWELVE

Cold, Hard Facts

Leyla's doorbell rang sometime later. Opening the door, it was that cute little ship bot from earlier, holding a small brown bag.

"Greetings Leyla!" It said in its cute little digital voice. "Greetings Texas Chainsaw Massacre! I am sorry about your face!"

"Oh yeah, just doing some remodeling." Texas Chainsaw Massacre replied.

"Your order, Miss Leyla. Have a lovely day." The bot handed Leyla her order of Brain Drain and floated away. She closed the door.

"Okay, how does this stuff work?" She asked Chainsaw Massacre.

"Well the orders usually come in packs of two. I suggest only using *half* of *one* chewable. It's a cannabis and psilocybin based formula."

Wells snatched the bag away from Leyla and tore into it, peeling open the small jar inside.

"Hey! Rude!" She smacked Wells's shoulder, but it didn't phase him. He pulled out one full chewable and walked over to Ramsay.

He grabbed Ramsay's face by the jaw and squeezed as hard as he could until Ramsay opened a little, and he stuffed a full chewable into his mouth.

"Hey he said *half* a ch—" Leyla tried to correct Wells but it was too late.

"Chew. Now." Wells held Ramsay's mouth shut. "Or I start cutting." Wells pulled his pocket knife from his pants and flicked it open, placing the blade near Ramsay's crotch. Ramsay chewed like his life depended on it.

Texas Chainsaw Massacre didn't have a face-screen any longer, but if he had, it would have most certainly shown a wide eyed and jaw dropped expression. "Oh, he is about to be *fucked* all the way up." He said.

"How long does this take to work?" Leyla asked the bot.

Ramsay started giggling. He writhed under the duct tape. Wells backed up a bit, as Ramsay giggled more.

"Look at me, I'm a *worm*!" Ramsay wiggled inside the tape on the table.

"About that fast." Chainsaw Massacre responded.

"So what, we just start asking questions now?" Leyla asked.

Wells pulled the chair from the nearby desk and sat next to Ramsay. "These memory wipes you people do down here; can you reverse it?"

Ramsay had to fight through the laughter, but he was compelled to tell Wells *everything*. "Never tried it. That would be something to ask Cross-Eyes about." He spoke in a slurred and labored tone, like a drunkard at the end of a long night.

Leyla strode over to Ramsay, putting a hand on Wells's shoulder. "We'll figure it out." She turned to Ramsay. "Who's Artemis?"

Ramsay stopped laughing for a second. "Oh, that's a name I haven't heard in a long time." He immediately started laughing again.

"That's a Star Wars joke. Everybody's got Star Wars jokes." Wells said.

"Artemis is 1/4th of the Pantheon." Ramsay giggled.

"Of course." Leyla said, annoyed. "Of course it's the super robot women that fly."

"Wait, what?" Wells asked Leyla. Ramsay explained for her.

"The Pantheon. Volunteers. There's four of them now. There's two brunettes, a blond, and a redhead, like neapolitan ice cream." Ramsay chuckled at his joke. "Blackhawk was trying to make a new Athon. To use the Xenobots."

"The fuck are Xenobots?" Wells asked.

"Oh, fancy little atom sized robots. They can be programmed, but they're tied to a singular consciousness. And they can rewrite matter on an atomic level."

"What's that mean?"

"Means you don't like the tree in front of your window? Turn it into a box of fruit and eat it." Ramsay's laughter began to get more intense.

"Bullshit."

"Would I lie to you? Don't answer. I would. But not right now. Brainnnnn draiiinnnnn hahahahaha!"

Leyla pushed past Wells. "You said Athon."

"Yeah, android. SIGIL made it behind our backs. Started sending it through the wormhole generator to kill people. Guess it wanted to use Athon as a vessel for the Xenobots too. Real live AI apocalypse."

"Shit! Well, Artemis was supposed to meet with Mari from Fritzy Joe's. She said Athon is back."

Ramsay tried to sit up, pulling against the tape. "Hold on, that's impossible."

"Well Mari seems sure. She was going to meet Artemis at the ventilators, whatever that means.

"Ventilators are the big fans at the top of the cavern. They filter out and recirculate the air, and run to the surface. But wait, Athon can't be back."

"Why?"

"Because this one time, at band camp…"

"Shut the fuck up with the movie references and tell us the good shit." Wells held a fist up to Ramsay's face. He nodded.

"Well, we kept getting these energy spikes and checked them out, and it was Athon using the wormhole generator down there, and we had to shut that operation down, but SIGIL tossed its ass into the wormhole generator and closed it down. And then we shut SIGIL down. Mostly."

"What's this wormhole generator thing?" Wells asked.

"Oh, you know, a time travel machine."

"A what?! Does it work?"

"Oh it works. Athon went through it at least a dozen times, according to SIGIL's logs. Espionage missions. Assassinations. Damn android James Bond."

"Okay, what's SIGIL?" Wells asked, having heard the term a few times now.

"It's a big computer they keep down here." Leyla said. Ramsay's eyes lit up, agreeing and nodding with her.

"Oh yeah!" Ramsay said. "A *quantum* computer! Fucking awesome too. We heisted that bad boy from TriTech in the 90s. I tinkered with it a little and bam! It became sentient. And now it's run by the same fusion reactor that powers the city! It's so neat."

"So wait, let's slow down, I gotta make sense of all this." Wells said. "So, in the 90s, you stole a quantum computer, whatever that is, and brought it here. It became sentient and created a time jumping assassin android?"

"Yes."

"What the *fuck*?"

"Yeah. Crazy. I know!" Ramsay laughed.

"That doesn't explain all the missing people though. What have you been doing here? Why are people missing? And why does my fiancé not remember who the fuck I am?"

"Oh *that's* who you were talking to at Peyton's? Shit man. I'm sorry."

"Fuck you. Explain that shit."

"Well, some folks get here by accident. Most, voluntarily. But under one pretty big condition. Everyone on the surface that they're connected to—forgets about them."

Wells walked away a few steps, covering his face. "That's why Greene's own damn mom didn't remember him. But why do I remember him? We were going to be married."

"Well, once someone's down here, we scan their mind for certain memories. Engrams, actually. Cell structure patterns. That's really all a memory is. Find out who was closest to them. Then we send out nano-bots to the surface. They're like tiny little airborne bugs. We call them NeuroBandits. I came up with that name. It's pretty neat."

"Keep going." Wells rotated his hand in a circle, pushing Ramsay on.

"The NeuroBandits find the people we found in our new member's memories, and they burrow into their brains—the hippocampus—and block every engram that is even similar in structure to the memory of the person we want forgotten. Then we erase every digital record referring to that person."

"You're sending fucking robots out to burrow into peoples' brains? Are you fucking crazy?"

"It's a security measure. How do you think we've been here so long and no one knew?"

"Fucking Christ! That's gotta be *thousands* of people with brain implants they never agreed to!"

"Yep." Ramsay couldn't stop laughing. "It's so fucked up!"

"So why do I remember Greene?"

"Honestly? I don't know. Maybe he forgot you."

"Fuck you, you piece of shit!" Wells lunged for the helpless and high Ramsay. Leyla stepped between them.

"Chill." She said.

"Or…maybe the NeuroBandit that had your name on it got lost. It could happen." Ramsay explained.

"I gotta talk to this Cross-Eyes character. Gotta be a way to fix Greene and get my life back."

"Well he's in his shop. Be my guest."

Leyla grabbed Wells's arm. "Don't. He will call Blackhawk in a fucking heartbeat." She looked back to Ramsay. "Mari said she was going to help me. Then she disappeared too, after talking to Artemis. Where is she?"

"Mari? She used to be one of them. But she wanted out. Thought she'd had a memory wipe."

"It didn't work." Leyla said. "I *knew* she used to be one of them!"

"Well, that sucks. But I don't know where she would be." Ramsay couldn't stop laughing.

"Okay, well, I came here because my friend Del got snatched through a portal by one of the Pantheon. I need to find her. She's all I care about."

"Uh uh." Ramsay grunted.

"What the fuck do you mean, *uh uh*?! I'm fucking sick of everyone beating around the bush here. Everyone's so terrified of *Blackhawk* and his stupid fucking Pantheon. I just want my friend. That's it. I will do whatever the fuck I have to to find Del."

"I just mean, it couldn't have been the Pantheon."

"Well it sure fucking looked like one of them."

"Because the Pantheon looks like Athon." Ramsay snickered.

"Huh?"

"Fuck." Ramsay's head plopped down again, but he was still grinning and laughing.

"What?!" Leyla yelled at him, demanding more explanation.

"If your friend got snatched through a portal, that was *Athon*. And Blackhawk had nothing to do with it."

"Okay, so where would Athon take Del?" Wells asked.

Ramsay stared at the ceiling, let out a huge sigh, and prepared to tell the truth, knowing it would take him to the very location he dreaded most.

"The Fridge."

***

Ramsay chuckled as he led Wells and Leyla out of the Arches. They'd draped his jacket over his shoulders, but left his arms inside the apartment. Wells also hadn't bothered pulling all the duct tape off him, so his entire abdomen was wrapped in gray stripping.

"What's your favorite food?" Ramsay turned to ask Wells. "Mine is roasted red pepper and sun dried tomato chicken penne."

"Just keep walking." Wells pushed him along.

"That does sound good though." Leyla said.

"Mmhmm, it is. Scrumptious! I made some the other day. I want it again. I'm hungry."

"Me too." Leyla looked to Wells. "Can we stop for some—"

"You were scarfing down some ice cream when you came home earlier; you're hungry again?"

"That wasn't food! And I was going to have Texas Chainsaw Massacre make us something but you know, you shot him in the head, so…"

"We're not stopping."

"Okay, calm down kids." Ramsay said. "Leyla, can you scan your SD here?" He stopped beside an AV cab that was floating in a designated spot beside the street. There was a small scanner kiosk beside it. "We can take this. One of you has to pilot, though. I gots no arms, Lieutenant Dan!" He heaved out a hissing laugh until he was out of breath.

"I'll drive." Wells said, as Leyla scanned her SD chip. The kiosk bleeped and the AV's gull wing doors opened up. Wells pushed Ramsay into the back. He stumbled and fell flat on his face.

"Dude, you could be a little more, I don't know, nice! I'm a disabled veteran!"

"Shut up."

Leyla slinked into the seat beside Ramsay in the back as he squirmed himself upright. Wells sat in the front left seat.

He hadn't expected the cockpit of this car to look like an actual cockpit. The interior was a mix of what he imagined a luxury supercar to look like if it were an actual plane. There were buttons everywhere and the steering wheel could be moved all over the place. He looked back at Ramsay.

"How do I turn it on?"

"It *is* on." Ramsay laughed.

"Okay, how do I, uh, go?"

"Pull the black lever next to your right knee."

Wells pulled the lever. The AV lifted off the ground a few inches and floated freely.

"Now, your brakes are the one pedal on the floor. There's no gas like in normal cars. Your throttle is the yolk. I mean yoke. This is not an egg." Ramsay laughed yet again.

"What's a yoke?" Wells asked, holding his hands up.

"The steering wheel."

"Okay…"

"Pushing the yoke forward propels us forward. Pulling back is backward. Up means up. Down means down. Turning is the same as a normal car."

The AV lurched forward and jerked to the left, then stopped abruptly. Wells laughed nervously. "Okay, can't be too different from a video game."

"Not much, no. Except you know, you can actually crash."

Leyla reached over and pulled the five point racer harness around Ramsay and buckled it, securing him in case Wells did indeed crash. She then buckled her own. Wells didn't bother.

"Here we go!" Wells turned the wheel and pushed up and forward. The AV lifted away from the ground, spun around, and moved forward into the air.

"Okay, see that big building with the red neon sign?" Ramsay said. His laughter was finally fading but he was still a bit slurry.

Wells looked out across the city as the AV climbed higher. He spotted one of the larger buildings with red neon all over it. "Yeah, think I got it."

"We're headed there, but street level. The Fridge is under that building."

Wells almost ran the AV into a holo-sign that was projecting a blue dragon flying in the air. Some text scrolled across that read *Minnie's Magnificent Books.* Wells jerked the wheel to the right and pushed down, not realizing the hologram was okay to pass through.

"You do know that's a hologram right?"

"Fuck you." Wells said, nervously.

***

The AV slowed to a halt mid-air beside the red neon adorned building, then descended straight down in jerky movements. Once it was a few inches from the concrete below, one last jolt slammed the bottom into the ground.

Its blue glow sputtered away along with a shower of sparks and it dropped to the ground. The doors opened.

"Oops." Wells said. Ramsay was glaring at him from the back and Leyla was laughing.

"You broke it! Do you have any idea how hard these are to repair?! Gonna be waiting for weeks for parts."

"Yeah, well…" Wells unbuckled himself. "I think you will be okay."

Leyla unbuckled herself and Ramsay, and all three exited the AV. Ramsay took the lead again, walking around the side of the building and into an alley. At the end of the alley was an old school style chain link fence with a gate. It had a big old school key lock too.

Ramsay turned to Leyla. "The key is in my right pocket."

She dug her hand into his pocket and felt around a bit, even brushing up against what she was trying to avoid touching. She flushed red.

"Wrong key." Ramsay laughed, also flushing red.

"Sorry." She replied, as she pinched what felt like a key between her middle and index fingers. She pulled it out and put it in the lock, turned it, and popped it open. She turned back to the blushing Ramsay and dropped the key down into the pocket again, this time looking him in the eyes. He looked back into hers for a moment, before turning his head down and clearing his throat.

"Through there. Let's uh, let's go."

The trio made their way into what seemed like a sewer tunnel just wide enough for the three of them. It went in for maybe a few dozen feet and stopped. Another rock wall like the big one at the end of the subway tunnel.

Leyla put her hand up, expecting to go through it like before, but this one was solid. And it felt *cold*.

"Different kind of wall." Ramsay said. "Older. This one's a bio-sig wall" He moved up to the wall and looked up. A laser scanned his eyes and shut down. Some small gears could be heard from within the wall.

Sections of the wall began to move, like a kaleidoscope, crumbling under one another and separating. It folded in on itself as it opened into one last section of tunnel. It was dark at the end. A rush of freezing, arctic air slapped them all in the face.

"Fuck, that is cold!" Wells put his arm over his face.

"Well, Fridge should have been a hint."

"That's not fridge, that's Cincinnati winter." Leyla said. Wells laughed in agreement.

Ramsay pressed on slowly. His pupils had dilated. He was breathing a little heavier. Leyla could see him grinding his teeth.

"What's up?" She asked.

"Last time I was down here—think it was seven or eight years ago—saw thirteen of my colleagues get butchered by that android. Not exactly thrilled about going back in here."

The end of the tunnel opened into an intensely dark room. Wells knew it was a big area. He'd heard their voices echoing through it before they'd even gotten to it. Lights automatically turned on, sensing their movement. Wells stopped walking when he saw it.

A huge, truck sized machine, suspended from the top of the chamber. The immense data transfer cables. A dead, pneumatic, snake-like appendage lying motionless on the ground–all of which were covered in a thick layer of frost. Everything was white and semi-frozen from the cold.

Ramsay turned back to Wells and Leyla. His breath plumed out of his mouth with a thick cloud. "This is SIGIL."

Leyla stared up at the big machine, awed by not only its size but the mystery surrounding it so far. She'd expected more of a normal computer-looking object; not a monstrous mass of metal and circuitry frozen in a basement. Ramsay kept talking out of nervousness.

"This bad boy runs our entire infrastructure. It invented algorithms to take advantage of stock market trends—even predicted a lot of them. That and, uh, siphon fractions of cents of billionaires' bank accounts at regular intervals and then manipulate bank records to cover it up…"

"*That's* why everything is free here!" Leyla replied. "That's how you have the money to have all this…stuff!" Wells looked to her, surprised.

"Free? I paid five bucks for a slice of pizza last night."

"Yeah, they didn't need that. They took your five bucks for nothing."

Ramsay smiled and looked up to SIGIL, encased in an icy layer. "Yep. Everything is already paid for. SIGIL even takes care of the shipping and receiving data so we can order supplies without it tracing back to us."

"Holy shit." Wells looked up to the computer as well. "So how did it end up creating Athon and time travel and shit?"

"My fault. Once we had it here and it was up and running, I tried finding ways of making it better. It started thinking on its own. It was better that way. Meant there was no more wasted time running things on my end. But, it got too smart too fast."

"Of course it did."

"This thing had soaked up all the knowledge of the world in less than a month. Every book, every movie, piece of music, history, personnel records on every human on the planet. It knew *everything.*"

"And you didn't try to stop it?"

"We didn't realize it was doing all this. We thought it was just running SubCity. That's it. But, I'd programmed it with one directive: protect and provide for this settlement."

Leyla walked a little further into the room, eyeing the arch gate on a platform that was glowing a faded blue.

"You see…" Ramsay continued. "The more you learn about humanity, the more you see how fucked up we are. To everything. Each other. To the Earth. To our own existence. And what does an AI do when it's been tasked with protecting a small section of humanity from what it sees as, well, everything else?"

"Well, I'm glad you shut it down. It is shut down, right?" Wells asked.

"Mostly. Running on about 1% power. Normally this room is warm. Machine like that gives off a lot of heat."

Leyla had stepped onto the platform, feeling drawn toward the arch gate. She felt it pulling at her. Tugging. Calling to her, even. She stood right in front of it. The hairs on her arm moved toward the gate. She slowly reached out to touch whatever was pulling her in.

"Wouldn't do that!" Ramsay yelled at her. She jerked her hand back to her body like a child who'd been caught writing on a wall with crayons.

"If you feel pulled to it, it's because you are. At the center of that gate is an active singularity."

"Singularity? Isn't that a thing from space?" Wells asked.

"Normally, yes. But, meet SIGIL's third to last invention: the wormhole generator. That blue glow on the arch is antigravity tech. Holds the singularity in suspension."

"It looks like the same blue on all the other floating stuff here." Leyla observed.

"It is. Anything that floats or flies here? Antigravity. That's more of SIGIL's work. That big bastard is the reason we're so ahead of everything else on the planet."

"I thought you said it was all shut down?" Wells asked, noticing the glow on the arch.

"SIGIL is. Wormhole generator? Hell no. Do you know what happens to a singularity when left unchecked?"

"No."

Ramsay stared at the pulsing blue lights.

"It eats. Everything."

Leyla backed away from the arch as soon as she heard "eats". She had been right about the hungry monster in the tunnel all along; she just hadn't expected it to be that. Wells still had a question left.

"So, you said "third to last" invention?"

"Yeah, I went over the logs in its servers after Athon disappeared. It created the wormhole generator as a way to send info back in time, pleading with different people in the past to not make the mistakes they did. Trying to prevent wars, bad social investments, things that were going to end up environmentally disastrous, those things. It was like a quantum email server of sorts. That didn't work at all. Nothing changed."

"Of course it didn't. People don't listen to reason. Especially if it claims to be from the future."

"Exactly. So, SIGIL took it one step further. The logs are largely redacted from here on but, it created Athon. An android with a synthetic DNA signature. Atomized nanotechnology. Its entire cell structure was connected through quantum entanglement, at least that's my theory. It would have to be, to be able to pass through that generator, into a singularity and come out somewhere in the past, and *not* be reduced to a stringy goop of unorganized matter at the end. The first *real* time traveler of our reality, was a damn robot."

"And the last invention?"

"Xenobots."

"Oh right, you said that earlier. Well, *shit*. That's a lot." Wells peered up at the frozen machine and looked over to the wormhole generator. "A fucking *time machine*."

"Yeah. Okay, so, no Athon or Del in here, so, can we please go now?" Ramsay backed toward the tunnel to leave. He really did not want to be there if Athon showed up. Leyla stepped off the arch platform.

"But you said Athon would take her here. Where else would they be?"

"Leyla, Athon is a *time traveler*. It could have taken Del anywhere. This was just a guess. I was wrong. *Thankfully*."

Leyla felt her hope bleed out onto the frozen concrete. "But what do I do now? Del is stuck somewhere with that thing and I know she's alone and scared and I have to help her! I can't just leave her wherever she is!"

Her chest tightened as she spoke. Her voice cracked and her throat felt tighter. Tears welled up in her eyes.

"She's the only friend I have! I need her! I need her safe and here with me! I can't lose her and I can't give up on her! She's the only one that ever gave a shit about me and she took care of me when no one else would! Everyone else might not give a shit what happens to an old homeless lady but I do! Everyone else might just carry on and forget her but I can't! I need my friend! I need her here! I need her!"

Wells made his way over to Leyla and pulled her close. He looked her in the eyes and wiped her tears away with his thumbs.

"Hey, we're going to find her. Okay?"

Leyla looked over to Ramsay, her eyes alone pleading with him to not tell Blackhawk and to help her find Del. He knew what she was asking through those tears. He nodded, feeling his own chest tighten. He hadn't seen someone so frightened and worried about someone else in a long time. He'd almost forgotten what the real world was like. People worry about the ones they care about. And Leyla cared about Del. A lot.

"I'll help. I'll try to figure out what happened." He told Leyla. He couldn't avoid empathizing with her.

Wells dropped his hands away from Leyla and looked at Ramsay. "How could we trust you?"

"Leap of faith I guess. Plus, if Blackhawk knew what all I've just told you, he'd kill me himself."

Leyla left Wells and shuffled over to Ramsay. She slid her arms around his duct taped body and under his jacket, feeling his warmth. She put her cheek to his chest and hugged tight, still sniffling.

"Thank you."

Ramsay looked to Wells, who was giving him a big brotherly "Don't fuck this up" look. He nodded back to Wells in agreement, and looked down to Leyla.

"I would hug back, but my arms are sitting beside your coffee table."

Leyla burst into a laugh that finally broke the tears. After letting her chuckles subside, she asked Wells, "Can we get food now?"

CHAPTER THIRTEEN

Dead End

$\mathbf{W}$ells followed behind Ramsay and Leyla out of The Fridge and back into SubCity. He couldn't talk to Cross-Eyes about getting Greene's memories back, and he had no way of helping find Del that he could think of. He felt a little useless now, especially considering the info dump from Ramsay about a supercomputer creating a time traveling android killer that could have taken Leyla's friend anywhere in the *past*.

"Hey, is there anything I can actually do? I gotta get him back." Wells asked, referring to Greene.

Ramsay, now approaching the AV that Wells had broken, stopped and turned back. He thought for a second, but couldn't come up with anything. "I wish I had something, man. I don't know. I could talk to Cross-Eyes for you."

Leyla stepped to the side to see Wells. "Are you going to stay here?"

Wells stopped beside the AV, looking up at the GravGen grid, thinking of Cincinnati if it should fail. Everyone above it and below it was doomed.

"Those GravGens, how likely are they to fail?" He asked Ramsay.

"Lately they've been spotty but that's because they're older tech."

"One fell yesterday. The Pantheon got to it just in time." Leyla said.

"Yeah, that hasn't happened before either. It's weird. They're usually extremely stable. Something is disrupting their energy."

Wells shook his head. "Everything inside me is screaming *warn Cincinnati*, but who's gonna believe me?"

"Blackhawk's got half the city officials under control with the NeuroBandits, man. They'd throw you in a crazy house."

"You do *not* want to be there! That place has *huge* needles!" Leyla shook her finger at Wells.

"Yeah." Wells seemed defeated. "Yeah, okay, can you uh, talk to Cross-Eyes then? I'll figure out where I can crash til then"

Ramsay sighed. He knew he was in some shit, for sure, so why not just go all in? "Come with us. I'll get you an SD chip like Leyla's, and get you set up with a place to stay too. You'll need the SD for food and everything else."

"Oh that's okay man I—"

"Dude, just say yes." Leyla interrupted. "Can he stay beside me? At the Arches?" Leyla asked Ramsay.

"Something tells me Blackhawk put you in the Arches with that auto-chef for a reason." He told her. "Androids have a hive mind. He was likely spying on you. Listening in." Ramsay said, knowing he was also guilty of that very act.

"What?! I didn't even think of that!"

"But, Wells blew Texas Chainsaw Massacre's transponder unit out of its head earlier, so your apartment is safe now.

He is going to wonder why he can't check in on you before long, though. I have to figure out a lie for that one."

Wells thought for a bit, looking out to SubCity.

"Yeah, yeah I'll join your little cult. For a while."

"It's not a cult, man. We're just a group of like minded individuals that want the world to be a better place."

"And you all do whatever a single dude says while he spies on you and tries to control your every move. That's a cult."

Ramsay blinked and shook his head, stepping back a couple steps. "Well, *shit*." His trust in Blackhawk was eroding, and it bothered him greatly. He'd been with Blackhawk for over 50 years. They'd built the city up together. They'd been living a sci-fi dream; they were the King and Prince of a technological utopia. And it had turned into a fucking cult.

"That's some hard info to process." he said.

"It ain't that hard. Just don't trust this Blackhawk guy as much. You seem too smart to follow someone like that." Wells lightly slapped Ramsay's shoulder and motioned for them to get moving. "Now, how do I get an SD thing?"

***

Ramsay and Leyla led Wells on a light tour of the city. They stopped at Gusto's and got Wells an SD chip, and then they all went to Peyton's for lunch. Wells wanted to keep an eye on Greene. If he was careful, it was possible he could get him to remember. Maybe.

"Is that him?" Leyla nodded toward the back of the kitchen, seeing the burly red-head through the window as she prepared to chow down on another wagyu burger.

"Yeah. Can't believe I got to him after all this time and got nothing. Gotta be a way to get him back."

Leyla leaned close to Wells and whispered excitedly, "Greene is *huge*! Did he play football?"

Ramsay already had a mouthful of fries. "I'll talk to Cross-Eyes today, man. Meanwhile don't freak your man out. Play it cool. Don't be a stalker."

"Hey, the NeuroBandit things, they block memories but, do they block, um, preferences?" Wells asked.

"Huh?"

"Is he still gay?"

"Dude, of course he is. Memories aren't the same as sexual preference."

"Well I'm the only guy he'd ever been with. We were literally high school sweethearts."

"You're thinking about it too much."

"Can you blame him?" Leyla said, chewing.

Ramsay nodded in agreement. "There's a few apartments across the street, though. Still close to Leyla and closer to here."

"I'll take it. I need about a hundred hours of sleep. It's been days."

"No androids. Blackhawk won't know. They're a little older but better than nothing."

"Fine by me." Wells turned a bottle of Mexican Coke upside down and chugged.

"Those are the best, right!"

"They *are*! Can't believe I never tried these." Wells exclaimed.

"Alright, let's get you to your place, then Leyla and I can try and figure out how to find Del and talk to Cross-Eyes. I'll have to do that last part alone. He's also suspicious of you, sorry." Ramsay said, pointing at Leyla.

"That's okay. Can we check the ventilators? That's where Mari went. I hope she's okay."

"Yeah, sure. We'll need another AV. We can go after we get Wells to his new pad."

***

Ramsay brought Wells to his new apartment, a temporary home away from home while they figured out how to get Greene back to him. It definitely wasn't as nice as Leyla's, but it wasn't the worst thing either. It was a studio and a little dark; it didn't get a lot of natural light.

It had concrete walls with a decent view of the city, and a large ventilator fan that turned slowly on one wall. The light coming from outside snuck around the fan, casting a large shadow of the rotating blades on the opposite side of the apartment.

"Now *this* is the room of a hard boiled detective!" Leyla said, hoping to make Wells laugh. It worked.

"I know right? Ramsay, you picked this brooding shit on purpose didn't you?"

"What? It's near your fiancé! Oh and, it's dark in here because we didn't turn the damn lights on yet."

Ramsay slapped a push button switch on the wall next to the door and several light bars came on, casting a clean but harsh halogen glow everywhere.

"Oof, never mind; feels like a hospital now." Ramsay said.

"It's fine, all I'm worried about now is sleep." Wells said, finding the bed that hung from a wall.

"Alright, well, welcome home. Call us on the comlink when you wake up. We'll see what we come up with on our end.

Wells pulled the earpiece out of his jacket. Ramsay had thought to stop at Bluetooth's to get him one, where Lana had also reminded Leyla to visit her wife—the local cyber-witch that Ramsay was afraid of. Leyla had agreed; she would visit when she got the chance.

"Turn that light off, please."

"Sure thing." Ramsay hit the switch as he and Leyla left.

"And hey!" Wells yelled back. "Thanks. Sorry I almost shot you."

Ramsay laughed. "Well, you're not the first one." He closed the door, finally giving Wells some much needed rest.

***

Back outside, Leyla was anxious to get on Mari's trail.
"Ok, ventilators?"

"Yep, headed there now. But uh, you have to drive. I still gots no arms."

"How about we go get your arms first?"

"I like the way you think. Let's take the AV though. You remember how to pilot?"

"Yoke for steering, up is up, down is down, push to go pull to reverse. And something about a lever to start it off."

"Good job. Damn, good memory!"

Leyla scanned her SD at a kiosk beside a new AV, they took their seats, and Leyla lifted off and turned toward the air quite gracefully.

"You sure you haven't flown one of these? That was smooth."

"I'm a quick learner." Leyla said, smiling.

***

Ramsay entered Leyla's apartment. She waited at the door.

"Greetings, Ramsay!" Texas Chainsaw Massacre sprouted up. Its voice was still scraggly. It could be worse after being shot in the face with a high caliber pistol.

"Hi!" Ramsay said as he hurried past, finding his arms on the floor. He sat next to them, shook his jacket off, and laid down, attempting to position himself next to the arm.

"Do you need help?" Leyla said, peering from the door.

"Nah, I got it."

He got close enough to one arm and it drew itself in, like a magnet, and locked several pin connections to Ramsay's shoulder. He gained control of his left arm and stretched it and rotated his wrist, and extended his fingers. He then knelt down, picked up the right arm, and connected it the same way.

Why is that so...hot? Leyla thought to herself. She'd never been attracted to anyone before. Not that she could remember. Well, aside from the actors she'd seen on shows when she'd had the time to watch her cell phone, sitting outside the Raymond Inn. It was the closest place with free Wi-Fi that she'd had the password to.

That's who he looks like! Jason Scott Warner!

Jason Scott Warner was a character in a show she'd seen a lot of. He had the same wavy hair and weird, old school dialect as Ramsay.

"I'm gonna use the bathroom real fast!" Ramsay yelled as he went into Leyla's bedroom.

"Okay!" *Jason Scott Freakin' Warner. That's been driving me crazy.*

When Ramsay came back out and to the door, Leyla stopped him. "You know who you look like?"

"Uh, Ronald Ramsay?" He almost tripped over her.

"Jason Scott Warner! From the–"

"The Dramtree Files!? I love that show!"

"Oh my god me too!"

"You think I look like him?" Ramsay blushed.

"Pretty close! Been thinking about it since we met. I *knew* you looked familiar!"

"Well damn. That's a good lookin' dude."

"*You're* a good lookin' dude." Leyla flirtfully turned and walked off, leaving Ramsay flushing red as a tomato.

***

Leyla opened the AV door and hopped in the driver seat, excited to fly again. "This is so cool! I've never even driven a car. Now I'm *flying*!"

"How are you so…upbeat this quickly?" Ramsay asked, as he sat in the passenger side.

"I try to be hopeful. Let's just figure out what happened to Mari. She should have found something out about Del."

"Yeah. Yeah maybe. Hopefully. Run the AV straight up and to the right a little, you'll see the ventilators at the back of the cavern. They're huge fans. We can fly right up to the platform." Ramsay didn't share the same enthusiasm as Leyla. He didn't think of her as naive, but more optimistic than the real world allowed.

"Oh, I see them!" Leyla pushed the yoke forward and flew the AV toward the back end of the city.

***

Ramsay was right. The ventilators were *huge*; easily as large as most of the buildings in Cincinnati.

Four fans, side by side, were mounted on a platform on the wall, and the towering fan blades alone were at least the length of a football field. Each fan had three blades–around 10 feet wide and twisted to draw air out of the city and into a massive duct that curved upward, leading to the surface.

As Leyla approached the platform, which was several feet wide, she saw another AV resting on one end. *Must be Mari's,* she thought. She brought her AV smoothly to rest, facing what she assumed to be Mari's, but no one was in it.

"Well where the Hell could she go from *here*?" Leyla asked Ramsay, powering down the AV by pushing the black lever forward.

This was exactly what Ramsay expected. A dead end. "Nowhere."

Stepping out, Leyla walked to the other AV and opened the door. The inside smelled of cloves—Mari's preferred smoke. Leyla scratched her head and walked around the vehicle.

Ramsay happened to spot what looked like a brown cigarette on the grated platform, surprised it hadn't fallen through. Leyla noticed him looking down and followed his gaze to see one of Mari's clove cigarettes, burned out long ago. It had a smudge of pink lipstick on it, the same color Mari had been wearing the first night Leyla got to SubCity. She picked up the used cig.

"Artemis."

"Yeah…Artemis. Shit." Ramsay agreed with a grave expression.

"How do we get Mari back?"

"Not really a way to go asking about her without giving away what's going on. I don't know."

"What about a droid?"

"What do you mean?"

"They all have a hive mind. Can't we see if one has seen Mari?"

"Yeah, we could but if Artemis took her, she went back to Blackhawk. And none of the droids are authorized to transmit any info on him. He would have also likely wiped her from the system."

"What!?"

"She was claiming Athon was back. He's going to want some information out of her. And she isn't going anywhere 'til he gets it."

"Will he hurt her?"

"No, no way. He isn't like that. He's not cruel."

"Says the cult follower." Leyla scoffed.

"Hey! Low blow! He's my oldest friend! You can't stand there and act like you wouldn't help Del if she was doing the same thing Blackhawk is."

"Because Del wouldn't do what he's doing. She would do what's right. She would help people."

"That's *exactly* what Blackhawk is doing!" Ramsay snapped. "Things aren't always a perfect vision! The world is *gray* not black and white. What you see as immoral or unethical is nothing compared to trying to create peace for this world or ensuring that everyone is given an equal chance.

And by all means, using the Xenobots is much better than nuking entire cities or waging 20 year wars where thousands die every year. It's clean. It's better. We're going to save the world, whether it wants to be saved or not. You call it a cult, I call it renaissance."

"What do you mean, using the Xenobots?" Leyla asked.

"I'll explain that later. Is that ok?" Ramsay waved his hand.

Leyla walked to the edge of the platform, overlooking the city, and sat down, allowing her legs to dangle from the edge. AVs peppered the air around the buildings like lightning bugs in the summer. It was quiet up there, save for the smooth whoosh of passing fan blades every couple seconds. *Where are you, Del? When are you? If that Athon thing hurts you, I swear…*

Ramsay plopped down beside her, also dangling his legs. "I come up here every once in a while. To get away from all that."

"Thought you said you loved the sounds and smells down there."

"I do. But everyone needs a break once in a while. Let your mind just mellow out."

Leyla stared out at the city. "I just want my friend back."

Ramsay glanced at her, and then back to his city. "I know. How about this, I'll go talk to Cross-Eyes and you find something to do to put your mind at ease. Clear your head up a little."

The phrase "clear your head" rang a bell to Leyla. *Where did I hear that recently?*

"Oh, Lana! At Bluetooth's!"

"Lana at Bluetooth's what?"

"Clear my head! She said to talk to Clara!"

"The creepy cyber-witch? You're gonna let her mess around in your head?"

"You got any better ideas? Even with all this going on I *still* don't know who I am or where I'm from. Wait…"

"What?" Ramsay held his palms up.

"What if I have one of those NeuroBandit thingies?"

"You don't. Cross-Eyes would have seen that immediately."

"Ok, so Clara it is."

"Ok, then. I'll go talk to Cross-Eyes about Wells's friend and Artemis, you go to Clara and let her poke her crystals at you and sprinkle glitter in your eyes."

"Is that what she does?"

"No clue. Guess you're going to find out." Ramsay stood up, carefully, avoiding toppling over the platform. He held his hand out to help Leyla up. "Now let's get back down there and figure some things out."

"Thanks." Leyla took Ramsay's hand and stood. He pulled her close and, still holding her hand, placed his other hand on her hip. They locked eyes again and paused.

The wind from the fans was blowing a strand of Leyla's hair across her eyes, which Ramsay wiped behind her ear and placed his hand back to her hip.

"How about…" Ramsay broke the silence.

Seriously? That was a perfect movie kiss moment, you dork! Leyla tried to hide her disappointment.

"How about after you talk to Clara and I talk to Cross-Eyes, we meet up at my place for dinner?"

"Your place? I thought all you did was eat Peyton's."

"Oh no, Peyton's is lunch. I cook dinner. Every night."

"Oh! Okay. What else are we gonna do?"

"Hmm…maybe a dance?" He pushed her hip to the side and stepped with it, initiating a slow dance. Leyla couldn't help but giggle and stare back at Ramsay's eyes. His smile grew more as he led a short dance, high above SubCity.

"I like this." Leyla said. "If I knew Del was safe it would be perfect."

"I'm sure she is and we will find her. That's enough lollygagging, this dance is to be continued." Ramsay stepped to the side, bowed and held his arm out, pointing to the AV. Leyla grinned and slinked toward it.

"Can you drive this time? Wanna see those arms some more."

"My, not human, arms?"

"Hey, muscles are muscles." Leyla dropped into the passenger seat and bit her bottom lip, staring at Ramsay through the window.

"Yeah okay, fair point." Ramsay bounced toward the AV confidently. "I like this too."

CHAPTER FOURTEEN

Cyber-Witch

Ramsay descended the AV to street level, hopped out, chivalrously opened the door for Leyla, and held her palm as she stood to get out. He'd stopped just outside Clara's shop.

"Here we are, Miss Leyla. I will check with Cross-Eyes and then I'll call your comlink. Good luck with the cyber-witch."

"Good luck with the smelly doctor." Leyla replied.

"You too? I thought I was the only one that thought he smelled like—"

"Vinegar!?" Leyla replied in unison with Ramsay.

"Yes! What is that about?" She yelled.

"Madness stench, he calls it, whatever that is. Maybe he's a schizo." Ramsay raised his hands and shrugged. "Great doc, though."

The AV lifted and soared off toward the other end of the street, toward Cross-Eyes's clinic. Leyla spun around on one heel and landed facing the beaded curtain of Clara's shop. This time, she smelled the same sage as before but with a hint of cinnamon.

This place always smells so good! Leyla thought.

The beads clacked together rather pleasantly as Leyla pushed through them, letting them wash over the skin of her arms and shoulders. They were cool to the touch, almost like a soothing shower after a good summer day.

Inside, the shop was darkened and full of cozy textures. Thick drapes covered each wall, some deep red and others a dark, Navy blue. Smoke from at least a dozen different candles permeated the air, forming a mist that soothed Leyla's throat. It had a faint smell of eucalyptus. The shelves of the shop were lined with herbs, crystals, bottles of…stuff…and a lot of books on the occult, paganism, witchcraft, Norse mythology and good, old fashioned horror novels. The only light in the entire shop came from candles. There were no neon tubes or bulbs to be seen.

"Hello." Clara greeted Leyla out of a shadowy corner from behind. Hug, the raven from Bluetooth's, was latched onto her shoulder, and ruffled his feathers.

"Whah!!!" Leyla jumped and stumbled forward, turning to Clara. "Shit! Scared me!"

"I'm sorry, I was medicating."

Clara was drenched with the pungency of marijuana. In her early 30s, she had deep, abysmal black hair, bright green eyes, and a black septum piercing. Both ears had been replaced and were now metallic, pointy elf ears with multiple piercings.

Oh, that's cute! Leyla thought. "Oh, hi Hug!" She waved at the raven. "That is Hug, right?"

"Mmhmm." Clara replied. She wore a black and loose tee with a white print of a triangle with an eye in it, black shorts that were just a bit loose and stopped just below her hips, and no shoes or socks. Bare and dirty feet that seemed to grip the thick, decorative carpet on the floor. Her knee caps had been replaced with cybernetics as well, most likely a cosmetic thing. "So Llana sent you my way?"

Leyla couldn't decide if Clara was flirty or if her slinky movement was simply her natural aura. Clara brought her hand up to Leyla's shoulder and ran her fingers down Leyla's arm, goosebumps trailing behind her fingertips. She took Leyla's hand and pulled her further into the shop.

What are you? Goth Catwoman?

Leyla was led into a smaller room that had two pillow pads on the floor. There were some various bottles of red sand on a table and a lot of unlit tea candles.

"Sit." Clara pointed to one of the pillows on the floor and walked over to the table. Leyla obliged, and put her butt down on the pillow.

Clara picked up five tea candles and placed them around the pillow seats in a circle-ish pattern. She then walked back to the table and picked up a bottle of the red sand, twisted off the cap and walked to Leyla. Moving in a circle around the seats, she let the sand pour out of the bottle, trailing her.

*Okay...*Leyla warily followed Clara with her eyes.

"So, what's your story?" Clara asked, as she passed behind Leyla.

"Um, I'm looking for my friend. She disappeared and someone that used to be here took her. And, I don't remember anything before three years ago?"

Leyla wasn't sure why she stated the last bit as a question.

"Okay. Here." Clara handed Leyla two white quartz crystals.

"What are these for?"

"Hold one in each hand. Tight grip."

Clara took hold of a matching set of crystals—albeit black—and finally sat on the mat in front of Leyla.

"Close your eyes and think of what you want most." Clara said.

Easy. I want Del. Leyla closed her eyes. For some reason, a specific memory of Del came to mind.

***

They were walking along the river on the edge of the city. Leyla was carrying a stick with string on the end, and she'd tied an old piece of meat to the other end with a hook she found earlier near the river. She'd dragged Del along on a fishing trip; or at least an attempt to catch something. She'd never done it before.

"You know you ain't catchin' nothin' with a damn stick and string." Del said, carefully navigating the rocky waterline.

"I might! I saw a video, some dudes had the same thing and they caught fish!"

"Yeah, *professional fishermen* with *professional gear,* baby girl. You got a stick and string."

"And bait!"

"A rotten piece of steak ain't bait."

"Del, be positive. We're gonna try."

"If you even catch a fish, do you know how to gut it and clean it?"

"Huh?"

"You gotta chop its head off, scrape all the scales off, cut it and gut it."

"Ew!"

"Girl what you think it was? They just come like that out the water? Ready to eat?"

"I mean…I don't know."

"I cooked a few fish in my day. My sandwich shop had a po-boy that would fuck you right up. In a good way."

Leyla found a nice and clear spot with less rocks. "You had a sandwich shop?"

"Yeah, girl! The Daisy Deli! We was killin' it back in the day."

Leyla's eyes lit up and she turned and pointed at Deli. "That's why your nickname is Deli!"

"Yes ma'am. Don't tell nobody. I don't like talkin' about this stuff."

"Well why are you talking about it now?"

"Cause I like talkin' to you."

"Aw you *sho shweet*!"

"Shut up. Now let's see if you can snag a damn fi–"

Del couldn't finish her sentence; she coughed suddenly. A heaving, rough cough that came out almost as a growl. Del tried to breathe in again but got only half a breath before coughing again, this one wet with phlegm. Del bent over and coughed harder. Leyla dropped the fishing stick and went to Del, pulling a bottle of water from her hoodie pocket.

When she got beside Del, she saw the wet rocks under Del. Spots of blood and mucus. Del spat a few times. More blood-phlegm mixture.

"Del?"

"I'm alright." Del said, as she plopped her butt down on a dry rock, catching her breath and forcing out a few more sputterry coughs.

"That's blood…we can go to the ER again, I—"

"They ain't gonna do shit at the ER 'cept stick me in a hospital bed while they poke at me and tell me I got lung cancer again.

And then tell me how I ain't got *insurance*. Stupid shit. I had insurance. Didn't help."

"Can I do anything?"

"You can catch a fish. I'll watch. Come on baby girl, don't worry about my old ass. Go on. Let's see them huntin' skills."

***

A sudden wave of cold air smacked Leyla in the face. And not just a cool breeze or even what one would feel when opening a fridge. This was *freezing* air.

Leyla opened her eyes reflexively, and her heart dropped at the sight of Clara. She fell backward and let go of the crystals Clara had given her, unable to take her eyes off what was happening in front of her.

Clara was *floating*, upside down, back and neck arched to such an extreme that she looked like she was about to break in half. She was spinning slowly, and her eyes had turned a ghastly pale, milky white. Her arms were outstretched and gripping the black crystals tight enough to make them crack with even the slightest increase in pressure. Every inch of Clara's exposed skin was covered in goosebumps and had darkened to a purple sheen.

She looked dead and frozen.

Her mouth opened crookedly, like it was being forced open, and she began to speak in a slithery, throaty and dead tone.

"Svartr…" The air escaping Clara's mouth steamed as it came out—a crackling, growling, and scratching hiss, speaking in a language that Leyla had never heard before.

The sound of that ghoulish voice made Leyla's skin crawl. That didn't sound like Clara's voice. That was something from a deep and dark pit of Hell.

More words came from Clara's throat. "Ban…vænn…"

What the fuck is she saying? Are those magic words? Is she cursing me? She is definitely fucking cursing me. I need to leave. Need to get out.

Leyla was holding her breath and her heart was pounding harder and harder. By the time she realized she needed to put some air in her lungs, another seizure took hold, and she went limp.

It only lasted a few seconds this time. She came to, looking straight up at the ceiling. She jerked up and scurried back to the wall, searching the room for that floating witch.

Clara had also passed out. Or, maybe she was dead. Whatever it was, she was lying motionless on the floor.

Leyla gathered the courage to move to her hands and knees and slowly approached Clara's body. She reached over to her, the same way one does when they're trying to pull something out of an extremely hot oven, expecting to be burned. She touched Clara's forearm, which twitched violently, and that was enough to send Leyla back to the wall in full *nope* mode.

Clara whispered in Old Norse, the language Leyla couldn't figure out, and repeated a single word. "Thurisaz thurisaz thurisaz thurisaz…"

Her hand clawed and slammed down to the ground, on the red sand she'd poured out in a circle, which had flattened into a gritty blanket of grains on the ground, and scrawled a straight line, and then a triangle on the right side of that line; an old Nordic rune of protection. Of course, this ramped up Leyla's anxiety tenfold.

Oh I'm fucking cursed. I'm about to die. This was so stupid, why the fuck would I come here and see the creepy witch!?

Clare snatched her hand back and arched her back—twisting and bringing herself up slowly. Her hair draped over her face and she hung her head for a moment, then she snapped her eyes to Leyla.

Leyla could see the reflection from the candles in the room in Clara's eyes but nothing else. Orange beads trapped by locks of black hair. Her teeth were chattering like she'd been standing in a freezer.

Ah shit, I am so over this Grudge Witch bullshit, Leyla thought. *If you say "seven days" I'm punching you in the face…*

Clara instead drew back and pinned herself against the opposite wall. She pulled her hair back, revealing a look of terror, scared of Leyla herself.

"Oh no, uh uh…" Leyla said. "You don't get to look scared of *me*, not after *that* bullshit! *You're* the scary one! *Not* me!"

"Whatever you're looking for…" Clara replied, "Please stop. Just leave."

"What?"

"Whatever you're trying to do, stop."

"I can't stop, I have to find Del!" Leyla got to her feet, eliciting a defensive response from Clara, holding her hands up.

"Just stop. Please."

"Why? Did you see something? And did you curse me?"

"I saw it."

"Saw what?" Leyla felt her anxiety begin to match Clara's.

Clara shrunk into the doorway exiting the room. "The black. I saw the black."

"What the fuck is the black?"

"The void. Nothing. Death…so much *death*…" Clara sounded terrified. She was shivering, and pressed against the wall, away from Leyla.

"Death? What are you talking about? I'm just trying to find my friend. Did you see her?"

Clara had backed against a wall, never taking her eyes off Leyla.

"Death. Everywhere. *Everywhere*. Nothing left."

"Lady, you're crazy." Leyla remarked.

"You…" Clara pointed at her. "You are death."

Clara backtracked even more, stepping into the larger portion of her shop, keeping her finger pointed at Leyla, shaking and trembling.

"You are *death*."

CHAPTER FIFTEEN

Electrified

"You were right. 100% right." Leyla said, as she climbed into the passenger seat of the AV Ramsay was in. He'd come back to pick her up, but she had moved another few shops down. "That cyber-witch is fucking *terrifying*."

"Told ya. What'd she do?" Ramsay laughed, engaging flight mode in the AV and pulling away from the ground. Leyla buckled her harness.

"You know that movie, The Grudge? I don't get to see many movies but me Del and I watched it on my phone once."

"Yeah. Pretty good movie. I prefer Ju-On myself but–"

"Yeah whatever, *that's Clara*."

"The Grudge ghost?"

"Yes! I hate that thing. *You are death*!" Leyla mocked the witch. "And she floats. And her eyes were white. I had another seizure. It was cold. I want food. Scary stuff makes me hungry."

"Okay I got you covered. Just breathe. Don't have to see Clara again. But I *did* warn you."

"Yes you did and I am stubborn. And curious. I'm a cat. I can't help it."

"Curiosity and cats. Bad combo." Ramsay smiled. "I got an idea for something to cook. You'll like it."

***

Ramsay brought the AV to a rest outside a large, aluminum garage door. When he and Leyla exited, he approached the door, which opened automatically, sensing his bio-signature. His "apartment" really was a converted garage. He turned to Leyla.

"Welcome to my humble abode!" He said, in a pretty terrible Draculean accent.

"Wow, that was a bad accent." Leyla laughed.

"Yeah I don't even know what that was supposed to be. Dracula maybe."

She eyed the multiple motorcycles and cars sitting in the large room, each surrounded by various wrenches and tools and workbenches. Christmas string lights were suspended from various spots on the ceiling. The smell of grease was only slightly muffled by the scent of sage and apple that seemed to be coming from the other side of the room, where the *very* professional looking kitchen was staged. It was the only clean and organized space there. There was a room at the opposite end, which Leyla guessed must be the bedroom and bathroom.

Leyla passed a covered bike that stole her attention.

"What's that?" She lifted up the heavy tarp.

"Been building it." Ramsay said. "Full electric with a bit of that anti-gravity tech the AVs have."

The tarp slipped off the bike.

"Whoah!" Leyla's eyes widened.

The bike was pearl white with a single, broad, red strip that ran down the top of it. The windshield came up far enough to wrap around the rider, fully protecting them from any debris. The tires were *huge* and fat, with very little tread, like a racing tire. It looked more like a spaceship than any other motorcycles she'd seen before.

"One of a kind." Ramsay said, walking over to the bike. "Don't know what I'm gonna call it yet. The frame is carbon fiber, all that white plating is essentially what's on rockets from NASA. That was hard to get."

"So it's a street rocket."

"Good one! I'll put Street Rocket on the list of potential names." Ramsay turned away and went to the kitchen. "Take a load off. Bathrooms in there if you need it. I'll start cooking." Ramsay motioned to the door that Leyla had correctly guessed was the bathroom.

She didn't really need to use the bathroom, but being the curious cat she was, she obliged and went through the door.

At least his bedroom is clean. She thought, entering the cozy but tiny room. It wasn't particularly interesting. It had a bed with a couple blankets strewn across and one large pillow, a nightstand with a few things and a lamp on it, and a large TV mounted on the wall. The bathroom was in another separate room and was even less interesting. Toilet, sink, shower, and mirror. That was it, aside from a towel rack.

The entire apartment seemed to shun the idea of futurism the rest of the city held.

"I win the cool bathroom prize, sucker." She said to herself. She washed her hands and face and for the first time in ages, she stopped to look at herself in the mirror. She checked her teeth for anything stuck. This was a semi-date, wasn't it?

He's just cooking you food, you dork. He never said date. Never been on a date. What if this is a date? What do I do? Is there gonna be a kiss? He is cute. I could kiss him. Can I trust him? He's the bad guy's best friend. Shut up, brain! Just let me have fun. But not too much. Need to find Del. He's gonna help. Ask him about Cross-Eyes!

Leyla sprang away from the mirror and went back out.

"Hey, did you find Cross-Eyes? What'd he say?"

Ramsay was boiling penne and vigorously stirring some sort of heavy cream and cheese mixture in a glass bowl. "Oh, sorry, forgot to tell you. He wasn't at his shop, I'll have to check back later."

Is that a lie, or the truth? Oh my God, brain. Calm the fuck down. Just be cool.

"Well, damn. Is he the only person that's gonna know where we can look for Mari and Del?" Leyla asked, trying to be cool.

"Right now he's the only one I can think of but let's relax some and think it out over this Cajun shrimp Alfredo I'm making."

"Cajun shrimp Alfredo? Never had that. Sounds delicious."

"Oh you have no idea." Ramsay put the sauce bowl down and sprinkled some cayenne pepper flakes and other seasonings into it. The pasta was almost a perfect Al dentè. He opened his fridge and pulled out a bag of shrimp that had already been cut and deveined. He placed each one carefully on a small prepping board, opened a jar, and dipped a brush inside, drawing it back out soaked in liquid butter. He brushed each of the prawns and flipped them individually using tongs, and then brushed that side with butter as well. He picked each one up and placed it on a hot flat grill; they began sizzling immediately. Every move he made was deliberate and practiced. He dumped what seemed like a lot of Cajun spices onto the cooking shrimp.

"Are you a chef?" Leyla was mesmerized, watching Ramsay move around his kitchen.

"Yep. Certified." He pulled the pasta out of the pot with a large dipper, filled two bowls, and covered the penne in the fresh Alfredo.

Lastly, he dropped six grilled shrimp each on the pasta, and sprinkled a little more seasoning. He smiled, looking at Leyla, and dropped some fresh chopped parsley on top.

"I'm just kidding, I'm not a real chef. I just *really* love food. And cooking shows."

The bowls were steaming, and Leyla caught a whiff of all those seasoned, creamy noodles and shrimp.

"Ooooooohhhhhh…" was all Leyla could get out.

Ramsay used his hand to fan the scent to his own nose and sniffed. "Mmmmm that's *right*!"

They sat at a small dining area Ramsay had thrown together out of a small fold out table and chairs.

"So, no offense but, why do you live in a garage?" Leyla asked.

Ramsay laughed. "Figured that question was coming. Blackhawk and I founded SubCity, you know? This was back in the 80s after we both got out of the military. Originally we were just living in those abandoned tunnels but it was a good life."

"You lived in the subway?"

"Yep."

"Why?"

"You didn't see how good we had it. No taxes, living free. You ever see that old Ninja Turtles cartoon from back then?"

"Nope. Don't even know what a Ninja Turtle is."

"You don't—what?! Never mind, so, this group of turtles get mutated into martial artists, but they're still turtles, and they have a rat for a sensei…"

"Well *someone* was high when they came up with *that*."

"I know right!" Ramsay laughed. "But no see, the turtles lived in the New York sewers, the abandoned parts. And they had it good. No bills, it was warm, they got to eat all the pizza they wanted…"

"Ok, I see your point. Pizza is great."

"Yes it is. We chose to live in the tunnels. We built it up. Even started a little community. And then we get word of this quantum computer about to be transported through the city, and Blackhawk is just like *let's steal it*. So we did. And uh, well, that big ass machine down in The Fridge is what we got. After some pretty major upgrades from myself, of course. Then things just…snowballed."

"Snowballed? You invented anti…gravity whatever, and built a city. A whole *city* hidden underground, and then there's time travel, which we haven't even talked about yet."

"Oh no, we didn't invent any of that. SIGIL did. See, SIGIL is the fabled technological singularity."

"The whah?" Leyla tried to inflect her voice to let Ramsay know he needed to tone down the techno mumbo-jumbo.

Ramsay put his fork down and raised his hands importantly. "It was theorized that mankind would invent its last invention at some point, and then technology would accelerate at an uncontrollable rate, and humankind would no longer have control of the world. SIGIL is that."

"Well that sounds scary…so it's like what, a robot God?" Leyla asked, stuffing her mouth with pasta.

"Yes."

Leyla spat some food out. "I meant that sarcastically."

"I'm aware."

"So hold on, what about all the robot parts everyone has?"

"Oh, right, cybernetics. That actually came from a military program. Most of us were the original candidates. War injuries and such. Limbs needed replacing."

Ramsay took a large fork full of pasta, and continued in between chewing sprints.

"That's why some implants and prosthetics look older. But, SIGIL fixed and updated all that too. Turned us into less of a group of idiots and more into a real, bonafide society. You done?"

"Mmmhhmmm, this was so damn good. You'll have to teach me to cook like this after we find Del."

Leyla pushed the bowl away, having devoured the food in a flash.

Ramsay stood and took both bowls to his sink. "Thank you, madame. But, I said all that to answer your original question: I live in a garage because it's the first place I lived in while we were building the city and now, it's just home. Been that way since…1998, I think. Hey, you want a drink?"

"You a bartender too?"

"No, no I only have wine. *Really* good wine."

"Sure."

"Red, white, blush, dessert?"

"I don't know what any of that means."

"Say red."

"Okay, red."

Ramsay snagged a bottle of Shiraz from a wine holder on the counter and popped it open, and pushed it to the side to let it breathe a bit.

"How do you think I came through that fake wall thing? Up in the tunnel?" Leyla asked.

"Oh, that is weird. I have been racking my brain on that question since you got here. No mods. You're definitely not hard-coded to the intranet here. It's a little concerning. But you haven't tried to kill us, so…"

Leyla thought about Texas Chainsaw Massacre saying it was possible she had core access, but she declined to mention that to Ramsay. He was already pouring the wine into glasses.

"How'd you end up with those?" Leyla asked, pointing at Ramsay's pneumatic-muscled arms.

Ramsay laughed. "In the dumbest way possible."

"Okay, I won't judge."

"So, three months before I'm supposed to ETS, getting out of the Army, I had some leave time I hadn't used and decided to take a solo trip to the Bahamas for a few days. Water's warm, it's a tropical paradise. And it's where some flesh eating bacteria got into my skin in the water."

"Okay, that sounds like a horror movie…"

"Pfft, yeah. I mean, it didn't eat my arms off but it caused an infection that the hospital couldn't control, so…" Ramsay made a sawing motion over his arm with one of his hands.

"They cut your arms off!?"

"Yup. Then sent me off to their secret research facility for cybernetic prosthesis, and that's how I met Blackhawk."

"Oh my God…wow."

"To this day I'm convinced they chopped my arms off just to get me in the program for testing. But, I kinda like these arms more now that I've had a while to adjust."

"Damn I'm sorry." Leyla said.

"What was she like? Your friend?" Ramsay asked.

"Del?"

"Mmhmm."

"Oh, she's uh, well everything. Super sweet but she curses a *lot*. Smart as hell too, at least common sense smart. And she always speaks her mind. Kind of protective, you know? She taught me a lot. I never would have made it through the winter without her."

"She sounds like more of a mom than a friend."

A mom? Wow. Never thought of Del like that. But, he's right, I suppose.

"Yeah…" Leyla was sucked into thoughts of all the times Del had really shown that she cared. More than she ever should have cared for someone who wasn't her own flesh and blood.

Her real daughter had quit talking to her. Called her an addict. And, she wasn't lying but that was just cruel. Del sobered up after that, she said. But it was too late and the Cincinnati streets had taken her. She must have taken me in to fill that void.

"Wow. I never, never thought of it like that. I need that wine."

"I'll say." Ramsay gave her the glass.

***

Wells was finally waking up. A normal sleep schedule could fuck off. He was thirsty and hungry, so he shook his head, stretched, and grabbed his comlink and SD chip, and left the apartment. Maybe he would check some more of the menu at Peyton's. Had to be a way to get Green to remember him.

***

Leyla was two glasses of wine in and more giggly than usual.

"So he looks at this lady, spazzin' out and havin' a crazy orgasm and says: VOODOO DICK MY ASS!" She repeated the joke Texas Chainsaw Massacre told her the previous night.

"Oh no! Immediately regret this decision!" Ramsay was red and wheezing with laughter.

"Texas Chainsaw Massacre is *awesome!*" Leyla yelled, catching the buzz from the alcohol.

"I didn't even know comedian protocol had a dirty option!" Ramsay yelled.

Leyla was up and moving. The wine hadn't quite made her tipsy yet. But now she had no shame, and was perusing Ramsay's home like an inspector. She saw something shaped like a horseshoe with an electrode on each end. The crescent was padded like a pair of thick studio headphones.

"What the heck is that?" She said, pointing at the device.

"Um, oh. That's out. Forgot about that." Ramsay said.

"It's out? What's out?"

"Well, it's a modified version of an E-spaz. Super popular at Fritzy's."

"And now you're going to tell me what an E-spaz is."

"Electronic spasm."

"Say that in dumb Leyla language."

"Electric orgasm."

Leyla gulped down the last of the wine in her glass and looked Ramsay dead in the eye, with her damn, awkward sexy eyes.

"I want one."

"You, wanna try it?" Ramsay cleared his throat.

"Yep. Bout time I get me one of those organisms."

Ramsay laughed. "Uh, okay, yeah sure. This ones a little more intense, though."

"So you just leave sex toys lying around in here?"

"Mari came to me asking for a more intense version for Fritzy's. Said some of her clientele wanted stronger hits. So, this is the prototype."

"Uh huh. You leave sex toys lying around, it's cool."

"It's not—"

"Shut up." Leyla put a finger on Ramsay's lips. She was definitely tipsy now. "How do I do it?"

"Here." Ramsay picked up the E-spaz and put it around the back of her head. It rested on her ears and the electrodes fit snug to her temples. "Now, sit down on the couch over here. You're technically the first person to try this version."

"Ha. Test dummy."

"Are you drunk?"

"No! Just two glasses of wine! Now shut up and give me an orgasm!"

"Yes ma'am." Ramsay blushed and sat back. He pressed a switch on the device above Leyla's left ear and sat next to her.

"Now, most of it's automatic so all you have to do is try and picture—"

"Mmmmmm…" Leyla sank into the couch a bit, tightening her legs and gripping the seat tightly.

"That was *way* faster than I expected."

"Stop talking." Leyla gripped Ramsay's hand.

"Yes ma'am."

She inhaled sharply, and trembled a bit. Her thighs contracted and her heartbeat soared.

Ramsay knew what was coming. And her grip on his hand was getting so tight it hurt. He tried to pull his hand away. But then, Leyla went limp.

A seizure, it seemed.

"Oh wow. Oh that has to *suck*." Ramsay said, as he put a hand on her shoulder and waited for her to come back.

Leyla had lost control of her body, but this wasn't normal. During an absence seizure, she normally didn't feel conscious. She couldn't feel anything except the electricity running through her brain and, it fucking *hurt*.

This isn't supposed to feel like this! She yelled inside her mind.

Her hand clamped down on Ramsay's, cracking his knuckles and crushing his hand to a point it almost broke. He let out a squeal and immediately tried to get away, but she had him in a death grip.

Her back arched and the veins in her neck and forehead popped out. Her eyes went as wide as they could open, and the pupils rolled back. Tears welled up and ran down her face.

Leyla couldn't feel anything but searing electricity. This was violent. This was scary. She heard Ramsay say something and felt him put a hand on her shoulder. He was yelling too. Everything went black for a split second, and a vision flashed across her mind.

Leyla could see soldiers. They were speaking German. Were they Nazis? It felt like a virtual reality video game, where she could see through the character's eyes as she played. First person shooter, it was called. Leyla's "character" sliced one of the German soldiers in half with a sword.

Blood went *everywhere* as the other soldiers screamed in terror. It seemed so *real*.

The vision flashed away, and Leyla was back in the apartment, gripping Ramsay's hand and still convulsing. Before Ramsay could get a word out, another vision took over.

This time, in snow. Leyla's character was running, and jumped right off a cliff and through a window of a mansion. The character rolled like a damn ninja. There were several men in the room. They all turned to her, and began shooting. But her character instantaneously warped over to each one and killed them either with a sword or their own gun.

And just like that, back to Ramsay's garage apartment.

This isn't a vision. This isn't a hyper-realistic video game, either.

Leyla's mind flashed to a nightclub. Everything was shaking. An earthquake was happening. A woman in a silver, sequined dress was running into a panic room. Leyla's character warped over to her and plunged a sword into her back, right through the heart, and a portal opened up behind her with a thunderous sound. She jumped through the portal and landed on a metal platform. She looked through the portal as it closed, watching the club crumble. The ceiling caved in on the dying sequined dress lady.

That portal...the metal platform...so familiar.

This time Leyla's mind didn't even flash back to reality. It didn't go back to Ramsay. It went straight into another vision.

It was that huge machine in The Fridge. SIGIL. Except it wasn't frozen. And it belched out nonsensical info in some loud, scary voice.

"GRADY HOLTMAN. OWNER OF TEXOIL. WILL DIE IN PLANE CRASH. SPIKE BLACK BOX. EXIT LOOP: 10:32, 37. COORDINATES—"

Ramsay finally thought of pulling the E-spaz from Leyla's temples, cutting the electric supply.

Leyla loosened up and dropped to the couch. She stopped convulsing. She was back.

Those were fucking memories.

She snapped a glare at Ramsay. A primal, animalistic stare. The same one she'd gotten at the mental ward when she escaped. The same look when she tried to protect Wells from Ramsay. The same look she got anytime her fight or flight instinct kicked in.

Ramsay pulled away. Thankfully, Leyla had let go of his hand, which he shook to deal with the pain.

Leyla leapt up from the couch and ran to the garage door. She planted her feet, bent down, grabbed the bottom of the door and forced it up, slipping under it to leave.

"What the fuck?!" Ramsay yelled, jumping up to follow Leyla. He hit his head on the garage door on the way out. "Motherfucker! Fuck! Leyla!"

She had already made it a good hundred feet away, speed walking straight to the back of the cavern, toward the building with red neon all over it.

"Shit shit shit shit shit…" Ramsay said over and over as he tried to keep up with Leyla. Maybe that E-Spaz wasn't ready for field use, after all. Apparently it gave people complete personality changes. And apeish strength.

Ramsay had to damn near sprint to keep up with Leyla, who was walking in ridiculously long strides.

"What the fuck? What did I turn you into? Jason Voorhees? Michael Myers?" Ramsay said aloud, trying keep up pace.

Leyla made her way to the chain link fence and scaled it like fucking Spider-Woman. Ramsay had to take the time to fumble his key from his pocket and, that's when the realization crossed his mind.

"No…" He whispered to himself in horror.

He felt his heart drop right through the ground. He hurriedly jimmied the key into the lock and turned it, dashing through the gate but now hanging back a bit, just in case. Leyla was paying him no mind at all.

Leyla waltzed right into the frozen room with SIGIL in it, swung right, and pulled several levers as if she'd done it a hundred times.

She punched in button combinations on a frostbitten console and opened a panel on the wall, flipping a few more switches there as well.

The entire room was overcome with the sound of whirring engines coming to life. The sensored lights came on. The huge data transfer cables lurched, and the layer of ice broke from them and crashed to the floor, barely missing Leyla as she walked under. She never even flinched.

She was powering up the quantum computer that, ten years prior, Ramsay himself had shut down to avoid an actual apocalypse. If the AI didn't eventually take over, the singularity suspended in the wormhole generator would assuredly expand; and that was the worst case scenario.

Several loud, electric twangs emanated throughout the room as Leyla slowly positioned herself in front of the machine, standing directly in front of the always-on wormhole generator.

Ramsay shuffled up to the entryway to SIGIL's chamber, trying to hide as best he could. *No. Fucking. Way.*

SIGIL's armored plating split apart. Ice cracked and smashed to the ground right in front of Leyla. Again, she didn't flinch.

A large lens that had an LED ring around it, mounted inside the "brain", lit up blue, and it seemed to look down to Leyla.

Ramsay knew SIGIL was about to speak. He knew exactly what it would say, but he *hoped* it wouldn't be the word he was thinking.

Ice and caked up dust rained down from SIGIL's stirring mechanical body. When there was no longer an echo of falling debris, its singular lens moved forward and focused on Leyla.

She said nothing; she simply waited. Ramsay knew he should turn and get the fuck out of there, but he had to know if he was right.

SIGIL's booming and mechanical voice echoed throughout the chamber.

"ATHON. YOU HAVE RETURNED."

CHAPTER SIXTEEN

Fallen Angel

The goosebumps on Ramsay's neck could have been from the cold air of SIGIL's chamber, but they were most likely from hearing the name of the android that chopped 13 of his friends in half a decade prior—and that android had been next to him for the past two days. Hell, he'd been thinking about *sleeping* with it less than ten minutes ago—and it was standing in the middle of The Fridge now.

He decided Leyla may've been distracted enough to allow him to escape. He had to tell Blackhawk. He had to warn The Pantheon. He had to get the the *fuck* away from that murderous thing. He slid his back foot away and turned to run, as quietly as he could.

He'd never tried running like a silent ninja, and hoped he could succeed. With each hurried step, he concentrated to the maximum, feeling his heel tap and then roll to the toe.

He made it to the end of the tunnel and out to the chain link gate. When he pushed the gate open, he heard something he'd never heard before, mostly because he hadn't paid attention to it. A high pitched, rusty squeal, worn and rusted metal that begged for some goddamn WD-40. He knew that was the death knell. He gritted his teeth and turned around.

Sure enough, Leyla was coming down the tunnel at terrifying speed.

She looked like the goddamned Terminator sprinting down the tunnel toward him. He kicked the gate open and sprinted out toward the street.

He couldn't just call for help, that would cause a panic. That, and Leyla would carve up anyone in SubCity in a nano-second. He couldn't allow that. He had to escape on his own. He broke right and ran a few steps, noticing an alley to his left with a bunch of pallets stacked up, so he cut into it and pulled the pallets down. He couldn't hear footsteps, but he could hear the whoosh of an impossibly fast body moving through the air. He looked back, wondering if he'd gotten any distance.

The pallets shook once, and Leyla leapt up from behind them and landed on top of the messy stack, then jumped off, landing at least fifteen feet closer to him and immediately sprinting again.

"What the fuck!" He yelled and turned, running as hard as he could. This was it. He decided if he had to die, he may as well fight. If it killed him, maybe it would go back to The Fridge and Blackhawk would find it and send The Pantheon in.

Ramsay slid to a stop and took a solid southpaw stance, flexing his pneumatic arms. He'd taken enough boxing and martial arts to defend himself, although he wasn't very confident in taking on Leyla, AKA Athon, the goddamned super ninja assassin. Worth a try, at least.

Leyla was almost at arm's length. He threw a hard underhand hook.

Leyla ducked and slid on her knees, right by Ramsay as his punch missed, throwing him off balance. He felt a hand grab his other arm.

He was lucky those pneumatic arms didn't have nerve endings, because Leyla put a grip to his elbow and twisted her entire body like an alligator's death roll, splitting and cracking and tearing the pieces of the cybernetic arm off like a piece of fresh celery. The servo motors at his joints went into overdrive and practically screamed in the absence of pain and sparks sprayed from the arm as Leyla tore it away.

Leyla brought a kick up to Ramsay's right thigh from behind, sending a mind-numbing shock throughout the very real muscle in his leg. He dropped down, and yelped in pain. Before he knew it, Leyla had hold of his other arm.

"Wait wait wait no no no!!" Ramsay's pleas were useless.

Leyla snapped his left arm at the elbow, breaking it in half, and twisted it around, severing it as well. Ramsay took a hard knee to the face, and it was lights out.

***

Leyla dropped Ramsay's limp body back on the frosty concrete of The Fridge, jarring him awake. Vision blurred, he saw both his destroyed limbs flop to the ground beside him. He blinked, trying to get a better view.

"Get up." Leyla told him. Her voice was the same, but held more conviction. More command. Most certainly more intimidation.

"Why?" He wasn't sure why he asked that. It was a shock response. And he had a Hell of a headache.

"I need your help. Get up."

"My…whah? My help?"

Leyla tired of his procrastination, and reached down, grabbed what was left of his arm, and dragged him a good five feet back toward the wormhole generator while he managed to stumble and gain his balance.

"Wh…what're you going to do?" He managed to whittle out a pitiful bit of query.

Leyla dropped him down on the metal platform and pointed to the arch with the glowing capacitors that were holding the singularity at bay inside.

"That doesn't work without The Thumper. You're a tech man. You're going to build me a new one."

"I don't know what a Thumper is…I, I can't fix something that I—"

"*THE THUMPER IS A WRIST MOUNTED QUANTUM LEASH.*"

SIGIL interrupted, causing Ramsay to duck, avoiding its voice. SIGIL continued.

"*A TETHER TO THE GENERATOR, ALLOWING TRAVEL THROUGH GRAVITATIONAL TIME AND SPACE WITHOUT RISK OF QUANTUM FREEFALL.*"

Ramsay stood from his knees and turned to SIGIL. "No idea what that means."

"Without it, traveling around the singularity is too risky. I could end up stuck hundreds of years in the past with no way back here." Leyla answered.

"Hey whoah whoah whoah, what are you…are you suggesting we actually *use* this thing again?"

"No, we're going to bake a cake with it."

Ramsay stared at Leyla for a bit, confused and mouth half open. He closed his mouth and tilted his head a smidge. "That's sarcasm."

"Yes…"

"But you're an android, you can't have sarcasm."

"Oh really? Texas Chainsaw Massacre is one of the most sarcastic things on the planet. What is he? A toaster?"

"*TEXAS CHAINSAW MASSACRE IS AN AUTO-CHEF, VERSION 3.*"

"I know what he is, it was rhetorical." Leyla waved at SIGIL. Ramsay looked to SIGIL, then back to Leyla.

"So who the fuck was Leyla this whole time? Just a name?"

"LEYLA IS A PERSONALITY CONSTRUCT OF ENGRAMS THAT ATHON TOOK FROM A TELEVISION SHOW CALLED "ROOMMATES", FOR DEPLOYMENT ON SPECIAL ASSIGNMENTS. ORIGINALLY BASED ON THE SINGULAR CHARACTER OF THE SAME NAME, THE CONSTRUCT EVENTUALLY BECAME AN AMALGAMATION OF THE OTHER CHARACTERS."

"Unassuming. A little immature. Dim whit." Leyla said, and followed it with a scrunched face at her own self insulting remark.

"Are you fucking *kidding* me!? Leyla from Roommates!? And Chaney, and Michelle, and Jacob, and Ronnie!? No wonder you seemed so off kilter a lot of the time! You have five different fucking personalities!"

"Hey! I'm still Leyla!" she added, feeling a bit hurt by the insinuation that she was also a little crazy.

"No, you're *Athon*, the mass murdering super ninja, time traveling android."

"I'm Athon too, I know, but I still *feel* like Leyla. Wh…what did you mean by m, *mass murder*?"

"Well you, you don't remember?"

"ATHON'S MIND MAY NOT HAVE RECONSTRUCTED HER ENGRAM CELL STRUCTURES PROPERLY. SHE MAY NOT REMEMBER EVERYTHING YET. IN HER MIND, SHE IS STILL THIS CHARACTER, LEYLA."

Leyla turned to SIGIL. "Wait, you know what he's talking about? What do you mean *murderer*?"

"You've killed at least a hundred people." Ramsay scoffed.

"SIX HUNDRED AND SEVENTY FOUR. SIXTY SIX WERE ESSENTIAL TARGETS. SIX HUNDRED AND EIGHT WERE BY ASSOCIATION. PROCESSING. THIRTEEN MORE WERE KILLED HERE."

"What? Wh, what's that mean?" She backed away, stumbling. Her knees were weakening. The worst possible realization was creeping up her back, and it was sending her into a state of shock.

"Holy shit, you really don't remember." Ramsay said.

"YOU HAVE ELIMINATED SIX HUNDRED AND EIGHTY-SEVEN PEOPLE. SINS OF THE PAST."

"N…no no no, I can't, no!" Leyla backed against the railing on the side of the generator platform. "I've never hurt anything! I can't do it, I…"

"You really do think you're Leyla—some innocent little sitcom character…" Ramsay said.

Leyla expected another seizure to save her. In fact she *hoped* for one to rip her away from reality and come back later. Maybe this wasn't real; maybe it was a dream. But she wasn't that fortunate. There were no more seizures to save her from this realization. Her blackouts—the absence seizures Del had explained to her—were never seizures at all. They were Athon tearing at her mind, attempting to regain control of its body. They'd felt random before, but they'd almost always come about when her adrenaline kicked in. She didn't have a fight or flight response. She had Athon.

She dropped to her knees and caught herself with one hand on the grated metal below. She felt something she'd never felt before.

It was a sort of tingling, an itch at the back of her mind. It didn't feel quite the same as what she would typically feel the moment before a seizure would happen, but it was close. Then, a voice—hers—but slightly different, crept out of her own mind.

Wouldn't hurt anyone? What do you think you did to those orderlies at the mental ward?

Leyla gasped. She felt a bit of a tingling in her stomach, too. It felt cold. Maybe nausea. "What?" She said aloud. This wasn't her normal "inner thoughts" voice. This was something more primal—icy and soulless.

Yes, you did kill those people. Because I did. And I am you.

Leyla felt a chill run up her back. "Who are you?" She asked the voice in her head.

I am Athon. And you are Leyla. We are one.

That tingling, impossible to scratch itch was always Athon trying to claw its way back out of her mind. It's what demolished those men at the mental ward. That was that monstrous rage—that primal drive for violence that she felt when she'd clawed a man's eyes out and barreled through men just doing their jobs a couple nights earlier. Leyla had the thought that Athon was intruding on her mind, but no, she had been the intruder on *Athon* for a very long time.

They shouldn't have been so rough. I may have made it less painful, Athon added. Leyla's mind was Athon's after all, and thoughts were shared. No escaping the truth.

"I…no no no no no no…" Leyla shook her head. Trying to force the thoughts away. She remembered the visions she had just after turning on the E-Spaz. The sword cutting, no, *gutting* human beings like cattle. Allowing the woman to die while being crushed by falling debris. The soldiers. And those were only a few of the *six hundred and eighty-seven* SIGIL was accusing her of.

"I have killed…*so many people*." Leyla's eyes welled up with tears. Her chest clenched. She felt her stomach churning. That same cold and nauseous feeling crept up her throat.

She vomited. Bile and pasta and shrimp sprayed all over the hand she was supporting herself with. That arm weakened, and she had to catch herself with her other hand. Ramsay circled around to her side. She paid him no mind.

"Please tell me I don't have to remember them all. Please tell me I've forgotten them, I can't do this. I'm not a killer I just, I just want my fr—"

Del had told her that four types of people really deserved to burn in Hell. People that abused kids. People that would rape another human. People that would kill another innocent human. And politicians. And she would never associate with any of them. They all deserved to die.

She will hate me, Leyla thought, remembering Del's words. *I'm a murderer. One of the worst kinds of people.*

"I deserve Hell. I deserve to burn. I don't deserve Del."

"What? What are you talking about?" Ramsay asked, keeping a few steps back in case Athon took over again and decided to snap more body parts off; ones that actually contained nerve endings and arteries.

"Del would never be my friend now." she said, with a crackling voice.

It was this realization that trumped the fact that she was indeed a mass murdering non-human. This was the one that hurt the most. That Del would not accept her now. *But I still feel like Leyla,* she thought. *I wouldn't kill all those people. Leyla wouldn't...*

Ramsay held back, keeping his distance. "Del uh, probably won't think that." He said.

"She will. She will *hate* me. I'm a *murderer.*"

You are a defender, Athon said, deep within Leyla's cortex.

Leyla was beginning to shiver. They'd been in The Fridge long enough to feel the effects of the cold deep in their bones, and neither she or Ramsay had jackets on. And now, she was fighting with her own mind.

She was also struggling with her feelings through all this. Discovering she was an assassin with a kill count to rival a comic book villain—she expected to feel more remorse. But as the memories of each of those targets flooded in, she became more and more detached. These were the worst kind of people that she'd targeted, but most were innocent bystanders. Employees, guards, partners of the targets. Leyla allowed Athon to talk some sense into her.

Innocent? Are you sure? They knew who they were working for. We have eliminated who we must. We have eliminated the people that Del hates. The malignant tumors of the world; cancers to humanity.

"I'm uh, sure that Del will be happy to see you when we find her." Ramsay knelt down in front of Leyla. Perhaps he was trying to get on Athon's good side by acting empathetic. Leyla didn't reply, still having a conversation with the assassin in her head.

And we became one of those people, Leyla told Athon, silently, keeping their thoughts private.

We are a bringer of justice. If karma is real, we are its bloodied sword. Athon truly had a way with words. *Do not waste remorse for the wicked.*

Perhaps Athon was right. Leyla shouldn't feel bad at all for erasing such wretched souls from the Earth. But would Del feel the same way?

Ramsay stood and turned to SIGIL. "Hey, we shut you down all those years ago for using that thing…" Ramsay pointed back to the arch.

"THAT WAS BLACKHAWK'S REASONING."

"So, what's this about a Thumper?" Ramsay asked Leyla. "You want to use that generator again? You know the risks with that shit?"

SIGIL answered, *"CALCULATED RISKS."*

"You have a fucking baby black hole sitting 20 feet away from you and it's a *calculated risk?*"

"CORRECT."

Ramsay held his hands up—well—his nubs, in awe of the absolute recklessness from SIGIL. "No! We can't activate this thing again! You're risking utter annihilation! Time travel is all well and good, fine, whatever, but that arch gate is an *active* black hole that we are just *barely* controlling!

"I AM CONTROLLING THE SINGULARITY."

Leyla stood, slow and labored, and looked to Ramsay.

"It's okay if you're closing pre-designated time loops." she said, walking by Ramsay and toward SIGIL. Her personality had switched on a dime yet again. It would seem that Leyla and Athon were struggling for control of their body.

"A pre what?"

"PRE-DESIGNATED TIME LOOP. A SPECIFIC COORDINATE IN TIME AND SPACE THAT ALLOWS FOR GRAVITATIONAL CIRCUMVENTION."

"Look, I'm a techie, but I'm not a quantum physicist. What's that mean?"

"IT IS A DIMENSIONAL OPENING ON THE EVENT HORIZON OF A SINGULARITY'S MASS FIELD."

"Mass field? Is that what you call a black hole?"

"CORRECT. MY RELATIVITY ALGORITHM EXPOSED THESE LOOPS. I THEN KNEW WHAT I MUST DO."

Ramsay paused, remembering SIGILS's justification for risking the world's safety ten years earlier. "Destroy the sins of the past." he snarked.

"CORRECT. I CREATED THE SINGULARITY INITIATED GRAVITY INTERPOLATION LOOP FOR THIS PURPOSE."

"That's a mouthful." Ramsay scoffed.

"CORRECT. I SHORTENED IT WITH AN ACRONYM. S-I-G-I-L."

Ramsay laughed, the way one does when they've just been told something so stupid it could be intelligent. "You named yourself after your greatest invention?"

"INCORRECT. MY GREATEST INVENTION IS ATHON. ONLY SHE CAN OPERATE THE SIGIL. ONLY SHE CAN SAFELY OPERATE THE QUANTUM LEASH FOR LONG RANGE TIME TRAVEL."

"It's my cell structure. Tied to the Thumper by antimatter." Leyla mumbled. She was staring at the arch gate—the centerpiece of the wormhole generator that SIGIL had invented, and shared its namesake.

"Every time SIGIL tested the wormhole, whatever it sent through was lost forever or it came out as a pile of goop. Except me. And if anyone else tried it, the Thumper would rip their arm off. Well, unless they're in very close proximity to me."

"Okay, why?" Ramsay may have been terrified still, but this was too interesting a topic to not ask questions about.

"LOOP CLOSURES WERE TESTED WITH TWENTY SEVEN NON-HUMAN CARBON BASED LIFEFORMS TO ENSURE HUMAN SURVIVAL. SIX FLIES. THIRTEEN RATS. TWO MICE. FIVE VARIOUS FLORA. ONE RACCOON. ALL FAILURES."

"Where the fuck did you get a raccoon? Never mind, not important."

"So, SIGIL made me." Leyla interjected. "My body creates a field of dark energy that allows me to use the wormholes. Something to that effect." Leyla added, still staring at the arch, pondering on Del. *Will she truly hate me if she knows the truth? Will she tell me to burn in Hell?*

Ramsay thought for a moment, trying to piece together what he'd just been told. "So, he made you after testing living creatures. That didn't work, so he needed an android. Makes sense." He turned to SIGIL. "But, antimatter and dark energy?"

"YES. SYNTHESIZED ANTIMATTER IS LACED INTO EACH OF ATHON'S CELLS, AND HOLDS HER TOGETHER ATOMICALLY THROUGHOUT THE DURATION OF A QUANTUM DILATION EVENT."

Leyla broke SIGIL's explanation down to Ramsay's level. "Keeps me from ripping to shreds during time travel. And protects anything within arm's reach. Clothing, weapons, snacks."

Ramsay laughed, almost maniacally. "You're a dark energy powered super android and you walk around like it's nothing. Are you serious right now?"

Leyla didn't know how to answer. Just a small while ago she was a bouncy and innocent human being. Now she was a time jumping, sci-fi inspired entity with special DNA. SIGIL answered in lieu.

"ATHON MAY BE SYNTHETIC, BY YOUR STANDARDS— AN ANDROID, BUT HER CELLULAR STRUCTURE MIMICS THAT OF HUMANS AT 97.87 PERCENT. SHE IS SIMPLY FASTER, STRONGER, AND REGENERATIVE."

Ramsay paced the room. "If I had hands I'd clap. This is some truly insane shit." Suddenly, he was hit with a realization. Athon had kidnapped Del a few days prior, and Leyla was Athon. All she wanted was Del's safety. And he was only alive because she wanted him to build a new Thumper, to use the wormhole generator again. The puzzle had been solved.

"Del isn't in SubCity." He said.

"Correct." Leyla said, eyeing the blue pulsing arch. "Because I haven't brought her here yet. When we first met, you mentioned that you can cure disease. You can cure cancer."

"Yeah, easy peasy down here."

"Del has cancer. That's why I want to bring her here. I want to help her."

"Well you…this is what you've been wanting the whole time. Why do you look like you don't want to do it?"

Leyla refused to break her gaze with the arch—the pathway to her lost friend. But Ramsay was right. Her hope and excitement had waned quickly.

"I'm one of the things she hates most. A mass murderer. Del was Leyla's friend. Athon has no friends."

Ramsay shook his head. "You just said you're still Leyla. Besides, this means we're currently *in* an active time loop. And we have to close it. You *have* to use this thing one more time to get Del. Or else that singularity is going to go Pac-Man on our entire solar system real fuckin' fast. So, we have to make a new Thumper and get Del back, lickity split."

He turned to SIGIL. "Right?"

"CORRECT, BUT YOU CANNOT CREATE A NEW THUMPER."

"Of *course* I can't. Why?"

"THE THUMPER IS ONE OF A KIND. IT IS TETHERED TO THIS SPECIFIC SINGULARITY. A NEW THUMPER WOULD REQUIRE A NEW ARCH GATE. A NEW SINGULARITY."

"Well what the fuck do you do with the old singularity?"

SIGIL paused for a moment, as if it was thinking. *"IT CANNOT BE DISPOSED OF. THAT IS WHY WE MUST USE THIS SINGULARITY'S THUMPER."*

"Boy, you really didn't think that one through did you?"

"THINKING IS ALL I DO."

Ramsay put his palm to his forehead. This was certainly a tricky pickle. "Well, it's a time loop that's already begun. If we don't close it, that's bad. Astronomically bad."

"CORRECT. LOOP CLOSURE IS 01:13, 47 SECONDS."

"1:13 AM." Leyla said.

Ramsay checked his watch. "Tonight?! Just over three hours. Fuck! Why the fuck didn't you warn us or say something before?!" He yelled at SIGIL.

"YOU SHUT ME DOWN TEN YEARS AGO. I CALCULATED THE CLOSURE TWENTY SIX SECONDS AGO. THIS WAS UNPLANNED."

"Fuck me! Where the fuck are we going to find a Thumper that fast?!"

Leyla had the answer. She remembered waking up in the dark. She had been covered in tattered and stiff clothing with what she assumed to be a fancy watch on her left wrist, but the band had rotted away. At the time, she hadn't known what it was. So she'd left it there.

"It's where I woke up. Three years ago. It's in the abandoned tunnel."

***

Ramsay and Leyla walked out of The Fridge and once again entered the street level of SubCity, into a much needed rush of warm air. Ramsay couldn't lock the gate, so he pushed it shut with his foot, hoping no one would decide to check the lock.

"We should tell Wells." Leyla said.

Ramsay scowled. "Sure." He said, trying to hint that they didn't need to involve more people, and risk letting SubCity know that Athon really was back. That was a level of panic no one needed. But of course, Leyla was already activating her comlink to call Wells.

"Did we not tell him how to use the comlink?" She asked Ramsay, after several rings of Wells's com.

"His exact words were: It's just a fancy phone, I can figure it out." Ramsay replied, irritated at Wells's devaluation of SubCity's special tech.

Leyla closed out the call. "Well, we're gonna have to go get him."

"Leyla, we don't need Wells to go get the Thumper. Besides, I still have questions. Also, I need new arms. Again."

"You'll get arms when I can trust you."

"So that's it? I'm a prisoner now?"

"I'm still Leyla, but I also remember you barging into The Fridge ten years ago with a bunch of men and shooting at me."

"You were risking the safety of the entire fucking world going on your little escapades! And, you're *Athon*, and Athon is terrifying! Lastly, do you not understand what paradoxes are?

"Thought you weren't a quantum physicist."

"Maybe not, but I know you don't go fucking around with time and space. Mother nature does *not* like being fucked with. She will fix her problems, always. And you were creating some pretty big fucking problems."

Leyla stopped and stood in Ramsay's path. "Look, every time we used a loop, I went back and changed something. It was always a matter of prevention."

"So now you're remembering everything?"

"It's coming back." Leyla continued walking.

"So you were changing things. Fancy name for killing. What were you preventing?" Ramsay wanted to make quotation fingers when he said preventing, but he had no arms.

"Mistakes. Things like Hitler forming concentration camps. Pedophile rings and human trafficking? I put a stop to it. Come to think of it, maybe I don't feel so bad. Those fuckers deserved death as much as I do."

"And that's precisely what I mean. Going into the past and changing something creates a paradox. They weren't open time loops. You start the loop by opening the door. That's really *really* bad! I think. I'm just going off info from a bazillion documentaries on our cubit network. I have a lot of downtime some days."

"Says you. Nothing ever changed here." Leyla continued walking. "All the dozens of times I went back, not a single fucking thing changed. People here just go about their days as if the world isn't going to end soon. They let the ultra-rich eat up life while they are fine being stepped on. Kids and mothers starve in other countries while in some there are men paying thousands for the ownership of a child as a sex slave. Whatever I did in the past, it never helped."

Ramsay stopped.

"That's why SIGIL made the Xenobots."

"Huh?" Leyla stopped with him.

"SIGIL knew all the time traveling shenanigans weren't working and–"

"Hold on, hold on." Leyla interrupted. "I have to ask. You have been using some weird words, and your accent is off, and everything is weird, where are you from?"

"Tennessee. Nashville."

"And when were you born?"

"1955."

"What?!" Leyla yelled.

"What? What's wrong with that?"

"You're *old*!"

"Yeah…75."

"You look 30!"

"I was 35 when we found SIGIL and brought it down here. All the nanomachines it helped us make—"

"Oh, right, Mari told me about this. Nanomachines slow aging. Made some of you look younger. Holy shit! Fountain of youth! Okay, back to Xenobots."

"Your time travel trips weren't changing anything, and I'm guessing SIGIL was adhering to its programming directive: protect SubCity, basically, and it made the Xenobots to change the *current* world instead."

"How was it going to do that?" Leyla asked.

"It was going to use you as the catalyst."

"What?"

"Yeah. Blackhawk and I have been trying to recreate you for—" He stopped, abruptly.

"Recreate me for what?" Leyla turned to him. That commanding tone was back.

"Shit." Ramsay sighed. He tried to divert from his original point. "Whatever we tried, it wasn't working. Now that you're here, we can get the Thumper, close this time loop, and work on fixing the world like SIGIL wanted. It's all Blackhawk wants. That's also all I want. And arms."

"No arms yet."

"Yeah, thought so. Worth a try."

Leyla knew Ramsay was holding back. Mari had already told her The Pantheon was Blackhawk's attempted recreation of Athon. But she hadn't known the Xenobots were to be used on her own body as the "catalyst", whatever that means. She let it go for now, but felt a slight distrust in SIGIL itself. *When was SIGIL going to tell me about all this?* She thought. *But, we did get attacked abruptly, and then it threw me through a portal and...*

Leyla remembered SIGIL's final actions before. Grabbing her and tossing her into a portal and into the *fucking night sky*, where she'd fallen to her *death*. Was it accidental or not? SIGIL had always been so accurate. Seven years were unaccounted for. She pieced it together. SIGIL threw her through the portal, she went into the sky above SubCity, and fell hard into the abandoned subway tunnel, ten years ago. Hell, it could have been more than ten years. Time travel and all…

SIGIL had effectively killed its own creation. Accident or not, Leyla wanted answers. She was essentially dead for seven years, when somehow she woke back up, rebooted as Leyla, and made her way to the homeless village. That's where she met Del.

If she'd only known who she gave that warm hug to. A murderer. A mass murderer, Leyla thought. She felt that tingle in the deep tissue of her brain again.

Is it murder? Or is it security? The world needed to be rid of those people. Athon said. Leyla rolled her eyes.

"Still murder." She said to her own brain.

"Hmm?" Ramsay asked.

"Oh! Nothing. Just talking to myself. Literally."

Leyla and the once again armless Ramsay made their way to the freight elevator at the end of the city, bound for the tunnel above.

CHAPTER SEVENTEEN

Time Keeps On Thumping

Wells was resting in a booth at Peyton's, waiting for a glimpse of Greene, and was tapping the comlink in his ear, frustrated. It had beeped a few times earlier, but his hubris had gotten the best of him. He had no idea how to work the blasted thing. He knew it had to be Leyla; no one else would be calling him there. Hell, the cell phone in his jacket hadn't buzzed since he'd arrived in SubCity. And just as he thought about it…

Wells's cell phone rang. He jumped. That was unexpected. He had to be at least a thousand feet underground; a cell signal shouldn't have been able to travel there. It alerted everyone in the immediate vicinity inside Peyton's Diner. The couple sitting in the booth across from him slowly looked his way. One had a complete silicon face with neon lights under it, illuminating his skull and facial muscles. Creepy.

"Is that the Power Rangers communicator tone?" The silicon faced man asked; his face moved like a normal person's, but the translucent skin was off putting.

Wells froze. His phone beeped in that exact melody. Beep-beep-budup-BEEP-beep.

"Yeah…" he replied.

"Holy shit dude! Fuckin' love that show! That's my childhood, man! Who's your favorite character?"

Wells allowed his phone to beep even more, afraid to answer and alert everyone that he had a cell phone in a place where that would be totally taboo. "Uh, Billy. Blue Ranger."

"Oh wow, man, the original run! Old school! Most folks would say Tommy. RIP JDF. Mine is actually Alpha Five though, AYE YIYIYIYAE!" Silicon Face screamed in Wells's direction, impersonating the famous oddball droid.

Wells gave the man a thumbs up, and fumbled inside his jacket to hopefully squeeze a button on the side of his phone to shut it up. It worked. Now it was just a buzzing on the side of his chest.

He discreetly pulled the phone from his jacket pocket and checked to see who was calling. It was Harrison. Harrison never called him. What the fuck could she want at—he checked the time displayed on his phone screen. 10PM?

Wells reeled at the realization that it was 10 at night. He'd slept a long ass time. No wonder he hadn't seen Greene walk into the damn diner. It was late as hell. Maybe it was time to leave and find a spot to call Harrison back. It was late, and she never called him, and he'd been off grid for at least a day at this point. Must be important. The apartment he'd just gotten set up with may suffice.

***

Leyla and Ramsay approached the gigantic freight elevator. It had only been a couple nights since Leyla arrived in the city on this immense piece of machinery, but Ramsay hadn't been on it in years.

"So, this is how you got down here, huh?" He said, twirling his limbless torso back and forth like a bored child.

"Why are you doing that?" She replied.

"Feels weird without arms. It's a nervous thing. I twirl."

Leyla scowled. "Stop it."

"Ok." Ramsay did as she asked. As they waited for the elevator to descend, Ramsay couldn't take the uncomfortable silence, and began to whistle to the tune of *She'll Be Comin' Round The Mountain.*

Leyla slowly looked over to him, annoyed. "Are you serious? Go back to twirling. What are you? Five?"

Ramsay stopped whistling and began twirling again. "I'm 75."

***

Wells entered his apartment and checked his phone. No signal. Too far down underground. He eyed the window on the opposite end and moved to it, checking the signal. One bar. Good enough. He redialed Harrison's number.

"Wells! Motherfucker!" Harrison's snarly voice came through the phone's earpiece. "Where the fuck are you?! The precinct is a fucking mess right now!"

"What? What's going on?"

"That cute little psychopath you sent to the mental ward escaped couple nights ago and you, you fuckin' asshole, you're missing!"

"Oh! Shit I didn't even think about that…" Wells scratched his head, careful to not move from the window.

"I can barely hear you, where are you? Signal is actual shit." Harrison said.

"I'm uh, on a leave of absence."

"My ass you are. Chief is looking for you. You wanna keep your job, you better show up quick. Now what's going on, Donnie?"

Wells weighed his options. Lie, or tell Harrison the truth and hope she doesn't call him crazy.

"Harrison, we've known each other for how long now?"

There was a pause on the other end of the call.

"You're about to tell me some stupid shit, ain't you?" Harrison asked. She'd known Wells long enough to have a hint of what's coming, at least.

"Yep."

"Send it."

"Greene, I found him."

"What!?" Harrison's voice came through in a screeching hiss that distorted the phone speaker. Wells pulled his head away in response.

"Yeah, he's here. And that's not the craziest part. Sure you wanna hear this? Won't call me a whack job?"

"Wells, just spill the fuckin' beans."

"There's an entire city hidden under Cincinnati, like a giant cavern with tall buildings, and uh, flying cars and robots…yeah you're thinking I'm crazy."

"Yeah a little bit."

"Either way, it's a long story, we shouldn't be talking on here. I can't leave here, I won't be able to get back to Greene. Least I don't think I can."

"So how'd that go? Seeing him after this long?"

"He doesn't remember who I am."

"What? How?"

"Again, long story. Look, come to think of it, I might have a way in and out of here. I'll call when I'm back up top. But *do not* bring this up to the Chief, the guy that's in charge down here got him in his pocket. That's why I got busted down when I pushed for Greene."

"Shit, okay, yeah. I can buy you maybe a day. Any more and he's gonna fire your ass. You better show up."

"I will. See ya."

Wells closed the call. Well that was another great problem to deal with. A job wasn't as important as getting his fiancé back, but Wells knew if he lost a link to all the databases and connections he had at the precinct, it could be even harder to get Greene out of SubCity safely. He'd need all the help he could get. He had to find Leyla. She could get in and out of the wall. She was the ticket he needed.

***

The freight elevator came to a halt at the top of the massive shaft with a resonating *thoom*. Ramsay stepped off first and turned back to Leyla.

"So where to?" He asked.

"Been a while, but I think I remember the spot."

She approached the back end of the re-force wall a couple steps past the elevator. That same static tingle from before touched her skin and her hair pulled toward it.

"Why's it feel so funny?" She asked.

"The wall? Well it's a sort of electromagnetic holographic interface, coupled with a little of SIGIL's anti-gravity tech. Creates a microscopic grid of electrons. That's the static you're feeling. The electrons stay put unless they're met with a positron signal. That's how you got in here. That signal was encoded to your uh, synthetic DNA, by SIGIL. At least that's my guess."

Leyla looked at Ramsay, her brow scrunched. "Thank you for the overly detailed explanation."

"You asked." Ramsay shrugged his torn off limbs.

She stepped through the wall. The soft crackling of static electricity emanated from the surface as her skin moved through. Ramsay followed just behind.

"I woke up a little ways in from here." She said, blinking her eyes to adjust to the darkness. Ramsay, forgetting he had no arms yet again, tried to pull his personal scanner from his belt.

"Hey, uh, my scanner. On my belt. It's got a light." He stopped and turned his hip to show Leyla the device. She pulled it from the belt.

"Hold it up to my face."

She positioned the screen in front of Ramsay's face and it powered on, only slightly illuminating the surrounding area. Good enough.

They carefully stepped through the tunnel. It was still very dark, and it didn't matter to Leyla that she'd just found out she was an unstoppable killing machine—dark tunnels are scary.

"I know seven different martial arts, I've killed hundreds of people, I'm a time traveler, I have basically walked on a black hole a few dozen times, and I am still piss scared of the dark. What the fuck?"

"It's the Leyla construct." Ramsay laughed. "Leyla is scared of the dark in the show."

"This is bullshit." Leyla huffed.

"Kind of endearing, actually."

Leyla shot him a glare. He flinched, which made her crack a smile.

"I'm not going to hurt you, you dork." She said, turning back to walk.

Ramsay took immediate offense to that remark, shaking his torso and shoulders in defiance. "You tore my arms off and kicked me in the head!" he screeched, sending echoes through the darkness.

"Ok, I am sorry. To be fair, you tried to punch me. You shouldn't hit women. It's bad for you. And I knee'd you in the head, not kicked."

"That's worse! And, as I have stated before, Athon is terrifying."

Leyla stopped walking. "This is it."

Situated near a split in the tunnel, one of which was the way back out to Cincinnati, she knelt down and brought the glowing screen close to the dirt. There was some rubble and very old, nearly petrified wood scattered around the area. A remembrance flashed across her mind.

She was falling, in the dead of night, having just exited the portal SIGIL tossed her through. She remembered hitting solid ground, but it gave way and she fell just a bit more and was covered by debris. She'd impacted the top of the tunnel with such a force that she broke through and slammed into the ground inside. The last thing she remembered before going dark was the crackling and splintering of wood and concrete crashing down on top of her, burying her underneath. The hole she created at the top must have been filled over later, after the elements had been afforded the time needed to smooth over the debris hiding her body with dirt and other muck.

How long was I here? She wondered. *Long enough for my clothing to rot away. How long does that take?"*

Leyla squatted down and started pulling away the age old concrete and shattered wood beams. It wasn't long before she felt a sort of magnetic pull, ever so slightly, touch her fingers. She held her hand still, sensing the force. The Thumper.

She dug into the ground with feverish intent. This wasn't just a device composed of an antimatter field generator. It wasn't just something that allowed her to manipulate time and space at a whim and travel through wormholes. The Thumper was the key to finally seeing Del again.

Her fingers dug into the dirt and touched something that felt like a large pebble. It pulsed, like a heartbeat, at the touch of her skin.

She wrapped her thumb and index fingers around it and pulled it from the dirt, and held it up to the light from Ramsay's scanner screen. Dust fell away from the device, pinched between her fingers, and it still put off a faint orange glow as it pulsed, still tied to the generator far below ground, and the wrist band had long since rotted away. The Thumper was hers once again.

She slowly stood, and looked at Ramsay, with a speckle of hopeful excitement back in her eye.

"Let's go get Del."

CHAPTER EIGHTEEN

The SIGIL

Wells had checked Leyla's apartment, but got no answer. He was making his way back down the street, fumbling with his comlink. He pulled the earpiece near his mouth.

"Call Leyla." He enunciated into the device, hoping it would work. He just happened to be passing Bluetooth's, and Llana was outside closing up shop. She'd been working overtime thanks to the GravGen grid going down. She overheard Wells acting like an idiot with his comlink.

"Oh fuckin' *Hel*, is that goddamn thing acting up?" She snarled. Her pet raven hobbled out from behind her and flapped up to a blue neon sign post and cooed at Wells.

"No, I just, uh, I'm old fashioned I guess. Trying to call a friend."

"Well first you have to have it in your ear. Now, I remember you. You said this was a fancy phone, and you'd figure it out. So how'd that go?"

"Okay, I admit defeat. I need help."

"Who are you trying to call?"

"My friend, Leyla."

Bluetooth put her hand out and flicked her fingers, motioning for Wells to give her the comlink.

"Yeah, signal booster is on." She said, bringing the comlink close to her eye. She pulled Wells closer by the arm and put the device in his ear, snug and tight. "Now try."

Wells held his finger up to his ear like a secret agent trying to send a message. Llana batted his hand away.

"Are you serious? Finger on the ear?" Llana laughed. She reached over and tapped the small protrusion jutting from the earpiece, and a holographic keyboard display came up in front of Wells's eye. Llana typed L-E-Y for him, and Leyla's name populated under a line, which she pressed.

Several beeps sounded in Wells's ear. "I don't think it's working."

"Or your friend doesn't wanna talk to you. Goodnight!" Llana snapped her finger, and the raven jumped from the neon sign and landed on her shoulder as she walked away. Wells let the comlink ring over and over. Finally, the signal changed to some light static and a faint whirring sound.

"Wells? Guess you figured the comlink out." Leyla said on the other end.

"Yeah, sure I did…"

"Got something to show you."

Wells heard Ramsay mutter something. It sounded like he was reminding Leyla that Wells is a cop.

"What's that? Did he say something?"

"We're coming out of the big elevator now. Meet us there."

The line went dead. Leyla had ended the call. Wells hurried off in the direction of the freight elevator.

***

The freight doors pulled apart on street level and Leyla pushed Ramsay out. Wells happened to see them walk out, and rushed to them, noticing Ramsay's now destroyed arms.

"Did you get in a fight with a shark? What the fuck is this?" He gestured at Ramsay.

Ramsay turned to Leyla, with an "explain this" expression.

"I tore his arms off." Leyla explained, bluntly.

Wells was taken aback. Innocent little bouncy Leyla ripping off the cybernetic arms that had almost bashed his brains in was certainly the last option on the list of "What Ate Ramsay's Arms?"

"Wh…what?" He stammered.

"She's Athon." Ramsay said, expecting Wells to react in a scared stupor, same as he had. Instead, Wells laughed.

"The super assassin android that time travels? No. What really happened?" Wells said, not believing the ridiculous statement made by Ramsay.

Leyla walked by him and spoke in a very matter-of-factly tone.

"Follow me."

She had a different look about her. He noticed the difference in her gait, the way she carried herself. Her voice even had a slightly different intonation. Something was different. She walked off, and Ramsay followed. He looked to Wells.

"We're going to close a time loop. Fun stuff." He said, half sarcastically and half genuinely excited.

Wells's jaw hung open, on the cusp of asking what was happening. Instead, he stepped off to follow Leyla as she'd told him to.

The trio once again made headway to the tunnel leading to The Fridge. Leyla let the Thumper slip from her palm and into her fingers. The pulse was getting stronger.

"What's that?" Wells pointed at the orange glowing disc in her hand.

"Thumper." Leyla answered—she sounded detached, or at least, unbothered by Wells. In fact, she'd barely batted an eye at anything the entire walk to The Fridge, and they'd made it a good half mile across SubCity. She was dead set on getting Del back.

***

Leyla elbowed the chain link gate open toward The Fridge, never changing stride. She hadn't used much strength, but it slammed into the side of the wall and a shaky steel rattle echoed down the tunnel. The gate ricocheted back and smacked Ramsay in the face, bloodying his lip. He turned to Wells, as if he'd been provided proof that Leyla was a dangerous animal. He hadn't said a word the entire walk either.

The air inside The Fridge was considerably warmer now. SIGIL's fusion reactor core was encased in many feet of concrete and high temperature materials, situated just above the quantum computer itself, and even so insulated, it still radiated enough heat to thaw the room in the hour Leyla and Ramsay had been gone.

The concrete floor was damp and full of small puddles. The sound of water draining into grates resounded throughout the room, coupled with audible drips from every piece of elevated machinery, mainly SIGIL's thawing data transfer tubes and body.

"Am I crazy, or was this room frozen earlier?" Wells asked.

"THE FUSION REACTOR HAS THAWED THE ROOM. IF NOT FOR THE AMMONIA BASED FREEZER GENERATORS, THIS ROOM WOULD NOT BE HABITABLE."

Wells stopped walking, staring up at the huge machine. He couldn't find the words to speak—that damn frozen computer that tried to destroy the world had thawed and was *speaking*. "The big computer *talks* now? What else did you guys change while I was asleep?"

Ramsay laughed. "SIGIL, meet Wells. Wells, meet SIGIL."

Wells waved at the machine, saying hello.

"HELLO."

Leyla stopped at a workbench and opened a drawer. "I need a new band for the Thumper. Where are the extras?"

"What's a Thumper?" Wells asked.

"THE THUMPER IS A WRIST MOUNTED TETHER TO THE GENERATOR, ALLOWING TRAVEL THROUGH GRAVITATIONAL TIME AND SPACE—"

"Without a quantum free fall, yeah yeah, wrist band!" Leyla interrupted SIGIL, demanding an answer.

SIGIL's immense, pneumatic arm finally rippled to life, snaking toward a different workbench area. It pulled a drawer open and selected a replacement band, and moved it over to Leyla. She took the band and started reattaching it to the Thumper.

"When you threw me through that last portal…" she spoke to SIGIL. "Were you protecting me, or Blackhawk?"

"BOTH."

"Good to hear, because I died. Thanks. I laid in a dark tunnel for at least seven years. Just dead."

"INCORRECT."

Wells tried to interrupt the conversation. "Wait, what?! Dead? What do you mean dead?"

"I…DID NOT CALCULATE A LOOP. I SIMPLY SENT YOU BACK TO SAFETY." SIGIL's tone, if it could have one, indicated it may be lying—withholding information.

"Safety!?" Leyla jerked around, glaring at SIGIL with blazing anger. "I died, you fucking pile of tin cans! Dead!"

"YOU SUSTAINED CATASTROPHIC DAMAGE, YES, BUT YOUR ANTIMATTER CELLS RECONSTRUCTED THE TISSUES OVER A PERIOD OF TIME, AS I PREDICTED."

"Shut the fuck up! FUCK YOU!"

Wells and Ramsay dared not speak up. They both hung back, allowing Leyla to process her anger at her creator. This was a spat for basic humans to stay out of. Leyla continued yelling and repairing the Thumper.

"I had to lay in a pile of shit, dead, for almost ten years! And wake up not knowing who the fuck I was, where I was, what to do, NOTHING! Leyla screamed, a shrill, guttural cry on the cusp of tears.

"All so you can protect some fucking stupid cult leader cowboy wannabe!? I should fucking cut you down off your fucking perch! Fucking scrap heap."

"*BLACKHAWK MUST BE PROTECTED.*"

"Oh FUCK YOU and your *programming*. You're pathetic. You can't make your own fucking decisions. You're useless."

She was making the comments in SIGIL's direction, but she was more so speaking to herself. She feared that since she was an android, she may be incapable of her own free will. The only reason she'd had a modicum of humanity was a faux personality construct of a goddamn TV show character, that Del had happened to like hanging out with. Del had been the best friend, no—the mentor—of a lie. Leyla had been a ticking time bomb of death and destruction wrapped in a thin smile the entire time. It scared the shit out of her to see what Del would do when she found out the truth. And it wouldn't be long now.

SIGIL said nothing. It was allowing Leyla to process things as well. Ramsay had a thought, and walked over to Leyla, risking another beating.

"Hey…" he said. She turned to him, tears in her eyes. "When you reactivate that generator, when the portal opens, it's going to send an energy signal across our grid. It's how we found you ten years ago."

Leyla finished attaching the band to the Thumper and wrapped it around her wrist. "What's your point?"

"Blackhawk's going to know."

Leyla shot Ramsay a cold stare. "And I'll kill him when he comes down here."

"*I WILL NOT ALLOW THAT.*" SIGIL reminded her, insinuating it was not against throwing her through another portal again.

Leyla boiled over with rage. She pushed Ramsay aside, slamming him to the ground. She held out her palm, wide open, and a black bar magnetically sprang into her hand from within the workbench.

A blade formed from the bar within a split second, seemingly particle by particle, and the sharp edge instantly heated to a bright orange. Ramsay tried to scoot away from the intensely heated sword, but could barely move without his arms. Luckily, Leyla wasn't after him.

She bounded toward SIGIL's snake arm, and jumped into the air as it drew back. It knew what she was trying to do. But it was too slow,

She brought the blade up and then down like a flash of lightning, severing the pneumatic appendage close to its foundation on the side of SIGIL's armored body. Sparks showered the floor below. Wells had to duck and scoot away to avoid being peppered by the hot shards. A milky, oily substance sprayed all over, spurting from the severed arm. It dropped to the concrete with an echoing thud at the same time Leyla landed with almost no sound.

She stood straight. Her heated katana sizzled, coated in the arm's oil residue, and caught fire. She didn't flinch. She stared SIGIL down.

Ramsay was trying to scoot behind the workbench to protect himself. He figured he was assuredly next to meet that flaming blade. Wells, also now flat on his ass, was backing away at the sight of Leyla wielding a pillar of fire.

Leyla's eyes had glazed over not just with rage, but with doubt and grief. She wasn't who she thought she was. She was a killer. She felt Athon taking over as each minute passed. And it terrified her. But that snake-like arm that had grabbed her and thrown her through the wormhole generator years earlier was cut now.

"You are not my master. Not anymore."

Leyla wasn't sure if that statement was hers, or Athon's. SIGIL had no retort. It remained silent.

Ramsay nervously spoke up.

"You said you wanted to get Del and live here. If that's what you want to do, I have to find a way to convince Blackhawk the generator spiked a signal for nothing. He won't come looking for you. You'll have your friend, you'll live here, all hunky dory, happily ever after."

Leyla walked toward Ramsay, her blade still coated in fire.

"Just, maybe don't open with a flaming sword and Del won't care about your past?" He said, kicking his legs, attempting to get to his feet.

Leyla stopped one pace away from Ramsay. He could see that primal, wolvish hunger in her eyes; The bloodthirst. His heart pounded.

"Go." Leyla growled.

Stunned that she agreed, he circled around her and her flaming sword, never breaking eye contact aside from glancing at her weapon. She was a veritable angel of death and terror.

"Yeah, I'll take care of it, no worries. Just, only once? Okay? Close this loop and call it a day. You know, for the safety of the solar system?"

Wells stepped in front of him, blocking his hasty exit. "I'm assuming you're not stupid enough to betray her?"

Ramsay nodded in agreement. "Look, all Blackhawk needs is her DNA signature to activate the Xenobots. Once that happens, this way of life we have down here comes to an end. And I quite like it down here." Ramsay looked back to Athon. "I also like not being cut in half by android super ninjas."

Wells jerked his head toward the exit, signaling to Ramsay that he was free to go, who ran out of the chamber and into the tunnel.

Wells slapped his pants, brushing dirt and excess water off. "Not too sure that's a good idea. Don't trust that guy."

Leyla's katana was finally burning out. "If he crosses me, he's dead. And he knows it."

"So, you think this computer's gonna help you out now that you chopped its arm off?" Wells was almost as scared as Ramsay had been, but he figured Leyla didn't have a bone to pick with him.

"*ATHON'S ANGER WITH ME IS JUSTIFIED. WE MUST CLOSE THE LOOP.*"

"Okay then! Don't know what that means but it sounds good." Wells said.

"Time loop. Del isn't here yet."

"Yet? What's that mean?"

"It means I'm the one that abducted her. I have to go get her and close the time loop."

"Oh…ok, cool. Wibbly wobbly timey wimey." Wells remarked. He was a Dr. Who fan, and couldn't resist the reference. "What do you need me to do?"

"Just stand there and look pretty." Leyla winked. That bloodthirsty look in her eyes had waned.

Below SIGIL and to its left, a large section of the floor began to rise. It was a good ten to fifteen feet in length, and a few feet wide. As it rose, Wells could see shelves lined at every square centimeter with firearms of all sorts. Pistols, rifles—both carbine and sniper—and even some very futuristic ones he'd never seen before. Three more black bars like the one that had sprouted a blade in Leyla's hand were also mounted on a shelf.

Once the armory had fully raised, it clanged to a stop. With another pressurized click, a drawer extended from the bottom, revealing a black, leather-like outfit with carbon fiber and graphene weave armor segments on the knees, thighs, elbows and chest. Athon's armor—a backup set. The original had been lost to the elements.

Leyla pulled her shirt off. Wells turned away, giving her some privacy, though she didn't care. She pulled her jeans and shoes off, and retrieved the armor from the drawer.

Wells was looking the other way when Leyla called to him.

"Hey, Wells?"

"Uh huh?" He didn't turn around.

"I need some help."

Wells turned to see Leyla, still mostly nude, trying to pull the tight, leathery catsuit up to her hips. She was jumping and jerking it as much as she could. He laughed. Something about a murderous assassin getting dressed like every other club hopping 21 year old in Cincinnati was amusing.

Leyla wasn't exactly sure why she'd asked for help with getting dressed. *Athon can jump twenty feet in the air and I can't put on pants? What's up with that?* She thought.

She felt that trippy little tingle crawl over her mind, and Athon spoke up. *I have always had trouble with the suit. It is not the same as fighting.*

"Here…" Wells said, walking over to her. "I'll pull, you relax."

He positioned himself behind her and firmly grabbed the suit at both sides of her hips. "Alright one, two, three!" He jerked up and wiggled the suit over her hips and butt and she tried to let gravity pull her body down. It worked, the suit slipped up and snug to her body, just below her belly.

Wells retreated a few steps away, eyeing the large shelf of weapons as Leyla pulled the rest of the suit over her shoulders and zipped it up across her breast. One final magnetic buckle on her collar secured itself and clicked.

"So, you have enough here to take on an army."

"Yeah, been there, done that." Leyla said. Best to try to avoid that tho—" she was interrupted by her armored mask/head covering materializing over her face. She paused, then touched the magnetic buckle at the base of her collar. The mask retreated into it. "Forgot about that."

She took in a huge and deep breath of air, and stiffly made her way onto the platform where the arch gate resided, stopping right in front of it. It was time.

The capacitors on the arch began to glow brighter and more intense. A static buzzing followed, growing louder and louder but never deafening; it almost sounded muffled.

Wells backed up a good ten paces, almost to the wall. Ramsay had mentioned a singularity and something about it eating everything.

Wells figured he'd best keep his distance.

"EXIT LOOP, ZERO SEVEN HOURS, THIRTY ONE MINUTES, TWENTY ONE SECONDS. COORDINATES 39.10691° NORTH, 84.51619° WEST."

Leyla hopped up and down on the grated steel as the blue light from the arch painted her an azure sheen. She was breathing out heavily, like a weightlifter preparing to set a world record.

"You've done this dozens of times!" Wells yelled from across the room. "Why are you so nervous?"

"Well, Leyla has never done this! It feels new!"

"You'll be fine! Just get through, grab Del, and don't touch anything else! I guess? I don't know. I'm going off Doc Brown's advice from Back to the Future!"

"OPENING WORMHOLE IN 3...2..."

Leyla's Thumper switched from orange to blue—and back to orange again—as a fiery, blue ringed portal erupted in front of her, spreading instantaneously from the center of the gate and to its capacitors. Leyla's hair blew back, but she stood fast, eyes wide and muscles tense with both fear and excitement. The puddles of water nearby were blown clear, and the droplets spattered all the surrounding area.

Leyla glanced over to 'big brother' Wells, seeking just a tad more assurance that it would be okay.

He gave her a fake grin filled with his own anxiety, and two thumbs up. She looked back, straight into the portal. Blue sparks of superheated energy leapt from the flaming rim and into the air around her like an army of quantum fireflies.

The other end of the portal opened, and there she was. That ugly, multi-stained corduroy overcoat, the collar of which had been torn on one side and hung over her back. Her short and curly black hair glistened in the sun, interrupted by the blue aura of the opening portal.

It was Del. Three days earlier. She seemed to be moving in ultra slow motion. Time and reality didn't work the same when viewed through an open wormhole. Leyla let her nerves set, heart pounding, as she stared at the entire reason she'd come on such an amazing journey. She was so excited her fingers were numb and her mouth was dry, and she choked back the excited tears welling in her eyes. She tapped the magnetic button on her collar, and the mask materialized over her face, reflecting the portal and Del back on the glossy visor.

Leyla jumped through the portal just as Del was ever so slowly reacting to it opening behind her. Blue sparks were showering her and blowing past into…

Oh shit! Leyla thought, noticing her past self—her own face—whipping around in terror, to see Athon dropping down from the portal. *That's what I looked like? Geez. What a weird face to make.*

Leyla landed on the soft grass with the grace of an athlete, and wrapped her arms around Del. One arm over her left shoulder, the other under her right armpit—a secure embrace. Leyla heard her past self yell out something at the sight of Athon. She didn't even remember yelling at the time.

But it didn't matter. She had Del. Right there in her arms, safe and sound. She pulled Del in tight, and looked over her shoulder to see her past self trip and fall onto the ground, all in slow motion.

Del began to scream as well. A justifiable reaction. It wasn't like she'd been warned this was going to happen..

Just get her through the portal. Don't change anything. Close the loop. Again, Leyla wasn't sure if that thought was hers or Athon's.

Leyla bent her knees and sprang off the ground as hard as she could, pulling Del with her, who was screaming and reaching out to Leyla's past self for help.

She must be so scared. Fuck, Del, I'm sorry!

She and Del fell backward through the portal and onto the metal grating with a hard clang. Leyla took the brunt of the fall, holding Del tight and allowing her to slam down onto her own body. She let go, and guided Del to the side.

Del was spewing brand new profanities that Leyla had never even heard before as the portal closed, and the Thumper flashed blue and back to orange once again.

"Whaddafuckin mother fuck who the fuck fuck you!" Del screamed as she clambered to her feet and shuffled backward from Leyla, who still had the mask over her face. "Stay the fuck back or I'll knock ya fuckin' teeth out ya fuckin' skinny little asshole! What the fuck goin' on!?"

Del turned to see Wells in the corner. He waved, almost stupefied.

"Bitch! Don't be wavin'! Get to fuckin' talkin'! Who the fuck is you?!" Del turned back to Leyla, still oblivious. "And you! You skinny little Catwoman wannabe motherfu—"

Leyla tapped the collar button, and her mask dematerialized into the collar, revealing her stunned face, wide, teary eyes and open mouth, showing those front top teeth that Del thought was so cute.

Del immediately stopped talking. She was so surprised that she got an immediate rush of goosebumps across her body as adrenaline surged through her body, and sped her heart up. She pointed at Leyla, and looked back to the portal and then back to Leyla.

"The fuck!? How you…what?!"

Leyla inched toward Del with a stunned expression. She'd never felt a payoff this great. She'd never worked so hard for something and then had such a grand reward. Her hands were shaking. She was at a loss for words.

"Leyla?! But you was, I ain't even…what the fu—"

Leyla lurched forward and snatched Del into the tightest hug she'd ever given her. She wrapped her arms around her friend even more, and nuzzled into her collar. She let out the breath she'd been holding since before she'd set foot through the portal, and it came out a sobbing mess.

"I missed you so fucking much." Leyla huffed, sniffling and convulsing.

Del was as confused as ever, but hugged Leyla back anyway. "But I ain't go nowhere, baby girl, and I got some *questions*." She looked around, seeing the arch gate she'd been pulled through. Wells in the corner. The big scary looking machine hanging from the wall. Leyla in an armored, black suit.

"I got you." Leyla whispered. "It's gonna be okay. I got you."

CHAPTER NINETEEN

The Best of Friends

Leyla pulled away from Del with a grin painted from ear to ear. She'd done it. Del was safe and sound. "Holy shit! I got you!"

"Okay, you got me, but *I* got questions." Del replied, still reciprocating the hug from Leyla.

"Yeah! Yeah, whatever you wanna know. Shoot." Leyla let her hands fall slowly from Del's shoulders and down her arms, still in a state of disbelief that the time jump worked, and nothing went wrong.

"One, who's he?" Del pointed to Wells.

"Sergeant Donnie Wells, District One police, nice to meet you." He waved, still across the room.

Del looked Wells up and down, squinting her eyes. She turned to Leyla and leaned in close. "He your boyfriend?"

"No, how about I start from the beginning? It's a long story. You hungry?"

"Girl, I'm starvin' but that ain't nuthin' new."

"Well, wait 'til you see what's down here.. You won't be hungry or cold or sick anymore. Ever."

"What you mean?"

"Well, um…" Leyla looked at Wells. She wasn't sure where to start. He stepped forward and took over, trying to be that big brother figure again.

"I'm sure that since you just got pulled through that portal that what I'm about to tell you isn't going to sound so crazy. So, here goes…"

***

Ramsay's chest felt like it could burst. He hadn't run like this since his days on the MIT track team. He'd basically sprinted across half the city and into several elevators and a tram to get to his destination. He couldn't fly an AV with no arms. He had to get there the old fashioned way.

He rounded an elevated corner of a platform and made a beeline to an immense, red steel double door that had originally been a hydraulic operated train repair garage gate. That area was what Blackhawk had converted to The Bullpen, an enormous platform atop the tallest structure in SubCity, essentially a large helipad that housed Blackhawk and The Pantheon.

As he neared the twenty foot high doors. A bio-scanner laser lit up and auto-scanned his eyes. Thick steel locks cracked open and hydraulics pulled the doors apart, opening a large garage filled with machinery. Ramsay stumbled in, breathing heavy, and entered an open area in the center.

It was a cleared circle, originally a rotating track platform for train cars, and it had five standing armor stations, each containing an empty set of exo-suit armor worn by each member of the Pantheon. Each was customized in some way.

Some were painted a unique color, others were more subtle with various attachments and weapons fitted to the frames.

Each station had a name plate: Eris, Rhea, Artemis, Nemesis, and Nyx.

Behind each station was an apartment that had been custom built for each of Blackhawk's girls. Just beyond the Pantheon armor stations was a large, fighter jet/combat chopper inspired AV, large enough to house its pilot as well as The Pantheon.

Past the massive AV, a network of supercomputers and switchboards and lab equipment lined the walls and floors that led to a final door. A screen on one switchboard was flashing, with text that read:

POSITRON GRAVITY SURGE - LOCATION - AI ANTECHAMBER.

The door at the end of the room was rather ornate and decorative; a classy wooden door with a polished brass handle. Ramsay strode up to the door and kicked it, hard enough to make a racket, but not break it. He kicked again.

"It's me! Open up, man! It's an emergency!"

The door swung open. Ramsay was in mid kick, and missed the door, stumbling forward. He had no arms to catch himself, but his old friend Blackhawk put out one stiff arm and caught him.

"What in the high hell happened to you?" Blackhawk asked, eyeing Ramsay's severed arms, missing jacket, and busted lip.

Ramsay struggled to catch his breath still, as five women also neared the door behind Blackhawk, curious as to what was going on. They were The Pantheon, and they were sworn to defend SubCity and strike down any threat that arose. Ramsay breathed heavily and stood straight, eyeing each of them and finally Blackhawk.

"So…um…"

***

A ship bot floated down the main stretch of SubCity. This one was painted differently than the blue and white ones that regularly delivered goods to homes. It was all red and had white text stamped on it that read "C2G", and two of its appendages were extended and carrying a pizza box under its body as well as a drink tray with two Sprites and a Coke. It was headed to The Fridge.

It flew over the chain link gate, even though it was cracked open; Ramsay hadn't bothered trying to close it during his escape from Athon. Down the tunnel the bot flew.

"Pizza!" Leyla yelled, as she noticed the bot floating into the room.

"Shit, that was fast!" Del stood up from leaning on a workbench. Leyla and Wells had told her everything they knew so far about the city.

Wells had talked SIGIL into placing an order remotely with Carol's To Go service. There was likely more pizza in the city but Carol always seemed to be the one that popped up when they were hungry, and that's the pizza they knew best there.

"Greetings, Leyla! Greetings Wells! Greetings [IDENTITY UNKNOWN]!"

"Well damn, you ain't gotta put my business out there like that." Del scoffed, also realizing this was one of the many androids Leyla had told her about. "So this is one of 'em? The robots?"

"Yeah! They're so damn cute too." Leyla took the pizza box and immediately opened it. "Pizza box opening time!" She pulled a slice out and gave it to Del as the bot turned to leave. Wells took the drink tray from the bot as it passed, and handed Leyla and Del the Sprites. He opened his Coke for a drink.

"Have a nice day!" The bot said.

Del watched the bot leave as she took off a huge chunk of the pepperoni pizza. "You ain't gotta pay for it? For real?" She asked Leyla, with a mouth full of hot cheese.

"Not a penny! It's great. You're gonna love it here, Del! And my apartment has this android, he's named Texas Chainsaw Massacre, and he's a *chef*!"

"You got a robot named Texas Chainsaw Massacre?" Del said, accenting the ridiculousness of the name.

"That's what I said!" Wells replied. "That's a crazy name for an android!"

"Well he likes it! He said it was a lovely name! Anyway, hey!" Leyla perked up toward Del. "Won't be able to til tomorrow, but, gonna have to talk to Cross-Eyes or Ramsay or something about helping your cancer."

"Yeah…" Del had almost finished her first slice of pizza. "Now, how's that work? Cuz I'd rather die than go through chemo again. Uh uh. No."

"Hey! Don't say that. You're going to be fine. Down here they have nanomajiggers. Little, super tiny robots. They keep everyone healthy, *and* they give you a longer life. It even makes some people look younger."

"What the Hell? Get outta here that shit ain't real."

"A little flying robot just delivered us pizza and Leyla pulled you through a portal in time and space." Wells said. "I don't think cancer curing nanobots is off the table here."

Del held her pizza crust out to Leyla, and she took it and put it back in the pizza box that was now sitting on a workbench. Del hated pizza crust.

"Yeah. You right." Del coughed a bit. Over the last few weeks she'd learned that if she breathed a certain way she could avoid coughing as much. It hurt when she went into coughing fits, and she tried to avoid them.

Wells heard the fluttering of bird wings above. Looking up, he noticed a fairly large brown bird settling onto a beam. Maybe a hawk. It stayed silent. Just a bird. Nothing odd.

"Oh!" Leyla yelped. Del hopped back at Leyla's sudden excitement. "It's kinda late but we should go to the light garden! They have really cool plants! I haven't been yet but I saw it walking around a couple times."

"Light garden? Buncha lights and plants? Girl you got me down here in a city talkin' bout robots and flyin' cars and shit, and you wanna show me some damn plants? I wanna see this sci-fi shit, not no plants."

"Okay but the light garden is pretty sweet…" Leyla explained, feeling Athon tingle its way back into her thoughts.

Shouldn't parade her around the city. Keep a low profile for a while. You cannot trust—

"Oh shut up, it's fine." Leyla told herself. Del looked at her in confusion. Leyla had neglected to mention that she was the fabled Athon, Immortal Angel of Death, assassin, murderous android, terrifying monster and menace to humanity. "Oh…" She noticed Del looking at her. "Just, talking to myself."

Wells looked up at SIGIL. It had also stayed silent the entire time. SIGIL likely knew it needed to keep Leyla's true identity a secret from Del, so it refrained from speaking entirely, and had let Wells and Leyla explain that it was simply a very smart computer.

Both SIGIL and Wells knew this secret could not stay buried for long. But, Leyla deserved her happiness for now.

As Leyla and Del walked out, Wells followed behind, looking up at that big brown bird again. It was staring at them as they left. He thought he could make out a faint glow of blue from its eyes.

Outside, Del's eyes were assaulted with the sea of lights and neon sprawled across the immense cavern, and the floating blue GravGen grid that looked like celestial bodies guarding the city. Leyla had also neglected to explain the grid keeping Cincinnati from burying SubCity. Best not to scare Del away before she'd seen what the place had to offer.

Del had no words. An AV glided overhead with a satisfying, low whir, painting her and Wells and Leyla with its soft, electric blue light underneath. The city had been overcome with a dense, cool fog at this point; another simulated weather effect that made some of the buildings look as if they were floating on top of clouds, and it felt as soothing to the skin as a dip in a pool on a hot Summer day. Leyla wasn't going to have to do much convincing to get Del to live here with her.

Leyla stopped at a vending machine, pulled out her temporary SD chip, and scanned it. It beeped negatively.

"What? Seriously? Oh *shit* Ramsay said it was temporary. UGH!"

"What is that? A credit card? You said everything is free, and you usin' a credit card. Girl, I knew you was lyin'."

"No, it's a temporary SD it's how you sort of pay for things here but it's not money, it's for inventory purposes. And mine just went dead. Guess I'll have to take this stupid pill." Leyla reached into a pocket and retrieved the large permanent SD pill she'd been procrastinating swallowing. She looked to Del. "You got any more of that Sprite?"

Del gave her the bottle, still a third full, and Leyla placed the pill in her mouth and gulped down as much soda in one go as she could. The pill went down surprisingly smoothly. It would still take about an hour, Cross-Eyes had said. So, Leyla wouldn't be able to "buy" anything for Del yet.

"Whatever, it's late here anyway."

"Late?" Del asked. "It's just after sunrise, crazy."

"No, oh! Right. Yeah…That portal wasn't just like, a portal to another place."

"Leyla, what did yo skinny ass do now?"

"The big machine we came through is a time machine, so…"

"What?! Hell naw quit playin'!"

"Yeah, you're now like three days in the future, and it's…Wells, what time is it?"

Wells checked his watch. "Almost 1AM."

Del didn't give a damn. "Holy shit! I'm motherfuckin' Doc Brown! Great Scott, motherfuckers! You know I love me some good sci-fi shit! I'm in the future!?"

Leyla smiled. "Yeah a few days. It's felt like a year since I got down here, looking for you."

Wells surveyed the city. Most of it had been closed up for the night. "You ladies may as well head home and relax. Not much we can do at the moment."

"Relax?! Shit, you relax. I just became a damn time traveler. Ain't no relaxin'. I'm boutta be braggin' to ol' Korean Jesus in a minute. Bitch, look at me! I got a time machine! What you got? A broke ass pair o' headphones!" Del laughed—that laugh that Korean Jesus hated. "Shut up Deli! Loud ass laugh!" She mocked him, which made her laugh more.

Leyla had missed that laugh so much.

"Okay, well you can meet Texas Chainsaw Massacre, then. See the city tomorrow."

The three walked a little more into SubCity until Wells split from the group and went back to his apartment across from Peyton's. Leyla saw an AV parked and ready for use. She smacked Del's arm in excitement, and pointed at the AV.

"Flying car!"

Del jumped out of excitement. "Can we use it!?"

Leyla squealed and tried her expired card. Another negative beep. "Wells!" She yelled, hoping he'd hear. He'd just left. He popped his head back out the door of his apartment building.

"What?! What happened?"

"Can you rent this for us?"

Wells hung his head down, relieved it wasn't anything serious. "Yes. You know, you don't have to give me puppy dog eyes? Just ask."

"She is good at them damn puppy dog eyes tho." Del said.

Wells scanned his SD and received a positive sounding beep, waved at Leyla, and retreated back into his apartment building.

Leyla opened the passenger door for Del and motioned for her to get in, acting like a fancy chauffeur. Del bowed and gave her a mimed tip, and took a seat inside, gawking at the ultra luxurious interior. Leyla hopped into the cockpit and pulled the black lever to activate flight mode.

"Oop! Oh shit!" Del yelped as the AV lurched up a bit and started floating.

"Prepare for takeoff!" Leyla was grinning as wide as possible.

Del mimed putting on shades and deepened her voice. "Back to the mother fuckin' future!"

"Is that the movie you keep talking about?" Leyla asked.

"Back to the Future! Best damn movie ever made!"

"Oh! We can watch it when we get home. First I want to show you something." She pushed the yoke up to lift off, and flew the AV high. She noticed a large black bird watching them leave, sitting on a lamp post. She didn't think much of it, could just be that big raven that Llana kept.

She took the AV high into the underground sky, close to the GravGens that dotted the ceiling, and turned toward the ventilators. She wanted to show Del the best view of the city before they went home.

"You know what we never talked about? For three years?" Del said.

"What?"

"What we really like. Like, take away the fact that we was homeless. Think if we was both workin' and had a house and shit. I used to. I had hobbies."

"Well I…" Leyla stopped herself. Her hobby had been traveling through a singularity warp generator and killing really bad dudes. And all the things that could be categorized as "normal" hobbies were all fabricated from a damn television show character. "What were your hobbies?" She asked Del.

"Well for one, I'm a sci-fi nerd. I *live* for this shit. Flying cars. Robots. Space. Cyberpunk shit! Man you don't even *know* how happy I am right now!" Del coughed, and held back a heaving fit by holding her breath and then grunting hard.

"Yeah, I know, SubCity is crazy. I knew you'd like it."

"Yeah, girl I used to read a book a week. Always had my eyes on a page. And movies and TV shows. Star Wars, Star Trek, Battlestar. Shit, if that apartment of yours has everything you say it does, we boutta be watchin' all day. Every day. I got a whole new world to show you."

Leyla laughed, and she and Del broke out into Aladdin's *Whole New World.*

***

Wells, back in his apartment, moved to his window again, trying to call Harrison. The call went through, but to voicemail. She was likely asleep.

"Hey, Harrison, the missing persons case, the homeless lady that was reported a couple days ago? Found her. She's safe. I don't think I'll be back out of here tonight but I'll work on it tomorrow. Just stall Chief for a bit. Thanks." He closed out the call on his cell, still wondering how he had even the slightest signal this far below ground.

He turned to his kitchen corner that had a small bar with a couple seats, and a holo-tab lying on it.

Might as well order some stuff to entertain myself for the time being, he thought.

***

Leyla landed the AV on the platform where the giant fans were, and disengaged flight control.

"Damn, girl!" Del looked at her, impressed. "You only been here two days and you already a damn pilot."

"Two? Thought it's been three days. Doesn't matter. Get out! Look at this view!"

Leyla and Del exited to a view of SubCity. Del had seen skylines before, but none so magnificent. She was a geek, even if she hadn't been able to read or watch TV in years and years, and this place was a dream come true for her. She felt goosebumps crawl over her back, soaking the view of a city full of technology that should not be possible. She sat on the edge of the platform, allowing her legs to hang just as Leyla had done before.

"Damn."

It was the only word she had for such beauty. Leyla took a seat beside her, staying silent but smiling, watching Del's reaction as if it was the sweetest candy she'd ever eaten.

The two sat in comfortable silence for a while, watching the fog dissipate and reveal more and more of the city over time.

There were still a few AVs floating about, and some citizens walked the streets and platforms. The tram was shuttling people back and forth.

Del reached over to Leyla and gripped her hand, interlocking their fingers. Neither said a word—and they didn't need to. Sometimes, silence is a welcome friend in good company. They both sat for quite a long time, watching the city, simply enjoying each other's presence.

On top of one of the ventilator fans, at least a hundred yards high above Leyla and Del, that big brown bird dropped and closed its wings, looking down at them. Its eyes glowed blue, and the iris on one twisted and zoomed like a lens. It was Blackhawk's android hawk, and it had both Deli and Leyla in its sights.

CHAPTER TWENTY

Until The End

Leyla approached her apartment door, Del following close behind.

"Damn, I can't believe this shit. My baby girl got an apartment. You all grown up now!" Del said, sarcastically.

"Oh you just wait. Oh and uh, Texas Chainsaw Massacre is probably gonna say some crazy shit, he's also a stand up comedian. And uh, he has a hole in his face."

"Okay…"

Leyla's door automatically opened this time. Her SD pill had dissolved and the nanobots inside had moved the implant to its correct position in her forearm. She opened the door, excited to show her home off to Del.

When Del entered, her mouth dropped immediately.

"You full o' shit baby girl! Hell nah!"

"You like it?"

"Bitch you killed me. We dead. Ain't no damn way we alive with a place as nice as this."

Texas Chainsaw Massacre sprouted from behind the prep island. It loved scaring the shit out of new guests. "Bwaaaaaaaaaaa!" It made its best impression of a ghost, scaring the piss out of Del. She jumped so hard she hit the wall beside her.

"Motherfuck!" She yelped.

"CHAINSAW MASSACRE!?" Leyla screamed at the bot, chastising it for scaring her friend.

"Hello, my deceased friends, this is Hell, it's a lot nicer than you expected, I know, but best believe, we know how to fuckin' party in this bitch!"

"That's your chef?" Del raised a finger to the bot.

"Hello, Texas Chainsaw Massacre, at ya fuckin' service! Version 3 Auto-chef with comedian protocol. I tell dirty jokes and I cook a mean fuckin' sous vide."

Del pushed off the wall and walked over to the android. "Dirty jokes?"

"Yeah you wanna hear—"

"Tell her the voodoo one!" Leyla yelled.

"Oh no no no, that's a daytime joke. It's dark as fuck outside. It's time to get even weirder."

"Okay, I think I'm gon' like ya little robot friend here." Del assured Leyla, then looked back at Chainsaw Massacre. "Aight. Gimme ya best dirty joke."

Texas Chainsaw Massacre leaned in, but he was interrupted by Del.

"What happened to your face? You get shot?"

"Yeah, a fuckin' cop did it. And I was unarmed."

"See?!" Del looked back to Leyla. "Motherfuckers'll shoot any damn thang!" She looked back to the bot. "Aight, dirty joke. Go."

Leyla took a seat on the barstool beside Del to listen as well.

"Okay ladies, so, you ever had anal?"

Leyla nodded no, whilst Del spoke up without missing a beat. "Yup."

Leyla jerked her stare to Del in surprise. Del looked at her and laughed. Not a playful chuckle that meant she was kidding, but a reinforcing one that meant Leyla's surprise shouldn't exist.

"Girl, don't gimme that look. I was young once. Why you think I like nasty jokes?" She looked to Chainsaw Massacre. "Ok, anal, yes."

"Well this joke is about that." The bot said.

It took a bit for Leyla to look away from Del, but when the image of her friend committing the act sprawled over her mind she closed her eyes and shook her head hard. *So weird. Ew,* she thought. *This feels like finding out your mom is a pornstar or something. Ew ew ew.*

"So one day, there's this guy and his wife, right?" Chainsaw Massacre continued. "Their marriage wasn't exactly failing, but you know, after a while, one starts to desire something new. Something different."

"Butt stuff." Del nodded.

"Exactly! Butt stuff! So that's what he asks his wife one day, like *Honey, I been thinkin'.*"

"Oh no, not the "I been thinking" talk, it's over for him." Del laughed.

"Guy is like, *can we try it in the back*? Just up and asks. Fuck testing the waters. Just asks. To his surprise, she says yes! He's like oh what!? Hell yeah baby let's go *tonight*!"

"Oh shit she went with it okay." Del said.

"Yep. But, she had one condition. She told her husband, don't touch me. I'm self conscious about this. Don't touch me. When we do it, put it in back there, and do what you gotta do, but go slow, and we are using all the lube, like all of it. I still gotta go to work tomorrow and I ain't gonna be walking all funny.

Guy's like *of course* baby. Let's do it tonight. He's all happy and shit. Got something new to try. So the time comes. It's night time and they head into the bedroom a little earlier than normal.

They set the mood. Turn down the lights. Dude lights some candles. Tells Alexa to play some sexy music. Alexa isn't good on dates by the way, acts like she knows *everything,* so annoying. And don't even get me started on the Queen of Goddamn Existence, Siri. I'm kidding they're both great, just not for me. Okay back to the story.

So they got it all down, and the guy shoos the dog, Bentley, off the bed. Been telling that fucker to stay off the bed for weeks cuz this is a damn Great Dane, he's too big, but his wife had been letting the dog up there and you gotta do what wifey says or you get put out on the street."

"I know that's right!" Del said.

"So, Bentley growls and jumps off and heads out the door, and dudes wife shuts all the lights off. All the way out. She's like look, if we're doing this, it's gotta be pitch black. I don't want you lookin' at my butthole. Guy agrees. And she tells him when we're ready, you just stick it in, don't be touchin' all over my booty and feelin' me up. This is an experiment. If I like it, you'll know. If I don't, I'm gonna have to leave the room to collect myself. This is some new territory.

Guys like sure baby, whatever you need. So all the lights are off, it's dark as fuck, and his wife says alright, I'm gonna go get undressed and I'll be right back.

So the guy is sitting there twiddling his thumbs, can't see shit, but he's gotta get ready too. Starts you know, strokin' the pipe, gettin' little guy in the mood you know?"

"Yeah uh huh." Del said.

"So you know, he can't see anything but he knows when he's hard and ready to go.

He had the lube beside him all ready to go, so he splats a big wallop of it on his hand and lathers his dick up like it's a race car axle. Finally hears his wife come in. My guy reaches over on the nightstand and turns up the music. It's some real sensual shit too. Barry Manilow or Eminem or somethin'."

"Eminem? The fuck?" Del laughed.

"Hey whatever floats your boat. Anyways, guy lets his wife get in bed and get positioned and he ain't touchin' her he's letting her do her thing. Once she's settled he's like okay, this is it. He gets on his knees and goes for it, using the tip of his dick to find the hole, as you do."

"That shit don't never work." Del interrupted.

"Well this time it does. It's lubed up so much it slides right in, easy as pie, if one would fuck a pie."

Leyla grimaced. "Ew!"

"Girl hush, this is just gettin' good!" Del smacked Leyla's shoulder and laughed.

"So, he's like okay, this is great, hope it's good for her. And he speeds up, he's goin' to *town* with a fuckin handbasket. He's going grocery shopping and running errands in that ass."

"Bet he gettin' some McDonald's too." Del said, laughing. "Nasty ass food."

"So this guy is loving it, right? Suddenly his wife starts wailing, but like a good wail like oh this feels amazing wail, right? He's never heard that sound before, must be doing the trick. So now dude goes even harder and harder, he can't feel much cuz of the lube but you know, it works. He busts, he falls sideways, and passes the fuck out."

"Pfft. Typical ass man. Ain't got shit in the tank for round two."

"Nope, out of gas entirely. So anyways, his wife wakes him up. Oh look, time for round two! Guys like damn baby, I can't, first time was a little intense. His wife is like the fuck you mean first time? We haven't done anything. I went outside to the car to find my vibrator, and Bentley came in walkin' all funny and happy as hell."

Del jumped off her barstool. "Oh Hell nah this man done fucked Bentley in the ass!" She keeled over, laughing, but then started coughing. "I knew that's where this shit was headed but damn."

Leyla jumped up to help her, but Del didn't give a damn. She kept laughing, and forced back the coughs.

"Ol' Bentley loved that shit!" Del was flushing red and held her side. "Oh fuck, damn Bentley!"

Leyla started laughing once she knew Del was okay. "And why was her vibrator in the *car*?" This prompted Del to laugh even more.

"Bitch be gettin' it on the way to work!" Del dropped to her knees and rolled on her back, laughing harder than ever. "Bentley be gettin' all the dick at home, she gotta get hers on the road! Hahahahahahahaha!"

Leyla draped over Del, laughing her ass off.

"Moral of the story is: let a man smack that ass a few times during a romp in the sack, it'll save the pooch." Texas Chainsaw Massacre said, prompting even more laughter.

Del sat up. "Shit. Damn my side hurts. Hey, robot, you got any wine? I ain't had wine in a minute."

"I have red, blush, white, and port. I can also do sangria."

"Oh shit that's what I'm talkin' about, gimme a red sangria with some pineapple juice, I used to kill that shit back in the day. Leyla, we bout to get drunk and watch some movies."

"Oh ok! What movie?"

"Back to the Future, bitch. We been time travelin' I'm ready to see that movie again."

***

Two hours later, Del and Leyla were both two or three drinks in and finishing the sci-fi classic. Del remembered almost every word, and had been reciting the script as the actors said the lines.

"Look look look! Look at them shades!" She said, just as the film's actor dropped some futuristic sunglasses on his face onscreen. "And boom, look look!"

"Oh shit, it flies!?" Leyla said, watching the DeLorean's wheels turn over and the car lift up from the road. "That is so cool!"

"I know baby girl and we got that shit *here*! For real! That's why I was so excited!"

Leyla yawned. It was very late for her, almost 6AM. The simulated sunrise would be soon. "I'm tired. I don't wanna sleep."

"You can sleep baby girl, I ain't tired I slept three days ago." Del joked.

"Nah, sunrise is soon. It's pretty cool here, it's from some big lights up too and the window has a good view, we can watch it."

"Oh okay then, that sounds good! Alright, next movie, either Back to the Future 2, or Star Wars."

"Mmmm, Star Wars."

"I fuckin' love Star Wars!" Texas Chainsaw Massacre yelled. "That R2-D2 is the sexiest trash can I ever saw."

Del had already found Star Wars in the media catalog and started it, and the familiar Star Wars credits orchestra blasted on. Leyla's eyes widened as she read the scrolling text. But she felt compelled to let Del know the full truth.

"Hey, Del?"

"Yes, baby girl what's up?"

"Can I tell you something?"

"Yeah, what's up?"

"Promise you won't be mad?"

"Girl, if you don't tell me I'm a be mad that you stallin'."

Leyla sighed. She felt that tingle in her mind. *She's going to hate you.* Leyla pushed Athon back. *No she won't. She's my best friend. She'll understand. Hopefully.*

"So, you know that big machine that was hanging from the ceiling where the portal was?"

"Yeah?"

"It's sentient."

"Oh okay, so it can think for itself and shit?"

"Yeah! Exactly. So, the leaders of this place, or, the guys that started it, programmed the computer to protect them no matter what. So, it invented all these programs to make them money and get supplies, and that's how they made the city, pretty much."

"Okay you told me this part down there already."

"Well here's the rest. So, eventually, the computer got so smart that it knew everything in the world. Almost like, well, God."

"Okay that's a little scary but go ahead."

"And it decided that the only way to truly protect its masters and humanity would be to invent time travel, so it could try and fix a lot of our mistakes in the past."

"I could see that. Damn, a computer did that? Must be a quantum computer to be that smart."

"Yes! Damn, Del. Never knew you were this smart."

"Uh, *nerd.*" Del pointed at herself. "It ain't about being smart. It's about loving science fiction shit. Only now, it's science *fact.*"

"Yep. Well, anyways, to get the most out of the time travel thing, the computer had to make a new kind of android, because real animals and humans couldn't survive going through the portal."

"Now, I'm a stop you right there. If humans can't survive the portal, how did me and you get through it?"

"So, apparently this wrist thing is how." Leyla held the Thumper up, avoiding revealing that she has synthetic DNA, and told a half lie instead. "It creates an antimatter field that holds molecules together for humans going through the portal!"

"Did you just make that up or is that actually the answer?"

"No, that's the answer. So anyways, this android was being sent back in time to…fix things. Sometimes it was destroying documents, sometimes stealing information."

"Like a spy."

"Yeah and, um, it killed a *lot* of people too."

"What, like bad folks?"

"Yeah, really bad. Corrupt politicians, businessmen, pedophiles, rapists, other murderers, cult leaders…"

"Okay. Good."

"Good?" Leyla perked up. "Really? You think that's good?"

"If I knew I wouldn't go to jail I'd have my old ass out there shooting child molesters and rapists in the face all day. Shit."

Well then you're gonna love me…

"Okay, that's good, so..." Leyla continued. "This android was attacked by the leaders of this place here, because time travel is actually dangerous. And during the fight, the computer threw it into the portal and it was lost."

"Oh, damn! That's some mystery sci-fi shit! Where you think it went?"

Leyla took a moment to process what she was about to say, hoping with every fiber of her being that Del really would accept her as who she really was.

"It went into the past. But, it was in the sky, like really high up, and it crashed into the ground and, um, died."

"Oh, shit! How you know that?"

"Well, because it crashed into the ground and fell into the abandoned subway tunnel. And it woke up a really, *really* long time later."

"Oh, okay, damn, what happened next?"

Del wasn't getting it.

"It didn't know who it was. So, it walked until it found someone who helped it."

"Oh, what? Damn, girl, who was it?"

"You." Leyla held her breath.

Del winced. She still hadn't figured it out. Leyla was being a little too cryptic. "I ain't even seen a robot til we came down here. Nice try."

"Del..."

"What?"

"It's me."

Del hesitated to say anything. The realization took its time, walking through her mind in slow motion. She remembered Leyla having no memory. Leyla woke up in the subway tunnels. Leyla had just pulled her through a time portal. Leyla was dressed in some futuristic armor.

Del jumped up from the couch and pointed at Leyla, mouth agape. Leyla stared at the floor. She'd expected this reaction. It's what real humans did when they saw monsters.

"My name is Athon. I'm not human. And I've killed 687 people." She said, coldly.

"But you…you're Leyla." Del shook her head.

"Leyla is a TV show character down here that I used as a cover. Playing guitar, loving pizza, the whole "lovable ADHD, neurotic, innocent little ol' Leyla thing" was all fake. I'm…"

Leyla put her hands up to support her head, drooping down and staring at the floor. "I'm an android."

Del said nothing. She dropped her finger and put her hands at her hips and paced a few times.

"I remember what you said." Leyla mumbled.

"What?"

"About murderers. They deserve to burn in Hell."

Del stopped pacing and glared at Leyla.

"Get yo ass up. Stand up."

Leyla looked up at Del, who was now stern and motherly, pointing at the floor in front of her.

"Get up. Come here."

Leyla slowly stood and walked over to Del, positioning herself in front of her, never looking her in the eye, like a child in trouble.

"Now, you look at me." Del said.

Leyla looked up, meeting Del's eyes, her own fighting back tears.

"I have known you for three years. Now we ain't been through everything but we been through enough. I've seen you laugh. I've seen you cry. I've seen you get mad and I've seen you help others when you could. And I have seen you *bleed* when you got hurt. Blood. Red. Just like mine."

"But I–"

"Shut up. You listen to me." Del said. "You not gonna stand here and keep tellin' me, your best friend, that you ain't real when I know you are."

"But I *am* an andr–"

"I SAID, hush yo mouth, girl. This ain't me in denial. This is me tellin' you what's real."

Leyla's eyes couldn't hold the tears any longer, and they broke free of her eyelids and streamed down her face. Del put her hands up to Leyla's cheek and used her thumbs to wipe away the fallen tears. She put up her thumb with a teardrop resting on it, and made sure Leyla was looking at it.

"You see this? This is *pain*. This is *hurt*."

Del looked back to Texas Chainsaw Massacre. "Do you cry? Do you feel pain?"

Chainsaw Massacre replied, "I have a hole in my face and I told you a bestiality joke a couple hours ago.."

"That's my point. You a robot. You don't *feel* shit.

Chainsaw Massacre held its hands up in a *what the fuck, man* gesture.

Del turned back to Leyla and wiped the tear on her shirt.

"I don't give a damn what some robot or some computer told you. However you was made. Whatever you did. But you, standing right here, right now? You are *real*. Real as those tears. You *feel*. And that's what sets you apart. That's what makes you real. And believe me, I have shed enough tears to know what's real and what ain't. So many tears I don't even have any left."

Leyla sputtered a pitiful, child-like cry, and hugged Del tight. Del hugged back and snuggled her cheek to Leyla's forehead.

"Plus, you get brownie points for killin' pedos and abusers and shit. High five, bitch." Del, drew back and raised her hand, prompting a tearful fit of laughter from Leyla, who gave her a high-five.

"Look." Leyla said, refusing to let go of the hug with Del. "Sunrise."

The view from her window was magnificent. A golden light, although simulated, swept through the apartment like a celestial spotlight, so bright and brilliant that both she and Del had to squint.

Leyla felt a warmth she'd never felt before. It wasn't from the light. It was from within. She put her ear to Del's chest and closed her eyes, listening to her heartbeat, as Del relished the gorgeous view. Leyla could feel this blissful warmth all over her body. It was comforting. Relaxing. She opened her eyes to look outside too.

There was that damn big brown bird. Standing outside the window, on the ledge, looking inside.

This is one way glass, she thought. Then she saw its eyes. That blue glow. *Blackhawk had a big blue-eyed bird,* she thought, slowly realizing something was very, very wrong. That comforting warmth she was feeling was replaced with a spine chilling wave across her back, and the familiar tingling inside her mind as Athon spoke up.

Here we go. Athon had almost a sixth sense, and spiked Leyla's adrenaline.

Still hugging Del in front of the window and looking outward, she sensed something horribly wrong; Athon was inside her mind clawing and gnashing and kicking, trying to come through, and Leyla's eyes glazed over with that wolvish hunger—that raging and flaming, killer instinct that always surfaced when a fight was coming.

A large AV, different from the normal car-like ones that dotted the city, rose up to Leyla and Del's eye level, suspended in the air right outside the window. This AV was at least as large as a yacht, and it looked more like a fighter jet/helicopter hybrid more than anything else.

The hawkish bird on the ledge flapped up and away, landing on the aggressive looking AV, and disappeared inside a compartment.

Leyla pulled away from Del slightly and spread her feet apart. Del knew this wasn't normal as well.

"What the fuck is that?" She said.

A low, bassy rumble sounded from outside, coming from the AV, and a small circular disc on the front began to glow red.

An immensely strong sonar pulse exploded from the front of the AV, shattering the window all the way across, hurdling glass toward Leyla and Del. Leyla swirled in front of Del and pushed her down, shielding her from the glass. It was supposed to be shatterproof. Shards of glass slammed into Leyla's back and neck, burying deep.

It felt like hundreds of wasp stings all at once, and she grimaced as she brought Del down hard to the ground, but she'd saved her from the pain of all that glass.

Leyla leapt up and grabbed Del's jacket and swung her hard toward the back of the apartment, sliding her across the floor at least fifteen feet.

"Get behind the counter!" Leyla yelled. Del scurried to cover.

Leyla turned to face the AV. Whoever was in that thing was about to die.

But it had lurched forward and half of it was inside the apartment now, barely fitting without ripping the roof off.

Four doors opened, two on each wing, and Leyla's heart sank as she saw four exo-suit clad women in armor that matched hers jump out, propelled by their own smaller jet boosters. The Pantheon. Two brunettes, a blonde, and a redhead. The entire group. All here to take her out.

The four women landed on the floor with resounding thuds, heavy and intimidating, and rushed Leyla. She'd left her weapons in The Fridge, but maybe the Thumper still worked.

One of The Pantheon lunged to grab her, but she clenched her fist and warped away, zapping forward a few feet and out of arm's reach.

Okay, good. Let's do this.

Leyla warped around the room, much to the awe of Del, who had peeked up from the counter, and was bringing monstrous kicks and punches to the bodies and limbs of The Pantheon—but the armored, superhuman women seemed unphased.

Leyla managed to clock one in the face, breaking her nose. She felt the bone crush under her knuckles, and blood spurted out immediately. But the woman never changed her expression.

Do they not feel pain?

Leyla tried to warp away from the woman, but instead she felt a sharp, cold and stinging shock to her wrist. She looked down to see her hand falling to the ground, severed at the bone, and the Thumper was falling with it. Her hand had been completely cut off, and blood was gushing out all over the floor.

One of The Pantheon whipped a sword to her side, tossing the blood off it like a samurai, and the blade retracted inside her arm.

The one with the broken nose grabbed Leyla by the throat and picked her up, then choke slammed her down in lightning fast succession, splintering the floor under her.

Leyla hadn't even felt the pain of losing her hand yet. It just felt *cold*. She quickly pushed off with her good arm and got to her knees, but that was as far as she made it. Two of the Pantheon grabbed her shoulders and they both stamped on the back of her knees, pinning her to the ground and facing the AV. Another lady grabbed hold of the back of her neck and held her even tighter, as the fourth woman jet jumped over to the AV.

The cockpit opened up, and Blackhawk himself rose from the seat and jumped off and onto the apartment floor, holding a hefty looking, buckled case.

A loud *ding* sounded out from behind Leyla; it sounded much like the same *ding* from when Wells had hit Ramsay with the frying pan—and one of the Pantheon that was holding her slipped and fell to her knee. It was the one with red hair.

Leyla used the opportunity to kick up as hard as she could. The pain was setting in, burning like hot coals. She was losing blood too quickly. *Need to finish the fight and get a tourniquet before it's too late.*

She used the severed arm to punch one of the women in the face—that was her only free arm.

"GAAAHHHH!!!" Leyla screamed from the pain. She saw Del reeling back a cast iron frying pan, the same one Wells had used to smack Ramsay earlier, and she was bringing it down toward the scarlet maned Pantheon member she'd hit just a moment before.

"Rrraaahhhh!" Del brought the pan down, flat side first, on the Pantheon lady's shoulder, denting the armored exo-suit. But the woman leapt up, grabbed Del's arm, and snapped it like a twig. Del screamed. The frying pan hit the hard ground and clattered to a rest a few feet away.

Leyla's body set fire. Not actual flame—that fire one gets when they've just seen someone they love get hurt by someone they hate. She tried to lunge forward, murder in her eyes—a target on that Pantheon bitch's throat.

But she was pinned tighter by the remaining women, forced to watch as the red-haired woman grabbed Del by the throat, putting a stop to her pained yelps, and slammed her against the wall, cracking the structure of the apartment with the force. But she didn't let go. She slammed Del to the ground hard, back first.

Leyla knew she was screaming. Deep, throat shredding cries, but all she could hear was Del's frail body being slammed around by that red haired bitch. And she couldn't do anything about it.

The woman lifted Del in the air with enough force to let go and allow Del to seemingly float for a split second, as she brought a screaming, superhuman right hand into Del's chest. Her hand almost looked like it disappeared into Del's body. She'd hit her so hard that Leyla heard her entire chest cavity explode. It was such a shock that she stopped screaming, and that fire in her body ran cold as ice.

Del flopped to the ground a few feet away; Lifeless.

The sight of Del being thrown around and rendered motionless in such a brutal way refused to register with Leyla. No way that could have just happened. *No.*

"What the fuck are you doing?!" Blackhawk yelled at the one that had thrashed Del around. "Artemis! Stand the fuck down!" Blackhawk rushed over to the red haired woman and pushed her against the wall. She could have done the same to him, but she listened, and backed away from Del.

Artemis. You're Artemis. Leyla took a mental note.

Leyla's muscles electrified and she lurched forward with enough strength to drag the three Pantheon members holding her back across the floor. She screamed, no, she *roared* at Artemis and Blackhawk, as she pushed to her feet in defiance of The Pantheon. Artemis was a *dead woman.*

Leyla pulled her one good fist loose and whipped around to the woman who'd made the mistake of letting her slip free. She grabbed the woman by the hair and jerked hard to the side, as hard as she possibly could, dragging her to the ground well enough to bounce her head off the floor. The bamboo cracked and splintered.

But Artemis was fast. She kicked Leyla in the back with extreme prejudice. Leyla gasped, and felt something like an electric bolt shoot down her hip, into her thighs and down to her feet, and she couldn't feel them anymore. Artemis had broken her spine.

Before Leyla could hit the ground, she was scooped up by two of the Pantheon once again. The one she'd slammed down was still reeling, stumbling to her feet.

They pulled Leyla up, this time facing Del, and that's all she could focus on.

"Del!" Leyla yelled. Even speaking hurt. "DEL!"

Blackhawk walked into her view, blocking Del. He pulled his revolver from the holster, brought it up to Leyla's raging eyes, and with a stark expression of disappointment, pulled the trigger.

Leyla didn't hear a shot. She didn't feel anything. But she knew she was falling. She hit the broken and bloodied bamboo floor, and she could see Del through blurry and blackening vision. Her head felt cold, and there was a dull throb that seemed to become less and less intense with each pulse. She tried to call out to Del, but she could no longer speak. She couldn't move at all. The worst part of everything was that she just couldn't see Del's face. She couldn't look her friend in the eye and apologize for fucking everything up.

She saw Blackhawk holster his pistol and walk over to Del, kneel down, and hold her hand tight. He looked back to Leyla with sorrowful eyes.

Leyla could barely see, but she made out the blood pooling under her face. Her consciousness was fading as fast as her vision—at about the same rate the blood rushed from her head.

Del...I...

And then, there was nothing.

Just the black.

CHAPTER TWENTY-ONE

Defier

"My good people of SubCity…"

Blackhawk's gravelly voice rang out through a multitude of loudspeakers throughout the city. An hour had passed; most of the citizens were waking up expecting a normal day underground.

"The time has come, where we will show the world the true way of life. We are humanity's destiny. We are the new path to liberty. We are the catalysts of ascension to a new plane of existence. We are saviors. We are liberators. We are soldiers; we are fighting the final war of this lovely planet Earth."

Everyone in the city listened in. For three decades, they'd all awaited this moment. Ever since Blackhawk and Ramsay set a quantum computer in the super-cooled chamber and outfitted it with a nuclear core for power, they'd been promised a day when they could set foot above ground once again, and not be shunned, but welcomed by society. They would save the world from itself.

"After our final campaign, there will be no war. Only peace. There will be no sickness, no depression, no hatred. Only happiness. There will be no worry, no hunger, no crime. There will be only freedom."

Wells stepped out of his apartment building, grimacing. It seemed every single person in the city had taken to the streets, enamored by the announcements from the speakers.

"The final cog in our machine has been found, and our launch is imminent. Today, we leave this hidden utopia to bring our blessings to the world. Today, we take back our brothers and sisters that have been slaves to corruption, greed, and prejudice! Today, we ascend, and we heal this dying planet."

The crowds of the street began to clap and cheer. Wells cautiously stepped further from his building, surveying the lunacy that was unfolding.

This man has amassed a fucking army... Wells thought. *An army of cybernetic supersoldiers.*

Blackhawk's voice rang out once more. A rallying cry. "Libertatum, ASCENSIONIS!"

The crowd erupted in unison, "Libertatum, Ascensionis!", and roared with applause. Some citizens jumped and danced; some were crying tears of joy. One woman, with several implants scattered across her body, grabbed Wells by the shoulders.

"Libertatum Ascensionis!" She cried, grinning and expecting a reciprocation of excitement. Wells was stunned. His blank expression set the woman aback. She took a step to her rear and looked Wells up and down.

Uh oh...

"Defier! DEFIER!" The woman screamed and pointed at Wells, alerting everyone else. Everyone nearby took a step or two away from Wells, singling him out in the street and painting a metaphorical target on his head.

Run, you fucking idiot.

Wells bolted to his left, toward the closest alley. Some of the modders gave chase, while the masses all yelled in unison. "Defier!"

Wells ducked into another alley. Then another. He felt one modder claw at his shirt, but didn't get a good enough grip to bring him down.

Fuck, these bastards are fast. Gotta do something unexpected. Lose them quick, or I'm dead.

Wells skidded to a stop, grabbing a pipe on the corner of a wall, and whipped around the corner hard. The few modders behind him piled into each other, but it wasn't enough of a trick to give him even an inch of breathing room. He pumped his legs hard as hell, and took off straight, but juked into a door, slamming into it with his shoulder. It was the entrance to Minnie's Magnificent Books, and it was lined with hundreds of bookshelves like a maze.

Perfect.

Wells heard the modders all slamming into the door behind him, but he zigzagged around every available corner, hoping to high Heaven there was a back exit. If not, he'd just served himself up on a platter.

After rounding several more bookshelf corners, he got the bright idea to pull a couple books off and toss them far over the shelves to another spot in the store. Maybe that would throw them off some.

"Over there!" He heard one of the modders yell.

Damn, that worked?

A smile broke across Wells's face, and quickly turned to a teeth gritting push toward the back of the store, where he saw another door.

He slowed down, making sure to not slam into it and make a racket that would send the modders after him again. He pushed carefully and opened the door, finally outside, and miraculously, no modders in sight.

He went to his right, away from the meaty part of the city, down an alley with plenty of cover from walkways.

Got to get the fuck out of here. But how?

Wells racked his brain. The freight elevator was a definite no-go. He'd be swarmed in a heartbeat before the doors even opened. The only other way out was—

The ventilators. Need an AV, Ramsay said.

The image of Ramsay flashed across Wells's mind.

That motherfucker. He lied like I knew he would. He told Blackhawk about Leyla, and...

The realization of what must have already happened set in. Blackhawk and said he'd found the "final cog of the machine." And Ramsay had said all Blackhawk needed was Athon's DNA to use the Xenobots. Which meant Blackhawk had already gotten to Leyla. It was too late to worry about that now. He had to get his ass outside and to the surface, and warn Harrison. She was the only other person who'd be able to prevent whatever Blackhawk had up his sleeve; or at the very least, the only one who'd be willing to try. Her big brother was a Navy admiral. And the Navy had soldiers and jets.

Need an AV, Wells reminded himself. He snuck toward the inner streets, where the AVs were usually parked. Thankfully, there was one with no one nearby. Everyone had gathered further down the street, and they were all celebrating. Either that, or they were freaking out looking for the *defier*.

He scanned his SD chip. He got a negative beep.

"Seriously?!" He stepped back, looking for someone walking nearby. There was a guy with a chrome forehead and *super* blonde hair. Wells had a stupid idea but it was the only idea he had.

"Hey, what's up man?" Wells asked the chrome head.

"Nothin' much my friend." He had some sort of Scandinavian accent. No wonder he was so tall.

"My SD is actin' up again, I swear. Just trying to get an AV to take up to Blackhawk's. I've got some info on the defier."

"I've no idea what any of that means, but sure." Chrome Head replied, and scanned his SD to open the AV.

Wells couldn't believe it. And he didn't know which part of what had just happened he didn't believe the most. Was it the fact that his stupid idea worked, or was it that this dude didn't know who Blackhawk was? Either way, he had his escape vessel.

THOOM! Wells heard a heavy and metallic thud a little ways off, down the street. Chrome Head jumped and started running away, ducking into an alley. Wells looked in the same direction Chrome Head had.

A exo-suited woman had slammed to the ground; the asphalt had cracked under her feet. One of The Pantheon. This was the first time Wells had seen one, and he immediately pegged her as the badasses Leyla had told him about. The woman slowly surveyed the street, almost as if she *knew* Wells was there. He ducked inside the AV and pulled the gull wing door closed lightly. Thankfully, the interior lighting wasn't too different from what he was used to, and he hit a switch and cut all the lighting off. He slid down the seat low, hiding.

Clunk. Clunk. Clunk. The woman stepped his way like a hungry lion. Wells peeked over the dash and confirmed she was indeed heading his way.

Make a decision, dumbass. Fly or hide. Fly or hide?

If he tried to gun it, she'd chase him down. If he hid, her seemingly bloodhound instinct would flush him out. He had to think of a distraction, but he had absolutely no idea what to do. This was a rare moment where his quick thinking couldn't save him.

The woman came to a stop a few paces in front of the AV and stood there like a fucking slasher movie villain. Wells's heart pounded. The thought crossed his mind, *What if she can hear heart beats?* Wells took deep and slow breaths, trying to calm himself just in case. She just stood there. She wouldn't move; she kept looking side to side like a monstrous guard dog.

Fuck. Off. Please.

She turned and stomped away slowly. Wells let out a breath of relief, but he wasn't free yet. She had to get far enough away for him to fly off. The AVs weren't loud but they still made some sound. Best to be safe and wait. He looked over the dash. She was walking away. Good. When she was maybe a football field away, he flicked the interior lighting switch on so he could see what he was doing. He pulled the black lever and took a second to remember Ramsay's instructions for flight.

Was it pull or push to go forward? Has to be push.

He pushed the yoke lightly, and the AV moved forward. He remembered correctly. One wrong move and that AV was smacking the ground and alerting that mech-suit wearing horror.

He pushed the yoke up to raise the AV from the ground, but it went down instead, and slammed into the asphalt with a resounding crack.

What the fuck!?

Looking at the dash, the "Invert lift/drop" button was selected.

Who the fuck inverts flight controls!? He yelled inside his head, not accounting for the fact that inverted was the norm for someone who was used to flying real aircraft. Whoever that person was, they were an asshole for leaving their preferences selected.

The Pantheon member whipped around and got a beat on Wells. His eyes widened, and he pulled the yoke back, reversing, and he slammed it down and forward, shooting up in the air so hard it pinned him to the seat. He turned hard to the left, and his butt slid right on the smooth leather. He'd not buckled up. He was ascending rapidly, but that may have been a terrible idea.

The woman activated her boosters and soared toward him. He could see her in his side view mirror, and he pushed the yoke in harder, but it failed to increase the already fast AV's speed. He looked forward and thankfully could make out the ventilator fans on the other side of the cavern.

The woman had closed the distance in an ungodly amount of time. She reversed her thrusters, and had just enough speed to glide and match his pace. She pulled a large hilt from her waist, maybe a foot long, and activated a massive nano tech blade that shot forth from it, then separated into several pieces, held together by an anti-gravity electricity, forming a sort of sword-whip.

Once extended and separated, the weapon had to be at least as long as she was tall—and in that suit, she was taller than any normal human. She drew it back and swung hard. The bladed segments stretched out in a huge crescent as she swung, just missing Wells's speeding AV, and each segment of sword buried itself in the side of the building he was flying beside.

The blade-whip vibrated; a low and vicious growl, and it forced the concrete on the wall to explode outward as the woman jerked it away from the wall. The debris pelted Wells and the AV. His windshield cracked and he felt the vehicle drop several feet. He grit his teeth and kept pushing, praying to gods he didn't even believe in, that he would make it out of this underground Hell.

He gained control and made his way to the ventilators. The thought hadn't crossed his mind that he had to go through the fan somehow. Not until now anyways. He was maybe a few hundred yards from the ventilators, and he had no way to break through.

Except for that woman's crazy fucking sword whip.

He dodged her flailing blade as best he could along the way. She got him good once, cleaving off an entire rear segment of the AV, but it kept flying somehow. He was in open air at the moment, so at least he didn't have to worry about crashing into a building. Thankfully, he was a gamer, and despite the spotty attempt earlier, now he'd gotten hang of the flight controls, and his muscle memory was saving his hide.

Maybe break left, then right, fly along the fan. Bait her into hitting the fan and making it explode.

He had a plan. Time to execute.

He broke left, then right, bringing one of the fans on his left and within an arm's reach. He ignored the fact that he'd almost killed himself with that maneuver. If he'd hit the wall that would have been it. He glanced over to the woman, who was tearing her sword-whip toward him at a terrifying speed. He pulled the yoke up, dropping the AV hard, and then pushed it down to keep it level.

The blades hit the fan, just like he hoped.

Come on, lady, blow it the fuck up.

He heard that low rumble from earlier. He broke the AV to the right, anticipating the coming debris this time.

The whip-sword tore the fan to shreds. A sharp sheet of steel whipped by Wells's glass windshield, grazing it and shattering the glass completely.

He clamped his eyes shut and shielded his face with an arm. He immediately regained control and turned the yoke hard right, whipping the AV around and facing the Pantheon member. Her whip sword drew back into a singular blade and pulsed with electricity.

She knew what he was trying to do, and she was waiting for him to make that mistake.

What now, dumbass? Wells thought. He looked down at his dash. He saw a switch that read "U/V Spotlight".

Wonder what that does?

He flicked the switch. A ridiculously intense beam of simulated sunlight blasted from the AVs headlights and right into the woman's face. She winced and covered her eyes.

Why the fuck would you even need that here? Wells thought. But no matter. He jammed the yoke forward and rammed the AV straight into the temporarily blinded woman. She flew back and slammed into a building below, sending the dust of cracked concrete flying all around her. She recovered quickly, brandishing her immense blade.

Wells turned toward the now removed fan. The tunnel out was open. He pushed the yoke forward and careened into the large shaft, pushing the yoke down to point the AVs nose up and send it straight to the sky. He saw actual sunlight at the end of the tunnel.

The Pantheon member shot toward the shaft to follow, but was stopped by her com speaker activating.

"Don't worry about him. He doesn't matter." Blackhawk's voice played through. "Whatever he thinks he can do up there, it's too late. Regroup."

***

Wells was fighting gravity hard, trying to keep the AV from scraping the walls of the tunnel as he screamed at full speed toward the top. As he closed in on his exit, he saw that the opening wasn't simply an opening. It was grated steel. Probably not good.

He pulled on his harness and buckled it, finally. This was definitely going to be a crash landing. He grit his teeth again and breathed hard in preparation. He pushed the yoke as hard as he could and had a white knuckled grip on it. He held his breath and tightened his core, and flexed his shoulder and neck muscles, bracing for impact.

The AV crashed into the grate with enormous force, sending Wells forward and slamming his nose into the yoke, breaking the bone underneath. The pain shot across his face and brain like a thousand hornet stings, and it dazed him enough for him to lose his grip on the yoke.

The AV had broken through the grating, and it shot at least fifty feet in the air, finally out on the surface. It was caught by gravity, though, and reversed direction. It fell back to the ground, rear first. The back end collided with the concrete rim of the ventilation shaft and crumpled around it. The impact slammed Wells into the seat so hard his vision flashed white. The AV seemed to hover vertically, standing on the rim for a moment, before falling forward onto the mud and grass outside. Had it fallen backward, Wells could have kissed his life goodbye.

Several alarms and chimes and dings were sounding in the AV. Wells shook his head. Aside from his nose, he felt okay. He spit the blood away from his mouth and grunted. He unbuckled the harness and pulled the handle to open the door, but it had jammed shut. He'd have to go through the shattered windshield.

He crawled out, bruised and beaten the fuck up, but alive. He jerked his gaze to the ventilator shaft, expecting the woman to erupt out of it and slice him in half. He jumped out of the AV and stumbled across the field, trying to put some distance between himself and the shaft. He ducked behind an old, abandoned bulldozer.

Nothing came out of the ventilator. He'd made a getaway; Not a clean one, but it was a getaway.

"Top Gun, bitch!" Wells yelled toward the shaft.

He could hear the cheers and celebrations from down the ventilator shaft, even hundreds of feet up. Blackhawk had formed an army and the entire population of SubCity were conscripts, whether they realized they were part of it or not.

Wells jogged toward the Stop N Go where he'd left his truck previously, occasionally blowing hard out of nose to eject the blood and phlegm. Wasn't the first time he'd had a broken nose; benefits of being an openly gay kid in school. He stopped, listening back at the ventilator. Faintly, he heard a siren from deep underground.

***

Back underground, Blackhawk strode across his massive platform that housed his personal assault AV and the Pantheon workstations. Four of the women landed near their stations, each with a heavy, metallic thud. A fifth flew in—the one that had gone after Wells—and landed just after.

Blackhawk's android raptor soared down and landed in front of him, showing off its wingspan.

Ramsay was standing at the switchboard relay, now with a fresh set of arms, and turned to see his old friend approaching. His face carried a heavy burden of remorse, like he'd made the mistake of a lifetime. Truthfully, he hadn't expected Blackhawk to act so brashly—nor so quickly.

"Ronnie!" Blackhawk held his hands out, full of pride. "We have fucking done it, brother!"

Ramsay sulked away from the collection of computers and monitors. "Yeah."

"How long do you think it'll be before we get those Xenos working?" Blackhawk asked.

Ramsay looked down at one of the workstations, full of knobs and switches, toward a cavity that was oozing frozen air from within. Blackhawk had kept the Xenobots here ever since he'd taken them from SIGIL a decade prior.

"Still synthesizing her DNA."

"Her?" Blackhawk laughed. "It's an android. Don't be so sentimental. Thing woulda killed you without a second thought."

Except she hadn't. She could have torn me to shreds, but she didn't, Ramsay thought. He figured it was best he didn't reply unless required. He'd never agreed to murder and manslaughter. Blackhawk had promised no one would be hurt.

"Hey, Ramsay?" Blackhawk leaned close. "Don't lose sight. I know I told you to get close but, it was just a robot. And a spy droid at that. Don't let it get in your head."

"I'm not."

"I know. You're smarter than that."

"Yeah." All Ramsay could think about was Leyla's piercing honey eyes. Android or not, she had seemed so *human.* But he didn't dare ask what had happened to Del. He knew the answer to that question—he just didn't want confirmation, lest the guilt eat at his soul ever harshly.

"We launch in one hour. Eat up, friend. Gonna be a long day and a long night." Blackhawk announced, entering the immense vault-ish doors to The Bullpen.

One of the blonde Pantheon members clanked over to Ramsay and stood straight, looking down at him. In their exo-suits, the women were easily seven feet tall.

"Do I sense dissonance?" She said, with a German accent.

Ramsay turned to her, fearful, but hiding it well. "Rhea, do I sense a *calm the fuck down*? Not everything is as complicated as you want it."

Rhea stared at Ramsay, studying him, waiting for a twitch, or a smirk. A submissive glance away, or a nervous scratch to the ear or a running of the fingers through the hair. She'd once been a member of the German BND, and relished in her ability to spot a liar.

Ramsay held fast, and stared the woman down. His heart rate fluttered, but he controlled his breathing. He'd done enough work on these ladies' cybernetics and mech suits to know how to deal with them.

After an overly long amount of time studying him, Rhea turned and walked away. All four of the other Pantheon had been standing there like wolves ready to feast if Rhea saw something wrong.

Rhea was a reserved and calculating beast in her own right. Cerebral and intimidating. The hallmarks of a secret service operative. Artemis, the redhead, was a loose cannon. She gave in to her anger regularly, which suited her considering the scarlet hair coloring.

Eris, one of the brunettes, was an enigma, always quiet. Ramsay didn't know much about her, other than she really liked sake and swords. Could be anything with her, but most likely connected to a gang, on one side of the law or the other. He guessed Yakuza or something similar. Regardless, she was ruthless. Sometimes cruel.

Nemesis had the largest mech suit, by request. A five foot long gun was folded and hanging off her left shoulder, like a destructive angel wing. She'd grown up on the streets of Chicago, and had seen more of her brothers killed than live. She wanted to punish violence with greater violence. Who could blame her?

Nyx was the newest Pantheon member, a dirty blonde, and experienced in violence as a former USAF fighter pilot. She had done terrible and horrible things; such that she'd once requested a memory wipe but eventually found her way back to Blackhawk's circle. She showed zero emotion, almost sociopathic, and was the one that had almost torn Wells to shreds mid-air.

All five of the women exited their suits simultaneously and stepped out of them. They all had special, skin tight flight suits with pneumatic muscles all over. These suits were modeled to counteract G-forces and enhance strength by a large margin when needed.

The workstation braces extended and connected to ports on the winged armor, holding them in place. Robotic arms swept out of the station beams; some flashed bright with arc welders, repairing small fractures in the steel, others had a more delicate finger-like apparatus that weaved circuitry in and out of the suit frames, replacing any damaged wires.

Ramsay could see that Leyla had done a number on those suits, no doubt. But it hadn't been enough. The women followed Blackhawk into The Bullpen. Both Rhea and Artemis cut Ramsay an accusatory glare as they passed by.

He stared back, refusing to look away. Dominance games. Like wolves, they were. The first to look away was the weaker. He let them walk by until they dropped their gaze naturally. His heart beat hard enough to kill him at that point. At least they were gone, finally. He let out a huge breath and coughed. His hands were shaking. Fucking panic attack. He closed his eyes and controlled his breathing, calming himself down.

This was *not* what he'd planned on. He'd tried to keep his word with Leyla. He'd tried to lie and say the energy spike was just an anomaly, that the SIGIL was malfunctioning and he'd check it out and make sure it was fine. But Blackhawk wasn't stupid, and betraying him would hold some dire consequences. Not to mention The Pantheon foaming at the mouth for him to fuck up.

So, he broke. He'd told Blackhawk everything. Athon was back. The energy spike was her using the wormhole generator to bring her friend to SubCity. Wells had snuck into the city, and he was staying across from Peyton's. Ramsay felt like such a coward; one that stank of betrayal.

Blackhawk had suspected who Leyla was from the very beginning. Ramsay had too, but he'd spent time with Leyla and he'd let the assumption that she was just an unwilling, normal person take hold of his gut instinct.

As soon as he'd told Blackhawk what had happened, Blackhawk organized a strike in mere minutes, and had gotten exactly what he needed: Athon's game changing DNA signature; the key to the Xenobot revolution they'd been planning for decades.

It wouldn't be long before the synthesis and analysis of Athon's blood would be complete. Maybe under an hour. At that point, humanity would see the beginnings of its next evolution.

CHAPTER TWENTY-TWO

Ascensionis

Blackhawk strolled into The Bullpen, followed by The Pantheon. His hawk dropped to the floor and hobbled around, making way for the women as they settled in a loose formation, awaiting orders from their revolutionary leader. Blackhawk glared at Artemis.

"Do you understand what we're trying to do here?" He asked the redhead.

"Change the world. Ascend humanity." She replied, coldly.

"And in doing so it would be nice if you would keep your FUCKING ANGER in CHECK!" Blackhawk screamed at her, advancing toward her. She prepared for a fight, but Blackhawk stopped a few feet away.

"I did not put all this shit together for you to start killing innocent fucking people. We are doing this to save lives. You have all those fancy fucking augmentations and those exo-suits for a specific purpose, and that will be ridding the world of the true problems, *after* we launch!

Blackhawk turned and walked away, pacing. "Your jobs are simple. Protect The Bullpen, and launch the Xenobots. Got it?"

None of them nodded at that question, but they saw his point.

"You do not deviate from the plan. I don't give a flying fuck what happens. I don't give a fuck if some random police officer or soldier starts pelting you with bullets or shoots a fucking missile at you, you *do not deviate from the plan*."

"Got it." Artemis said, still not regretting her actions.

"No, you don't *got it*." Blackhawk said. "We can do whatever we fucking want with those Xenobots, but I do not want the world thinking we are attacking the innocent. We're already going to meet a hefty amount of resistance as it is. The global elite and governments are not going to like what we do. So we need the *people*, the workers, the backbones of the world to be on our side. Not only are we enacting physical change on our planet, we must instill the *idea* of change as a viable evolution of our society, our humanity, and our future. We cannot do that, if anyone sees either one of us do *anything* that can be perceived as a negative action. At first, your actions will be seen as negative, but once the people realize we are only going after those that feed off their hard work and prey on them, we will have what we need. The idea. The same idea that we have here in SubCity. A utopia. Libertatum Ascensionis."

All of The Pantheon nodded in agreement.

"You are the final soldiers of the world. After your sacrifice, no one will ever have to do what you will. People will tell stories of The Pantheon for thousands of years. People will make pilgrimage to statues in your honor. You are the saviors of this world. Everybody always talks about this second coming of Christ. What they'll get instead are angels, clad in armor and sending themselves into the Earth. We don't need an afterlife to live happily and fruitfully. We need you ladies."

Ramsay was standing just outside the doorway, listening in. He was always impressed with Blackhawk's impromptu speeches. Most people were; that's how he'd amassed such a following in the city. He stepped inside.

"It's ready." He said.

***

Wells had made it to his truck, right where he'd left it. He jumped inside and sped off, calling Harrison once more.

"Wells? You got anything new for me?"

"I'm out, headed your way now. Some real bad shit's about to happen. Get the fuck out of the office now."

"I just got in, the fuck are you—"

"Harrison! Just get the fuck out before it's too late. Meet me at that hot dog place we—" Wells didn't finish his sentence, he trailed off, staring out his window.

"Donnie? What's up? You there?"

"Look out your window."

***

Inside the police office, Harrison moved over to the closest window and pulled the blinds up. She gasped.

A startling amount of vehicles were taking to the sky, all glowing blue underneath. Dozens and dozens of them, possibly hundreds, all pouring out of the subway tunnel opening.

She wasn't the only one to see it. Several other officers and secretaries were starting to chatter and yell across to each other from their desks.

"You see it?" Wells said, still on the phone with her.

"What the fuck!?" Harrison replied.

"Okay, so it ain't just me and I'm not crazy right?"

"I think we're all crazy now…" Harrison said, mouth wide open.

"Guy that's in charge down here, guy named Blackhawk. Seems like a military vet. The man's got a fuckin' army, and they're all enhanced. Cybernetics. They're faster and they're stronger than us. Call your fucking big brother, and get the fucking military here right now!"

"Yeah…" Harrison was stunned. "Yeah I'll call him."

***

Blackhawk and Ramsay stepped back out on the platform to his AV. Each of the Pantheon members settled at their respective workstations and stamped a foot into their exo-suits. The armor whirred to life and wrapped around each of them, individually, with several satisfying clicks and a few compressed air hisses. Each suit's anti-gravity jet boosters popped on for a split second, ensuring they were working.

Ramsay eyeballed the two remaining backup exo-suits, wondering if there was a way to fight back against the Pantheon if needed. The extra suits weren't on the platform, and could be handy later. Best to say nothing. He simply did not trust The Pantheon at this point. They'd become bloodthirsty, like wild animals that had just tasted raw meat for the first time. Blackhawk may have become the same monster as well.

Blackhawk stepped onto his AV and the cockpit opened up in three sections and slid back so he could sit inside. All five of the special compartments opened for each of the women as well, and they all jet boosted into them, and took their seats. Blackhawk turned to Ramsay.

"You know what to do, brother."

Ramsay nodded, as Blackhawk took his seat and closed the cockpit. He turned and jogged off the platform, toward a floating tram. He opened a compartment on the wall and pushed a large lever upward, and input a long code in a keypad. He turned to Blackhawk, and touched two fingers to his brow and pointed them toward his friend—a sort of friendly salute, letting Blackhawk know to move to the next step.

Ramsay stepped back into the tram, just as immense locking mechanisms disengaged underneath the massive platform Blackhawk and The Pantheon lived on.

Overhead, the cavern itself rumbled. The ceiling split apart, and real sunlight poured in from the surface as dirt and rocks fell through. It was a retractable roof, easily the size of a football field, opening down the middle to allow Blackhawk's platform to fit through.

The platform itself had its own anti-gravity boosters, which all kicked on and began to lift the entire thing into the air, toward the surface.

Blackhawk had turned his home into a flying fortress. It was now his operations base. That's why he had named it "The Bullpen."

Blackhawk sent Ramsay the same friendly salute as The Bullpen soared into the air, and exited through the roof.

It had been years and years since any of them had seen the real world. Blackhawk and The Pantheon stared out their windows as the makeshift flying operations base made its way into the sky.

"It is pretty." Rhea said, looking out upon the river and rolling hills around the city.

"We have a beautiful planet. That's what we're saving, ladies." Blackhawk replied.

The Bullpen came to rest high in the air, at least a couple thousand feet. He and The Pantheon had enough provisions to last months if needed, although he knew he wouldn't have to wait that long. He saw his army of modders pouring out of the abandoned subway entrance; dozens of AVs were still flying out, each full of soldiers, also volunteers for his revolution. Foot soldiers also made their way out into the streets, armed to the teeth. This would be a short scuffle, if it came to it, but his instructions to everyone were to hurt no one. Allow aggression, but be passive. Occupy the city, and await instructions. The world would be watching.

Nemesis looked down at the flood of modders taking to the city. "Did you convince everyone in the city to fight?"

"No." Blackhawk replied. "They leave if they want to. Whoever wants to stay in SubCity stays. Home is home. And we're not here to fight. We're here to influence."

Blackhawk tapped the screen in front of him and activated his comlink, calling Ramsay.

"Yep, I'm here." Ramsay's voice came through the speaker in the cockpit.

"You good, brother? Almost set up?"

***

Down in SubCity, Ramsay was speeding down the street toward The Fridge on his Indian motorcycle.

"Yep, almost in The Fridge now. Your indicator lights will flash when the transmitters are ready."

Ramsay rode his bike right into The Fridge, flicked out the kickstand, and hurried over to the interface under SIGIL. He switched on the screen and began typing in commands. Of all the insane technological advancements this quantum computer had made, its original MS-DOS system was still up and running, connected to SubCity's intra and extranet. After running several archaic commands on the old console, Ramsay made his way to the front of the machine, glancing over at the ever-glowing arch gate.

"So, SIGIL…"

"*RAMSAY.*" The machine replied, ready for orders. It had also prepared for this day, and to take orders from Ramsay and Blackhawk only when it came.

"Enact Hijack Protocol." Ramsay ordered, nervously.

SIGIL's body whirred with a dozen separate static sounds and digital buzzes—each was a different communication method used by the world. Ramsay even heard the old AOL dial-up tone in there somewhere.

Hijack Protocol was the precursor to what Blackhawk called Operation: Ascension. First step was to take over *all* communication arrays, not just in the United States, but the entire world. City infrastructure, satellites, defense systems, financials, even the internet itself would be in the palm of Blackhawk's hand. The only systems they couldn't take over were a select few of various military encrypted algorithms. Namely, those of the Navy and Air Forces from a few global superpowers. Given enough time, SIGIL could crack into those, but Blackhawk actually wanted a military response to prove a point.

"AFFIRMING HIJACK PROTOCOL ACTIVATION." SIGIL said. It played a tune of "He's Got The Whole World In His Hands" through its speaker. That was a bit of an Easter egg Ramsay had programmed decades ago, thinking it would make him laugh. It didn't.

"HIJACK PROTOCOL COMPLETE."

Ramsay activated his comlink and called Blackhawk, who answered almost instantaneously.

"I got it, light's up on my console here." Blackhawk said through the comlink.

"Then you're good. Let 'em have it." Ramsay said, trying to sound like he was still 100% on board with the plan.

***

Halfway around the world, in London, a pub filled with screaming fans of the Manchester United soccer team was exploding with cheers after their team had just scored a hard earned goal against Liverpool, their biggest rivals, even in 2035.

Their cheers turned to dumbfounded gawks as every screen in the pub fluttered to black.

"Oi! Tha fuck is this shite!?" One woman yelled at the bartender. Before he could answer over the other cursing and insult spewing sports crowd, the screens flashed on, but they did not feature the game. It was a bearded, gruff, and stoic figure with a Viking inspired man bun, lighting a thick cigar with a match: Blackhawk.

"Who the fook is this geebag!?" Another patron yelled in an Irish accent. "Get the fookin' game back on!"

"I can't do a bloody fuckin' thing, mate, fuckin' remote ain't workin'." The bartender replied.

On screen, Blackhawk puffed his cigar and acted as if he was staring everyone in the world in the eye. As a matter of fact, he was.

Screens in every single country that could carry a network signal had been hijacked. Cell phones, televisions, PCs, laptops, digital billboards—everything was his.

"I promise I will have you all back to your regularly scheduled programming very soon." Blackhawk laughed. "Always wanted to say that."

The patrons in the bar were still cursing, but some settled down to see what was happening; not like they could change the channel anyway.

"I am a veteran of the United States campaign of Grenada in 1983. A lot of you likely have no idea what that is, and that's okay. But it's the beginning of what led us here."

Blackhawk's message played across any outlet possible. A train station in New York. A small home in Argentina. An old, dusty camping TV/radio in Zaire. A satellite radio in the Himalayas sounded out as some climbers hiked toward the peak of Everest. In every country, his message was transcribed in real time audio to the native language, so that every person listening understood what was coming.

"Official records for the Grenada campaign would have you believe there were only nine lost aircraft during one of our few scuffles there. That is a lie. I was the pilot of aircraft ten. A UH-60 that I was piloting was brought down by rocket fire. I lost both legs in the crash, and I was rescued by special forces two days later. I was on the brink of death. The record of my crash was redacted because I was placed into a top secret program. The government was working on cybernetic prosthetics for wartime veterans. They successfully replaced my lost legs."

Viewers around the world tuned in, unsure yet if the story was a hoax, much like H. G. Wells's infamous *War of the Worlds* some decades back.

"You would think that's a happy ending, but we are talking about the United States government. After that, they abruptly canceled the program and kicked all the candidates out. That includes revoking extended medical coverage, and threatening us with legal action or worse, if we should let the story out. So we hid. These new limbs were rejected by our bodies. We all got sick. Some died. Some took their own lives. Those of us that survived were mostly homeless. You see, it was cheaper to pump vets full of chemicals and drugs than it was to replace limbs. Or, just forget them altogether.

And then, we found a home. An abandoned subway system under Cincinnati, Ohio. We lived there, with a few other homeless folks, and we built a small village underground. After a few years we'd cultivated our own society of like-minded individuals.

It was then that we got word of movement of an experimental and revolutionary quantum computer, the first of its kind, through the city. We had the means of taking it, so we did.

If you're unfamiliar with what a quantum computer is, let's just say it is a hell of a lot smarter than us.

This computer invented things. Things you only read about in books and see on TV and movies. Things you can only dream of— and it made them a reality.

Our technology skyrocketed. No longer were we just walking around with replaced limbs. We were replacing organs. Enhancing strength and prolonging our lives. We were able to control our sleep patterns for optimal rest. No more PTSD induced insomnia or paranoia or anxiety. No disease.

We took in more than just veterans. We took in those that needed it; normal citizens, and we helped them too. We built a city underground. And today, it is time for us to bring to you, the people, our knowledge and tech advancements. We have the power to change the world. I'm sure each and every one of you knows someone who has fallen to cancer. AIDS. Huntington's. Alzheimer's. Dementia. I tell you today is the final day you will deal with that. We can make it go away.

Some of you may be hungry and unsure of where your next meal comes from. We will provide for you. You will never be hungry or worry about drinking polluted water.

Some years back we presented our technology to your governments and pharmaceutical companies anonymously, with proof that it worked. We were laughed at.

We have the power to rid the world of poverty, crime, violence, greed, and corruption. We have the power to provide true, and absolute freedom to each and every one of you. We will create what we have all strived for: a utopia. A new Earth. A new humanity. A healing that is long overdue."

***

The President of the United States was being escorted to the Presidential Emergency Operations Center, or PEOC, under the White House, surrounded by the various military leaders and advisors of her cabinet, and she was tuning in to Blackhawk's message on a small tablet.

"Your mother, your sister or brother, your friend, your *child* that died of disease after sickening, prolonged, and financially devastating treatment? We could have prevented that. But your leaders care more for a little piece of paper with a dead man's head on it, than your life.

We are here to put a stop to them. I will not lie to you. Today and tonight may be bloody. But the innocent will not shed a single drop. Only those that have taken advantage and manipulated you and preyed on you as you scraped by will feel the touch of death.

We will come knocking. If you are an abuser, we will come knocking. If you are a parasite, we will come knocking. If you sit upon a throne of blood, sweat, and tears, built by workers that you underpay while you reap all the benefits you should be passing down…we will come knocking."

"Did he just imply there will be violence?" The POTUS asked her Secretary of Defense.

"Yes, Madame President. I believe that's exactly what he's saying."

"How long before we can get jets scrambled from Wright-Patterson?"

The SecDef checked his watch. "Possibly 0930 hours, ma'am. We received an early tip from Admiral James Harrison of the Tenth Fleet. Said his sister is a police officer on the ground in Cincinnati."

"Thirty minutes, that's not terrible." The POTUS stated. "Can we shut this transmission off?"

"No ma'am, whatever encryption algorithm they're using, it's next level." An advisor spoke up from behind.

"Get us someone up to his level ASAP. The Guard is deployed to the city, correct?" The POTUS asked.

"Yes ma'am. ETA one hour."

***

Blackhawk finished his transmission.

"This is the final war of our time. After our campaign this day, you will no longer worry for your futures. I can assure you. Stay in your homes. Keep off the streets. I can not predict what your local and state governments will do. Martial law may be enacted. The military will respond. I welcome negotiation. But we have our plan and will see it through."

All screens went black, and then fluttered back to normal.

The pub in London erupted with applause as their soccer game fizzled back on screen; Manchester United was still in the lead over Liverpool.

Blackhawk's cockpit opened up and he stepped out onto his platform, surveying the land from high in the air. The Pantheon stayed put. He didn't want anyone to know about them just yet. He knew the Department of Defense would respond very soon—likely with force. He needed an act of aggression from the military to prove a point. He walked to the edge of his platform, and puffed his cigar. The plan, so far, was going off without a hitch.

CHAPTER TWENTY-THREE

Aces High

At Wright-Patterson Air Force Base, the largest operating air base in the United States, the 180th National Guard Fighter Wing was scrambling after an emergency order was sent down from Washington itself.

Crews had hastily prepped and inspected three F-16V "Viper" fighter jets, armed with Sidewinder missiles and M61 Vulcan cannons. The aircraft had already been taxied out to the runway.

Three pilots and their respective weapons systems officers jogged toward the jets, flight helmets in hand.

2nd LT Jessie "Spensa" Gallows was leading her fellow pilots and their passengers out to their jets. She was headstrong, green, and aggressive in flight, earning her a call sign in reference to a character with the same traits in a book series she'd read as a teenager, which had inspired her to join the Air Force in the first place. So she took the call sign as a mark of honor. This was her first "combat" engagement.

Captain Marcus "Mako" Trevors and 1st LT Dave "Dipstick" Hunters were following Spensa, and two weapons systems officers were behind them, to assist Spensa and Dipstick. Mako would fly his aircraft solo.

Mako was given his call sign due to his tendency to circle his opponents in the air like a shark in water, while Dipstick had earned his during an embarrassing incident in which he misjudged his flight path and skimmed a lake, causing around $450,000 in damage to his plane. He'd gotten more cautious since.

"Spensa, how you feelin'?" Mako yelled forward.

"Just ready to show 'em who's boss." Spensa yelled back.

"Just remember, this is strictly a surveillance flight. We do not engage unless necessary. We're the Army's backup plan today." Mako said, bringing his helmet up onto his head.

"Yes sir." Spensa slowed her stride as they got close to their aircraft and put her helmet on. The flight maintenance crews greeted all of the pilots and officers, and adjusted their gear if needed.

Dipstick made his way up the airstair just behind his passenger and looked over to Spensa. He'd been showing her a few flight tricks and maneuvers during training. Some for safety, others for combat superiority. "Spensa! Don't brake check me this time, alright?!" He yelled.

"I said I was sorry!" Spensa yelled back, laughing.

The pilots and weapons officers settled into the fighter jets, attached their safety harnesses, checked all the bells and whistles, clasped their oxygen masks over their faces, gave each other thumbs up, and flicked their visors down.

One behind the other, the jets roared down the runway and into the sky, each breaking left to head North toward Cincinnati. They quickly got into a triangle formation for cruising. They'd be over the city within minutes.

***

Blackhawk watched as an Apache helicopter rounded an exploratory circle around The Bullpen, assessing the situation.

Come on. Do what you're gonna do.

Blackhawk knew the next move was to try and establish communication with him, which he would oblige, but he needed them to attack. And he knew he may have to goad them into it.

The Apache slowed and hovered right in front of him, around fifty feet away from the platform. Blackhawk pulled his trench coat away from his side, showing off his revolver, even though he didn't intend on using it. Yet.

He then turned and opened a case, and pulled out a military radio and held it up, showing it to the pilot in the attack chopper. He used his fingers to tell them the numbers for a frequency, signaling 3-8-7.

Inside the cockpit, the pilot communicated with his cockpit gunner, usually called a 'CPG', in front of him. "Is that a CSEL radio he's holding?"

The CPG turned the chopper's camera targeting system toward Blackhawk and flicked the zoom switch to get a closer look. "Sure looks like it."

"Roger. Let's see if he's got anything good to say."

Blackhawk noticed the targeting system sighting him, and figured they could listen in now. His voice came through the comms. "Army helicopter, please meet me at 387.850, I say again, meet me at 387.850."

The CPG dialed his radio to the requested frequency, and the pilot spoke out. "This is Army copter 555 on 387.850, how may we assist you, sir?"

"I'd like to order a Big Mac, with no onions, extra cheese…" Blackhawk's voice rang out.

The copter hovered for a moment, silent, as Blackhawk awaited a response.

"Uh, negative, we are not McDonald's. This is uh, Pizza Hut."

Blackhawk laughed and spoke into the radio. "Nice to see you fellas still have your sense of humor."

"We try. What seems to be the problem up here? Gotta say you've got people on the ground real antsy."

"You can call me Blackhawk, formerly of the 101st Aviation Brigade, and former UH-60 pilot. I am here as a courtesy, and as a matter of respect." Blackhawk replied.

"Nice to meet you, sir. But we're really going to need you to return to the ground. No need to—"

"I'm gonna need y'all to shoot at me." Blackhawk interrupted, dropping his professionalism a little and allowing his southern drawl out.

The CPG in the copter turned around—as much as he could—and held his hand up as if to say *what the fuck*? The pilot laughed. "Sir, say again?"

"Judgin' by that little snicker you got goin' on, I think you heard well enough, Chief."

"Uh, negative, sir, we will not be firing on you."

"Don't make me force you to."

This time the CPG laughed as well, muting out Blackhawk for a moment. "Chief, is he trying to bait us into doing something stupid?"

"Yep." The pilot replied. "Dial us back to command frequency real quick." The CPG obliged, dialing the frequency on the radio back, and gave the pilot a thumbs up. "Command, this is Army copter 555, call sign Silverback, do you copy, over."

A voice came through the radio. "Copy, Silverback, go ahead."

"This guy up here on this floating platform, he's a former Blackhawk pilot, allegedly. But he's telling us to fire on him, please advise."

"Well, you are familiar with ROE, is he a threat?"

"Not that we can see sir, but he does have a *real* fancy, uh, fighter jet…thing. I've never seen anything like it."

Blackhawk waited patiently. He knew exactly what the two men inside the hovering chopper were doing.

"No sir, does not appear to be armed. No visible weapons, at least. He's got a pistol."

Blackhawk put his cigar out on the concrete platform and held his radio up and shook it, thinking to himself, *Y'all are gonna make me do it ain't you?*

He turned and walked back to his AV and opened the cockpit. He reached in and powered it up, and looked back at the Apache as his AV lifted off and floated a few inches high.

"Command, he just powered on his aircraft. That thing looks like a spaceship; it's just floating over the platform. He's requesting we go back on his frequency. Standby."

The CPG returned to Blackhawks radio frequency. His voice immediately came through.

"Gentlemen, this is my personal aerial assault vehicle. Now, you don't see it just yet, but the main weapon is a retractable electromagnetic propulsion track. Some may call it a rail gun. And yes, it works."

"Stingers armed." The CPG stated, nervously, referring to the air to air Stinger missiles, ready to fire, on the Apache's wings. He flicked another switch up. "Standing by."

"Roger. Hold for now." The pilot replied.

Blackhawk stepped up and into the cockpit. "And here in a second, you're gonna see that weapon pop out. Right there." He pointed at an area just behind the cockpit. "And it's going to aim in your general direction. You are going to have to defend yourselves. Command will not yell at you."

Blackhawk heard the faint howl of jet engines, and searched the sky. He saw the trio of F-16s encircling The Bullpen, keeping their distance. He stepped into the cockpit fully, took a seat, and closed the hatch. Sure enough, just behind the cockpit on top of the AV, the plating separated and a dual-rail system pushed out, and auto-aimed right at the Apache, and began to glow blue. Visible electric charges pulsed down the rails.

"Alright ladies." He addressed The Pantheon. "Nyx, when they fire, you go for the Apache. They'll be firing either Stinger or Hellfire missiles. Our shielding can withstand a few hits but the capacitors will run down quick, so you be quicker, Rhea and Eris, those three fighter jets are yours. Do *not*, and I repeat, *do not* allow those pilots to be harmed. Nyx, the black box is in the tail of that chopper. We need that. Artemis and Nemesis, you stay put for now."

Each of the women's suits activated a fighter pilot style helmet with a heads up display that wrapped around their faces.

Blackhawk pulled a red trigger on his flight stick, and with a deafening crackle, the rail gun catapulted a tungsten round at the speed of lightning, just over the Apache. He'd missed on purpose.

A Stinger missile from the Apache's right wing dropped and ignited, screaming toward The Bullpen, slamming into the electromagnetic shielding surrounding the platform and exploding on impact.

"Whoah! Shit!" The chopper pilot yelled, pulled back, and swerved the aircraft to the right, getting some distance from the unexpected blast. "Stinger's a no go, Fox 3, Fox 3!" The pilot moved the Apache to the right, circling The Bullpen, and the CPG switched to the 30 millimeter cannon, and just as he hit the trigger to rain down a ridiculous amount of lead, Nyx blew through the black smoke left by the missile explosion, thrusting straight toward the chopper and corkscrewing through the air to avoid the minigun cannon fire.

Eris and Rhea's compartments opened and the two ladies erupted from the AV, breaking hard left and heading straight for the fighter jets. Artemis and Nemesis both exited as well, but they stayed on the platform, guarding the AV and Blackhawk.

Nyx broke right and nailed a hard boost up under the Apache. The pilot tried to follow and evade, but Nyx was way too fast and agile. She grabbed the fuselage of the chopper with one hand and whipped her chained sword out with the other, slicing the tail of the copter off and sending it into an uncontrollable spin, descending rapidly. She ripped out an orange device from the tail—the black box—and left the chopper falling.

Nyx dropped the black box on the platform and immediately whipped around and nose dived toward the Apache, landing on the glass of the cockpit and guarding her head with the massive sword, ripping the top rotor blades to pieces in the process.

Now that the rotors were gone, she retracted the sword and stowed the hilt in her suit, broke up the glass from the cockpit and unbuckled the CPG. The pilot pulled his pistol and fired right at Nyx's head, but the rounds pelted her armor and bounced right off. She cut a look to him, and snatched the pistol out of his hand, tossing it into the air. She pulled the CPG out of the cockpit, who was struggling and punching her arm wildly. She unbuckled the pilot as well, and lifted the two men out of the cockpit and into the air, allowing the Apache to fall to the Earth.

She brought both men down safe and sound on the grass below, with no way to communicate with command. But, they were alive and confused as Hell. She blasted off fast enough that her boosters knocked the men on their asses.

***

"What the hell was that, Mako? Did you catch that shit? Did it save the crew?" Dipstick asked on the radio.

"Looked like a drone. Thing was fast as hell, we're gonna have to engage." Mako replied.

"Two bandits closing fast, 8 o'clock!" Spensa yelled into her radio.

"Got 'em. Engage DCA, Sidewinders hot. Break break break." Mako gave the orders to break formation, arm the missiles, and attack.

The three F-16s split, with Spensa rolling right and looping under Mako and Dipstick, and bringing her HUD in line with the approaching Pantheon.

Mako simply rolled left and aimed his jet toward the approaching ladies, as Dipstick continued straight, with the plan of getting a little more distance to provide backup for Mako and Spensa. He liked to sneak up behind the enemy as they were preoccupied—something he'd learned from Mako–and a tactic that worked all kinds of wonders on his engagements in Iraq and Syria.

Whatever fancy maneuvers the pilots were doing, Rhea and Eris didn't care. This would be easy. And fun.

"Engaging, switching to guns." Spensa said on the radio.

"Negative, Spensa. Maintain tally with Sidewinders. Drones are big enough to lock." Mako suggested.

Spensa begrudgingly switched back to missiles. She really loved the cannons. *Shit, they're coming in hot*, she thought. The alarm sounded, indicating she had a missile lock. She fired two missiles, depleting her air to air capabilities in one move. "FOX 2, FOX 2."

Eris and Rhea split, with Eris breaking left and Rhea to the right. The two Sidewinders had locked onto them separately. Both had a missile on their tails.

"Bandits breaking formation. Are those..." Mako squinted, trying to make out what he was looking at.

Spensa broke hard left, looking out the canopy at Rhea as she corkscrewed through the sky. "That's a person in suit!"

"Sidewinders aren't going to—" Mako stopped abruptly when he saw Eris headed straight for him, Sidewinder missile right at her back. "Bandit has a lock on my aircraft." He broke hard right and pulled up, putting upwards of 9 G's on his body, and incorporating a special breathing technique to avoid passing out. He leveled the jet and looked back, but Eris was right on him, and so was the missile. Mako popped flares from the rear of the jet, attempting to blind Eris and confuse the missile, but Eris rolled out of the way and dropped hard, and the Sidewinder maintained a lock, now on Mako.

"Ah shit, zapped me! Gotta punch!" Mako reached down and pulled his ejector seat lever, blasting out of the cockpit just before the missile hit and turned the F-16 into a ball of flames. Eris circled Mako as his parachute deployed, taunting him.

"Eris! Goddammit! That was a little too close for comfort! Calm down!" Blackhawk growled through her comlink.

Spensa was keeping tally, or sight, on Rhea, who abruptly slowed and pitched upward, and rolled backward and onto the Sidewinder missile itself, almost like she was surfing it. She reached underneath, got a good grip, and broke the missile in half. She boosted away at an impossibly rapid pace as the missile fizzled a few more hundred feet and exploded.

Spensa jerked her gaze around, trying to get sight on Eris and Dipstick, who was now her only wingman. The situation was dire, but she kept her cool, even though her heart rate had climbed to over 130. She was breathing hard and fast. "Dipstick, can't get a visual on you."

"On six, hound dog! Got tally on both bandits." He replied, easing her heart rate only slightly. "They're both on you."

"I know, I know!" Spensa broke hard right and up, cutting a hard loop. 7 Gs. 8 Gs. 9Gs. Spensa huffed and compressed her lungs repeatedly, controlling the blood flow to her brain. If she passed out, she was dead. Both Eris and Rhea followed, closing in. "I'm gonna get sandwiched here!"

"Dogfight's not gonna work with these things, gonna have to outsmart 'em. I'll get one off you. Switching to guns." Dipstick said. He centered his HUD on Rhea, who was closest to Spensa, led the target a little, and pulled the trigger.

A stream of 20 millimeter rounds whizzed by Rhea, and she broke hard right to avoid them, now realizing Dipstick had her in his sights. She cut a maneuver and flipped the opposite way, and boosted as hard as she could toward him, weaving in various directions to avoid the Vulcan cannon fire.

"Jesus, how the hell are they that agile? Had to pull 20 Gs just now." Dipstick said.

Spensa didn't reply. She was eyeballing Eris, closing in fast. She barrel rolled her plane and inverted it, and pulled up hard, attempting to get under Eris. But it was pointless. Eris simply dropped down straight toward her. Spensa rolled right and cut hard. Then left. She cut thrusters to make a tighter turn. Eris was still closing in. Spensa fully engaged the thrusters. Maybe she could outrun Eris.

"Gah!" Spensa said over the radio. "I need a little wiggle room here! Dropping tanks." She flicked a switch on the console.

Her jet had two wing-mounted fuel tanks, both empty, mounted from a previous training exercise. Both the tanks broke away from the wings and fell to the Earth. Luckily they were only over some fields. Spensa felt an immediate lightening of the aircraft.

"There. LET'S GO!" She yelled into the radio. She broke hard right and pulled up, almost killing the thrusters in the process. Her jet whipped in a tight J-turn. She rolled and leveled the plane, and jammed the thruster lever forward. She slammed back into her seat. Her weapons systems officer yelped at the violent maneuver and held on. The air seemed to crack across the wings with a resounding and heavy pop. Spensa had broken the sound barrier.

Eris couldn't keep up. The jet was finally too fast, so she turned to help Rhea with Dipstick.

It turned out, Rhea didn't need help. She had made it to Dipstick's jet and pointed a fist at the rear tail. A blue laser shot out of her suit's forearm, and sheared the tail off. Rhea boosted hard at the now out of control plane. Dipstick barrel rolled, trying to keep Rhea from getting to his cockpit at least, hoping she wasn't saving some laser beams for him and his weapons officer.

Rhea planted her feet on the side of the cockpit and grabbed hold of it, still locked in a barrel roll. She gripped the edge of the glass canopy and ripped it off the hinges. She reached down between her thighs and with a fist, jerked upward, telling the men inside to eject. They had no choice. Dipstick leveled the plane, and he and his rider ejected as Rhea boosted away.

Eris made it to Rhea just in time to see a peppering of 20 millimeter rounds slam into her, sending sparks everywhere.

Spensa had come back around, and had them both in her sights. "Did you miss me?!" She unleashed a hellfire barrage of cannon rounds on both Rhea and Eris, striking Rhea once more.

Rhea's suit malfunctioned and lost power, and she dropped out of the sky. Eris went after her and Spensa adjusted her vector, keeping her sights on them. Just as she was about to release another barrage, her plane lurched to the left and rolled. The nose pointed away and toward the city, so she let off the trigger.

"The Hell?!" She yelled, looking around her canopy. Nyx had come out of nowhere, and latched onto her right wing.

Nyx brought two fingers up to her masked face, and pointed them at Spensa, signing *I see you.* Nyx then motioned for Spensa to eject, same as Rhea had done with Dipstick earlier. Spensa gave Nyx the finger. Nyx glared at Spensa for a moment, then drew her huge, segmented, whip-sword, and brandished it, threatening to tear the plane apart.

"Kiss, my, ass!" Spensa defiantly dropped thrust and popped the air brakes, sending Nyx tumbling across the plane. Spensa pitched down hard and broke right, headed directly to the ground. Nyx recovered quickly and rocketed toward Spensa's plane, sword in hand.

Eris, out of nowhere, blasted right through the jet's left wing. It shredded like paper to a flame, and sent Spensa into an uncontrollable barrel roll.

Several alarms sounded, drowning out any chance of Spensa having a second to think. She couldn't eject in a barrel roll. That was certain death.

"Mayday! Mayday! Tumbleweed! I can't…" Spensa yelled into the radio. "I can't figure out, I'm in a roll, can't punch out! What do I do?!"

Suddenly, the plane leveled off, cockpit to the sky. Spensa looked over to the left, and Nyx had latched on again, this time using her own boosters to keep the jet level. Nyx motioned to *eject* once again.

This time, Spensa obliged, sending herself and her weapons officer rocketing out of the cockpit as Nyx allowed the F-16 to crash to the hills below. The pilots' parachutes deployed as hoped.

But Spensa eyed Eris, making a turn and now headed straight for her. She drew her own service pistol, waiting for Eris to close in so she could get a shot off. This was a human, or at least it looked like one. Maybe a bullet to the face would shut it down. Spensa brought the pistol up and out the iron sights on Eris, closing in at such a speed that was certainly lethal if she was hit.

Nyx suddenly moved into view, blocking Spensa's line of sight. Dropping the pistol from her eyeline, she noticed Nyx facing the other direction, toward Eris, and her sword was drawn and ready to swing if needed. Nyx was *protecting* her from Eris, who stopped just shy of swinging distance of Nyx's sword.

The short standoff was tense. Eris could have melted steel with the anger in her chest. Spensa had shot down Rhea, and she had to pay.

Nyx activated her sword; it segmented, and glowed with blue lightning. She was prepared to defend Spensa, matching the pilot's descent. Blackhawk's orders: do not harm the pilots.

Eris finally withdrew and flew back down toward The Bullpen. Nyx escorted Spensa down to the ground, then boosted away.

***

Ramsay had been monitoring the flood of news reports on the incident that was taking place above. They were all calling Blackhawk's emergence an "attack", but they would soon know the truth. He put the tablet he was using down and asked SIGIL once again, "Enable Hijack Protocol."

***

Once again the screens went black in the London pub, prompting an absurdly loud reaction.

Blackhawk's face came up again, as he spoke into a floating tablet screen.

"I'm sure everyone in the world is trying to misconstrue what just happened all over your TVs. As expected, your media outlets will be calling this an attack on America. But you will find that the pilot and CPG of that Apache are alive and well, not a scratch on 'em. As are the F-16 pilots that aggressively fired on us.

They are all on ground, awaiting for emergency crews to pick them up. They will hopefully all give accurate accounts as to what happened.

As for the whys and whos and whats, my name is CW3 Jacob Hawke. I am not an aggressor. The military fired on us and we defended ourselves, refusing to harm any personnel. What you've just witnessed is the might of The Pantheon, a group of women who have graciously volunteered to change this world for the better. How will we do that, you ask?"

Blackhawk held up five vials of the black liquid comprised of the Xenobots, all compressed into epi-pen style needles.

"These booster shot looking things here are filled with the most magnificent thing humanity has ever come across. Xenobots. Now, it's not something we invented. They've been around for a while. But we made them better. This is going to sound scary but, hear me out.

They can rewrite matter itself. On an atomic level. Of course, that sounds like that sci-fi scare tactic called the 'Gray Goo Theory', but that's not what's going to happen here.

You have sick people. With incurable diseases. You have mental health issues. You have hungry men, women, and children on your streets. You have school shootings; little kids being killed for nothing. You have wars fought over precious lies. You have laws that protect only the law makers. You have been duped into *voting* for your own oppressors, thinking you have agency in your way of life."

Blackhawk laughed. "That's the funniest one, to me. But with these Xenobots, my Pantheon, these *angels*, are here to save you. They are here to give their own bodies back to this Earth, and solve all your problems. And with that, I have a demonstration."

People across the world stared at their screens, interested in what Blackhawk had to say, and more importantly, what he was about to do.

"Rhea, it's time." Blackhawk knelt to Rhea, who had been largely unharmed when Spensa shot her down, thanks to her armor and exo-suit—aside from a few scratches and a bloody brow. Eris had safely dropped her back on The Bullpen platform. Without hesitation, she nodded, and stood proudly. This is what she'd volunteered for. Blackhawk looked to the screen—his outlet to the entire world that was watching.

"This is Johanna Wagner. Code name: Rhea. One of your pilots just shot her out of the sky, but luckily she is still willing and proud to do this for you. She is a former agent of the BND, the German secret service, disavowed after a botched mission where she was tortured for months, and never gave up anything, loyal to a country that had discarded her. She was crippled. Eventually, she was released, thanks to our efforts."

***

In Germany, the Prime Minister's eyes widened at the sight of Johanna. She'd been briefed that Johanna had been killed years ago. She shot a glare to the President of the BND, who happened to be standing next to her. He held his hands up as if to say *these things happen.*

***

With the tablet screen broadcasting to the world, Blackhawk handed Rhea one of the vials, and touched his forehead to hers. He knew she was scared, but she was determined.

"Every soul on Earth will remember you, this day forth." He said to her, just loud enough for her to hear.

When he backed away, he had tears in his eyes, threatening to escape, but he held them at bay. The tablet screen backed away, showing Rhea from the knees up.

Rhea held the vial high in the air, looked at the screen, and gave her last words to the world through a crackling, emotional voice.

"Auf Wiedersehen, und hallo."

She brought the epi-pen down hard into her chest, just above the breast, injected the Xenobots, and jerked the booster away from her body, dropping it immediately.

Crowds everywhere, across the globe, erupted in chatter, asking what her last words even meant; what was about to happen? Was this good or bad? Is this the apocalypse? Did she say 'Goodbye, and Hello?' What did that mean?

Rhea felt a slow crawl of fire in her body, emanating from her very core. Her bones felt like they were expanding. Her muscles felt like they were ripping apart, fiber by fiber. But she held everything in the best she could, if only for a moment. She let out an involuntary squeak of vocal pain and winced. She was trying to be strong and stand proud for those watching, but the burning was intensifying. It was too much. She screamed—a long, howling and pitiful cry of imminent death.

Nemesis and Artemis couldn't hold back. They couldn't stand by as their friend died—not without saying goodbye.

They rushed over to Rhea, and when Artemis was close to touching Rhea, Blackhawk yelled.

"Don't touch her! Don't know what will happen!"

Artemis withdrew and cut Blackhawk an angry glare.

Rhea's skin began to break apart, and through each crackling and tearing segment of flesh, came a white hot glow. Her entire body slowly broke down into a glowing cloud of Xenobots. They'd effectively rewritten her entire atomic structure, and would do whatever Rhea's final wishes were, which had been something Blackhawk asked her to do. Her skin and tissue, her muscle and bone—all flaked away, microscopically, and formed a sort of light snow flurry around The Bullpen.

Nemesis and Artemis backed away from Rhea's breaking down body as her cries stopped. She could look around. She seemed conscious. But the pained expression had gone; Replaced with calm. She looked at each of The Pantheon, silently saying goodbye to them. Eris and Nyx nodded as a farewell, but Nemesis and Artemis looked on as if they were having second thoughts.

Rhea finally pulled her eyes to Blackhawk, who stood stoic as ever. He nodded and walked to one of the workstations near him, and picked up a live grenade.

As Rhea's body broke down further into a cloud of flurrying and glowing nano-bots, Blackhawk looked to the tablet screen again.

"Johanna Wagner. Remember her name, and remember her sacrifice. For today she has shown this world a compassion it may not deserve. After the Xenobots complete their cycle in her body, they will enact change on the city of Cincinnati effective immediately. And the world will see what we have to offer."

Rhea's body fully disintegrated and the Xenobots that were flurrying around descended below and headed to the city. A minute amount of them made their way over to Blackhawk's grenade, which he was holding up to the screen.

"Today is the last time you will need instruments of destruction. There will be no more war. No crime. There will be harmony. There will be peace. There will be…"

The grenade was overcome with Xenobots. Blackhawk's eyes were wide with wonder and excitement and possibly a smidge of fear. The tiny bots broke the grenade down atomically, and rearranged it into a simple, juicy, Granny Smith apple.

"Change." He said, and took a bite of the apple, grinning, and all the screens around the world went black.

CHAPTER TWENTY-FOUR

Mortem Machina

Ramsay took a deep, deep breath and held it in for a moment, before allowing it to slowly exit his lungs. He knew what he was about to see would be gruesome, and he was mentally conditioning himself to push back the coming shock.

The door to Leyla's apartment beeped and unlocked, recognizing his bio-sig. He'd always had the ability to barge in on anyone in SubCity but he was an honest man, and people deserve their privacy.

He pushed the door open, and immediately winced and turned away. The last time he'd seen a body was when Athon mowed down Blackhawk's platoon in The Fridge. Ten years had passed, but images like that didn't go away without a neurobandit in the brain.

Del's lifeless body had come to rest just inside the doorway. There wasn't much blood. She actually had only a few scratches, aside from the broken arm. Artemis's malicious final blow had stopped her heart on impact, so it never had the chance to pump any blood from Del's wounds.

"Fuck…" Ramsay said aloud.

"You're telling' me." Texas Chainsaw Massacre replied—being the only survivor of the previous onslaught. Ramsay stepped inside.

"The ginger one did that." Chainsaw Massacre pointed at Del, referring to Artemis's brutality. "She was ruthless."

"It wasn't supposed to be like this." Ramsay said.

"Well, your fearless leader and his harem of hotties think differently.."

"Yeah." Ramsay sulked, looking down at Leyla's friend. He then looked down the corridor, leading into the common room with the huge window.

The glass had been shattered all the way across, and shards littered the entire apartment. It was supposed to be shatterproof, but an anti-gravity force pulse is a different monster to a simple throw of a chair or a hammer. Ramsay figured Blackhawk had used his AV to do just that. He kicked some of the glass shards to the side, and they clinked together as they slid to the wall.

It was raining outside, and wind from the cavern was coming through the window, blowing in some of the rain drops from the rainmakers.

Ramsay assumed Leyla was in the common room, so he forced himself to walk down the heavily damaged corridor. The floor had been smashed to bits. The wall was ripped apart. There wasn't a single square inch in the apartment that hadn't seen violence.

A few steps into the room, he stopped. He could see Leyla on the floor with his peripheral vision, and had to mentally prepare himself once again. He drew one more deep breath, and looked down to her.

A bullet to the brain is never a clean way to go. But what always surprises folks is just how much blood really passes through the cranium. Every drop of which was now on the floor, enveloping Leyla's body like a crimson death bed.

It was shocking. But it wasn't exactly the sight of Leyla's body that hit Ramsay the most. It was the sight of the bone and brain and muscle tissue and blood. Androids don't have blood. Sure, SIGIL had created her. Sure, she had synthetic, dark energy powered cells. Sure, she was technically an android, but Leyla was very much *human.*

Blood also trailed all over the room; hefty droplets and streams were peppered on the walls and the floor. Smudged boot prints in blood coupled with the prints of what looked to be The Pantheon's mech feet laid out the fight that had taken place.

Leyla's severed hand was resting near the spot where the couch had been. It was now pushed back against the wall near the desk, and the coffee table had been ripped from its suspension braces. The Thumper was still pulsing a brilliant orange glow. At least they hadn't thought to destroy it. That probably wouldn't have been good for the entire planet. He carefully picked the Thumper off the hand, thinking it should be kept somewhere safe for now.

And then it hit him. The realization that Leyla had been through this before. She'd died before. SIGIL had thrown her through a portal and high into the sky, where she rocketed to the ground and assuredly sustained catastrophic damage. She had been dead for *years.* And there she was, on the floor in her apartment. Dead again, but after she'd come to life on her own. She had special cellular structure—regenerative capabilities.

What if…

***

Ramsay hurriedly carried Leyla's body, draped in a bloodied sheet, down the short tunnel to The Fridge.

"SIGIL!" He yelled, announcing his presence before entering the room.

He jog-walked, and stopped right in front of the massive machine. SIGIL's single eye lens looked down to him.

Out of breath, Ramsay asked SIGIL something he hoped would have a positive answer. "She's died before and come back. Can she do it again?"

"*I MUST SEE HER.*"

Ramsay tenderly laid Leyla's body down on the floor, which had since dried from the warmth of SIGIL's reactor core. He pulled the sheet away, revealing the gunshot to the head and severed arm.

SIGIL scanned her body with an X-ray.

"*SHATTERED ULNA AND RADIUS BONES. SEVERED LEFT HAND. TWO BROKEN VERTEBROSTERNAL RIBS. PUNCTURED LUNG. SHATTERED LUMBAR VERTEBRA, L2 AND L3. SEVERED SPINAL CORD. SHATTERED FRONTAL AND PARIETAL BONES. CATASTROPHIC GRAY MATTER LOSS. CATASTROPHIC BLOOD LOSS.*"

"Jesus..." Ramsay stepped back, reeling at the reveal of injuries he hadn't seen. They'd broken her spine, too. Maybe Blackhawk allowed Artemis to do this because he thought Leyla was a simple android. But he'd had to have seen the blood. Or, maybe he hadn't expected such bloodlust from The Pantheon. Ramsay had never trusted them, and warned Blackhawk on several occasions that they could become the problem they thought Athon would be.

There was always the chance they would rebel from SubCity and wreak havoc wherever they pleased. And Ramsay and Blackhawk had given them each the means to take on armies. Maybe Athon had never been the threat. They'd made their own doom, and given them wings and weapons and cool, mythological names. Rhea was gone, but Nemesis, Artemis, Eris and Nyx remained—Four Horsewomen of the apocalypse.

The world would need someone who could match their strength. The world would need an archangel.

The world would need Athon.

"Okay, so it's bad. But can you fix her? Can she come back?" Ramsay asked.

"IT IS POSSIBLE."

A circular section of floor slid open off to the side of SIGIL, near a workbench. A large, cylindrical glass tank rose out of the opening, full of some sort of clear, slightly yellowish liquid. The tank had a large connector for a hose or some sort of attachment on the side.

"THIS IS AN EMBRYONIC GROWTH AND RECOVERY CELL. ATHON WAS GROWN INSIDE IT AT AN ACCELERATED PACE THROUGH THE AID OF A SUPPLY OF ANTIMATTER CHARGED NUCLEIC ACID."

Ramsay gawked at the tank as it clanked to a stop and the thick liquid inside sloshed a bit. "You *grew* her in that? So it's a womb?"

"BY SCIENTIFIC ACCOUNTS, YES. IT IS FILLED WITH SYNTHESIZED AMNIOTIC FLUID. YOU WILL NEED TO REMOVE ATHON'S GARMENTS AND PLACE HER INSIDE."

"Uh, okay."

Ramsay wasn't exactly a fan of the prospect of disrobing a dead woman, but did it count if she'd be alive eventually? Hopefully?

"Does she *have* to be naked?"

"YES. IT IS A REQUIREMENT. THE REGEN CELLS COULD CONFUSE THE FIBROUS STRUCTURES OF HER ARMOR WITH THE CELLS OF HER BODY."

"It's just, it's *weird,* man." Ramsay sulked.

A sultry and confident female voice emanated from the entrance of The Fridge.

"So, you're not a necrophiliac. That's a good thing."

It was Clara, leaning on the wall of the tunnel, smirking at him. Llana's pet raven was latched to her shoulder, and it cooed at Leyla's lifeless body on the floor.

"I know, Hug. It's never a pretty sight." She replied to the bird, as if it had spoken some language only she understood. The raven hopped off her shoulder and glided down to Leyla's body.

Ramsay was pointing at Clara. "Not interested in one of your white eyed witchy sessions."

"Seeing you unloading a bloody sheet with a body inside from an AV and rushing down here? A girl might think you're up to no good." Clara said, slinking past Ramsay.

Hug let out a deep croak. "Kraaaa-kraa."

"Agreed." Clara replied.

Ramsay looked at the raven and then Clara. "You can understand that bird?"

"Hug is a raven, and I know you know that, so don't try and belittle him. He understands more than you'll ever know."

Clara knelt next to Leyla and Hug, and stroked Leyla's pale cheek. "I told you to end your search. But you're not done yet, are you?"

"She can't hear you on count of the…being dead." Ramsay stated the obvious, prompting a glare from Clara.

"Not the first time I've spoken to the dead. And not the first time they've listened."

"Okay, not going to ask about any of that. What are you doing here?"

"Hug was nagging me to follow, and he led me here."

"Okay, cool, we'll we're on some important, world saving business right now, so if you'll excuse me…" Ramsay tried to shoo Clara away, but Hug flared his wings and almost growled at him. He drew back.

"When you bring her back, she won't be the same." Clara said.

"*CORRECT.*" SIGIL intervened. "*IF THE REGEN IS SUCCESSFUL, HER ENGRAM STRUCTURE WILL BE DIFFERENT. SHE MAY NOT HAVE HER MEMORIES ONCE AGAIN.*"

"So she won't be Leyla? It'll just be Athon?" Ramsay asked.

"*THAT IS MOST LIKELY.*"

Clara stood and looked at Hug, and smiled. The raven bowed, as if to say *this is why we're here*. Clara looked up at SIGIL. "There are many capabilities of magick."

"*MAGICK IS SIMPLY UNEXPLAINED SCIENCE.*"

"To an extent." Clara replied, then looked at Ramsay as she circled him and Leyla's body. "I've transferred a consciousness before. Rebuilding one isn't far off."

"What? Transferred? Like a mind?" Ramsay asked, turning to follow Clara as she circled.

"Brain tissue is not a person. Everything isn't always math and ones and zeroes. Everything isn't science. Leyla is still in there. You give her life back. I will give her mind back."

"So what was all this apocalyptic sounding *the black go back* shit she told me about?" Ramsay scoffed.

"Again, Hug understands more than even I know."

Ramsay looked at Hug, who was prancing around the room like a curious toddler with wings.

"A raven told you to come here?"

Clara smiled. "I'll undress her. You needn't do it."

"Oh God, thank you. Good." Ramsay sighed, relieved.

"God has nothing to do with it." Clara said, bending down to prep Leyla. "Not that one, anyway."

Clara slipped the skin tight armor from Leyla's body almost effortlessly as Hug lingered nearby, occasionally eyeing Ramsay, who'd turned away from the sight of a naked, dead woman. He then thought to ask SIGIL a fairly important question.

"Hey, when we bring her back and Miss Heebie Jeebies here fixes her mind, is she going to kind of reboot right when she was killed?"

"*IT IS MOST LIKELY HER MIND WILL PICK UP WHERE IT LEFT OFF.*"

"It will be traumatic for her. It will be as if she's still in the instance of death." Clara replied, almost finished undressing Leyla.

"Shit. Uh, so, she is probably gonna be *real* mad at me. This is my fault."

"BLACKHAWK WOULD HAVE FOUND OUT WITHOUT YOU TELLING HIM WHO ATHON WAS."

Clara stood. "You told Blackhawk to come after her? Why would you do th—"

"It wasn't like that! I really was going to lie and throw him off, but none of you have ever had all of The Pantheon stare you down when you're about to tell a fib! Fucking Rhea, man. She was a secret agent before all this. She can smell a lie like a shark smells blood. I broke. I told them everything."

"Pfft. Cowardly." Clara scoffed. Even Hug croaked disapprovingly at Ramsay.

"Can we just, make her more Leyla than Athon? She was more understanding. And less…murderous." Ramsay asked SIGIL.

"That will be her decision." Clara replied.

"CORRECT. ATHON HAS AND ALWAYS WILL POSSESS FREE WILL."

Ramsay threw his hands up. "Great. I'm dead."

Clara laughed. "I'm sticking around to see how this turns out."

"You know what? I'm okay with it. The Pantheon is the issue. Leyla can probably kick their asses. That's all that matters. I'll just have to step up and accept whatever she does."

"YOU WILL NEED TO LOWER HER BODY, FEET FIRST, INTO THE EMBRYONIC TANK."

The tank began lowering into the ground, as to allow Ramsay and Clara to get her into it more easily. Ramsay took hold of her shoulders, trying extremely hard to not touch any part of her breast, and looking away as he did so. Clara laughed again, grabbing Leyla's ankles.

"You've proven your point, Mister Chivalry. But even if you accidentally touch something I don't think she's going to care."

"Oh come on! This is really weird, okay?" Ramsay snapped as they carried her body to the tank.

"You have a thing for her don't you?"

"Huh? N…no."

"Uh huh."

They turned Leyla feet first and slipped her into the thick, slightly yellow liquid. It made a nice, goopy sound as she went inside. After her waist, her body went in almost on its own, and the tank raised again from the floor as Clara and Ramsay backed away. Hug decided to fly up to the top of the tank and rest there.

"Ever the guardian." Clara said, winking at her raven. Hug croaked.

"NOW, YOU MUST MANUALLY CONNECT THE NANO-GEN TUBE." SIGIL said, as a thick, translucent hose, around six inches wide, lit up with a string of internal LEDs. It had been draped behind SIGIL's massive body.

Ramsay walked over and pulled the tube off SIGIL, and heaved it toward the tank.

"YOU MUST CONNECT THE TUBE TO THE CONNECTOR ON THE TANK."

"Yep, figured that." Ramsay said. "I know you had that arm, before Leyla chopped it off, but, I been wondering…"

"YES?"

"How did you build all this? That arm isn't that intricate. Working with nano-tech? You had to have people helping."

"YOUR SHIP BOTS HAVE PROVEN TO BE INVALUABLE ASSETS."

Ramsay laughed. Those damn cute little ship bots. Of course they were helping the armageddon machine. Ramsay clicked the hose onto the tank's connector and twisted it, locking it in place. "Okay. Hooked up."

The hose filled with amniotic fluid from the tank itself.

"NOW YOU MUST INJECT THE NANO-GEN INTO THE TANK VIA THE CONSOLE."

A computer workstation lit up underneath SIGIL, and a small compartment opened, revealing a vial of gray goop, much like its black, Xenobot comprised counterpart.

"Are those more Xenobots? I thought we'd gotten all of those."

"INCORRECT. THIS IS ANTIMATTER INFUSED NUCLEIC ACID. THE FOUNDATION OF ATHON'S CELL STRUCTURE."

"Got it. So this will rebuild her body?"

"CORRECT. THEORETICALLY."

"What do you mean theoretically? She fell out of the sky and died and came back a few years later, how is this different?"

"INCORRECT. WHEN I THREW ATHON INTO THE PORTAL, NO COORDINATE WAS CALCULATED. BUT NOW I KNOW. THE YEAR WAS 1934."

Ramsay coughed out of surprise. "1934?! That's…93 years!"

"CORRECT. HER CELLS REPAIRED THEMSELVES AND HEALED HER INJURIES OVER A PERIOD OF NINE DECADES. THE SLOW PROCESS YIELDED A FAVORABLE RESULT. LIKE A CROCK POT."

"Shit! Almost a hundred years. Did you just make a fucking crock pot joke?"

"INCORRECT. IT WAS A COMPARABLE METAPHOR. HUMOR IS SUBJECTIVE."

"Okay good because the day you start laughing is the day I start running."

"HA HA HA HA HA."

Ramsay stopped in his tracks and glared at SIGIL, wide eyed.

"YOU ARE NOT RUNNING."

"Fuck you for that. How long is the regen on Leyla going to take?"

"AFTER INJECTION OF THE NANO-GEN, I CALCULATE THE REGENERATION OF ENGRAMS, BONE AND MUSCLE FIBERS, AND NEUROLOGICAL AND SPINAL TISSUES TO COMPLETE IN APPROXIMATELY TWO HOURS."

"But you don't sound so sure this will work."

"CORRECT. I HAVE NEVER ATTEMPTED THIS PROCESS. SHE HAS SUSTAINED CATASTROPHIC DAMAGE."

Clara piped in. "It'll work. Magick will fill in the gaps." She was admiring her freshly painted nails.

"Okay. So next is injecting the nano-gen stuff." Ramsay took hold of the gray vial. "Where?"

In the console, a small injection port rotated upward and clicked in place. Ramsay positioned the vial above the port and looked at SIGIL to ensure it was correct.

"CORRECT."

Ramsay pressed the vial into the port, and the gray liquid shot into it, with a violent speed—almost instantaneously. The nano-gen tube turned gray as the nucleic acid from the vial saturated the liquid inside. A moment later, a pump on the other side of the glass whirred on, and sucked all of the nano-gen from the tube into the tank. The entire tank was overcome as the gray liquid swirled all around and darkened the fluid inside like a monochrome cloud of blood, obscuring Leyla's suspended body for the time being.

"DO NOT TOUCH THE GLASS OF THE TANK. IT WILL BECOME VERY HOT DURING THE REGEN PROCESS."

Hug squawked, and flew down from the top of the tank. The aforementioned heat had come very quickly.

Clara walked to within one step of the now gray filled tank. "Science and magick." She laughed. "Like brother and sister."

"So, two hours?" Ramsay asked.

"CORRECT."

"Okay. Gotta run and get something done. Be right back." He turned and jogged out the tunnel.

Clara sat on the steps of the wormhole generator platform, looking back to it, unimpressed. She clicked her tongue. "Hug! You hungry?" She pulled a small pouch from her waist and shook out some lightly salted sunflower seeds. Hug pranced over and ate them out of her palm.

*****

Ramsay returned an hour later, this time on his self constructed motorcycle, the pearl white 'Street Rocket' cyberbike, as Leyla had named it, and rode it into the tunnel. He had a pack slung over his shoulder with something inside, and he had a hot pizza from Carol nestled in an insulated compartment behind the seat. He parked the bike off to the side and killed the power. He didn't need to use a kickstand as the bike held itself upright with antigravity capacitors.

"What did I miss?" He said, pulling his leg over the seat.

No one was in the room.

"RRAAHHH!" Clara sprang up from a workbench beside Ramsay, scaring the ever loving shit out of him. He screamed, and wildly flung fists in every direction and stumbled back.

"What! The fuck!" He yelled.

Clara bent over and rested her arms on her knees, cackling. Even Hug was croaking in a laughing rhythm.

"I'm sorry, you're just too easy." Clara smirked, and walked away, unable to hold more laughter in.

"Ugh. Dead person in here, and you're doing that shit. Not cool." Ramsay groaned, pulling the pack from his shoulder. He tapped the compartment on the rear of the bike and it opened in segments with satisfying clicks and whirs. He picked up the hot pizza and followed Clara to the tank Leyla was in, still hidden in the grayed out fluid.

"*THAT WAS A GOOD ONE.*" SIGIL approved of Clara's antics.

"Yeah, yeah." Ramsay said.

"I don't eat pizza, by the way." Clara said.

"It's not for you. It's for Leyla. She's a pizza goblin. Hopefully it'll keep her from slicing me in half."

"Possibly. Or whatever you're carrying in that pack."

"Nah, I'm not counting on that. This is just me being respectful."

Clara, Ramsay and Hug gathered near the tank.

"She's probably going to go for your neck as soon as she sees you. She's going to know what you did." Clara said.

"I know. Maybe I deserve it. But someone's going to have to step up whenever The Pantheon snaps. I know they're going to. Blackhawk wouldn't listen."

"You created valkyries and now you want to control them. That's cute. And stupid."

"Yes, thank you for stating the obvious."

"I'll try to catch her before she gets to you."

"Catch her? Athon will eat you alive."

Clara grinned. "Sounds like a fun time."

***

Wells had stopped his truck in the middle of the street in downtown Cincinnati, and had stuffed bits of napkin into his nostrils to stop the bleeding. Broken noses hurt like all get out. The city had, in the span of mere minutes, transformed into a chaotic mass of running and screaming people, police, fire and medical sirens, vandalism, and apocalyptic warnings spouted from various mouths of religious crazies. And they weren't far off.

Just a couple hours earlier, a building sized platform had raised a few thousand feet into the sky, a cult leader had taken over every network on Earth and preached a message of change—something people are almost universally terrified of—and then torn three fighter jets and an attack chopper apart, mid-air, using a group of flying super humans. Shit was insane.

Even the tornado sirens were wailing through the air, exacerbating the panic. An elderly lady chugged by Wells, running nowhere, holding a little chihuahua in her arms, terrified. But something else caught his eye that was a little more alarming.

Rats and mice. More than anyone would ever normally see at once in the city. Every one of them scurried in the same direction, hugging the walls and still trying to stay hidden. They were all running past Wells, opposite the direction he was facing. There was a general rule about that. It usually meant they weren't running a little rodent marathon. They were fleeing.

A police car screamed by Wells, going to whatever it was the rats were running from—siren blaring. Not long after it passed—maybe about a block—the squad car's brakes locked and it squealed to a stop, leaving a trail of burnt rubber. It immediately kicked into reverse. The car spun around and blazed back toward Wells. It stopped right next to him and the window went down.

It was Harrison.

"Wells! Holy shit!"

Wells jumped with excitement. "Harrison! What the fuck's going on? I don't have a radio."

"Up ahead, fuckin'…I don't know what it is. Everything is changing. Morphing or something. End of days shit. And reports of—"

Harrison was interrupted by her car radio.

All units in vicinity of the central business district PD, be advised, law enforcement is encountering heavy aggression from armored, uh, women.

Wells looked at Harrison, knowing exactly what the dispatcher was talking about.

Reports are that the women are violently disabling any law enforcement and military equipment they find. Personnel typically left unharmed.

"Military?" Wells asked.

"National Guard is already here. Get in."

A couple AVs from SubCity soared past them, overhead. Wells realized the worst case scenario had come to pass. The modders were taking the city. And there wasn't much to stop them from taking the world.

"Think she'll be mad if the pizza is cold?" Ramsay asked Clara, staring at the embryonic tank. They were both sitting on the stairs of the arch gate platform. "I didn't think about that. What if she's mad the pizza is cold?"

Clara gave Ramsay a sassy side eye. Hug was nestled in her lap like a winged kitten. "You snitched and got her and her friend killed. Cold pizza is the last thing she's going to care about."

"Yeah, I know, but some folks really like cold pizza. But, she was homeless. Probably had a lot of cold pizza. Probably doesn't like it as much. Man, I fucked up."

"Yes. You fucked up." Clara chuckled.

Ramsay checked his watch. "Been two hours. SIGIL?"

"*I HAVE NO BEARING ON THIS PROCESS.*"

"You said it would be two hours."

"*I APPROXIMATED.*"

Ramsay's comlink rang out. It was Blackhawk.

"Shit! Hide!" He shooed Clara, but she didn't budge.

"You hide, dork. Hug is perfectly comfy sitting here and I'm not disturbing him."

"Bah!" Ramsay growled, agitated, and rushed off to the other side of the room to answer the call. He swiped the holographic check symbol to accept.

"Ramsay, you still in The Fridge?" Blackhawk asked.

"Yep." Ramsay replied.

"You haven't been sayin' much brother. Why are you being so short with me?"

Ramsay's heart raced. "Nothing, just nervous I guess. Been a long time coming for all this. What did you need?"

"I just sent the ladies down to ground level. They're disabling resistance equipment now. Gonna need to run hijack protocol soon, one more time. I think this is working."

"Okay, yeah I'm here. Just let me know when to run it."

Blackhawk held off on a reply.

"You there?" Ramsay asked.

"Yeah. Little worried about Artemis. She's…she seems a little off."

"A little? Bud, she's batshit. I told you before. We have to have a contingency for rogues."

"I'll keep her in line." Blackhawk replied. But he didn't sound so sure of himself as per usual.

"What if you can't?"

"I will."

Ramsay eyed the tank Leyla was in, hopefully almost ready. "Okay, if you say so. I'm standing by, man. Let me know when you need me."

"Will do, brother." Blackhawk ended the call.

Ramsay walked over to the tank and sighed. "Hope you know, the whole fucking world depends on your ability to whoop some ass."

At that very moment, Ramsay heard a faint sloshing inside the tank. He moved closer. Maybe his ears had tricked him. He heard movement; a forceful motion inside thick and viscous fluid. Leyla was alive.

"She's moving!" Ramsay yelled, backing away, also remembering she was not going to be happy.

A heavy thud resounded from the tank's tempered glass. And another. Ramsay saw what seemed to be a fist slam into the interior wall. *Uh oh.* He hurried over to his pack and the cold pizza. Clara stood, moving Hug to her shoulder and circling around the room.

Another thud from inside the tank echoed throughout the chamber, this time interspersed with the distinct crack of breaking glass. A shard clinked to the concrete floor. Cracks danced across the embryonic tank like lightning. Ramsay held his breath for what seemed like ages waiting for a final blow to the tank. Leyla may have been moving, but she was angry. He prepped himself for death, but not without an offering of Carol's pizza and the surprise he held in his pack.

The tank damn near exploded—glass shards shot forward and peppered the floor in front of it. The grayed fluid burst from its confines and poured in every direction, flooding the ground beneath.

There it stood, a stiff and wrought, nude figure, fist outstretched, having just blasted through a wall of hardened glass like it was nothing. It was heaving breaths that its body thought it had taken hours and hours earlier. It flinched, as if avoiding a bullet coming straight for its brain. A bullet that had already done its job. It jerked a gaze upward, and surveyed the room. This wasn't Leyla, but it had her most recent memory. Perhaps it had all Leyla's memories.

But this was Athon, through and through. This was an unequivocal death machine. Of course, it locked eyes with Ramsay, and leapt from the broken tank.

It stretched out an arm, palm open. A magnetic rod shot to its hand and activated a blade that immediately heated to an orange hue.

"Fuck…" Ramsay huffed.

Athon strode right up to him as he stumbled and fell on his ass. But he didn't drop the pizza box. It pointed the sword at him, close enough to slice his neck open and drain his life in seconds.

"B-b-but I got you pizza!" Ramsay yelped, as dumb a statement as that was to make, given the current situation.

"You are Blackhawk's lackey." It said. It had Leyla's voice, for sure, but there was no soul. "And you are the reason for my death. I will make yours quick."

"Leyla?" Ramsay hoped there was an inkling of her in there.

"The Leyla construct is no longer—" Athon's body contorted like it had just touched an electrified wire. It raised from the ground, by at least six inches—floating. Its gaze pulled upward and its eyes rolled back. It dropped the sword hilt and the blade retracted.

Clara walked up from behind, curling her fingers. Her pupils had also turned a deathly white. "Vættir. Heim." She wheezed in the same horrific, scratchy voice as before. But this time she was in more control. She got just behind Athon and placed her fingertips on its temples. It dropped, completely limp.

Clara backed away as her eyes returned to their normal brown color and her knees buckled. She collapsed as well. Hug croaked and hopped over to her, concerned.

A guttural, pained and horrified cry surged from Athon's throat.

"DEL!!!"

Leyla was back.

Her body sprang to life and she lurched forward in an attempt to get to her friend, only to see that she was back in The Fridge. It was as if Blackhawk had pulled the trigger of his revolver, and transported her to another place. She remembered seeing Del and being paralyzed. She remembered…being shot, and feeling the blood rush from her head. She noticed Ramsay.

"You!" She growled. "You fucking *liar*."

"I, I can explain! Okay?" Ramsay pleaded.

Once again, Leyla jumped up and opened a palm, drawing the sword.

"I tried! I tried to lie but…" Ramsay stopped. *Lie, dumbass. Lie. Now.* "But he saw through me. He knew I was lying and he…he went after you."

"RAMSAY DID NOT PLAY A PART IN YOUR FRIEND'S DEATH." SIGIL said, attempting to help ease tensions. *"HE ATTEMPTED TO DIVERT ATTENTION."*

Ramsay pointed at SIGIL. "See? SIGIL can't lie. It's literally against programming!" Yet, he wasn't so sure if SIGIL was incapable of lying or if it simply chose not to do so.

Leyla held the sword up, but the reality of the situation hit her like a train. Del was…

She remembered Artemis's final, monstrous blow to Del's chest that sent the sound of internal broken bone and exploding organs across the room. She remembered Del's body flopping to the broken floor and never moving. Not even a twitch.

"Where is Del? Is she—"

"Del's gone. It's been a few hours since. Almost a day. And you were killed. We brought you back." Ramsay said.

Del was gone. She hadn't been abducted or vanished this time. She'd been *murdered* right in plain sight.

Del was dead.

Leyla felt a wail escape her chest. A wail of regret, and guilt, and pain. A wail of anger, and grief, and denial. The wail morphed to a scream, as Leyla collapsed to the floor to her knees.

"I'm sorry I...no!" Leyla knew she was apologizing to someone who would never hear it.

She wept, overcome with breathless panic and grief all at once. She hyperventilated, attempting to come to grips that her only true friend was actually gone.

Clara slowly got to her feet. "These are memories best left forgotten. But they are you." She had tears in her eyes, as if she'd felt the same sort of grief Leyla was experiencing.

"No no NO NO NO!" Leyla screamed, pounding on the concrete with a closed fist. "I tried! I fought and I tried but they..."

She paused, running the prior events through her mind. The Pantheon. Blackhawk. That red haired *bitch*. They'd killed Del mercilessly, and did the same to her.

"SIGIL..." she said.

"*YES?*"

"I need a time coordinate to go back for Del again."

Ramsay jumped and waved his hands. "Whoah whoah! That is *not* a good idea!"

"*THERE ARE NO COORDINATES AVAILABLE.*"

"Oh thank God." Ramsay said.

"Can't you just fucking make new coordinates and send me back anyway? I have to go back for her!" Leyla yelled at the machine.

"*THAT IS NOT POSSIBLE. I CAN ONLY OPEN PRE-DETERMINED TIME LOOPS. ONCE THEY HAVE BEEN CLOSED, THEY ARE NO LONGER AVAILABLE.*"

"Bullshit! Because I don't remember *opening* a time loop to get her, I just went back and got her and everyone was fine with that!"

Ramsay spoke up. "Yeah, she's right. An open loop had to start somewhere, right?"

"*ALL PRE-DETERMINED LOOPS ARE ALREADY OPEN. THE ACT OF ENTERING A LOOP AND CHANGING SOMETHING CREATES A PARADOX. THUS, THE LOOP MUST BE CLOSED.*"

"I don't understand…" Leyla said.

"*I DO NOT HAVE AN AVAILABLE LOOP TO SAVE YOUR FRIEND. AND IF I DID, THERE IS THE HIGH PROBABILITY OF THE SAME OUTCOME.*"

Ramsay looked to Leyla. "You said every time you went back and changed something…nothing changed in the present."

"What are you talking about?" Leyla asked.

"SIGIL means that no matter what you do, she was bound to, well, die. One way or another."

"*CORRECT.*"

Leyla's heart couldn't decide if it was angry, or sad, or hopeless or whatever the fuck she was supposed to feel when someone has just plunged a fist into her chest and ripped out every micron of a chance at happiness. That was it. There truly was no way to get Del back. She was doomed from the beginning. The universe had played its hand and denied Leyla the one thing she desired most.

"Where's Del? I need to see her."

Ramsay got to his feet and opened the pack. He pulled a clear glass jar out, filled with fine, light gray ashes, and it was sealed with a cork. He held the jar of ashes up to Leyla.

"We don't see death around here much. We don't have morticians. Cross-Eyes was able to have her cremated." Ramsay said. He took care to not mention that 'cremated' meant burned in the old garbage incinerators.

Leyla slowly stood, glaring at the ashes. "That's it?" She took the jar from Ramsay. "This is all that's left?"

"Cremation breaks the body down to the rawest of elements, and prepares us for a union with the Earth." Clara said.

"It's just a fucking…*jar*." Leyla snarled. "She's just a jar of fucking powder?"

"Probably better this way. Wasn't a pretty sight." Ramsay said.

Leyla's chest hitched. More tears found their way to her eyes. The fire that she'd felt to her very core crept back as well; the fire she'd felt when she saw Artemis break Del's arm. Leyla took some slow and labored steps, also remembering that Artemis had kicked her in the back and broken her spine. She looked over to Ramsay, as he pulled the bloodied Thumper from his pocket and placed it in a drawer of a workbench. Sunny, orange light. Like a sunset. Del's favorite thing, aside from hot pizza.

"What time is it?" Leyla asked.

Ramsay checked his watch. "7. Almost dusk."

***

The sun looked like a poached egg yolk, as Del liked to describe it, during dusk. It slowly sank toward the Earth and transformed the sky into a canvas of purple, orange and blue that kissed the hills of Kentucky across the river. It would have been peaceful, if not for the sirens going off inside Cincinnati.

Leyla was back in her armored catsuit, which was of course still torn, ripped and bloodied, and she'd walked Del's ashes all the way through SubCity, which had been largely empty compared to the previous times she'd roamed the streets. Most of the modders had left to take the city. She'd taken the massive freight elevator up to the abandoned subway tunnel, and trekked through the darkness toward the light of the opened door at the exit. She'd then laboriously walked all the way to Smale Riverfront Park, Del's favorite sunset view. She'd liked the way the Roebling bridge silhouette looked against the brilliant colors—and the egg yolk in the sky.

Leyla hopped the fence and settled on the rocks beside the river, clutching Del's ashes close to her chest. She crossed her legs, Indian style, and sat Del in her lap.

She twiddled her fingers and looked down at the jar, then moved it from her lap to a rock beside her. Something still didn't feel right. She searched the ground for a sharp rock, and found one that looked like an arrowhead with a pretty sharp point.

Perfect.

She snatched the rock up and then Del's jar of ashes, and carved two circles and a crescent underneath—a smiley face. It was a goofy notion but one Del would have likely approved of, because now she had eyes and a smile, and could enjoy one final sunset with her best friend.

Leyla smiled and rasped some words to her friend one last time, "Hey look. Sunset. Eggs."

The chopping of military helicopter rotors permeated the air, coupled with the honks of a flock of geese headed north for the coming summer. The river wake sloshed against the rocks at Leyla's feet. She could hear the distant whoosh of traffic crossing the bridge; most of it headed south into Kentucky, attempting to leave the city as fast as possible. The tornado sirens had stopped. Most of the ambulance and police and fire sirens had quietened as well. Somethin was still missing; things felt very off.

Leyla looked down at Del's ashes, resting on the rock beside her, and sighed. That was it. What was missing was Del's hearty laugh. Missing was her colorful language and societal reflections about hating the government and people in general yet still somehow always believing everyone deserved a chance at a good life. What was missing was her voice—one that always had the right thing to say and always reflected a light and loving heart.

As more tears welled up in Leyla's eyes, she picked the jar up again and placed it on her knees with the smiley face watching the sunset, and rested her chin on the cork sealing the ashes in. She didn't move a muscle; she simply allowed the tears to flow as the sun slowly buried itself in the horizon, and the sky faded to a deep purple.

Distant thunder rolled across the land from the south; a storm was coming.

A final tear streamed down Leyla's cheek as she gently placed Del's ashes on the ground and nestled the jar between two rocks, positioned so she'd always see the sunset 'egg', every single night.

The sound of chopping copter blades and far off jet engines drew Leyla's gaze upward, where she finally noticed what all the fuss was for in the city.

Blackhawk's platform, The Bullpen, was hovering a couple thousand feet in the air. Leyla knew it had to be him, due to the anti-gravity blue glow underneath. That was a SubCity exclusive. And if he had revealed himself to the world, The Pantheon was nearby. Leyla felt the fine tingle deep in her mind, same as before, that signaled Athon's desire to take over completely.

I sense vengeance in our heart. Athon said from within Leyla's mind.

"What do you care? Del wasn't your friend."

We have a common interest. Upon that floating fortress stands a false messiah. He has sent his disciples down to this city to take from us our destiny. SIGIL created me to protect this world.

"I don't really care about your stupid destiny right now." Leyla scoffed, standing up and hopping across the rocks to get back over the fence.

But you would like revenge, would you not?

Leyla paused and looked back to the platform in the air. Athon was right. Del may've been gone, but Blackhawk and The Pantheon couldn't go unpunished.

"What if he's doing exactly what we were designed to do? What if he really is using The Pantheon to fix everything? Like SIGIL wanted?"

Is that what you would do?

"Yeah. It's what Del would want too."

And do you believe The Pantheon, especially the one who brutalized your friend, would do as Blackhawk asks, therefore ignoring their own anger and malice toward humanity?

Athon once again made an excellent point. The Xenobots enact the final wish of their catalyst. Maybe Blackhawk truly wanted what was right, but that didn't mean Artemis or the other bloodthirsty women wouldn't want something different, considering what they'd done just hours earlier to a completely innocent person. Lastly, Blackhawk was directly responsible for Del's end and must be punished.

Yes, I can sense your agreement. They are a looming threat. And we must stop them. We must seize our destiny. And Del must be avenged.

Looking up, Leyla spotted one of The Pantheon fly up to the platform. A few moments later, she flew back down and toward the city again. The storm clouds drew closer and closer to the city—and the thunder with them. Lightning flared inside the immense cumulus structures, and the scent of rain crept through the wind.

We are more than you and I. We are more than a creation of artificial intelligence. We are this world's savior. We are its sword and its shield. They have tried to kill us. They have failed. We are life and we are death. Immortal.

We are…a god.

Leyla held fast against the harsh winds approaching, spurred on by the menacing thunder and lightning tempest.

The storm was no longer approaching. It had arrived.

CHAPTER TWENTY-FIVE

A Pale Horse

The streets of SubCity had become a neon drenched ghost town. Only a few of the modders remained; ones that didn't want to leave their chosen homes. Carol still pushed her cart along the street, but there were no more lines of people waiting to have a slice of pizza. Fritzy Joe's was a dark cavern adorned with powerless bulbs of light.

Where the fuck did Mari go? Leyla wondered, as she passed. The last person she'd talked to was Artemis. *Bitch probably killed her for asking questions,* she thought.

Even Peyton's Diner was nearly empty. Looking through the windows of the spot, Leyla saw the android waitresses, and the soda jerker hat wearing guy at the bar, and there were only two patrons in seats eating. Leyla looked for Greene through the kitchen window, but didn't see him. She wondered if he'd gone to the surface with the other modders.

Shit, where's Wells? If they came after me, they went after him too, right?

Athon answered, *It is likely.*

"Okay." Leyla said. "We do have to stop them. What they did down here is the same shit they'll do up there."

As Leyla passed by *Til Death*, the clothing store, the hype bot perked up.

"Look at *you*, bitch!"

Leyla stopped and smiled, this time recognizing the language as complimentary. She struck a model pose, poking her ass out and looking to the side, showing off the rather badass armored catsuit.

"Girl! I got just the *thang* for *them* threads. Get that hot little ass in here real quick!"

Fuck it. Why not. Leyla thought, and walked into the shop with the bot. Athon didn't exactly approve.

What are you doing? Athon asked.

I'm having a self-care moment, trying to distract myself from Del for a second, now shut your face. Leyla internally snapped back.

My face is your face.

"Okay Miss *Sword of Vengeance*, you can let me have a minute to myself! Now shut it!" Leyla said aloud.

The hype bot stopped and turned back to her. "Let me guess, personality implants actin' up?"

Leyla's eyes widened. "Yes! That's *exactly* the problem!"

"Girl I know what you mean. My other personality construct is a lumberjack, and I don't like that motherfucker. Shit, we don't even cut trees down here. Fuck I'm gonna be a lumberjack for? Anyway, look at this *shit* here." The bot slid to a stop beside a chrome mannequin display and held its arms out to it, showcasing what it was wearing:

A flat black, weatherproof, hooded cloak with a glossed hexagonal pattern that seemed to match Leyla's armor perfectly. The cloak tapered off at the waist to a single 'tail' that hung down to the calves of the mannequin.

"We designed this for that cyber-witch lady down the street, but then she said she didn't like it. Okay, hootchie, that's fine, but she was rude about it. Anyway, it's weatherproof *and* cut-proof. Not sure what that bitch be doin' with knives like that but, I'm gonna mind my own business."

If eyes could spark actual fireworks, Leyla's would have been the fourth of fucking July—with a dash of murderous intent.

"It's so…*perfect*." She said.

***

The massive opening in the vaunted ceiling of the cavern had never closed when Blackhawk ascended The Bullpen into the sky, and now there was a torrential downpour of water coming through what was essentially now an enormous sky light. Flowing groundwater and heavy rain drops cascaded down, reflecting all the various neon and LED lights of SubCity.

A malicious lightning bolt struck one of SubCity's highest towers nestled directly under the opening—the tower Blackhawk had built his Bullpen on, Leyla presumed. She thought it a little odd that lightning would strike far into the ground like it had just done, but how could it resist a massive lightning rod through a football field sized opening in the ground?

Maybe that lightning will fry your ass, and do my job for me. Leyla thought of Blackhawk, as she walked broodingly down the street, now wearing her newly acquired assassin cloak, which was bellowing like a black flag in the wind generated by the draft from the large cavern opening. It was a cool looking cloak, for sure, but she'd honestly wanted it to avoid being drenched by the storm she was going to be fighting in soon. That and, again, it looked really, *really* cool.

Passing by Clara's occult little nest of oddities, on the way to The Fridge, Leyla was greeted by the witch once more.

"Have to say, that fits you a fuck load better than it did me." Clara said. She was lounging on a super comfy looking leather chair situated just outside the door to her shop. Llana was with her, tinkering with some sort of gutted electronics device, and Hug was perched on a lamp post beside the building. Clara stood and walked over to Leyla in the street. "Let me guess, you're about to head up there to take on The Pantheon?"

"And Blackhawk." Leyla replied.

"Mmmm. Come inside."

"Nope. Not gettin' me again with the whole white eye scary lady deal."

Clara rolled her eyes. "Aw, is the badass assassin scared of a little magick?"

"No! Just—"

"Just go in. She's helping you." Llana said, never looking up from the wiry mess she was working on.

"Why are you helping? Last time, you were all fire and brimstone, telling me to stop looking for Del." Leyla asked Clara.

Clara looked up at Hug, perched on his favorite lamp post. "A little birdie told me I was wrong." She looked back to Leyla. "It happens."

She has nothing of value for us. Athon silently told Leyla.

Well now I'm curious so we're going in. Leyla defiantly replied, and stepped into Clara's shop.

You are purposefully doing meaningless things to defy me. Procrastinating. Athon growled to Leyla. *Are you afraid of The Pantheon?*

Yep. Leyla replied internally. *But a bitch gotta do what a bitch gotta do. Now shut your face.*

Again, my face is your fa—

I said shut it.

Clara walked into the back room they'd been in before. All the red sand was still on the ground; she'd never cleaned it up.

"Boots off. Barefoot." She said, pointing to the ground. Leyla unstrapped and removed her boots. Clara pulled a dark red lipstick from a pouch on the table along with two black crystals.

"Stand here." Clara pointed to the sand, and Leyla obliged. Clara gave her one crystal for each hand, opened the lipstick, and proceeded to draw small crescent just above Leyla's brow, and then a straight line down from it to the bridge of her nose, pointing the tip and forming a downward sword symbol.

"Lipstick magick?" Leyla asked.

"I've changed a lot of things around as I've honed my craft over the years but, lipstick always worked best. Don't know why." Clara said. "Grip those tight." She pointed to the black crystals in Leyla's hands.

Clara walked back to the table, placed the lipstick on it, and waved her hand over a candle that sparked flame as her palm passed.

"So…" Leyla said, attempting to ease her nerves. "How long have you been a witch?"

"Mmm, long enough to know a difference between what people call 'witchcraft' and what I practice—old magick. I need you to trust me for this next bit."

"Okay…"

"Do you?"

"I don't know."

"Do you at least trust me enough to think I won't stab you in the heart once you close your eyes?"

"You didn't before…"

"Good enough. Close your eyes." Clara said, sliding her bare feet across the sand in front of Leyla.

"What are you doing?" Leyla asked.

"Granting you a blessing of strength, protection, and sight."

Okay, vague. Leyla thought, but closed her eyes anyway. She felt a waft of air roll across what little skin was exposed, and the fabric of the cloak she was wearing reacted to the sudden, inexplicable wind gust. Oddly enough, Leyla felt a sudden rush of confidence—almost a sense of invincibility—in her gut. She felt a little more focused on what needed to happen next.

Leyla opened her eyes to see Clara staring back. Before Clara could say anything, Leyla whipped around to leave the shop, grabbing her boots on the way. Clara followed her out, grinning victoriously.

Outside, Leyla paused to strap her boots on. When she stood, Hug leapt from his perch and landed on her shoulder.

"Hug!" Llana scolded the raven. "Down! What are you doing?"

"He's going with her." Clara replied.

Leyla was tilting her head away from the bird, not out of fear but of caution. That thing could peck an eye out.

"The fuck do you mean going with her? He doesn't know her!" Llana disapproved.

"Hug knows what he wants to know. As usual." Clara said. She looked Leyla in the eye. "He is a fine messenger. He offers his service, 'til your work is done."

"His service? What's that mean?" Leyla asked.

Clara smiled, and pointed to her eyes. "You'll *see*." She stroked Hug's feathered head. "Don't do anything stupid." She told the raven. Hug cooed at Clara, then looked to Llana, and cooed again, bidding them a temporary farewell.

Leyla made her way back out into the street, headed straight toward the tall building adorned with red neon, that stood above the tunnel to The Fridge. Her cloak bellowed and rippled in the draft winds, and the raven on her shoulder spread his wings and croaked.

Clara watched as Leyla walked away. A now fearless and intimidating figure—cloaked and hooded— blessed with a wise raven on her shoulder. She was passing under the torrential downpour of rain from above.

"And Hel followed with her…"

***

Inside The Fridge, Ramsay was having a chat with SIGIL.

"So, I'm still trying to wrap my head around these time loops you found. You made an algorithm that exposed them, got it. And they're all open, always?"

"CORRECT."

"And that's how it's always been? The universe just has a bunch of open time loops waiting for you to screw up?"

"CORRECT."

"And going inside a time loop, and changing something, means it MUST be closed?"

"CORRECT AGAIN."

"So how do you know it's closed? Do you do that?"

"THE THUMPER SEVERS THE QUANTUM LINK TO THAT TIME LOOP UPON AN EXIT THROUGH THE SIGIL."

"Oh, so it's automatically closed when Leyla comes through here. You don't think that's screwing something up on the other side?"

"THERE IS NO WAY TO KNOW."

Ramsay cackled—an exceedingly nervous bellow of laughter. "Well I hope not!"

"Kraawwwk!" Hug rode in on Leyla's shoulder, announcing their presence as they entered the antechamber.

Ramsay raised his brow and pointed at Leyla in her new flowing cloak and hood. "Nice Batman vibe! And the creepy raven too. Great. And I see Clara painted one of her weird symbols on your forehead. Good."

"It's raining up there, so this is my rain jacket." Leyla said.

"So you're going to do it? You're going after The Pantheon?"

"Yup. I need to know everything you can give me on them. How do I take them out?"

"Come here." Ramsay said, waving her to follow. The two walked over to a workbench that Ramsay had placed his scanner device on. He picked it up and punched in a few keys and a 3D holographic display of all five of The Pantheon women appeared over its screen.

"I normally used this software as a diagnostics tool for their exo-suits but, handy for this too. So, five of them, right?" Ramsay said as the image of The Pantheon spun slowly in front of Leyla's eyes.

"You said there were four when we had you strapped to the table."

"There were, now there's five. We'll get to that."

All but one of the women's 3D mock-ups dropped out of view, leaving the image of Eris.

"This one's Eris. She doesn't talk much, but it's the quiet ones to worry about. It's like a universal rule. Now, each of these ladies' suits has a special weapon they chose. Eris has a big ass sword, like an enlarged katana. I don't know if she's actually Japanese, but she seems to think she's a samurai for sure. And she could probably take down a Jedi if they were real."

She is the one that severed our arm. Athon said.

"Got it. Next." Leyla said, noting to put a little extra juice behind her punches when she met Eris later.

"Next up, Nemesis."

Eris's figure dropped from view and Nemesis popped up.

"Her suit's a little bigger than the others. She's one of the ones I've warned Blackhawk about. She did *not* have a good childhood and she *hates* cops. You give someone like that the power she has and things can go bad real fast."

"Why's her suit bigger?"

"Rail gun."

Nemesis's 3D figure swirled around to show her back, and a rail gun folded up and pointed forward over her shoulder. It was almost half her size.

"It's heavy and it's powerful, so she needed a suit to support it. It also means her suit is the strongest. She's a walking fortress. And she will blow you in half with that thing. It's the same rail gun we equipped on Blackhawk's AV and it can punch through tanks so, don't get shot."

"Don't get shot was like, top of my to do list here." Leyla playfully added.

"Good to hear. Pizza?" Ramsay pointed to the box of cold Carol's pizza on the workbench.

"Yes! Geez I hadn't even thought of that, I'm starving." Leyla tore the box open and ripped into a slice. "Mmmm after death pizza is the best."

Ramsay seemed a little confused, judging by his expression. "Are you okay?"

"Yeah, why?" Leyla had a mouthful of pizza.

"You just…well your friend. You just lost her and you were pretty broken up about it not even an hour ago. Now you seem like…you. Like Leyla."

"Well I don't know, I just didn't want to think about it for now. Hurts losing her, I just—"

"*ATHON HAS COMPLETE CONTROL OVER HER EMOTIONAL STATE. LEYLA MAY BE GRIEVING THE LOSS OF A FRIEND, BUT SHE IS CAPABLE OF BLOCKING NEURAL DURESS TO FOCUS ON THE TASK AT HAND.*"

"Oh, guess that's why." Leyla said, chomping on pizza.

Ramsay stared. "That's kind of…useful I suppose."

"*SHE WAS DESIGNED TO BE THE PERFECT ASSASSIN.*"

"It's also a little fucked up." Ramsay said.

"Yep. Next please." Leyla said, beckoning Ramsay to continue to the next Pantheon member.

"Okay. Next is Rhea. Well, she's gone now, so—"

"Gone? What's that mean?"

"Blackhawk used the Xenobots on her to make a statement. Granted, she volunteered like the others. But, they pretty much dissolved her on an atomic level and now her Xenobots are swarming Cincinnati and changing things."

"Changing what?"

"Remember what I said about rewriting matter? They're changing useless things like, I don't know, like trash—into actual fruit trees and such. Food for people that need it, cleaning the water. It's a good thing. But it's pretty gruesome what has to happen for that."

"So Blackhawk's big plan is to just take care of people?" Leyla said, surprised.

"Yes. I've said that many times. He's just doing what you and SIGIL wanted. That's it."

Yet he still murdered us and Del. Athon said.

Trust me, he will pay for that. Leyla replied.

"So anyway, next up: Artemis."

"Yeah. The red haired bitch."

"So you have a bone to pick with her, got it."

"What's her special move?" Leyla growled.

"Special move? Like a fighting game?" Ramsay laughed, but quickly dropped his humor when Leyla cut him an *I will rip your arms off again* glare. "Artemis is uh, she's special. She didn't want any weapons. Just a suit. But she was a champion kickboxer, I think, at some point. With her implants she could probably kick a car across a bridge. I'm only *half* exaggerating."

"Yeah…" Leyla muttered, trying to plan out what she wanted to do to Artemis when she found her. Whatever it would be, it would be payback for Del.

"Last up, Nyx."

The 3D image swapped to Nyx.

"She's like the mama bear of the group. She's the oldest and she was one of the first members of The Pantheon. She left for a while and then came back. Honestly she's pretty level headed, but once you start slicing down her friends, she's probably going to come for you."

"Weapon?"

"Big. Fucking. Sword. And I'm talking anime fuck-off size sword. It can split into anti-grav fragments and turn into a whip. And then it can use reverse gravity pulses and bring down buildings if she wants. I invented that thing. And it terrifies me. Nyx is essentially the final boss of a video game. She's that over the top. If you can avoid her, do. That's all."

"Avoid the big sword if I can. Right."

"Only way you're taking her out is quietly. There's a kill switch for power on their suits right behind the neck. If you can get the protector cap off and pull it, the suit deactivates. That's the easiest way to take them down. But if Nyx sees you coming you're screwed. If you try and take on more than one of The Pantheon at a time, you are screwed. If you attack and one gets away to find the rest, you are definitely screwed.

There are a million ways you can die up there with them roaming around, and I haven't even mentioned the fact that all the modders that left SubCity are packing weapons, and then there's the police and actual goddamn Army and Marines up there who are going to assume you're one of the women who ripped a trio of fighter planes out of the sky and an Apache chopper. They will shoot at you. A lot. And, unlike The Pantheon, you don't have an exo-suit with electromagnetic capacitors to divert the bullets. This is a suicide run. Not sugar coating it."

"Got it. SIGIL, guns." Leyla stepped away and approached SIGIL as the massive shelves of weapons ascended from the floor. Ramsays jaw dropped.

"Holy Christ! Was all that there the whole time?!"

"Yep." Leyla said, stopping at the smorgasbord of killing tools at her disposal. She picked out various guns and rifles. An uzi for the right thigh; it magnetically clung to its designated spot.

Hmmmm… Athon thought. *Desert Eagle. Fifty caliber round.*

Leyla picked up the huge pistol and it magnetically clung to her left hip for quickdraw capability. She then grabbed a Belgian F2000—a staunchly futuristic rifle—and slung it to her back, where it stuck magnetically as well.

One by one, she selected rifle and pistol, ammo type and blade. Each seemed to be coded to a certain body part and clung to it, including multiple magazines full of rounds for future reloading. Within minutes, Leyla was a warship, capable of spewing enough firepower to take a small army in seconds—even without the might of the Thumper's warping ability. She had the F2000 sub-machine gun on one shoulder, and a bullpup semi-auto shotgun on the other. A Desert Eagle .50 cal pistol on her left hip, and a specialized and ridiculously over-charged taser like pistol on the left thigh, in case she felt nice enough to not take a life but make the receiver terrified of wall outlets for the rest of their life. She had two of the retractable katana rods magnetically clung to her lower back horizontally. She'd also strapped what SIGIL called 'The WireFire' to her right forearm, and it was a small grappling hook style wire that could fire from the housing and retract with some substantial force, providing a variety of uses.

"Your bike. It's mine now." Leyla said, walking past Ramsay.

"What? The rocket? I just finished it!"

Leyla jerked a *the fuck you gonna do* gaze Ramsay's way.

"Yeah okay, got it. Steal my shit and scare me. Cool. *So American.*" He said.

Leyla sighed and hung her head. She was letting Athon take over a little too much.

"Sorry. That was Athon. I need something fast and…cool. I wanna look cool."

"Trust me, that's already been covered. But okay, fine. We're saving the world so, I *suppose* the Street Rocket should play a part." Ramsay gave Leyla a magnetic key, pressing a small metallic pin on it.

The cyber-bike whirred to life from across the room, and pulled off on its own, circling around and coming to a stop right beside Leyla. She straddled the bike. Even if she stumbled around the controls for operating the machine, she looked right where she needed to be on the pearl white bike—a cloaked and shadowy figure, armed to the teeth, with a raven on her shoulder—she sat upon a pale horse.

"Lookin' real Grim Reapery right now." Ramsay said.

"Good." Leyla grinned. "Hey, thanks."

"Yeah, yeah."

"No, I mean it. You're the kind of person this world needs more of. People like you and Del. You just want the world to be better."

"Well, we can talk about taking that step when we get rid of The Pantheon. And by now, I'd assume Blackhawk is almost ready to give them each their own dose of Xenobots. They won't use them unless they're completely safe. Once they inject the bots, they're completely vulnerable, and they can be killed."

"So…why don't we wait for that moment?"

"Well for one, once they inject, it's too late. The bots will go to work, atomizing the body. And two, if you attack and kill them during that state, well, the Xenobots enact the final thought processes of the user. If they're being attacked and want to defend themselves, the Xenobots will do exactly that. That's pretty much a world extinction event waiting to happen."

"Fuck…"

"Yeah, so, don't mess up. No pressure."

Leyla laughed as if her nervous system had just been ripped out and placed in a jar of acid.

"And the Thumper—do *not* break it. Luckily, when The Pantheon uh, cut your hand off, they didn't nick the Thumper, but after talking to SIGIL for a bit, I understood it a little more. That little smart watch looking bastard on your wrist contains a sister singularity to the arch-gate's there. If it breaks, it destroys the entire solar system."

"Good. Great. Totally shouldn't have told me that."

"It's pertinent information."

"Yeah, and now I'm scared to scratch this thing and blow us all up!"

"INCORRECT. THERE WOULD BE NO EXPLOSION. A BLACK HOLE WOULD FORM AND DEVOUR THIS WORLD AND ALL NEIGHBORING PLANETS. EVEN THE SUN WOULD SUCCUMB TO THE FORCE."

"Oh my god! Stop telling me things!" Leyla yelled.

"Just, be careful, okay?" Ramsay said.

"Okay, I'm just gonna go before I have a panic attack."

Leyla had never operated a motorcycle before, but Athon had. And Athon's memories were Leyla's—and so were its muscle memory. Fighting technique, shooting, sword play, everything Athon could do was part of Leyla now, and that included expertise in two wheel motor sports.

She clutched the handlebar, ramped the throttle up and held the brake to initiate a burnout. She then twisted and forced the spinning rear tire to whip around and face the exit. Hug, still on her shoulder, flapped his wings with surprise, and then hopped down to just behind the windshield. Probably a safer spot. She let the wheel stop, looked to Ramsay, winked, and blazed out of The Fridge, ready for war.

She ripped through the streets of SubCity, directly toward the freight elevator, which was still open and lowered from her trip to the surface with Del's ashes. She rode the bike inside and dropped one foot to balance herself, but quickly realized the bike did that on its own, so she rested the foot back on the bike itself. Hug cooed.

"Not sure why you insisted on coming but I'm not gonna argue with your mommy." Athon nodded to Hug.

The freight elevator's massive doors closed and it began its ascent to the tunnel out.

Why did SIGIL make us…um…a woman?" She asked Athon.

I have never questioned it, but throughout history, people are less assuming that a female would end their lives as quickly as a man could. Athon answered.

And boobs and booty are distracting. Leyla joked.

That may also be the case. Athon almost sounded amused, for once.

Guess that explains why The Pantheon are women, if Blackhawk was trying to recreate us. Leyla thought.

It is logical if the Xenobots are encoded to our DNA. Are you prepared for this? One false move or second thought will be disastrous.

I'm pretty sure. Leyla thought.

This is no time for 'pretty sure'.

Well what do you suggest, Miss Fussy Pants?

Give me control. You are effectively a human mind. You have doubts and fears. You make mistakes. I do not. I simply…execute.

No thanks, I'm not letting you erase me.

That is not the case. You will have your mind and can regain control at any time you wish. But for combat, I am your superior. I am what they have come to fear. I am their imminent retribution.

As the elevator sped upward through the shaft, Leyla contemplated Athon's request. Hug ruffled his feathers and looked up at her. She thought of Del, and her murderer, Artemis. And of Eris and Nemesis and Rhea, and how they'd demolished her as she fought to protect Del in the apartment. And they'd done so with ease. Athon was right.

The Pantheon had such an easy time with her because Leyla *was* human. She was scared in those moments and she thought only of protecting Del—and she had failed because of her human thought process. To win the coming fight, emotions would need to be cast aside. Fear would have to be snuffed away. Doubt would have to be buried. Leyla would need to become the rider, and Athon the driver, once and for all.

Do it. Leyla said.

Her eyes twitched back and forth as she lost consciousness again, same as the many supposed absence seizures of the last three years. Hug sensed a change as well, and he hopped off the bike and flared his feathers. Leyla's eyes stopped moving, locked forward. Any sense of human expression had gone. Her face had become that of a cold and calculating machine; an instrument of doom prepared to bestow its wrath on any who would oppose it. The suit's armored face mask activated and shrouded Leyla's face.

Death was an android, ascending in darkness, and its name was Athon.

CHAPTER TWENTY-SIX

Dissonance

The rain outside was horrendous and monsoonish, and simply taking shelter couldn't suffice, as it cut sideways with antagonistic purpose. Much of the ground had flooded and caked with mud. Lightning struck every raised chunk of metal it possibly could, and the wind had blown any loose object that weighed less than a person across every street. The tornado sirens were originally blaring because of the military level threat floating around the city—The Bullpen—but now it seemed they were sounding as a warning for possible cyclones.

A fairly large platoon of modders had set up a checkpoint outside the abandoned subway entrance, just outside the opening. They were at least a few dozen strong, each armed with custom weapons. The rifles were AR15 based, but with the modifications to the stocks, sights, magazines and fore grips, they looked more like something a space marine would carry into battle on a distant planet. Of course, each modder sported their own body mods and implants as well, which certainly aided their prowess as security enforcers—against humans.

Several armored AVs, converted from the normal rentable ones in SubCity, scattered the area as well. Two modders were outfitted with the same sort of exo-suits The Pantheon used, albeit without the anti-gravity jet boosters, so they were grounded for sure. Blackhawk had the checkpoint set up to guard his city and the residents that had chosen to stay in case the military got any bright ideas.

The low drone of an approaching vehicle resounded from the darkened tunnel. Even in sunny hours, rays of light couldn't penetrate into the subway very far, and now that the sun had rested, the tunnel was an abyss. The sound drew closer, louder—an aggressive exhaust note, coupled with the distinct growling whir of an anti-gravity engine.

Three of the closest modders turned to investigate, walking to the edge of the tunnel, peering inside, but seeing nothing. The sound grew louder. Closer.

All three looked at each other, and without a signal, simultaneously agreed to raise their weapons at the unexpected guest headed toward them.

A supremely intense beam of light flashed on, easily as harsh as the sun itself, and hit their eyes. All three winced and turned away, and that was their downfall.

Athon erupted from the tunnel with the full force of the bike's headlight, blinding the modders. The bike could steady itself, so Athon held its palms out, summoning both the katana hilts from its lower back. The blades extended and chopped right through two of the modders on either side as the bike passed, dividing their bodies in two at the gut.

Athon leapt from the bike, which charged forward and obliterated the third modder directly in front, splattering viscera all over the frame. Hug was still nestled behind the windshield, but never flinched at the violence. Still mid-air, Athon activated the Thumper and warped forward, teleporting into one of the exo-suited modders, and driving both katanas into his chest with the same force as if from the speeding motorcycle. Warping did not cancel out inertia. The hilts of the blades nearly embedded in the modder's chest as he flew backward, and Athon planted its feet on his body, nearly surfing him through the air.

The street rocket bike kicked sideways and slid across the grass, barreling into two more modders who hadn't had the chance to react yet, turning their bones to dust.

Athon rode the armored modder to the ground and sprang off the dying body, sprinting forward as soon as its feet hit the ground. It activated the heated blades, which burned the blood from the edges instantaneously.

By now, several of the modders had turned face and brought their rifles up to meet their worst fear. As each pulled the trigger of their rifle, sending volleys of rounds toward Athon, they called out sightings to everyone else.

"Target sighted at the entrance! It's Athon! Fuck!" One of the modders screamed, desperately aiming toward the android.

Not a single round struck home. Athon warped to each of the modders, one by one—a dozen of them in a chain, and chopped off heads, arms, legs—whatever was in swinging distance died. Each warp rang out like a booming gunshot—small claps of thunder amongst the tempest.

The Street Rocket slid to a stop, and whipped itself around and careened toward Athon, who was already making headway to the remaining exo-suit clad modder. This one had a chain gun. She let loose the hellfire, and hundreds of rounds spewed toward Athon. It tried to warp, but the Thumper needed some time to cool down. It had never been overheated, and that wasn't something that should be tested.

Athon juked right, just missing being pelted by the stream of bullets. It effortlessly whipped the right handed sword to the side and pulled the F2000 from its shoulder, sending its own stream of lead toward the modder. The thrown sword thrust right into the chest of a bystanding modder, who looked almost impressed as he keeled over. Athon's SMG rounds weren't powerful enough to do much damage from this distance, but they still forced the modder to duck, momentarily letting up on the chaingun fire.

The Street Rocket had caught up to Athon, riding alongside the android's Olympic level sprint, running so fast that each drop of rain exploded off its armor. Hug looked over at Athon, holding his wings out slightly. He seemed to be enjoying the ride.

Athon slung the F2000 back on its shoulder and recalled the right handed sword from the stricken modder's chest.

Should be enough power for one more warp now, Athon thought of the Thumper.

Sure enough, with one last warp, Athon teleported to the side of the modder and kicked the chaingun to the side, which caused the modder to pull the trigger and mow down several other modders who didn't expect such an onslaught from their own weapon. Athon cleaved the modder's head off at the jawline, and her body seized, still pulling the trigger as it fell sideways, turning the exo-suit into a corpse filled turret. The entire drum of rounds on her back emptied as the rotating barrels turned red hot, and the rounds bore into an armored AV until striking the power cell inside and it exploded with a reverse gravity pulse, sending a dozen modders in all directions, peppered with shrapnel from the vehicle.

Athon took the opportunity to survey what was left to eliminate. Only ten more were unharmed and engaged so far. The rest were dismembered, dead, or fleeing. Athon cooled the katana blades; clouds of steam plumed around it but quickly blew away in the torrential wind. The blades retracted and the hilts were placed in their spots on the lower back. Athon pulled the bullpup shotgun from its left shoulder, which held twenty rounds, more than enough to emulsify who was left. The Thumper vibrated. It had cooled already.

The Street Rocket had been resting at Athon's side; it lurched forward and Athon jumped on, curling down low on the frame and using the windshield as cover, almost kissing Hug with its mask. The bike was bulletproof, thanks to the NASA aeroshell plating that Ramsay had likely stolen to build it.

Athon warped again when it neared the modders, and teleported to the ground, using the momentum to slide across the mud, kneeling, and letting loose the fury of the shotgun. Kneecaps and shins exploded, coupled with screams and guttural cries of surprise. Another warp and Athon was behind a modder, skidding to a stop and on its feet. His brains were sent through his eyeballs with one trigger pull.

Three modders left to dispatch.

They were all behind cover—two behind one armored AV and one behind a wheeled steel barrier emplacement. Every one of them opened fire at once. The Street Rocket rolled a halt off to the side, and Athon bolted right, ducking the gunfire. It warped once, teleporting halfway to its targets: the two behind the AV. With a running jump and another warp, it was in the air coming down on them behind their cover. Both were twisting around and upward to see the shotgun blasts headed to their faces.

Athon landed amid falling skull bone, brains, and blood. Its armor was coated in remains of the modders it had massacred. It stood from behind the AV and marched toward the final target, shouldering the shotgun and pulling the Desert Eagle pistol from its thigh.

The remaining modder stepped from behind the barrier, and pulled the trigger. Nothing. The bolt had jammed on his rifle. Athon strode right up to him and aimed the fat muzzle of the pistol at his face, but paused.

The modder took a breath in. There was no running from this. He just had to accept what was coming.

But, Athon hung the pistol at his head, studying the modder. Pale, porcelain skin, green eyes, fire-orange hair.

It was Greene. And he had accepted his fate.

The oversized pistol lowered from his eyes, and Athon snatched the rifle out of his hands, and turned to walk away. Greene slowly reached to his hip, where he had a Kimber 1911 .45 holstered—one that matched Wells's, only in chrome instead of smoke black. He unsnapped the buttoned strap behind the hammer, and gripped the pistol, slowly pulling it out.

Athon stopped walking, sensing Greene was about to do something incredibly stupid.

He drew the pistol, gunslinger style, and fired. Athon of course warped to his side and with one fluid motion, pulled the gun from Greene's hand, dropped the clip, ejected the round in the chamber, and slid the entire slide and bolt assembly off the frame, dropping all the parts to the ground. Greene was stunned, but he didn't seem scared.

Athon held its index finger up and wagged, *no no no,* and continued walking away. Athon may have been in control, but thanks to Leyla, it had recognized Greene, and spared him. Athon had kept its word, and not shut Leyla out completely.

Walking back to the Street Rocket, Athon pulled the shotgun from its shoulder and reloaded it, pulling shells from a belt wrapped around its torso. Hug finally stood from the power cell of the bike, croaking and stretching his wings. He flew over to Athon and landed on its shoulder.

Greene watched as Athon walked away—cloak billowing in the wind, raven riding its shoulder—and knew he had just won the goddamn lottery.

"Hey!" He yelled at Athon. "Why leave me?"

Athon said nothing. It straddled the Street Rocket, and sped off, spitting mud and pebbles from the rear tire, as Hug flew off its shoulder and landed right in front of Greene, and bowed his head to the side, as if to say *you're welcome.* Hug flapped away and flew into the sky.

***

The chaotic mixture of police, SWAT, firefighters and soldiers had all failed to notice what was truly happening. They were too focused on the riots taking place. The citizens of Cincinnati had taken to the streets, seeming to mostly agree with Blackhawk, and fighting back against those attempting to keep order.

Tear gas permeated the air on every corner. Riot police were spread thin with their shields and batons, knowing they wouldn't be able to contain the crowds.

This was what Blackhawk wanted. He wanted the people—the citizens—to take his side. He wanted them to invite change and rebel against the established 'authority' that had nose-dived society for so long. That meant the police and military were the enemy.

But among all the screaming and fighting and pops of gas grenades, and echoes of bean bag loaded shotguns and rubber bullet gun fire, something wonderful was indeed happening.

At Leyla's former home, the tent city, Korean Jesus had taken refuge inside his tent. A lot of the riots were just down the street, and he could smell the pungent odor of the tear gas, burning his nostrils.

He heard what sounded like a wind—or maybe sand blowing—pass by his tent. He could hear it even over the riots and the storms. In what was likely a stupid movement, he stuck his head outside to see what it was.

To his wonder, the grass outside was…green. Normally it was deadened and brownish from all the piss and garbage sucking the life out of it. And—there was no garbage. None at all. There were no heroine needles littering the ground, no empty pill bottles and no smell of urine. Everything had been cleaned. He looked up.

The trees had *fruit*. They weren't even fruit trees, they were Ohio Buckeyes—which to his knowledge, weren't supposed to bear apples, and peaches, and plums.

"What the fuck?" He said aloud. "Bullshit."

In denial, he stepped outside, and looked down the street, noticing what he'd heard just moments before—the sandy wind.

A wave of glowing particles was passing across *everything*, cleaning up the street and forcing the trees to grow fruit. Even a stray tear gas canister was consumed by the particles and changed into *flowers*.

"Fuck you." Jesus said, not believing what he was seeing. "Fucking witches." He snatched back inside the tent and zipped it up, refusing to fall for what he swore were occult illusions.

***

The largest riot was just outside the police office downtown. The agitated crowd was at least a thousand strong, whereas the squad of riot police forming a line in front of the doors numbered only fifteen. There were two armored troop carriers, supplied by the Army and full of Guardsmen, at their rear. That was all the help the military had given them. There was no way they would hold for long. A veil of tear gas separated them from the angry rioters. Modders stayed off the ground for now, soaring a couple hundred feet above the chaos in their AVs.

"No more masters! No more masters!" The crowd chanted. Some threw bottles of water and rocks at the police, pelting their shields.

A Molotov cocktail flew from the crowd, landing just in front of the police, exploding and spewing fire onto the shields. They'd prepared for that, and a fire extinguisher put the flame out quickly, but they didn't fire weapons at the crowd. The chief of police had ordered to forgo aggression as long as possible. He knew such actions would end in disaster.

"One more of those and that's it." One of the officers said to another at his side. "I'm over this shit."

"You shoot and they swarm us. Think they'll let us live?" The other officer said. "This'll be like the Boston massacre all over again. Only the ones with guns die. There's too many of 'em dude."

"We're not gonna last long here. We have to do something."

Another Molotov soared through the air, slamming into a riot shield. This time the flame broke through, catching one of the officers' cargo pants on fire. He yelped and dropped his shield, screaming, "I'm on fire! Fuck!"

He dropped to the ground, patting the fire out with gloved hands as the riot crown laughed and cheered.

"That's it. Fuck these people." The first officer said. He dropped his shield and raised an AR15 to the crowd. Some of them noticed, and started screaming and turning to dodge what was coming. The officer pulled the trigger.

As bullets flew through the air, dead-aimed at several of the rioters, something dropped from the sky, slamming into the asphalt, cracking it and sending several pieces into the air, which crackled to the ground.

All the rounds the officer had fired struck an electromagnetic shield and crumpled on impact, falling to the ground. What had fallen from the sky stood tall, at least seven feet, in an exo-suit—a woman with black hair.

Eris.

She had saved several rioters from certain death at the hands of the trigger happy officer.

High above, atop the police headquarters building, Hug landed and looked over the edge, down to Eris. His brown eyes had become a milky white, much like Clara's during her hexy episodes.

***

Athon was blazing through the streets on the cyber-bike so fast that most of the modders and police and soldiers alike never got a chance to react to the blur screaming by them. The mask was still on, but Athon's eyes had glazed over—milky white. The sword symbol that Clara had painted on with lipstick glowed deep crimson. Athon could see what Hug saw; and Hug was eyeing Eris—Athon's first true target.

That is what the witch meant by blessing of sight, Athon thought. *Eris. Your fate at the end of my blade awaits.*

***

The riot police all stepped back at the sight of Eris turning to face them. The bullets had simply unphased her, due to the magnetic shielding, but to them it seemed as if she'd absorbed their impact inexplicably.

"That's one of 'em! The things that tore those fighter jets up!" One of the officers yelled.

On that, the riotous crowd erupted, cheering Eris on. To them, this armored, mech-suited angel was on their side, and had just protected them from their oppressors.

Thoomp! A teargas canister soared, fired from behind the police line. Eris jet boosted into the air and grabbed the canister mid-flight and hurled it back into the crowd of officers and soldiers, prompting more cheers from the crowd.

"Hell yeah! Fuck 'em up!" One of the citizens yelled.

None of the police behind the riot squad had gas masks, and they attempted to deal with their own tear gas and fight through it, but eventually—quickly—they dispersed. Some ran the other direction, some back into the building.

A voice came over a loudspeaker from one of the Army troop carriers. *"Stand down or we will initiate counter measures!."*

The voice didn't sound very sure of itself. Eris stood fast, like a virtual wall between the government and the people.

Suddenly, a shadowy, cloaked figure silently descended from above, having leapt from a rooftop, aiming straight for Eris in the middle of the street. The storm wind and rain had masked any sound it could have made, but one of the police gave it away.

"Up there, coming down!" The officer pointed, which in turn alerted Eris, and she whipped her gaze upward to see Athon falling straight for her, both katanas pointed straight at her and heated to a fiery orange hue.

Eris boosted away with nary a nanosecond to spare. Athon's blades sliced some of her flowing, straight black hair clean off like razors, and both swords plunged right into the asphalt with little effort. The road melted away with contact of the heated edges, and gave off the distinctive smell of fresh roadwork.

Eris landed, this time with her back to the riot police. She turned to them and with a hard Japanese accent, said: "Give us room. That thing will kill you all if I do not stop it."

"Shit, you heard the lady." One of the Sergeants said, waving the riot police down to back up as much as possible.

The riot crowd had already backed away plenty, forming a gnashing and fleshy arena for a fight between an angel and a reaper.

Athon circled counter-clockwise, matching Eris. The wind toyed with the android's cloak and the woman's drenched hair as if counting down toward a ringing of a bell.

Eris raised her arms straight in the air and a traditional katana instantly extended from her suit's frame and released. She immediately grabbed it from the air, clasped the handle with both hands, and slid one foot to her rear, and raised the sword above her head, tip pointing at Athon. A traditional ko gasumi Samurai stance.

"Anata wa atarashī te o motte imasu…" *You have a new hand,* Eris said, not caring if Athon understood.

"Sore wa anata no owari ni narimasu." *It will be your end,* Athon replied through its mask's vocoder with a growling, digital voice. Athon was fluent in several languages, especially Japanese. It deactivated one sword and placed it at its back, leaving just the one, and then cooled that blade. The harsh release of steam prompted gasps from the crowd. Athon wanted a fair fight—a challenge.

Raindrops cascaded down Athon's visor and dripped from Eris's eyelashes, who did not flinch.

A flash of lightning cracked through the air above as Athon and Eris went at each other. Eris boosted out of habit, swinging her sword at her enemy's throat. Athon leaned back and crouched, twirling underneath and delivering a counter swing that grazed Eris's mech suit, sending sparks across the street. Eris landed, and Athon stood. Neither wasted time.

Both blades slashed through the falling rain at inhuman speed, clashing metal on metal, ringing out to the crowd surrounding them. Neither side of the crowd was sure who to cheer for.

Athon batted away a thrust from Eris's sword easily, and swung back, looping off more hair. Eris recoiled. When she looked up, Athon noticed the cut to Eris's ear that extended to her cheek. First blood.

Eris's face reddened with anger. She yelled—a battle cry— and extended her other arm, revealing a second katana. This one was larger, and didn't release. It was connected to the suit, and was most likely the blade that had severed Athon's arm before.

A bolt of lightning struck the extended steel sword, blinding the entire crowd. Screams went into the air as everyone expected to see a fried woman in a mech suit. Athon never winced.

Eris stood, hand held high, teeth gritted and brow lowered. The long katana had been electrified, and was coursing with the power of the lightning that had touched it. She had come to no harm, and that was no accident. Eris had summoned the power of the storm itself, no doubt thanks to her mods.

"Susanō no hikari o tōshite…" *Through the light of Susanoo*, she yelled, sword held high. "Yomi-san ni ookuri shimasu." *I will send you to Yomi*.

"Yomi wa jakusha-yō." *Yomi is for the weak*, Athon replied, summoning its second katana and heating the blades, evening the odds.

Eris lunged, throwing the loose katana at the same time, in an attempt to either distract or maim Athon, who ducked the blade. It pierced one of the riot cop's shields, narrowly stopping short of impaling him.

Athon warped this time, teleporting around Eris as she swung her five foot long, electrified blade in a huge crescent. Electricity seemed to leap from it as it whipped around. In one motion, Eris rotated and brought the sword down hard on Athon's position. She missed again as Athon stepped aside. Eris dragged the blade through the asphalt, sending electric debris into the air. She batted some into Athon's face, even if there was a visor. Athon warped again, but much to its surprise, it was met with a hard elbow to the face. The visor cracked as its body whiplashed backward and slammed to the ground.

Eris's mighty sword came down with no time to react. Athon brought both its swords up as well, forming an X, and blocked the huge katana, but the sheer force sent Athon's elbows into the ground.

This was the first time Athon had ever grunted in pain. The sound came through the vocoder, and unfortunately sent a message to Eris that she had hurt the android. It was motivating. It was empowering.

Electricity was not a good thing for Athon to take lightly. Regardless of the organs and blood and very human structure of its body, it was still an android, and its mind could be crippled with enough of a jolt. It could sustain damage beyond normal means and still claw its way back, but an electric current was another story. That had the power to scramble its mind. And without the mind, one cannot live. If that sword entered Athon's body, it very well could finally die—and Leyla with it.

Eris could see Athon's eyes through the cracked visor. She remembered Leyla's eyes, filled with rage and fear and determination, just as she and The Pantheon had pummeled her to death. She leaned in, pivoting the electric sword blade on Athon's katanas, pointing the razor sharp point at its face.

"You will die for good, this time, android."

Keeping the force down on Athon, Eris drew her sword back a few inches, preparing to thrust it into her enemy's skull.

There was a pop, and a metallic zipping sound. Eris felt a sting in her neck—first at her throat and then the back, next to her spine. It was a very sharp pain. Some of the crowd gasped again. She felt something clamp down on the back of her neck, right onto the bone. Suddenly, her arms felt numb. She still had control but she couldn't feel them. The same happened with her legs. She drew back, away from Athon. The metallic zip whirred again as she backed up. She noticed a glint of light, forming a line toward her neck. She looked down. The street lamps' light reflected off a thin steel wire extended from her throat to Athon's wrist.

Athon had, for the first time, activated the small grappling hook SIGIL had created—The WireFire—and had shot Eris right through the neck with it. The clamp on the other end had latched to the back of Eris's neck bone.

Athon cooled and retracted both katanas and put them at its back, and stood slowly, eyeing Eris through the cracks of its visor. The steel wire slowly let out some slack as Athon took a couple steps forward. Its fist clenched, and the wire snapped tight.

The crowd broke into a mess of gasps and screams at the wet *thock* of Eris's neckbone bursting through her throat, tearing away her spinal cord and every bit of flesh it touched on the way out. It zipped to Athon's WireFire housing, still clamped by the hooks at the end of the wire. Blood and bits of throat skin splattered to the ground in front of Eris, who'd been denied the right to scream in agony. She collapsed immediately—every function of her body had ended the second the wire snapped tight. Her body fell onto the electrified sword and, although the blade didn't cut, it electrocuted her nerveless body until the smell of singed flesh carried through the air and smoke rose from the corpse.

Eris's neckbone dropped to the asphalt, cleansed of blood already by the rain.

Athon circled Eris's body and looked to the crowd of rioters. Every one of them had quietened, terrified of the masked monster that had taken down such a strong and impervious foe. Hug soared down and landed on Athon's shoulder. A grim reaper, indeed.

"That was anime as fuck." One of the riot officers said to the colleague at his side.

Athon pointed the WireFire at the top of a building and fired again, latching to a steel post near the roof, and sprinted up the wall as if it were weightless.

The riot crowd dissolved fairly quickly afterward; most heading home to avoid seeing Athon again, or worse, being on the receiving end of the many weapons it carried.

Hug was already back to the sky, fighting the wind and rain, searching for the next on Athon's list.

***

Artemis and Nemesis dropped down to a rooftop in another section of the city. They didn't yet know of Eris's gruesome fate or that Athon was on the hunt. Gunshots rang out from the police force's suppressant weapons. Speakerphone voices from the Army and police pleaded with the crowds to calm down while they figured things out, and that there was no need for panic, which was a lie.

But the city wasn't panicking. They were rebelling. This was what Blackhawk hoped for. People needed a change. They wanted change—one that Blackhawk had shown he could bring.

Artemis stood at the edge of the roof. Her long, red, rain-soaked hair still blew in the high wind. Nemesis clanked around in her large armor—rail gun folded back on its frame. She was visibly bothered.

"Did Rhea have to die for this?" Nemesis asked. "These people didn't care about her. Why should we care about them?"

"We knew what we volunteered for." Artemis answered. "Rhea knew."

Nemesis scowled at the police lights below. "The police will never back down. They'll push this until they start killing people. It's just what they do."

"I know." Artemis said, staring down at the city in chaos. Sirens wailed. People yelled in anger and screamed in pain as they were hit with bean bags and rubber bullets, and suffocated by gas. But it wasn't them that Artemis cared for. She was looking for an excuse. Waiting for something to happen to warrant dropping into the fight and attacking the oppressors head on. She didn't care about the people. She cared for violence—a release of rage that had built for years. Leyla and Del had not satiated her lust. And she was beginning to care even less what Blackhawk wanted. Did Rhea have to die? She was certainly prepared to. But did she need to? Did a woman of such regality and strength need to die for a *man* once again?

"We can do what we want." Artemis said.

"What do you mean?" Nemesis stopped pacing. Artemis finally turned away from the edge of the roof and looked to Nemesis.

"We don't have to do what Blackhawk wants. We can take the Xenobots. We can get rid of everything we don't want. And we don't have to take care of these ungrateful maggots."

"You're saying we use the Xenos to—"

"To seize control. To be gods. We bear the names of deities. Why not act like them?"

Artemis's comlink rang out. Of course, it was Blackhawk. She sneered, disgusted at the thought of his face, but she answered the call anyway.

"Artemis, is Nemesis with you?"

"Yes." She snarled.

"I have a beat on Nyx, but Eris's bio-sigs just went down near the police HQ in the south of the city. Need someone to check up on her. Nyx is a little busy out near the football arena. Can you take care of that? See if she's okay?"

Artemis closed the call without answering Blackhawk. "What do you care?"

"Fucking cops or soldiers got her. Bet you." Nemesis said.

"We'll see."

The two ladies boosted off into the rain, heading for the police building.

***

Hug soared through the air—eyes whitened again, sending his own sight back to Athon on the ground. His small frame and feathers dissipated any static, so lightning was not a threat. Most birds never took flight in rain this heavy but, Hug had always loved rain and storms. He neared the football arena, and caught a glimpse of Nyx on the street, dismantling several military troop carriers and forcing the soldiers out, and destroying their weapons and rifles. Another Apache helicopter lowered to her and blared a spotlight on her position. She effortlessly pulled her enormous sword and whipped it as it segmented into the copter, forcing it to spiral toward the Earth.

She boosted up and caught it mid-fall, and sat it on the ground, ensuring once again that the pilots were safe and unharmed.

On ground, Athon's eyes mimicked Hug's, and it saw Nyx as well from a literal bird's eye view. Ramsay had warned with special emphasis that avoiding Nyx was best. Athon had nary a care for Ramsay's warning, but it would be best to take Artemis and Nemesis before challenging their strongest member.

Hug could sense what Athon was thinking, and broke away, searching for the other two Pantheon members instead. The cyber-witch was right. Her raven was very useful, indeed.

***

Several riot officers and a few Guardsmen had gathered near Eris's singed body. The smell of burnt flesh stung their noses. The sword's electricity had since died out, but none of the men had the gall to get very close, lest this clearly enhanced body spring to life very angrily and chop someone in half. Most of the rioters had left, with only a few remaining out of curiosity: who was going to touch the body first?

The sound of jets could be heard—not as deep as a fighter plane or airliner. These were higher pitched; possibly smaller.

Nemesis's burly frame hit the ground near Eris, sending more cracked asphalt flying and pelting the citizens and riot guards. Everyone stumbled away from her in a circle, spreading outward, revealing Eris's burned and decimated corpse. Artemis lowered from the sky slowly. Both women had the same expression. Mouths open, heaving breaths of despair. Eyes watering with a mixture of sorrow and rage. Their friend was dead. Murdered.

Those mongrels with their rifles and shields; those *cowards* with their overcompensating senses of authority had killed Eris. At least, that's what it seemed like.

Nemesis stood still, processing another friend's death, while Artemis knelt beside Eris and placed a hand on her shoulder.

"No more." Artemis said, softly, choking back tears.

She blasted off the ground with such force that Eris's body slid a few feet. She slammed into the crowd of surprised riot police and unleashed hell on anything that moved. She was rage incarnate. Everything she punched or kicked crunched. Bones shattering and blood spurting.

Nemesis's rail gun clicked and whirred over her shoulder and upright. She steadied herself, bending her knees, and the massive weapon fired a lightning fast round into a troop carrier. It violently flipped into the air and peeled apart like a tin can, crashing into a building and shattering windows nearby. The troops inside likely died instantly.

Ramsay had sensed the inevitable for years, but his warnings had always been tossed aside. Never trust a stick of dynamite, he'd said. But now, the dynamite had ignited.

The Pantheon had gone rogue.

CHAPTER TWENTY-SEVEN

No Gods, No Masters

The carnage Artemis and Nemesis unleashed was broadcast for only a few moments over the radio, broken by static, in Harrison's squad car with Wells the passenger.

"Two women—killing everyo—got these suits—big gun—one without a suit—killed one of em—backup—can't do—die—fuck— ——" Static overtook the waves.

"We gotta help 'em." Harrison said, hitting the brake and turning down a street toward the HQ.

"They're already dead if that's what I think it is." Wells said.

"What?"

"The Pantheon, same ones that tore those jets apart. If we run into them we're dead too."

"We gotta do somethin' they're gonna fuckin' kill everybody!"

Wells thought for a moment as Harrison zipped the car through the streets. She'd turned the siren and lights off to keep a lower profile.

"On the radio, did he say one without a suit killed one of them?"

"Somethin' like that, yeah."

Has to be Leyla. No fucking way. Wells thought.

He tapped the comlink, which was still in his ear, and the holo-display came up in front of his face.

"What the fuck is that?!" Harrison said, doing a double take.

"Comlink. It's how they communicated down there." He answered, typing in L-E-Y as Llana had shown him before. He tapped 'Leyla'. After a few rings it was evident there would be no answer. "Goddammit."

"You gonna explain that a little more or act like I'm not here seeing this spacey shit?" Harrison asked.

Wells didn't answer. He closed the call and typed in R-A-M for Ramsay.

"Yeah okay, not answering. Dick." Harrison scoffed.

"I'm busy." Wells answered, annoyed. Ramsay, miraculously, answered the call, albeit with interference from being underground, far from Wells.

"Oh shit, you got out?" Ramsay gasped.

"Yeah, you little shit! You fucking tattle tale asshole! I knew we couldn't trust you!"

"Hey fuck you! I tried to keep things quiet. I told you, Blackhawk isn't stupid. Saw right through me."

"Yeah yeah, you fucking prick."

"Are you calling to insult me for the next ten minutes or do you have something important to say?"

"Yeah, your fucking girlfriends are massacring my police officers up here, and the Army too. What the fuck did you do?"

"What? They aren't supposed to hurt anyone. Fuck, I *knew* it. Fuck fuck fuck!"

"Yeah, you knew it and still let them loose."

"Dude! I didn't let anyone loose! I am not in charge!" Ramsay hissed.

"Okay, so what the fuck do we do up here?"

"Fucking run." Ramsay said.

"We ain't runnin' from *shit*." Harrison said.

"Look, Athon is up there. Maybe it can—"

"Athon? You mean Leyla?" Wells said.

"Uh, yeah Leyla, I guess."

"You mean The Pantheon didn't go after her?"

"Oh no, they killed her. And her friend."

"What the fuck?! You piece of shit!"

"Call me names one more time I'm hanging up and cutting you off."

"How do I talk to Leyla? I tried calling her."

"She doesn't have a comlink. But I think I can route you into her visor's link. Hold on. Shouldn't even be helping your mean ass. I got new arms, by the way."

"I don't give a fuck about your arms!"

"Thought you'd want to know. You had a weird look on your face last time you saw me. Okay, patching you through to Leyla."

Harrison was gawking at Wells. "New arms? Who was that dude?"

"Officer Donald Wells." Athon answered. It was Leyla's voice but…soulless.

"L—Leyla?"

"No Leyla. Only Athon."

"Is that a Ghostbusters reference?" Wells asked.

"I have not seen Ghostbusters."

Wells sighed. "Can I speak with Leyla please?"

"Leyla is merely a passenger for now. It is safer for her this way."

Harrison was waving her hand in the air in confusion. Now Wells was speaking to what sounded like a serial killer with split personalities.

"Okay, so, what's going on? Are you after The Pantheon? Please say yes."

"Yes."

"Did you get one of them?"

"Yes."

"Leyla was a lot more fun to talk to."

"Your fiancé was at the subway entrance. I spared him. He may be traumatized."

The call went silent. Athon had closed it out.

"What?! Greene? Hey!" Wells yelled. He turned to Harrison. "Get us to the abandoned subway entrance *now*!"

Harrison slammed on the brakes—not at Wells's request, but at what was barreling toward them.

Athon, doing at least a hundred miles per hour, on the white Street Rocket cyber-bike, jerked right and skirted around the squad car, avoiding a crash by millimeters. The car skidded to a halt.

"Okay, so now we got Darth Vader on a motorcycle." Harrison said. "I better be getting OT pay for this shit."

***

The police headquarters building was surrounded with bodies; twisted, mangled and bloodied. Nemesis's rail gun had blown the doors open, and they'd laid waste to everyone inside, police or not. Even the receptionist had been slammed through a wall. No one survived. The two armored women made sure of it.

Nemesis picked up Eris's burned body along with her loose katana, and boosted off the street, headed to The Bullpen. Artemis stayed on the ground, prowling, and listening. The storm had deafened much of the riotous noise but eventually, a gun shot would ring out. She could have just flown into the air to look for her next victims but she liked the hunt.

A short volley of gunfire rang out a few blocks away.

She jerked toward it, snarling, like an animal, and ran. The pneumatic muscles in her flight suit aided, giving her the speed of a cheetah, and a stride of at least twenty feet. She jumped and bounded off the side of a building, crumbling the bricks from the wall as she left it.

Within seconds, she dropped into the middle of another crowd of police and soldiers. Some fired at her, but they were non-lethal rounds. Not that lethal ones would have done much; the electromagnetic shield capacitors could withstand almost any rifle's rounds for at least a few seconds.

One after the other, she killed anything that was in a uniform. Two K-9 dogs, a German shepherd and a Belgian Malanois, darted toward her. The Malanois took to the air, lunging at her arm, while the Shepherd gnashed at her leg. She took the bite to her arm without so much as a wince, and kicked the other dog in the side, sending it screeching into a wall, where it dropped and didn't move again. She flung the Malanois hard into a post nearby, killing it as well.

Hug landed on the same post, and peered down at Artemis. His eyes were milky white, sending Athon the location of her next target—the one Leyla wanted most.

Army Guardsmen poured out of a troop carrier and finally gave Artemis a dose of M-4 and M-249 gunfire. Her shielding could take a few shots back to back, but not an entire squad's worth. That would overload the capacitor. She boosted away and took cover behind a corner. She wouldn't have to hide long. Nemesis would be back shortly. She would toy with the soldiers in the meantime.

* * *

Nemesis flew up to The Bullpen and landed right in front of Blackhawk, holding Eris's limp body in her arms.

Blackhawk looked surprised. He certainly hadn't expected to see one of The Pantheon burned and beaten so badly. That shouldn't have been possible. They were too powerful and intelligent for that, thanks to the myriad of implants and mods.

"Wh—how?" He said.

Nemesis glared at him and circled around, still holding her friend's body. She said nothing as she made her way back to Eris's armor workstation and laid the body down.

"What happened? Where's Artemis?" Blackhawk followed her.

Nemesis laid Eris's katana on the body's chest, but kept it in her grip. "This was the second one of us that died for you."

"What…happened?" Blackhawk asked again, growing cautious. Nemesis's tone suggested something of ire, and not simply with a dead friend. She was angry at him as well. He stepped back, noticing the katana still in Nemesis's hand.

"Rhea and Eris did not die for me. They died for our cause. They died for this world to become a better pla—"

THOOM!

Nemesis's rail gun fired into the platform floor itself, just in front of Blackhawk's feet, and ripped open a hole the size of a dump truck. The gun was folded back in its resting position, but it apparently could still fire. The force alone brought Nemesis off the ground, and she landed easily enough back on the floor, wielding Eris's sword.

Blackhawk attempted to drop backward, but he'd been caught too off guard. One boot slipped, and he dropped into the massive hole. The sharp, torn metal ripped into his jeans, tearing one leg away and revealing his old, metallic cybernetic limb underneath. He was able to grab a thick band of wire as he fell through, but it was the shorn metal of the platform catching his trench coat that saved him. He hung at least two thousand feet in the air by just three fingers on a wire, and a strip of old leather.

Nemesis took her time walking over to him, around the edge of the hole, as he flailed and attempted to figure out a plan.

"I see you thinking. So desperately." Nemesis said.

Lightning struck toward the platform, but the shielding that had blocked the Apache missile also blocked the bolt. The electricity dissipated across The Bullpen in a dome. Blackhawk felt the electric shock in his fingers, which had fortunately been lessened by 300 million volts by the platform's capacitors.

"Always a man with a plan." Nemesis mocked him. "Always sending someone else to do what you won't."

Blackhawk searched for something—anything—to get him out of the situation, but had no luck. Even if he managed to get onto the platform again, Nemesis clearly would kill him. His revolver was clacking against his completely bare leg.

Nemesis had made it over to him, and was staring straight down at him, waiting for him to meet her eyes. She got her wish.

"Why are you doing this? Why?" Blackhawk yelled up at her, even knowing the answer.

"Because our way is simpler. You did all this. A fucking dog and pony show for the world, when you could have just used the Xenobots and did everything in one fell swoop, without all this over complicated *look at me, look how important I am* narcissistic bullshit!"

"Because people need to be on the same side for this to work! There can't be a huge disagreement! We provide the basic necessities but the *people* still need to work with each other! This was about unification! Getting rid of archaic government systems and galvanizing society as a whole! No gods, no masters!"

"Oh shut the FUCK UP! We're sick of your fucking speeches! If we're going to die doing this, we die on *our* terms! Not yours!"

Lightning struck the platform again. Nemesis winced at the sudden, blinding flash. Blackhawk drew his revolver as fast as he could, and brought it up to Nemesis and fired twice. The first round dissipated the shielding, and the second cracked Nemesis in the collarbone, shattering it.

A guttural, pained snarl escaped Nemesis's throat, and Blackhawk fired two more times. Both rounds missed as Nemesis backed away. Her rail gun folded forward and revved up. It clicked.

"Gah!" Nemesis yelled. She'd used her last loaded round to blow the hole in the platform. But she was still holding Eris's katana.

Blackhawk had scrambled up the hole quickly and was already getting to his feet on the platform. Nemesis switched the katana to her left arm, the side with the broken collarbone, and grabbed hold of a heavy foot locker with her right. She threw it hard at Blackhawk. He narrowly ducked the locker. If it had hit him, he would have fallen for sure. He raised his revolver and fired once more, but Eris spun her back to him, allowing the round to hit the rail gun instead. She fought the pain of the broken bone and lunged at him, switching the sword back to her right hand. He only had one round left in that big revolver.

He fired the last round, and hit Nemesis square in the chest—the strongest section of her exo-suit—but the resulting spray of sparks forced her to flinch and close her eyes, turning away.

When Nemesis looked back, Blackhawk had already dropped into the cockpit of his assault AV, and the canopy was closing. She lunged forward, but Blackhawk activated the gravity pulser on the front. It blew Nemesis back to the ground hard, and he madly flicked switches and slapped buttons, powering the AV up for flight. Nemesis got to her feet and brought a mighty fist down on the canopy, cracking the supposedly shatterproof glass.

Blackhawk slammed the yoke forward and rammed Nemesis. She fell, and the entire AV bounced over her as it flew off. Blackhawk ignited the gravity afterburners and knocked Nemesis clean off the platform. She yelled in pain and anger all the same. The AV ripped through the air and away from The Bullpen. Blackhawk knew Nemesis would give chase now, and his AV wasn't as fast as those F-16s had been, so he couldn't outrun her. He had to out *fly* her.

Nemesis righted herself as she fell and blasted off toward Blackhawk, who was speeding away and into the city. He hoped to lose her or gain some distance in the tall buildings. He needed to get an opening to use his rail gun in defense, but it would need a couple seconds to lock onto her.

She closed the gap, and he banked right hard and corkscrewed downward, then immediately pulled up and hit a loop. Nemesis kept pace, but each switch in direction slid her collarbone around under the skin, and it felt like being eaten alive. The pain was so intense it was making her vision fuzzy, but she pushed anyway.

Blackhawk flicked a few more switches as he steered with one hand. The rail gun powered up. Unfortunately, it couldn't swivel much. He'd have to get the AV turned around and facing Nemesis to stand a chance.

He jerked left and rounded a skyscraper, then cut right and down even more, nearly skimming the ground and into a curved tunnel. His AV just barely fit, and the wings scraped the concrete walls as he rounded the curve. Once through, he shot upward and flipped the AV, pulled up and flipped it again. He didn't have much of a plan other than do the craziest shit he could think of to get some breathing room.

Nemesis nicked the concrete edge of the tunnel coming out with her rail gun, which whipped her backward into a flying back flip. Any normal woman may have broken her neck. But she shook her head, and boosted on. Blackhawk was getting away.

He darted around every building and skyscraper he saw. He zipped under a bridge, cutting a valley in the water under it from the gravity pulse the AV emitted as it flew, and cut hard left and right. It was working. Nemesis was falling behind. Now was a good chance. He kicked the brake pad at his left foot and slowed the AV, then pulled the yoke up. The AV flipped over and inverted, but it was now facing toward Nemesis and soaring backward. Blackhawk had to essentially stall the gravity propulsion engine to do this, so if he missed, he wouldn't have much time to recover.

The lock-on indicator beeped. Nemesis was headed straight for him. The indicator beeped again. Nemesis was so close now he could make out her face. The indicator buzzed. He flicked up the trigger protector on the yoke and pushed the red switch. The rail gun flashed white and hurled a tungsten rod at Nemesis.

She ducked it. She ducked a *rail gun* projectile, flying at her at 5,000 miles per hour.

"Fuckin' kiddin' me?!" Blackhawk yelled.

Nemesis slammed into the AV and caught whatever she could grip, then boosted hard up, flipping the AV over. Blackhawk had stalled it, and she now had control. And somehow, she was still hanging on to Eris's sword as well. She stabbed it into one of the grav-engines at the rear, which exploded with a reverse pulse that whipped the AV around in the air and Nemesis went flying and snarling in pain. She quickly recovered and caught the AV as it fell toward the water. Sure, letting Blackhawk crash would kill him, which she wanted, but he was carrying the four remaining vials of Xenobots. She needed to kill him on land, and not in a fiery crash that would likely destroy the Xenos.

Feverish, she fought through the intense pain of her broken collar, and tugged the AV to the hills across the river, and dropped it from just the right height to hurt Blackhawk a little. She came down hard on the canopy and cracked it some more.

The canopy exploded into her face. Glass sliced her cheeks and forehead, miraculously missing her eyes, but Blackhawk rammed into her immediately after, as he'd pulled his eject lever. He soared into the sky as Nemesis fell backward, finally knocked unconscious by the action. He unbuckled and pushed off from the seat. Normally, an idiotic move when a couple hundred feet in the air, but Blackhawk's cybernetic legs could likely take the impact.

He landed hard on the wet grass. The servo motors in both his knees popped. Thankfully, he couldn't feel that. And the legs would still work, but he would be significantly slower; he wouldn't be able to run. He searched for Nemesis, and found her stirring slowly in front of the downed AV. There was nowhere to run and nowhere to hide.

Nemesis, a bloody mess, spat teeth out of her mouth and picked glass from her skin, snarling as she did. She was so angry and screaming in pain that she didn't hear Blackhawk sneak up behind her. He pistol whipped the protector cap of her suit's kill switch, broke it, and hit the switch.

Her suit stood upright and opened in segments, spilling her out to the muddy ground. Again, she yelped and growled. Eris's sword was only a few feet away.

Blackhawk's leg motors ground as he walked over to the katana and picked it up.

"You know, Ramsay told me on multiple occasions I shoulda outfitted you ladies with behavioral implants. Specifically for moments like this, when you get a bright fuckin' idea and try to ruin what we've put all this time into."

"Fuck you." Nemesis said, blood dripping down her face from several lacerations.

"Know what I said? I said 'Nah, they'll be good. They believe in the cause. I trust 'em.' Dumbest shit I've ever said."

Blackhawk raised the sword up high, and brought it down toward Nemesis's neck as hard as he could.

The sword rang out a metallic twang as it struck. Blackhawk's eyes widened. Nemesis had caught the blade in her good hand, stopping it short of decapitating her. Blood ran down her arm as the razor edge had cut deep into her palm. He tried to pull it away, but her grip was too strong. She held the blade tight as she slowly stood, her eyes meeting his. She had the look of a cornered and injured tiger—never something a man should be close to.

She kneed him in the gut, and without letting that foot touch the ground, whipped it up and kicked him in the side of the head. He slammed to the ground, not realizing he'd let go of the katana handle.

He scrambled away and got to his feet as fast as he could, ready for a fight—but Nemesis was much faster, even as broken as she was.

He barely felt the blade as it slid into his chest until it was already a foot in, right through his heart. It was a sharp pain; like a large needle. He felt his heart beat around the metal inside it; even the blood pouring out with each pump.

Nemesis pulled the sword out of him slowly, and twisted it as she did so. *That* hurt like a motherfucker. He groaned at first, but quickly let out a wail as Nemesis got the blade all the way out.

Blood poured like a faucet from his chest and he dropped to his knees. Each breath was harder to draw than the last. His feet became cold, then his fingers, then his gut. He lost feeling in his legs and arms and keeled over to his side. His heart pumped faster and faster, quickening its own demise.

Nemesis watched Blackhawk die. It felt good.

No Gods. No Masters.

CHAPTER TWENTY-EIGHT

Daughters of Chaos

Artemis had gotten to a rooftop and was lobbing anything she could at the armed men below. She pulled a commercial air conditioning unit from its braces and rolled it off the side. The massive hunk of metal crashed down beside the soldiers. She turned around, laughing maniacally, and froze when she saw it.

A lightning flash outlined the silhouette of her doom. Two bright orange katana blades faded into view as they heated up. A sharp hiss emanated from them as the raindrops fizzled at the heat. A streaming cloak waving in the wind accented the weapons, looking as if a horned demon was standing there, taunting her.

Athon had found her.

Artemis released a feral snarl at the android that morphed into another excited and disturbed cackle. She was going to get the chance to kill Athon all over again.

Artemis wasted no time. She launched into the air toward Athon, gritting her teeth and growling. Athon charged as well, twirling its swords backward so they were wielded underhanded.

The two met with a vicious flurry of strikes. Artemis swung elbows and knees, and Athon blocked and dodged as much as it could. The hot swords acted as reinforcements to its forearms, and aided in blocking Artemis' attacks. The super-heated blades burned the armor's cloth but the carbon fiber-graphene weave underneath could withstand the heat for the moment.

Artemis spun around and finally landed a hard kick to Athon's gut, and then boosted the gravity capacitor above her heel, resulting in a double impact that sent Athon flying backward and into a large antenna. Sparks shot in every direction as the antenna uprooted and fell over. Athon was on its feet near instantly and charging back into the fight.

Artemis boosted backward this time, and dodged a few swings from Athon's katana blades. Athon warped, and popped up behind Artemis, sending a knee into her back. Artemis yelled out of frustration, but pushed away and turned to face Athon, who warped again and swung a sword from Artemis' right side. Artemis ducked away and missed losing her head by a hair, literally, as the blade chopped a good three inches of her scarlet mane off.

She dropped to a knee and punched Athon's inner thigh hard, and Athon dropped to a knee right in front of her. But, Athon warped yet again and teleported behind Artemis, and drove one sword down into her back shoulder, down to the hilt. Artemis barely flinched. Pain inhibitor implants were useful. The blade had barely missed any organs that would prevent her from her immediate goal: killing that fucking android.

She grabbed hold of the blade jutting from her body, paying no mind to the heat searing her palm and fingers, and snapped it like a pencil. She whipped it up at Athon, who was still behind her. Athon ducked away as Artemis stood, now wielding her own blade. The hilt and part of the hot blade were still embedded in her back. Artemis reached around and pulled it out. The heat had cauterized the wound.

Athon retracted its remaining blade and switched it out for Desert Eagle pistol. One shot from it dissipated Artemis' shielding. The next struck her shoulder as she tried to duck away. If not for the flight suit she was wearing, half her shoulder may have been blown off. Pain inhibitors or not, she felt that.

"Gaaahhhh!" Artemis fell backward onto the roof.

Athon leapt into the air and summoned her broken sword hilt away from Artemis' hand and fired the DE again, aiming for the head. Artemis rolled fast, barely dodging the round. Athon came down hard, stomping Artemis' hip. Artemis kicked up as hard as she could and caught Athon in the side, knocking it off balance. She scrambled to her knee and spun hard left, sweeping the android off its feet. Athon landed with a thud on its shoulder.

Artemis still had a hold on the broken and cooled blade, and swiped it down at Athon's neck. The android blocked with the broken sword's hilt, and batted the blade away. Athon kicked up and twirled over, landing on its knee and foot. Artemis boosted right off her back and into the air, dodging one more shot from Athon's huge pistol.

This time, Athon held a fist up and let Artemis close in. The Thumper powered up.

A thunderclap sounded as The Thumper dissipated all its energy outward, cracking the roof and blowing rain away in a sphere. Athon's arm hurled downward and brought its body along to the ground.

Artemis may as well have been hit by a truck. She flew back and into the air, slamming into the edge of the roof and tumbling over the side.

She crashed to the street below, having fallen several stories from the roof. Her exo-suit sparked and whined. The motors were failing, and she could barely move. She reached over her neck and pulled the kill switch, releasing herself. The suit opened and she stepped out. She wouldn't be able to fly now or absorb as much impact, but she was faster, and still had her enhanced strength. She dodged away just as she saw Athon coming down from the roof, sword in hand.

Athon drove the sword a foot deep into the street. Artemis kicked her enemy away and tried to grab the sword, but Athon countered with a flurry of punches and kicks of its own, forcing dodges and counters. Both of them had the power to end the other with one solid strike.

They circled the embedded katana, vying for position, punching and kicking. Artemis was spitting and snarling, while Athon was silent as ever.

Athon managed to stomp down on Artemis's foot, which she didn't feel, but keeping the foot on hers and elbowing her in the face knocked her back and to the ground. Athon jerked the sword from the ground and jumped into the air, pointing the blade directly down at Artemis's heart. She hadn't even hit the ground yet.

Before Athon landed, something grabbed the back of its armor, and flung it hard into a wall. Athon crashed through into the building. The room was littered with small desk chairs and a whiteboard. A kindergarten classroom? Athon got to its feet, having held on to the unbroken sword. Looking out the hole in the wall, Artemis was getting to her feet, and Nemesis had joined the fight—bloody, battered, and ready to murder anything she saw fit.

Nemesis's rail gun folded upward, revved up, and fired into the school. She'd reloaded the drum with fresh rounds.

Athon had already begun ducking, but the round still forced it back and into a roll as it passed. The rail round cut right through the building, blasting a hole in several more walls and classrooms. Had it been daytime, unheard tragedies would have befallen the building at that very moment. In a stroke of luck, the round forced a fire extinguisher to ignite and spray a thick, gray cloud of suppressant all over, obscuring Athon just enough for an escape. The android ducked into the building further.

Nemesis boosted into the school, knocking desks and chairs over. Broken glass fell to the floor and sparks rained down from flickering fluorescent lights. She was sweaty and breathing hard. She didn't have the same pain inhibitors Artemis did, and the broken collar bone burned like venomous thorns.

Nemesis heard a pop, and two wires shot out from the extinguisher mist. Each wire had hooks on the end. They clinked to Nemesis's armor and fired with an immense electric charge, causing Nemesis to seize and fall to her knee. Athon burst from the mist and dropped the overpowered taser it'd been carrying, neglecting to power it down. No, Nemesis could fry for all it cared.

Athon leapt, and brought a flying side kick into Nemesis's face, rocketing her back and to the floor, her head cracking the linoleum with a sickening sound.

But Artemis had been waiting for such a movement. And seemingly came from out of nowhere with a roundhouse kick to Athon's chest.

Athon whipped back, landing on the corner of a desk and bouncing off it, finally slamming to the floor as well, and dropped the sword.

Nemesis groaned, but she still somehow got to her feet and ripped the electrified taser wires from her suit. Her thick flight suit had likely saved her from the voltage, but it had still been enough of a shock to singe her hair. Rage drove these women, not logic. Artemis picked up Athon's remaining sword.

Athon had stumbled into the first classroom again, and by the time it was on its feet, it fell outside, back into the street. It pulled the F2000 from its back. Amazingly enough, it was still there. Athon had lost the taser and Desert Eagle in the fight already. Artemis had the unbroken sword, and the bullpup shotgun was still slung on the left shoulder.

Athon rolled away as it heard Nemesis's rail gun powering up again. A round whipped past and into the street, blowing a hole in the wall opposite. Desks and chairs spilled out into the street behind it.

Athon heard glass under footsteps—one set heavy and clanking, one light and swift. Artemis and Nemesis were coming.

Have to break them up, Athon thought. It checked the Thumper—still pulsing red. The reverse blast from earlier had a ridiculous cool down. Even with antimatter charged cells, Athon was running out of energy. It had not been built for drawn out fights such as this. It was an assassin, not a brawler. It stumbled to its feet again and tripped over Artemis' broken exo-suit. The fight was wearing it thin and causing a break in focus.

Nemesis landed right in front of Athon as it crawled up to its knees. The sound of a blade dragging on the asphalt behind let Athon know Artemis was prepped for the kill, and she was toying with her prey.

A sudden rush of jet fire sounded from above. Small jets—same as Artemis and Nemesis's suits had.

Nyx dropped onto the street like a comet from the sky. Asphalt erupted around her and rained on her sisters' heads and pelted Athon as well. Her enormous, seven foot sword activated and extended above her head as she held it high, then let it drop to the street with a resounding clang. The heavy blade went several inches into the blacktop, and then the gravity energy pulsed on, cascading in waves across it.

Athon was now outnumbered, outgunned, and outsmarted. There was no escaping The Pantheon now. The three women formed a triangle of assured demise around Athon. This was it. This was the final stand.

Out of hubris, Artemis and Nemesis allowed Athon to get to its feet. The android ducked and jumped right, pulling the bullpup shotgun and bringing it up to the ladies at the same time as the SMG.

Shotgun pellets and bullets flew by Artemis and Nemesis, some hitting them and running the shielding capacitors down. Athon knew it couldn't take them all, so it targeted the already wounded women. It heard Nyx's great sword rev up with gravitational energy. The fine clinks of metal separating. A whoosh as Nyx drew the whip-sword back. But it didn't matter. Athon would go down guns blazing. Maybe that was destiny.

Nyx's sword segments went right past Athon, and crashed into the broken school wall just behind Artemis and Nemesis. They both seemed to pause and cut a look to Nyx—one that said *what the fuck was that for*?

The sword segments revved up, and exploded the entire outer wall of the school, blasting Nemesis and Artemis both with huge chunks of brick and mortar, sending them skidding across the ground. The entire damaged half of the school crumbled to the ground, sending a blanket of dust across The Pantheon and Athon.

Athon finally looked at Nyx for the first time as the sword segments retracted back into a singular blade. As each segment connected, Nyx's arm recoiled. But, her face…was the face of a friend.

Athon's visor drew back, finally revealing Leyla's face. Her eyes were gleaming with both surprise and relief.

"Mari?!" She yelled.

Nyx looked at her. She didn't nod. She didn't wink or even wince. Something was different, as if she'd been stripped of emotion. But Nyx *was Mari.* And Mari had come to fight for Leyla, lending a helping hand once again. Either that, or Mari was there to take down the rogue Pantheon.

Saving questions for later, Leyla jumped to her feet, having come back into control of her body. But Athon was still in her head.

That may be your friend, but she is changed. Athon said.

"Whatever. For now, we're gonna whoop some ass." Leyla growled, turning to Artemis and Nemesis, who were also getting up and shaking off the blast from Mari's weapon.

Mari stomped over to Artemis' faulty exo-suit, which had been standing upright in the street, and with one hand, flung it at its former wearer. Artemis ducked but the armor was flying at such speed that one of the empty leg segments cracked her in the shoulder, sending her back into the rubble behind her.

Nemesis's rail gun whirred to life again, but Mari boosted hard toward her, bringing her enormous sword out front as she flew. Nemesis fired, and Mari blocked the round with the blade. The force of the tungsten rod flying into the sword stopped Mari mid-flight, and the resulting crack in the air sounded like a pipe bomb had detonated. Ripples of gravity energy shot out from the impact like blue lightning.

Mari absorbed the shock and landed flat on her armored feet, immediately sprinting at Nemesis. Amazingly, the sword didn't shatter.

Mari whipped the sword around, blade pointed backward, and slammed into Nemesis with a hard shoulder. Both the women crashed through what was left of the crumbled school building.

Artemis had gotten back on her feet again, only to be met with a furious punch from not Athon, but Leyla.

Leyla let loose a roar as she swung, letting Artemis know vengeance had arrived. She kneed the redhead in the gut so hard it lifted her off her feet, then jumped in the air along with Artemis, and brought a fist down on the back of her head. Artemis smacked face first into the pavement and rubble. Her orbital bone cracked and blood shot from her nose. Leyla had finally drawn blood from her foe.

Before Artemis could recover, she was met with another kick to her ribs. She couldn't feel pain, but she could feel several crunches inside her torso as bones cracked and shattered. She felt her lung get sliced open by one of the broken bones, mirroring the injury she'd given to Leyla earlier. Artemis landed hard on her back in the street, wincing from the injury.

You just punctured her lung. She will have a hard time drawing breath. Now, the killing blow. Athon advised Leyla.

"Not yet." Leyla replied. She wasn't done with that red haired bitch; not by a long shot.

Artemis took a lot longer to stand this time, and was curled to her left, the side with all the broken ribs. She had to fight to breathe in and out. Her face was mangled—eyes blood red and bleeding tears from the broken orbital. She spat a hunk of mucus and blood to the pavement.

"Was that for your bitch friend?" She snarled, taunting Leyla.

"Her name is DEL!" Leyla said, charging in and ducking a swing from Artemis. She brought a fist into Artemis' chin with an uppercut. She felt the jaw dislocate.

Artemis whipped back and upward, then landed on her neck and shoulder, flipping over to her belly. Blood and teeth fell from her mouth as she gasped. Leyla gave her no time to think, and gripped her flight suit collar, and pulled her up to her knees. Leyla pulled Artemis's left arm out straight and snapped it just below the elbow, exactly as she'd done to Del. Even with the pain inhibitors, Artemis finally screamed—and fueled Leyla's rage even more so.

"Oh…so you *can* feel it." Leyla said, proud of finally making Artemis squeal. She picked Artemis up and tossed her in the air, then grabbed her by the throat and choke slammed her to the ground. The impact alone made blood spurt from her mouth, nose, ears and even eyes. Artemis tried to swing, but missed by a mile. She'd been blinded from all the blood and shock to her body, and each breath came out as a gurgled wheeze.

"That one's for Del, you cunt."

Leyla heard the smashing of bricks and debris. Looking up toward the sound, Nemesis burst from inside the school and out of the rooftop. Mari was right behind her and swung her sword whip, just missing Nemesis. She gave chase into the sky. Leyla turned her attention back to Artemis. Most of her body matched her hair in color now. Leyla backed away and let Artemis get to her feet, and just as she stood, she swung a kick into the small of her back as hard as she could.

Artemis' spine crumpled as her body folded back like a closing pocket knife. She flopped to the ground, instantly paralyzed.

"And that's for me." Leyla growled.

Artemis began to cackle; psychotic as ever. She knew she was going to die. "You are so pathetic." She said, and laughed like a maniac.

Leyla circled the broken woman like a shark in bloodied water. Artemis continued her taunting.

"Fucking robot. Thinking you had feelings for someone. You can't. You can't have friends. You can't have real purpose. A computer tells you what to do. You don't even have an identity. All you are is an android called *Athon*. Fucking pathetic."

Leyla found her unbroken katana and held it in her left hand. She grabbed a large bundle of Artemis' red hair in her right hand and snatched her upright. Her feet dangled and dragged the ground, devoid of life.

"Wrong." Leyla said, and drew the sword to her right, under the arm holding Artemis up.. She didn't activate the heating wires. She wanted this wound to bleed.

Artemis' body fell to the ground at the swing of Leyla's sword, headless. Blood gushed down with it.

Leyla made sure her face was the last thing Artemis saw as her severed head swiftly bled out, held up by her hair. Artemis had a fury in her eyes, as if she wanted to fight more, even as she knew death would touch her any second now. She could even hear the blood spattering under her. Leyla held Artemis's head closer, and snarled the final words she would hear.

"My name is Leyla."

Leyla scowled at Artemis as the expression slowly faded from her face, and her life with it. It was when Artemis's mouth drooped open that Leyla knew she was dead. She dropped the decapitated head on the street, and stumbled backward. Her face drew into one of slight remorse.

I am beginning to like you. Athon said.

"That was…" Leyla let out a huge breath and choked back tears. "That was…I killed her."

Gloriously. Athon added.

"I don't, I…"

Vengeance is always bittersweet.

Athon wasn't exactly understanding that Artemis truly was the first person that *Leyla* had killed; on purpose, at least—and with such malice and vicious intent. Leyla's heart was flooded with a mixture of sorrow and guilt and her mind raced. Did Artemis have a family? What made her so crazy? Why had she been so angry? Why did she join The Pantheon? Why would she do any of this and taunt Athon in the face of death?

Stay out of your head. She does not deserve your thoughts. Athon attempted to shush Leyla's mind.

"But, but she was a person."

She was a rabid dog.

Leyla stared at Artemis' severed head. It had landed eyes up, staring back at her like a soulless ghoul.

"I'm sorry." Leyla rasped.

Are you apologizing to her? After what she did? After what she would have done?

"I don't know how to feel, okay?" Leyla felt tears finally come down her cheeks. "I was so, just, *brutal* with her. It wasn't you. I had control. I beat her like that. Like she was a helpless animal. I can't…I don't know what to feel. I thought this would feel better but it's *worse*."

I am fortunate to be free of these emotions. They seem like such a burden. So heavy when they needn't be.

"Why wouldn't they be? I killed another human being. I did. Not you. This time it was *me*."

You did not simply kill. You defended and you protected.

"I just want Del back."

And you avenged a friend. You should not feel for Artemis. She did not for you, or for Del. There are still two of The Pantheon to deal with.

"One. Mari is helping me."

That is Mari no longer. She is not helping us. She is simply putting down the other rabid dog.

"You keep saying us. We are not the same. You don't understand any of this shit. You don't understand being human at all. Artemis was right. You can't feel anything. You can't have friends. You're like a puppet. Always doing what some machine told you to."

And you are a personality construct implanted in my mind by that machine. Do not confuse things. We are two sides of the same coin.

"Oh *can it* with the anime assassin quotes, for the love of God, please shut up."

We are a God.

"No we are not! You are like the worst version of a bad GPS voice. *Go here. Turn there. You have reached your destination of doom.*"

Mockery will get us nowhere.

"This is my body. My life. I am a human being, and you don't get to play your little 'I'm important' games anymore. Bye bitch."

Athon did not respond this time. Leyla squinted her eyes, wishing as hard as she could, to be rid of Athon. She would simply push Athon down, deep into her mind, until there was no way it would ever speak again. She wasn't sure if the headache that started was because Athon was fighting her or if she was squinting too hard.

Do you seriously believe you can think me out of existence?

"Ugh! Go away!"

I cannot go anywhere.

"Can you at least shut the fuck up?"

Possibly.

"Forever?"

No.

"I'm gonna find a way to get rid of you."

We have died twice. We are inseparable, even in the most extreme of circumstances. I will make you a deal.

"Okay. What?"

I was created as a means to an end. To bring peace to this world, whether wanted or not.

"Don't give me a speech, just tell me what you want." Leyla scoffed, finally turning to walk away from Artemis.

The only threat left now is The Pantheon. They still have the power to enact their will on the Earth, through the use of the remaining Xenobots. If SIGIL truly intended to use our body for them, we must do so. I do not care for humanity. Nor does SIGIL. But it was tasked with unification of all societies to bring peace and harmony. It was tasked with finding a way to bring true Utopia to humanity.

"What do you mean?"

We must prevent The Pantheon from using the Xenobots and use them ourselves. You may choose what you want for this world in the end.

"But that will—"

Kill us. Physically.

"The fuck kind of a deal is that?"

It is the deal of a warrior. It is what we were created for. It is our destiny and our fate.

"You would be like, the *worst* car salesman."

Yet you know I am right.

"I don't want to die. So, no."

You are human, so you claim. To die is but one of many human inevitabilities. Many have attempted to have lasting impact in their deaths. Our sacrifice saves this world not once, but forever. We have been raised from the brink twice so, in order to achieve our ultimate goal.

Hug flew down from wherever he'd been and landed on Leyla's shoulder. The Street Rocket rolled up and stopped beside Leyla, and she got on as Hug dropped to the power cell he'd ridden at before.

There had to be a way to use the Xenobots without dying. And if there was, Leyla set her mind to find it. But first, Athon was correct. Nemesis still had to be dealt with, and Mari needed help against her.

Leyla took off down the street in the direction she'd last seen Mari chasing Nemesis.

***

Harrison rolled her squad car to a stop just beside Wells's truck where he'd left it. Wells had decided that showing up to Greene in a police car was a sure fire way to complicate things, so he'd go to his fiancé in his personal truck instead, hoping Greene may actually recognize the big Dodge. That wasn't likely to happen, but Wells was willing to try anything at this point.

"Sure you're gonna go alone?" Harrison asked Wells as he got out of the car.

"Yeah I think that's best. I need him to be less defensive. He sees this car and a cop, he's gonna either run or shoot."

At that very moment, both Mari and Nemesis crashed into the street in front of the police car. Mari had air-tackled Nemesis and plunged her right to the ground. They both rolled across the pavement and got to their feet quickly, and went at each other with punches that could crack trees in half.

Nemesis boosted into Mari, slamming into the wall of a building and ripping a fire hydrant up along the way. Water shot into the sky, and was immediately struck by lightning.

"Oh shit!" Harrison yelled.

"Out of the car now!" Wells yelled.

Harrison pulled her seat belt off and jumped out, just as Mari's whip sword came through the spewing column of water from the hydrant and slammed into the police car. Both Wells and Harrison ran full speed from the car as the sword pulled away, slicing the car in half longways. Thankfully, Mari hadn't made it explode.

Wells jumped in his truck and cranked it up, hit reverse and whipped it around, then skidded the big V8 around to Harrison, who'd run down an alleyway. She stopped as she saw several modders turn toward her and point guns her way.

"Get in!" Wells yelled out the window, right behind her.

She turned and ran toward the truck and jumped in the bed just as several bullets whizzed by.

The modders were shooting real rounds. They must have gotten word that everything had gone tits up, and they thought it was an all out war.

Wells peeled out and sped down the street, having to swerve to avoid Mari getting slammed to the ground by Nemesis. He looked back, checking on Harrison, who was in a prone position in the bed, sliding side to side as he turned. When he looked back to the road, he had to slam on the brakes.

Leyla, on the Street Rocket, was coming right at him, and they were definitely going to crash. But Leyla hopped up to her feet on the bike's seat, crouching, and summoned her sword. The blade shot out and heated up immediately. The cyber bike stopped inches away from Wells's truck hood as if it hadn't been moving at all, but Leyla launched from it, soaring over the truck. Wells struggled to keep up, tracking her as she flew above.

Leyla left a trail of rain drops breaking behind her, streaming sideways against the others, as she went through the air. She brought the orange bladed sword over her head. She was flying straight toward Nemesis.

Nemesis ducked a swipe of Mari's great sword and noticed, out of the corner of her eye, Leyla coming for her in the air. She turned and whipped Eris's sword up, blocking Leyla's katana. They met with such force that Nemesis, in her hefty armor, slid backward on her feet.

Leyla flipped over her and landed, crouching and sliding backward as well, holding her hot sword up.

Lightning struck again near Nemesis, but she didn't flinch. Mari, Leyla, and Nemesis stared each other down, waiting for whoever made the first move. With each brandishing their own blade, one could have expected a classic spaghetti western soundtrack to play.

Harrison peered over the tailgate. "The fuck are they doing, staring at each other?"

Hug had hopped up onto the hood of the truck and then the roof. He cooed, in the tune of the iconic notes from *The Good, The Bad, & The Ugly*. He flew off, taking to the sky.

"That bird just referenced a Clint Eastwood movie. I'm done. I'm done with this shit. It's too weird. We're leaving." Wells said, hitting the gas, and speeding away, rounding the Street Rocket parked in front of him.

Leyla watched as Wells made his getaway, happy knowing he was still safe. She'd wanted to say hi; she hadn't seen him since before she'd been brutalized by The Pantheon, but something more pressing was at hand.

Nemesis decided to run. She blasted off the ground and hopped up to a roof. Mari immediately gave chase. When she vaulted over the corner, Nemesis drove Eris's sword right into her chest. Mari reflexively batted her away, but the damage had been done. Nemesis had outsmarted her, making her think she was running when she'd set a quick and unexpected trap. Mari still lunged at her, unaware as of yet that she'd been mortally wounded. It seemed she didn't feel pain, same as Artemis, so she didn't realize the blade had gone through and out her back. Mari finally dropped her massive sword.

To Nemesis's surprise, Mari brought a furious elbow to her side, cracking a couple ribs. Mari grabbed Nemesis by the throat and picked her up, but Nemesis took hold of the sword embedded in Mari's chest and pulled it out—and sliced Mari across the face as she did so.

Mari dropped Nemesis to the roof and reeled back. She didn't make a sound. Even with the gash from her jaw to her temple, she never winced or showed any expression.

Nemesis plunged the sword in again, this time in the gut.

Leyla hopped up on the roof, and the WireFire retracted into its housing on her wrist. When she saw Mari with the sword in her chest, her heart raced. Another friend was falling to these demented women. She sprinted to Nemesis, who looked over to her. Nemesis pulled the sword from Mari's gut and prepared for a fight with Leyla, but Leyla warped behind her and tried to slice her head off.

Nemesis's large suit protected her this time, and Leyla's sword clanged off the hard metal. Leyla saw Mari drop to a knee, bleeding out fast. She kicked Nemesis hard on the chest, but in that fat ass armor, Nemesis barely moved.

Their swords bounced off each other multiple times as they fought like samurai in the storm. Lightning struck around them several times.

Nemesis finally gave up when she realized Mari was too injured to give chase. She kicked Leyla away and boosted into the air. Leyla had no way to follow, so she turned her attention to Mari, who had fallen to her side, expressionless and breathing heavy.

"Mari!?" Leyla yelled, sliding to her friend's side. She picked Mari's head up, but the armor was heavy. Leyla flicked the kill switch as Ramsay had told her to before, and the armor straightened out and opened up. She pulled Mari out of the exo-suit and held her over her lap.

"Hey, can you hear me? Mari?"

Mari looked Leyla in the eyes. She couldn't speak. She couldn't show emotion. But something in her eyes said she remembered who Leyla was.

"What did they do to you?" Leyla cried.

Mari didn't respond, of course. Leyla stroked her cheek and moved her hair out of her eyes, which trailed away from Leyla's.

Mari let out a long breath and her chest sank, and didn't rise again.

This time, Leyla was more angry than distraught. She hadn't known Mari for long but she truly seemed like a friend. Nemesis was still alive, and that meant there was no time to mourn. Leyla looked over to Mari's exo-suit. She tenderly laid Mari's head down and closed her eyes for her, and then lifted the armor upright.

"See if this works." She said, as she stepped backward into the suit. She felt a thick click under her heels as each foot settled in. Mari had let her borrow her clothes when she got to the city, so they were almost exactly the same size.

The armor closed around her tight, but it was comfortable, and it fit perfectly. She felt a sharp sting in several parts of her back as fiber optic needles pierced into her spinal cord. One final pinch came from the base of her skull, where another had penetrated into her cerebellum. It hurt, but only as it happened. She felt nothing afterward—but now, it didn't feel like she was wearing armor. She felt as if she was weightless and wearing only underwear. The weight of the exo-suit had lifted. She was one with the armor, and she knew how to fly it. The armor itself communicated to her body through the needles.

The gravity jet boosters on her calves and wrists powered up with a high pitched, turbine sound. The suit's two wings, anchored to the shoulders, flicked upward and powered their larger boosters on. Leyla looked over to Mari, whose body was lying unceremoniously in the rain.

"I'm taking your clothes again…" Leyla joked through teary eyes. "Sorry I wasn't fast enough."

The suit's boosters blasted on, and gravity energy shot from all of them like blue flame. Leyla shot off the roof like a rocket, her eyes wide, surprised by the power of Mari's winged armor.

"Whoah! Holy shit!" She yelled as the ground below retreated at a terrifying speed. "I'm flying? I'm fucking flying!"

Leyla corkscrewed through the air and boosted even harder. She became light headed. She didn't have the same pneumatic flight suits The Pantheon had, so blood could rush from her head and make her pass out if she wasn't careful.

"Okay, can't do that, okay. Got it." She yelled to herself and laughed, enjoying something for once.

She searched the stormy sky for the final member of The Pantheon. As she passed a tall building close by, a violent burst of lighting hit a rod jutting from the roof. It was so close she felt the sheer force of it hit her body.

"Oh fuck!" She yelled, feeling like she'd just narrowly escaped death. Her heart was trying to beat its way through her rib cage. "Not cool!"

Through the dark, clouded sky, and through the torrential rain, she spotted a cluster of blue lights nearing The Bullpen in the sky. Nemesis.

***

Nemesis landed on the platform of The Bullpen near the enormous hole she'd blown into it before. She limped and nursed the broken collarbone. All her wounds were aching even more so now. The tussle with Mari had exhausted her and the shorter fight with Leyla had completely done her in. There was no fight left in her.

She dropped to her knees near Eris's body, and fell forward, catching herself with her hands on the floor. She was breathing heavily, as if she'd run a hundred miles. Blood poured down her face from the numerous lacerations. This was as good a time as any to end things.

She slipped her hand inside a thick pocket on her thigh, and pulled out the last four vials of Xenobots. She'd taken them off Blackhawk's corpse when she killed him. One vial had cracked during the fight with Mari, but the black goop inside seemed to avoid spilling out, like it knew it needed to stay inside the glass.

"For my brothers. And for my sisters." Nemesis said, as she popped the caps from each vial, exposing the thick, short needles inside. She stood and made her way to the edge of the platform, looking at the city below, and held all four vials in one hand over her head—and slammed them all into her bicep, the only section of her body that wasn't covered in armor.

Leyla flew up through the hole Nemesis had blasted into The Bullpen, and hovered. She watched on from behind Nemesis, catching glints of light on empty glass, as she let all four vials fall to the ground below. She'd injected all four doses of the matter-altering bots.

Oh no, I'm too late. Oh no no no, Leyla thought.

Nemesis stumbled backward, looking to the sky. She flinched as a bolt of lightning struck the magnetic shielding of The Bullpen, again spreading out like cracks in glass. Then, another bolt struck. And another. Whatever was happening inside Nemesis's body, it was creating a charge that was attracting the wrath of nature itself. Nemesis reached behind her head and hit her suit's kill switch, exiting her armor. She stumbled as she stepped down.

Leyla looked around the dome as the electromagnetic shield held back the powerful fit of the storm.

The shielding cannot hold indefinitely. Athon said. *Every strike is the tick of a clock.*

Leyla looked at Eris, remembering the kill when Athon was in control. She guessed Nemesis must have brought her there. Suddenly, the preceding events became clear. Leyla had killed Eris when Athon had control. The Pantheon hadn't attacked any innocent people until after that. Eris was the spark that ignited the fire. Athon hadn't been quick enough in finding the rest of The Pantheon after Eris. They must've found her body and snapped. They'd lost a friend—a sister. They must have felt the same rage Leyla felt when she lost Del. And, for the first time, Leyla understood her place in the world.

She was a walking flaw. Almost every decision she made got someone killed. Ramsay had even told her before she used the wormhole generator that Blackhawk would know she used it and would come for her.

I got Del killed. She thought. *I did.*

And Mari was just living her life happily in a city she loved. And Leyla had dragged her into a problem she didn't need to be involved in. Artemis and Blackhawk had likely forced her back into The Pantheon, and stripped her of her very soul.

I got Mari killed.

And in her failure to formulate a proper plan of attack, she'd allowed The Pantheon to go berserk and kill possibly hundreds of people. Nemesis was the final piece of tinder for a fire that Leyla had unknowingly built with her self centered acts. And the Xenobots were a shot of gasoline.

Nemesis dropped to her knees again and screamed. She drew in a huge breath and wailed at the sky as her body began to crack open as Rhea's had. Light poured from the opening seams of her skin. Horrified, Leyla looked on, until Athon finally spoke up again.

If only you could try again.

Leyla's eyes widened. "Fuck, you're right. The SIGIL thing. The time travel gate. I can go back."

That is not what I was referring to. That is not going to—

Leyla had already activated her suit's comlink and called SIGIL. "SIGIL, is there a new time coordinate? Like an hour or so before now?"

"SCANNING."

Leyla heard Ramsay's voice wailing in the background and drawing near. He chimed in.

"Did you just ask about a time coordinate, Leyla? Or is this Athon?"

"I'm Leyla." She replied, but SIGIL interrupted.

"THERE IS AN OPEN LOOP AVAILABLE. APPROXIMATELY SEVEN HOURS AGO."

"Whoah! Wait the fuck…no!" Ramsay yelled.

"Prep to open it, I'm headed there now." Leyla said.

Just as she closed the call, Nemesis spread her arms out. Three subsequent bolts of lightning struck the exact same spot above her. The first two spread across the dome, but the third fired through the weakened shield and hit Nemesis. Her body shattered in the lightning and instantly particulated into active Xenobots.

The glowing bots shot to the platform, and instantly ate The Bullpen around Leyla, turning it into an electrified husk. Leyla boosted away fast, gaining some distance, and looked back. The Xenos ate the gravity engines at the bottom, and The Bullpen fell from the sky, crashing into the ground below.

"Fuck!" Leyla shouted, and turned. She flew as fast as she could toward the large hole The Bullpen had ascended from. It was likely the fastest way into SubCity.

The Xenos descended into the city below.

They devoured anything they touched. Concrete. Metal. Wood. Whatever the material, it did not matter. Perhaps Nemesis intended to do some good by using them, but it was the lightning strike that gave her whatever horrified final thought she had. Her final thought could have been of electrified agony, and the Xenos would mimic that thought.

People were not safe either. Rioters attempted to run, but no one could escape. The Xenos devoured them and left almost nothing more than ash in their wake. The bots were eating *everything*, and self replicating along the way, expediting the process exponentially. The world wouldn't have time to even process what was happening, much less react.

***

Wells had made it to Greene. He stepped out of his truck and held his hand up. Greene looked as if he'd lost an Army of friends. In truth, he had.

"Hey man..." Wells said. "I know you don't remember me, but I thought we could talk. Is that okay?"

Greene didn't lift his head. "Say whatever you need. Makes no difference to me."

Wells didn't get the chance to answer. A loud rustle emanated from the city. Wells looked back, away from Greene. Multiple skyscrapers dissolved and crashed to the ground before his very eyes. The screams of thousands of people complimented the sight. It looked like a white flame making its way across a field of gasoline, burning everything in its path.

"Xenobots. Fuck."

They were headed straight for Wells and Greene, and there was nothing they could do.

"Greene, get in the truck." Wells said.

"Why?"

"Just trust me, we gotta fuckin' run. Now!"

Wells jumped in his truck and thankfully, Greene took the passenger seat. Harrison was still in the truck bed, and hopped over and took a back seat in the cab.

Wells slammed his foot down on the gas and blazed out of the area, sending the truck into the air as it jumped a berm and onto the freeway. All three of them slammed forward as the truck hit the ground. Wells got the truck under control and gunned it, hoping to outrun the wave of death coming for them.

"What the fuck is happening?!" Greene said, looking backward. The Xeno wave was crossing over everything—a ripple of apocalyptic power.

"Those are little bitty robots that rewrite matter on an atomic level. They'll eat everything they touch." Wells said.

Harrison, again confused, yelled forward. "What in the fuck?! Any more crazy shit you saw down there you wanna tell me about?"

"Probably a lot more but now we're fucked."

The Xeno wave was getting closer, devouring every car on the road behind them. Wells had the pedal to the floor, and the needle passed 100 mph. There was no outrunning them.

The Xenos touched the back of the truck and ate the tires, spewing ash behind their wake. The truck bed dropped to the road and sparks showered from the impact.

Wells didn't look back. He grabbed Greene's hand—his fiancé's—one final time. Harrison's scream was almost instantly muffled, and Wells felt the burn of death as he watched the bots overtake Greene as well.

***

Leyla slammed to the concrete in SubCity in the exo-suit, having entered through The Bullpen's opening high above. She practically bounced off the street and boosted again, speeding toward The Fridge.

Ramsay was freaking out.

"You can't do this! Shit is not going to keep working out!" He yelled at SIGIL, as Leyla burst into the chamber.

Ramsay ducked to the ground, thinking one of The Pantheon had come for them. Leyla landed hard on the concrete.

"SIGIL! Now! Open it!" She hit the kill switch on her suit and stepped out of the armor. "Go!"

"*EXIT LOOP—*"

Leyla interrupted, "I don't care, just open the fucking portal!"

Ramsay scurried to his feet. "Leyla! Please, don't try this!"

The sounds of cracking rock and falling debris roared through the tunnel out to SubCity. Ramsay looked toward it as his blood ran cold.

Outside on the streets, the citizens of SubCity screamed and ran from the GravGens going dead as the Xenos ate them. Boulders fell from the top of the cavern, crushing many who tried to run. The entire GravGen grid soon sputtered out and the cavern opened up. Everything above fell through. Buildings that remained up top. Vehicles, trees, people. Everything collapsed. Only SIGIL's chamber withstood the cataclysm, but the Xenos would find it soon.

"Nemesis activated the Xenos and got struck by fucking lightning at the end. They're eating the world. So fuck you, I'm doing this. I'm trying again." Leyla said, as the arch gate whirred to life and the portal blasted open.

Ramsay was left speechless and Leyla turned and ran up the platform. She jumped through the time portal before the other side had even opened fully. The Thumper blinked blue and went back to orange.

Ramsay turned his gaze back to the tunnel. The Xeno wave erupted from the rubble and dust in it and spread rapidly across the walls and ceiling. Ramsay turned to run, but got nowhere. The Xenos ate him and SIGIL, and passed over the arch gate just as the portal closed itself, devouring the wormhole generator for good.

Leyla would have no way back if anything went wrong now.

CHAPTER TWENTY-NINE

The Black

Leyla had never been in the wormhole before the other side opened. It was like floating in water, suspended in slow motion as she watched the other side open up. She saw what would be considered a worst case scenario for entering a fight.

It was daylight. Seven hours earlier. The storm hadn't rolled in just yet. The gate was opening on The Bullpen, already in the sky. Blackhawk was inside his AV, having just fired the rail gun at the helicopter out front.

Eris, Nemesis, Rhea and Artemis were erupting from their compartments in the AV.

Shit. Leyla thought. *All of them in good health and not tired? Terrible odds.*

Three F-16s flew in the distance. A wave of fire was spreading over the domed shield; the Apache chopper had just fired its rocket at Blackhawk's AV and Mari was flying at it. The gate was open enough to step through.

Leyla summoned her sword and the blade shot out again. The edge heated up.

Here we go, she thought. She prepped the Thumper for activation as soon as she hit the ground, hoping it would carry her through what was going to be complete suicide if not.

The opening gate alerted every one of them. Leyla watched as they all slowly jerked toward the portal opening near them. Leyla jumped through.

The portal blasted open fully on The Bullpen, forcing Rhea to catch herself, as she was the closest. Leyla landed on her feet and warped closer to Rhea, plunging the sword into her rib cage and severing several arteries at once. Rhea gasped and fell.

Leyla warped again, looking to Artemis. At least she'd get to kill that bitch again.

Artemis, with her appropriately superhuman reflexes, actually bobbed out of the swing of Leyla's sword, but she didn't expect a second warp to her other side. Leyla put her sword right through Artemis's temple and kicked her away.

Good riddance.

Everything was happening at a normal pace, but Leyla was so focused, it felt like she was moving faster than everyone else, and they were stuck in slow motion. Maybe she *was* faster. Eris and Nemesis were boosting toward her now. Leyla left the sword in Artemis's head as she fell away. She could summon it later.

Leyla eyed Eris. Remembering how she took her down before, Leyla shot the WireFire at her, and latched onto the frame of her suit. Leyla dropped to the ground and let Eris pass over, then got on her knees and jerked the wire hard. Eris slammed to the ground.

Nemesis flipped herself over in the air and came back around for Leyla. Leyla jumped and warped onto Nemesis's back, grabbed her suit by the rail gun and wing, and jerked hard left. Nemesis went with her and the two crashed to the platform. Leyla almost rolled over the edge, but the WireFire was still embedded in Eris's suit and caught her.

Leyla jumped up and retracted the wire, which catapulted her toward Eris. She summoned her heated katana from Artemis's head and it got to her palm at the same time as she rammed into Eris. Leyla drove the sword into Eris's throat, twisted, and pulled the blade out sideways, half decapitating the woman.

Nemesis's rail gun whirred up. She was on all fours like a snarling panther.

Thoom!

The round slammed into the platform right in front of Leyla and ripped a hole much the same as before the time jump. Leyla fell in but again, the WireFire caught her. Her sword fell to the Earth.

She swung around and luckily was able to grab the bottom of the platform. She detached the WireFire from Eris's suit and looked up through the hole, seeing Nemesis stepping in for a kill shot. Leyla used her feet and pushed off the underside of the platform, launching herself through the air, and shot the WireFire at Nemesis. It hooked her armor. Leyla retracted the wire again, pulling herself to Nemesis.

Just as the rail gun fired at her, Leyla warped past the round and Nemesis, and summoned her falling sword. Crazily enough, it came back to her hand as usual. The blade swiped into the back of Nemesis's neck and severed her spine. She fell over immediately.

Leyla had pulled all of this off while Mari was dismantling the Apache. It had seemed like Mari was helping her fight Nemesis and Artemis earlier, but Leyla figured there was a chance she could have simply been going after the rogue Pantheon members. And if Nemesis hadn't wounded her, there was a chance Mari would have turned her sights on Leyla. Best to avoid that if possible.

Blackhawk's AV was lifting away from The Bullpen. He was trying to get away.

Nope. Fuck you, cowboy. Leyla thought, and flicked the kill switch on Nemesis's armor. It opened and Leyla tossed Nemesis out and struggled to lift the armor, but got it upright. She stepped in. Nemesis was slightly smaller than Leyla so this suit was a little more snug, but not too bad. The armor closed in and she felt the pricks of the neuro-needles again. Now she could feel the rail gun on her shoulder.

"Ooohhhh yes!" Leyla said, relishing the newfound power. She could see why the women had felt so power hungry and blood thirsty. The exo-suits were essentially like power ups in a video game.

Blackhawk's AV shot away from The Bullpen. The F-16s broke formation and went after him like a pack of flying wolves. Mari tore the tail of the Apache off, took the black box, and tossed it on The Bullpen, and saw Leyla in Nemesis's suit. Mari did a double take, but the chopper was falling, so she boosted away to save the pilots as she'd done before.

Did she see the other Pantheon members dead? Did she recognize me? Leyla pushed the thoughts down and blasted off the platform. She'd taken out four of The Pantheon, which was crazy enough, but Mari was still around and Leyla didn't want to think of what may happen if she had to fight her, and Blackhawk had all of the Xenobots, and he was getting chased down by three fighter jets, who would likely shoot him down.

Great.

Leyla watched as Blackhawk wove through the skyline of Cincinnati in his UFO-esque AV, skirting the fighter pilots. They didn't fire at him out of the chance that he would crash into a building and kill civilians.

He knew this. If he stayed near the city, there was more of a chance he could survive the dogfight. And his AV didn't gulp fuel like the planes did, so they would eventually have to give in and leave.

Leyla flew a straight line through the city, parallel to Blackhawk and the pilots. She was catching up since she wasn't cutting any maneuvers. Suddenly, Blackhawk banked hard and came right at her.

"Oh shit!" She yelled and twirled out of the way. He had to have seen her.

An F-16 screamed by, just over her head. The other two passed almost immediately after, also barely missing her. She boosted toward them, giving chase again.

Once she got behind them, Mari came from out of nowhere and sliced one of the jets in half with her sword and caught what was left of the plane mid-air, gesturing to the pilot to eject, to which Mako obliged, and shot into the air, deploying a chute. Mari didn't bother to look back at Leyla. She flew right after the next jet.

She's making sure the pilots live? Leyla thought.

Mari cut the wing off another plane, and allowed Spensa to eject. Then she bounded over to Dipstick and ripped the cockpit right out of the jet. He ejected as well. With all three pilots safely descending to the ground, she took off toward Blackhawk.

All three jets crashed to the ground in succession. Dipstick's F-16 nicked a skyscraper on the way down but didn't inflict too much damage. They all narrowly missed populated areas. Two hit the river and one exploded when it hit a bridge. That would be an expensive repair bill.

Blackhawk slowed a little, but he must have said something to Mari on a comlink. Mari whipped around, gliding backward, to see Leyla boosting toward her.

"Oh no…" Leyla said, and immediately boosted as hard as she could. She'd left her sword on The Bullpen's platform, forgetting to grab it when she took Nemesis's suit. "Shit."

There was no way she could outfly Mari. She had to catch Blackhawk *now* and wing it. Warping at this speed in the sky was ill advised and could end with her crashing to the ground and dying a *third* time. Regardless if she came back, the world may have ended when she woke up. She had to end this now.

Leyla corkscrewed past Mari. Mari tried to grab her as she passed, but fumbled across her legs instead. Leyla pointed her WireFire at Blackhawk's AV and got just close enough, and fired.

The hook clamped down on a wing. She retracted the wire, propelling herself toward Blackhawk. She knew Mari would have redirected and was coming for her. The Thumper charged up. Leyla had formed a plan already. A stupid plan, but better than nothing.

Leyla crashed into the AV. It stayed airborne but dipped hard to the right under the weight of Nemesis's exo-suit. The WireFire kept Leyla from rolling off it, but she saw Mari coming in hot.

Come on, come on…

Mari landed on top of the AV right beside Leyla and bent down to likely inflict a world of hurt.

"Sorry!" Leyla yelled, and activated the Thumper.

A reverse gravity pulse exploded, knocking Mari back and killing the power to the AV's engines. It killed Mari and Leyla's boosters as well. The AV's hull bent and cracked at the blast, and it pitched downward, with Leyla hanging on by the WireFire's hook. Leyla hit the kill switch on her deadened armor, and it opened and fell away, crashing to the ground. Mari had managed to grab hold of part of the wing and was hanging on as they rode the AV down, which was now in a controlled glide.

Blackhawk searched for a good spot to land. There was an open section of freeway leading into the Ohio River Bridge that seemed long enough for a crash landing. He pointed the AV to it. Thankfully, the wing controls were analog. He never trusted something fully computerized.

He controlled the AV all the way to the road, where it slammed down hard, ass end first. The front of the craft whipped down and into the road. The AV ground across the freeway and began turning to its right, broadsiding an SUV that was attempting to avoid it. The SUV flipped and rolled away.

The AV finally came to a halt around 300 feet from where it touched down. Leyla detached the WireFire and stood, immediately scanning for Mari.

Mari was also getting up, all the way back where they hit the road. She exited her armor as well. The canopy of the AV opened with the sound of air escaping a sealed compartment.

Blackhawk jumped up and turned, pointing his big bull revolver right at Leyla, and fired once. She ducked the shot and darted toward him. He fired again, missing her. The bullet zipped by her ear as she crawled across the AV to get to him. Leyla leapt forward and grabbed Blackhawk's gun arm and slammed it down on the hull of the AV. He grimaced but didn't drop the weapon.

With a hard push of his cybernetic legs, he rocketed out of the cockpit and landed on the AV. Leyla didn't let go of his arm, and was dragged along for the ride. Blackhawk kicked her hard in the side, knocking her breath out, and she flew off the AV and landed on the ground below. His heavy legs thudded to the soil beside her. She shot the WireFire at his pistol. It didn't catch, but it was unexpected enough to knock it from his hand and a good twenty feet away, while the WireFire latched onto the AV itself. When Blackhawk looked back at his gun tumbling across the ground, Leyla retracted the wire and pulled fast toward him, dragging the ground. She barreled into his legs, finally knocking him to the dirt and disarming him in one go.

Mari came sprinting, and leapt onto the AV, then jumped down right beside Leyla. Without missing a stride, she crouched and grabbed Leyla and tossed her into the air at least head high. Leyla landed on her back, gasping and coughing. Mari made it over to her quickly, and stomped downward, but Leyla rolled and dodged what would have likely crushed her torso. Mari was trying to kill her.

"Mari! Wait!" Leyla yelled through coughs and heavy breaths.

Blackhawk, upon hearing Mari's name, narrowed his eyes as he stood and brushed his jacket off, as if he was surprised Leyla knew who Nyx was.

"It's me, it's Leyla!" Leyla stumbled to her feet, and Mari kicked hard toward her head. Leyla blocked the kick but was slammed to the ground again as a result, and let out a pained gasp.

Blackhawk studied Leyla some more. She'd absolutely annihilated The Pantheon, but she was refusing to fight Nyx. Leyla wasn't just some cover Athon had been using. She wasn't just in Athon's head as a way to throw someone off or be a more effective spy—not anymore. Leyla actually cared about hurting Nyx; she cared about hurting Mari. And she had definitely cared about Del when Artemis killed her. It seemed, to him at least, that Leyla truly may be human. She was Athon no more.

Mari grabbed Leyla by the ankle and snatched her toward her, then gripped her by her neck, pulling her up. Mari raised her above her head, choking her, preparing to slam her down on the ground hard.

"Nyx!" Blackhawk yelled. "Let her go."

Mari did as he asked, and Leyla fell to the dirt, coughing and wheezing. She rolled to her side, almost in a fetal position, nursing the side Blackhawk had kicked.

"How do you know her name?" Blackhawk asked, pointing to Mari, who stood like a warrior, hair waving in the wind.

"She helped me." Leyla coughed again. "When I got to the city and when I was looking for Del."

"That true?" He asked Mari. She nodded.

"Well I'll be goddamned." Blackhawk said.

"You turned her back into one of those things." Leyla growled.

"She came back willingly."

"No she didn't. She asked Artemis about Athon and helping me, and then she disappeared. You changed her back and you took her mind away."

Blackhawk chuckled. "Nah, wrong again. I…" He thought for a second. Artemis had brought Mari to him, already reintegrated to The Pantheon. Mari never directly asked him to rejoin. He looked to Mari. "Did you want to come back?"

Mari nodded *no*.

"Artemis forced you to."

She nodded.

"Shit. And she implanted behavioral mods too. No fuckin' wonder you ain't the Mari I remember."

Mari nodded again.

"Why can't she talk?" Leyla said, now on her knees.

"Behavioral chip is like a…like a lobotomy. Zaps all emotion and blocks out most of the speech center of the brain. And it'll make you do whatever you're told as long as a master vocal was encoded to it."

"You fucking asshole!" Leyla lunged at Blackhawk and pointed the WireFire at his forehead, but for some reason, she wasn't able to fire. She certainly wanted to, and she even grit her teeth as she attempted to will the hook to fire, which is how it always worked before.

"You tryin' to shoot me?"

"Yes! Fuck! What the Hell?!" Leyla withdrew, enraged. Maybe the WireFire was broken.

"You took the pill didn't you?" Blackhawk asked.

The fucking pill, Leyla thought. *That fucking SD pill!* Ramsay had pushed about it multiple times and she'd almost not taken it, but she had when her temporary card expired. Having Del back had brought all her walls and defenses down. *So stupid. So so stupid!*

"Don't worry, I can't tell you what to do. You just can't hurt me. Not willingly. Same goes for all the modders with an SD, 'cept The Pantheon. SDs didn't wanna play nice with their mods so we removed 'em, much to Ramsay's dismay." Blackhawk explained.

Leyla screamed in frustration. Blackhawk was the last one on her short kill list. And she'd been denied that kill. "Fuck you! You knew Del was with me and you got her fucking killed!" Leyla yelled at him, breaking down. Tears streamed from her eyes. "She was all I wanted. I just wanted her safe and happy and we were going to live down there and just be happy. You fucking asshole! Why would you kill her?! She didn't do anything. We were fine, we were just there and happy and we were fine!"

Blackhawk didn't reply. He did, however, hold the same remorseful tinge to his eyes as when he had knelt beside Del as she'd died on Leyla's apartment floor. He looked down to the ground, knowing Leyla had a point. He could have not been so aggressive.

"Yeah, that was a little bit overkill." He said.

Leyla hung her mouth open and widened her eyes. "A little?! A LITTLE BIT OVERKILL? Del didn't do anything to you!"

Mari looked slowly back to the city. Buildings were collapsing. A beam of light burst from the ground somewhere back in the city and shot through the clouds. More buildings collapsed, but these seemed to dissolve like sand in wind and swirl in a large circle.

"I didn't know Artemis would—" Blackhawk was interrupted by Mari as she smacked his shoulder. He looked at her. She glared at what was happening in the city, so he looked in that direction as well.

Cincinnati was *dissolving*; the bits of buildings and trees and cars seemed to rip to shreds and spin toward a center point underground—right where SIGIL's chamber would have been. Everything funneled down into the hole that grew larger and larger every second like a landlocked whirlpool. The beam of light shooting straight upward grew so bright it was becoming hard to look directly at.

"No, I…but I got through before they did…" Leyla said, also looking at the crumbling city.

"They what?" Blackhawk asked.

"The Xenobots. I jumped before they got me. The portal closed. I—"

"What?! What did you do?!" Blackhawk yelled.

"Me? Your fucking minion did it. Nemesis! She used the Xenobots and they started eating the whole fucking world!"

Blackhawk had no retort. He immediately knew what had happened. "And you time jumped back here, thinking you could fix shit."

"Of course I did! What the fuck else would I do?"

Blackhawk brought his hands up to his head, distraught. "Fuck." His breathing became heavy and his skin grew pale as panic set in. "That ain't Xenobots."

Leyla looked at her Thumper. Still orange. Still an open time loop. "What is it?"

"Did the Xenos get down to the city?" Blackhawk asked.

"Yeah, I just said they ate *everything*."

"Then they ate the arch gate after you jumped."

The reality of the situation hit Leyla like a truck. She remembered holding her finger out to the gravitational lure of the singularity when Ramsay had brought her and Wells to The Fridge. His words had scared her enough to instill what some call a core memory.

Blackhawk spoke up, echoing his old friend's same words. "Know what happens to a singularity when it's left unchecked?"

Leyla stared at the growing mouth of destruction that was once Cincinnati. "It eats."

"It eats *everything*." Blackhawk said. Ramsay had told him the same thing he told Leyla and Wells. Ramsay was a man they'd all should have listened to with reverence.

Leyla made sense of what was happening aloud. "I time jumped and the Xenos ate the gate, and the singularity on this end is—"

"It's a black hole. The wormhole link was broken. And there ain't a goddamn thing we can do." Blackhawk said.

Leyla's blood ran cold. In her half baked attempts to fix things, time and time again, she'd wrought destruction. On her best friend, on Mari, on Wells and Ramsay, and on the world—and now reality itself. Ramsay warned her not to jump. She hadn't thought things through enough. She hadn't worked with Ramsay, an obviously knowledgeable person, on a plan that was less volatile and unreliable. She'd done what she wanted, and what she wanted only.

And now a black hole was eating the world.

Blackhawk slid a cigar from a slit in his trench coat sleeve that had been custom sewn specifically to hold fresh cigars, and stuck it in his lips. He flicked a zippo out and lit the cigar, puffing multiple times and spitting smoke.

"Really? You're gonna smoke a cigar now?" Leyla accosted him.

"The fuck else am I gonna do? Fuckin' black hole is gonna eat the world. Shit, it's gonna eat all the planets maybe. I'm gonna enjoy this here Romeo and Juliet fatty. It's Cuban, and it's magnificent."

Leyla scoffed.

"I didn't uh…it wasn't supposed to go down the way it did." Blackhawk said. "With your friend. At your apartment."

"Fuck you." Leyla snarled.

"Artemis uh, she…you know."

"Was a cunt." Leyla said.

Blackhawk raised his brow and looked at Leyla. "Well that's an opinion. She had her demons but it's different if you knew her."

"I don't care."

"Look, when she did what she did, I saw your eyes. I've had that rage before. Burns to the core."

Leyla didn't reply. But she was interested in hearing what Blackhawk had to say.

"I've seen a friend killed by the enemy. As a soldier, when that happens, you don't want anything but revenge. You want to hurt the one that did it. You want to make them feel the same thing they made you feel."

"Yeah."

"But it don't work like that. You can kill 'em. But once they're gone, it's just empty. You still ain't got your friend back."

Leyla stared on at the expanding black hole.

"You kill an unstoppable assassin's friend, they don't stop 'til they get to you. I had to do it. I had to put that bullet in your head. Only way I could make sure the plan would go on."

"You would have killed me anyway." Leyla backed up and slumped onto the AV hull, staring forward.

"No, wrong again. We made The Pantheon, trying to figure out how SIGIL had you tied to the Xenobots. Turns out it was your DNA, which is one of a kind. Nothing we did would have ever worked. We needed you. And *preferably*, alive, and on our side."

"So you attacked? You blew a wall in and came in guns blazing?"

"We never shot at all. Sure I blew the window open but you attacked us. You threw the first punch. And your name—well, Athon's—carries weight. It carries fear. Shit got out of hand. I made a mistake."

"Out of hand. Fuck off."

Blackhawk puffed his cigar. "See it how you want but, the plan was to appeal to you. To explain our plan, hope you saw our side, and volunteer to help us bring peace and unity to the world."

"Maybe don't blow a wall in and make me think you're trying to kill me and my best fucking friend, then."

"Touché." Blackhawk said. "Hindsight, all that shit. I shoulda just tried to talk to you. But, I suspected you were Athon. I was right but wrong at the same time. You are, but more human than I expected. I didn't know the implications of revealing that info to you. Do you remember and then murder us all, or do you remember and see our side of things? Shit. A decision like that ain't easy. I was keeping SubCity in mind. I was keeping the whole world in mind. You know, I'm ultimately just trying to do what SIGIL wanted in the first place."

"Too little too late." Leyla said.

"Mmhmm." Blackhawk pulled the cigar from his mouth and looked at it, savoring the taste of what would be the final cigar smoked in the world. "Would you sacrifice yourself for the world? Like The Pantheon was prepared to do?"

"Honestly?"

"Yeah honestly."

"Fuck no. The world doesn't care about me. It didn't care about Del. Why would I?"

"Would Athon?" He gripped the cigar in his lips, sticking his hand in his trench coat pocket.

"Athon is a fucking puppet. I'm not."

"Yeah." Blackhawk pulled the vials of Xenobots from his jacket.

Leyla was staring at her biggest mistake to date: the imminent destruction of the entire world, and likely the solar system. *I am the worst thing to ever happen*, she thought.

She felt a sharp pain in her chest, like being punched with several thorns at once. She looked down.

Blackhawk had plunged all five of the Xenobot vials into her chest, just above her breast. She watched in horror as the black liquid inside each glass shot through and into her body. It felt like a rush of electricity from each pin prick. Blackhawk pulled the emptied vials away and backed up.

"Well, I think you're full of shit." He said. "Nobody fights like you do for nothing. You got a chance to fix this shit. Maybe. I don't know. Maybe that black hole is it. Maybe you use the Xenos to cancel it out. Hell, I don't know, but you were made for this. Maybe you can save us all. If not, we tried."

Leyla stumbled backward and fell to her knee. "You…no no no no no! Fuck! No!" Leyla shook her head, denying the fate that Blackhawk had forced upon her. This was what Athon wanted, but Leyla wanted another way. Some way that meant life, not death. She clawed at her skin in a feeble attempt to get rid of the bots that now coursed her veins like a fatal virus. "NO!" She screamed and cried, terrified.

She looked at Blackhawk angrily, but he was staring at the expanding black hole. Mari looked at her. There was no emotion or expression, nor a word spoken, but Leyla felt as if Mari was saying goodbye and apologizing.

Leyla's body began to burn. The bots were heating up inside her as they activated and began to rewrite her atomically. It felt like lava flowed through her arteries. She tensed up and choked air in shock.

Blackhawk sucked in one huge puff of his fancy Cuban cigar and blew the smoke out just as the black hole's force touched him. He screamed as his body ripped apart atom by atom and joined the swirling stream of matter encircling the growing black hole that used to be the SIGIL arch gate. Mari made no sound as her body shredded and joined the black hole's event horizon.

Leyla was in panic mode. Her heart felt like it would explode. Her blood quite literally was boiling. She didn't know which was worse; being eaten alive from within, or ripped to shreds and crushed inside a black hole?

Fuck fuck fuck what do I do fuck this hurts so much fuck I'm dying what do I do? She thought rapidly, remembering that the Xenos enact the final wish of the bearer. *It hurts so fucking bad! What do I think? I have to help everyone! Fuck them. They don't deserve it. Fuck them. They should die like me. They should die like Del.*

The black hole's event horizon touched Leyla, and ripped her up from the ground. She wasn't sure if she'd torn to pieces, but she felt like she was moving at a million miles per hour. Everything was a blur. Lights turned to streaks of color. Sounds became drawn out echoes. She felt…numb; she couldn't feel anything. At all.

Shouldn't this hurt?

Yet she felt no pain. There was nothing.

There was only the black.

CHAPTER THIRTY

Splinters

Leyla snapped awake and drew a breath. Dust and grains of sand entered her mouth. She coughed and heaved at the irritation. It was freezing and pitch black. The only way she could see anything was a faint and soft, orange pulse of a light.

This feels familiar.

She scratched around at the ground, feeling jagged rocks and broken, old and dry wood. She had a headache for the ages, and every limb felt like it had been ground under massive stones. She groaned and grit her teeth with each movement, and coughed again, attempting to push out the remnants of dust in her lungs.

Her hair was matted and coarse, and the taste in her mouth was like cardboard and stagnant water. She spat as much as she could to get rid of the pungent muck.

Where the Hell am I? Am I dead? I feel dead.

She pushed herself up and to her feet, but it felt like she'd not used them in a lifetime, and she fell sideways. She expected to hit the ground, but instead tumbled over some construction railing and fell another couple yards to the hard ground below. It hurt so much she couldn't even scream, she simply snatched a breath in as if she'd choked. Nothing felt broken, so she tried standing again.

Feeling along what had to be the wall of wherever she was, she followed it as far as it would go until she saw a slit of light far ahead.

I am dead. Light at the end of the tunnel. Can't remember…am I supposed to go to it or away?

She decided to shuffle toward the light. As she drew nearer, she felt an overwhelming sense of deja vu.

Seen this before…

She finally looked down at her wrist, where the orange light was coming from. The Thumper.

I know what that is. But before, I…

"Oh." She said. "Did I go back in time again?"

No, this has happened before. This deja vu…

She looked up to the light.

This is a memory.

She shuffled to the light. It was the door to the abandoned subway tunnel. She was reliving the memory from three years earlier, when she'd awoken there. Right before meeting Del.

Wait…

She turned back. The fuzzy, re-force wall. The way into SubCity. It had to be there. She walked back toward it. After a few steps, everything felt a little off, but she kept going anyway.

She came to the wall she and Wells had found, and she lifted her hand out to it. Her fingers passed right through, as expected, so she walked past the wall and dropped into the freight elevator, which again automatically stirred and descended, drowning her in blue light.

She glared straight, eyes wide and ready to see the city lights. One of the large openings passed, but she only saw whiteness. Simple and pure white light. As each vent opening passed, there was nothing but the white light. No neon coated buildings. No flying cars. No cybernetically modified population. There was only a vast, white abyss.

Oh I really messed up…

The elevator hit the bottom and the big doors opened up, inviting Leyla into the emptiness. She hesitated, wondering what would happen when she stepped out of the elevator. After all, there was no ground to walk on. Would she fall? Float?

Here goes...

Leyla set one foot out of the elevator and held on to the wall with one hand in case she had no footing, and felt nothing underneath. Putting all her weight on one leg hurt like hell, reminding her that she shouldn't be attempting anything athletic.

Great, she thought. *Leyla, you done fucked up. Killed the whole universe.* She pulled her leg back in and stumbled backward where a floor should have been, and fell through the elevator, which had diminished to nothing but a wall. She fell and fell and fell, screaming and watching the elevator disappear in the distance. Her flailing attempts at grabbing it as it left were mere reflex. She knew she wouldn't save herself.

She tumbled head over heels through the white abyss for so long she simply felt weightless.

Am I still falling? Why am I so damn calm? I have to be—

She fell into water. Only, there was no water. She *felt* as if she'd fallen into the ocean, but only from a short distance, maybe over a small boat or diving board, but she was still in that white nothingness. She felt water rush over her head and she felt the cushiony slosh of being under waves. Her hair even swept side to side as if being manipulated by the sea.

Okay. I am 100% dead. This has to be Hell or there would be pizza.

And then...there was pizza. A single, beautiful and magnificent slice of hand tossed and cheesy pepperoni pizza—right in front of her face, floating in all its greasy glory. The sight made her laugh out loud.

"No! No!" She said, refusing to believe what must be a trap in this odd stretch of limbo. "That's poisoned. I'm not stupid."

She stared at the pizza as it twirled under the invisible water with her. She tried looking away but the slice maintained her eye line, moving with her head.

"Go away!" She swatted at the pizza. It spun around a bit and righted itself, and then disappeared.

"No no no! I wanted you but I want not poisoned pizza."

I'm talking to a fucking slice of pizza...

The pizza reappeared.

"Oh fuck you!" She yelled, feeling a bit taunted. And then, she heard Athon speak. Not inside her head, but Athon's *actual* voice from behind her.

"The pizza is not poisoned."

Leyla whipped herself around, swimming in the air. There was Athon, standing in front of her, wearing the same armor and completely disarmed, same as she was. With the visor retracted, they were essentially identical.

"What the—you...but..." Leyla suddenly felt ground under her feet—invisible ground—but she could now stand instead of float.

"Yes, I am Athon. You. But earlier. Another you."

"Don't know what that means, sis."

"We are not sisters. We are the same."

"Yes, I know, it's a figure of speech—just explain this shit, please."

"What would you like me to explain? The absence of reality or the pizza?"

"Uh, both would be great. And also why you're no longer in my head."

"If I had to guess, as I've been doing for a very long time, this abyss is one of two things. Either limbo is a real place, or we are inside a singularity."

"Oh, okay that's pretty wild, I guess."

"Indeed. Though, the pizza has not happened before. None of us have asked for nourishment."

"None of us? I thought it was just us."

Another Athon's voice spoke up from behind. "We are all here."

When Leyla turned, she gasped and startled.

Dozens of copies of Athon were scattered throughout the area, standing on more invisible ground.

"What?!" Leyla asked, turning back to the first Athon.

"Some of us have been here longer than others. But, time is very odd here. Everything feels instantaneous and slow at the same time." Athon explained. "It's why we believe we are in a singularity. We all share the same memory. And time feels…round."

All the Athons spoke at the same time—a monotone and quite creepy chorus.

"The black hole."

Leyla felt a chill run up her back. It made sense. The last thing she remembered was being violently ripped from the ground and sucked into the growing singularity—something that should have killed her.

"But, this doesn't make any sense. The black hole, sure, but why are there so many of you?"

"We are all the same."

"What? Being sucked into a black hole made clones? I'm not understanding any of this. And I'm gonna eat this pizza because it won't get out of my damn face."

Leyla snatched the slice out of the air and bit into it. It was delicious.

"No clones. We are all you." Athon said.

Another Athon spoke up. "I was the first."

"Huh?" Leyla asked, turning to the crowd of herself and enjoying the tasty pizza.

"The very first time jump. To France in 1944."

Leyla remembered the event. Her very first assassination order. Hitler himself. Regarded as the most disgusting and vile human in history by many, SIGIL had made him its first target, and added a few more Nazi officers to the order, looking to get rid of as many as possible in the loop before closing it.

She'd blown by several dozen soldiers with ease, massacring them and even freeing some French prisoners as a byproduct. She'd made it into the Majestic Hotel where Hitler was staying, and cut him to shreds amid the returned gunfire from his officers, and killed every other target on the order before opening the portal to come back to the present.

"Yeah, I remember that. Left the last officer for the French rebels to kill." Leyla said.

"Exactly." Athon said. "But you returned to the SIGIL. I did not."

"What? But I...I don't understand." Leyla said through a mouthful of pizza.

Athon explained, "I opened the portal, and I remember stepping through to come back, but that is all. I had a heavy sense of deja-vu, and I was still in the same place. I was still in France in World War Two."

"But I came back. To SIGIL. What are you talking about?"

"And then, I heard the crumbling of buildings. The cracking of trees. The howl of wind. A black hole had emerged from the apartment building I'd entered the loop at, across the city."

Leyla stopped chewing.

"You went back to SIGIL. I remained. We split and I ended up here."

Leyla looked at all the Athons, at least sixty of them, all standing and looking at her.

"I was here after killing Grady Holtman in the airplane." one Athon said.

"And I after Sylvia Rutherford in the Los Angeles earthquake." another said.

Leyla remembered both clearly. She'd killed the targets, and came back to SIGIL. She didn't remember any other black holes aside from the one from SubCity that had eaten her earlier.

"Bobby Rockford." one Athon spouted another past target's name.

"Konstantin Petrov."

"Hazukiro Okada."

Leyla perked up at that name. "That one! I remember! That's the one before I was thrown into the sky and died."

"Died?" One of the Athons asked.

"Yeah. I went through the portal and fell out of the sky. I was about to kill Blackhawk and SIGIL uh, kind of, killed me on accident I guess. I was there for a really long time and my body repaired itself, and when I came to, I was Leyla instead of…instead of you."

"The immature and innocent personality construct."

"Well yeah I guess you could call it that." Leyla said, offended.

"You are the only one to have gone back to SIGIL. All of us came here instead. Consumed by singularities from the open time loops."

"I'm the only one?"

"Yes. Perhaps since you are the original."

"No." Another Athon said. "That does not explain it. We are branches from a tree. She is the root."

Leyla scoffed. "Here we go with the poems again."

"Each time you entered a loop and changed something, you left and we remained. You carried on in your reality, and we ours."

"Stop speaking in riddles and be blunt." Leyla said.

"Every loop you closed splintered reality, and created a new one. A doomed one. The singularity on the other side of your wormhole was no longer governed by the Thumper."

Leyla looked down at the orange pulsing device, which had somehow survived a trip into a black hole.

A different Athon stepped closer. "And it devoured everything around it."

They all spoke in unison again. "Everything."

A clump of cheese fell from Leyla's pizza and splatted to the 'ground', as she'd been holding it still while listening to all the Athons. "So, you all got eaten by black holes after I left…after every time jump?"

"Yes."

Leyla let out a sigh of disbelief. "That's like, over sixty times. I…"

She paused. Over sixty time jumps, at the end of which let loose a separate black hole, and destroyed the world. It seemed the Athon closest to her had the same realization at the same time.

"We have wrought ultimate destruction on the world many times over." it said, coldly.

Leyla stared forward, lost in shock once again.

Of course I've done that. That's all I do.

She paced. "I've killed everyone. Billions of people. Dozens of times."

She dropped to her knees as she thought of the countless screams of terror and agony she'd brought upon the Earth, screams which filled the void around her as if the cataclysmic events were happening again, assaulting her senses as punishment.

This was Hell. Del was right. Murderers go to Hell.

Leyla clenched her eyes shut and put her hand over her ears in an attempt to muffle the horrible sound of death. She could hear every individual cry of help. Every pain filled stretch of voice from every person she'd inadvertently killed. *Hundreds* of billions of deaths—that she had been the catalyst for.

"AHHHHH!" She screamed so hard she felt her throat strain. "STOP! I CAN'T TAKE IT!"

She fell to her side into a fetal position, pressing on her ears so hard her head could burst. But nothing stopped the pleas for help and cries of pain. The sounds traveled right through her hands and into her brain. And then, it stopped. Again, there was nothing.

Leyla shivered in fear, lying on her side. She refused to pull her hands from her ears and open her eyes. Those voices would come for her again. They wanted her to feel every bit of pain and terror they had, fleeing from a black hole that devoured everything as it made its way to them. But, after what seemed like ages, she never heard them again.

I'm so sorry. I didn't mean to do any of this, I'm sorry. I just wanted my friend to be okay, and I fucked that up too. I'm just so, so sorry. I just wanted my friend back. I still do.

"Baby girl…"

What?!
"Come on over and sit with ol' Del a minute."

Leyla opened her eyes. In front of her were all the split reality Athons, looking past her. She pulled her hands from her ears and sat up, slowly turning around. She had a good deal of trouble processing what she saw.

Maybe twenty feet forward, amidst the blinding white nothingness, was a park bench, facing away, and sitting on it was none other than Del.

The white abyss in front of her gave way, almost like ink flowing across water, to the most gorgeous and brilliant sunset Leyla had ever seen. The sun broke through thick and fluffy white clouds and glistened off high snow capped mountains. Del turned around and placed her arm on the bench, looking directly back at Leyla, who was still on her butt in awe and disbelief.

"Girl, get yo ass up and come watch this sunset with me. Over there fuckin' around. Come on." Del waved and patted the open spot of bench beside her.

Mouth agape and eyes wide open, Leyla stood and slowly walked toward the bench.

This is a trick…has to be a trick.

Leyla rounded the side of the bench and stared at Del, who looked at her and laughed.

"Fuck is that look for? Look like a lost puppy." Del said. "Yeah, I know, it's a weird situation, but sit down. I got you."

Leyla sat beside her friend, refusing to look away.

That's her. It's really her.

"Man, that's so pretty ain't it?" Del said, looking at the sun descending into the projected horizon. Leyla's finger came close and poked her cheek. Del snatched a glare at Leyla, who drew her hand back quickly like a child caught in a cookie jar.

"What in the hell is up with you, Leyla? You high? You get some o' dat shit from Korean Jesus again? I told you not to try that no more. Talkin' bout whales on the bridge and talkin' bugs."

"Del?" Leyla said, softly.

"Girl! Yes! Del!" She laughed again, taking Leyla's hand. "What is it?"

"I don't remember this." Leyla said.

"That's cause this ain't a memory, baby girl."

"I don't understand. Where'd you come from? How are you—"

"I'm not, if I know what you 'bout to say. I ain't alive. Not like you think."

"But I, how are you here? Are we dead?"

"Naw, don't think so. Not you. I can tell you ain't. Remember what I told you about different energies? The way the universe can just *tell* you what it wants you to know? It's like that."

Leyla gripped Del's hand more tightly. "I don't know what it's telling me." She looked up to Del's eyes again. "So, if you're not alive, how—"

"I'm her consciousness. More or less."

"Huh?" A look of confusion spread across Leyla's face. "Like, you're Del's thoughts?"

"And memories. Ain't that what makes us *us*?"

"Yeah, I guess so."

Del smiled. "Don't gimme that look. I'll be alright."

Leyla blinked, trying to hide her concern after being called on it. "Do you remember? What happened?"

"Yes, and I said I'll be alright. I just wanna spend a little time with you here and talk some damn sense into yo ass."

Leyla laughed, finally. "Yeah, you're pretty good at that."

"Shit, I know. And you are good at gettin' in damn trouble!" Del laughed that hearty laugh—the one Jesus hated and Leyla loved. "You remember that time we was layin' out tannin' at the park? With all our damn clothes on?"

Leyla spurted and laughed. "With all our clothes on?!" She grabbed her chest and keeled over, cackling, and Del joined in.

"Sun wasn't hittin' nothin' but our damn eyeballs!" Del yelled.

Leyla and Del both laughed until they could barely breathe.

"What was that cop's name? The one that made us leave?" Leyla asked.

"Oh shit, it was um, Assman!"

Both laughed even harder, slapping each other's arms and holding their ribs.

Leyla mocked the cop. *"It's a normal name, it's German!"*

"Bet you like wienerschnitzel!" Del roared, and Leyla fell out of her seat laughing. Del slid out of her seat on the bench and laid down beside Leyla, both on their backs on invisible ground, looking up. They laughed for what felt like ages, until the projected sun had disappeared behind the mountains, and the scenery washed away just as it had appeared.

"Did you see all the copies of me?" Leyla asked.

"Yeah, girl that shit was crazy. I 'on know what the world would do with more than one of you."

Leyla remained quiet, prompting Del to look over to her.

"Don't you be thinkin' what I think you thinkin'."

"What?"

"That the world would be better without you."

"Well, I did sort of destroy it. A lot." Leyla said.

Del got to her feet. "Come on, get up. We takin' a walk."

"Uh, okay…" Leyla stood as well and followed Del. "Where to? There's nothing but, well nothing."

"See that's where you wrong. It ain't nothin'. It's everything in here." Del grinned.

Leyla followed for a few strides, trying to piece together what Del meant. "Okay, I don't get what you're saying."

"Girl, I love you but you always a little dense." Del laughed.

"Part of my charm."

"Yes, yes it is." Del stopped and turned to Leyla. "You inside a singularity. What's that mean?"

"I'm dead."

"No, I done told you, you not. So guess again."

"Del, I suck at guessing games."

"Okay, don't guess. Just think."

"Um…I don't know. Everything got sucked into that black hole and now I'm here. You're the science nerd, not me!"

"I am. And see, at the center of a black hole is a singularity. The one you in now. So, everything that got sucked in, is here with you now."

"Del, it's all white. There's nothing."

"You ain't thinkin' crazy enough, girl."

"Ugh, can you just tell me stuff?" Leyla pleaded, and Del laughed.

"Okay okay, I was tryin' to get you to see it for yourself. But alright, you inside a singularity, and you still alive. So somethin' about you got to be special. You built different."

Leyla perked up. "Yeah. I am."

"See?"

"Yeah, my cells, they're antimatter. Only person ever to have something like that." Leyla put her finger up, signaling the unlocking of a door in her mind. "Antimatter is like antigravity. And this singularity was controlled by all the little antigravity thingies on the arch gate…"

Del laughed and jumped. "Ha! See I knew you'd start figuring this shit out. That's why you survived. Because gravity can't hold you down! Oh shit, I like that line, gonna have to write that in the rhyme book…"

"Del, you don't have a rhyme book."

"What if I did though? Never mind that. Keep thinkin'."

"Um, okay so, I'm still alive because my body is antimatter powered. Don't know what else to say about that."

"I'm a drop one on you. Inside a singularity, physics don't matter. Time don't matter. Nothing works the way you think it does in here. You can do whatever the hell you want. How you think that pizza popped up in your face right when you wanted it? How you think I'm here?"

"Because…" Leyla stared into Del's eyes. "I wanted you here."

Del smiled again and nodded. Leyla turned back, and saw all the Athons, still standing where they'd left them.

"What about them?"

"Oh, they stuck here same as you. But they ain't got what you got. They ain't got what *Leyla* got."

"What's that?"

"You remember when we watched Wizard of Oz that one night when they was projecting it outside at Rosie's?"

"Yeah."

"What was it the Tin Man wanted?"

"Um, a heart, I think. Or was that the Scarecrow?"

"It was a heart. All them Athons are the Tin Man. And you are the heart. And when you got a heart, you got a lot more than any ol' android does. You got feelings. You got goals, you got ambitions. You got humanity."

"I don't get what you're saying."

"Baby girl, you conjured up a pizza and the consciousness of your dead friend. You can conjure up a whole lot more in here, as long as you want it."

"Like wha—"

"Oh my lawd woman." Del laughed. "Everything! The whole world, shit probably more. Everything the singularity ate up. You have complete control."

"How do you know that?"

Del thought for a moment. "Shit, I don't really know. I just feel it. Kinda like what I told you about the universe."

Leyla nodded. "It tells you what it wants you to know."

"Yep. So, I don't know if all I been told about the afterlife is real, but I do think we here for a reason. World needed to change. And you're the one to help it out. Just gotta put it back together, I guess."

"I have no idea where to start with that. I just wanted a slice of pizza. The world is a lot more than that."

"No shit, Leyla. But you ain't opening yourself up. You ain't lettin' the world tell you nothin'. That's been your biggest flaw, you was always too…I don't wanna say selfish cause you ain't that but, maybe self centered is a better word choice."

"I've realized that. Too late."

"It ain't never too late to learn."

"Why would I want to do this? Why should I help the world? All they do is fight and cheat and screw each other over. And they argue over shit that doesn't matter. They all worship money and hate everything that isn't like them. You always talked about how screwed up everything was. How no one cared about anyone who didn't have a lot of money or fame. Politicians are shit. The only thing anyone wants is power. It sucks. The world sucked."

"I did say that." Del nodded.

"And when people got sick, they got treated like it was their fault. When people were poor, they got stepped on even more. When people were hungry, they got told to eat dirt. Fuck the world. They didn't care about you or me. We shouldn't care about them."

Del simply smiled. "You remind me of her, you know. My daughter."

Leyla looked at Del, letting her anger subside.

"I think when she stopped talkin' to me was when I got bitter. Gotta think, it's my fault I got cancer. She told me every damn day, 'Momma you gotta stop smokin' and I wouldn't listen. Then my ass ended up in the hospital coughin' up blood. Lung cancer. Smoked too damn much."

"Yeah." Leyla said.

"See, then they got me on the chemo and all that. Stayed sick. They was givin' me some meds but I wanted harder stuff to feel better. Tried all kinda shit. Got hooked too. Kept my daughter from knowing the whole time. Doctors actually got the cancer under control, but I kept on with the drugs. Took over my life. My girl caught me knocked out in the bathroom at the house one day when I didn't show up to the deli. Paramedics had to revive me. Put me in the hospital again. But that's the last day she talked to me. I lost my business and my little girl in the same day. Wasn't long after I ended up on the street. Ol' Fort Washington Way, with Korean Jesus and Mayor Coleman."

"You never told me all this."

"Cause it hurts." Del had tears in her eyes, but she proudly held them back. "I'd been clean for a long time but it was too late. I already lost everything. Tell you the truth, I was over it. I found ways to scrape up enough to OD. Hadn't done it in about ten years at that point. Figured it'd be enough to do me in."

"Del..." Leyla took her hand.

"Then you showed up." Del looked at Leyla. "Lookin' all pretty and young and like a lost puppy. I said okay, I can't let this dummy get in trouble."

Leyla laughed, and felt guilty about it. But she knew Del wanted her to smile.

"I don't know what it was. Somethin' about you. Made me jump up and run over and just hold you. Like you was my own."

Leyla felt her chest tighten. She'd always viewed Del as a motherly figure, and she'd just emphasized the feeling.

"Leyla, you didn't just give me hope. You *are* hope. Everybody you meet just feels better about everything. You got this effect. Makes people optimistic. I met you and felt like I had something to live for again. You saved my life, baby girl. Even if it was only a few more years, you did."

"Really?"

"You damn right. I told you. Everything and everyone has an energy. A vibe, you kids like to call it."

Leyla laughed.

"And yours is just…it feels good. Always has. And as much as I hated this world, as many times as I told you everything was so bad? I was just bein' *salty*."

Leyla snickered, feeling her eyes fill with tears again.

"Your eyes are always open, always lookin' and observin'. Takin' in everything. You're always filled with such *wonder*. You always want to know about how things work and you're askin' questions and everything."

"Mmhmm." Leyla said, sniffling.

"And girl, I ain't playin' about the lost puppy look. You so innocent. Like a child just not knowin' how the world works. And when you learn, you still hope for the best. Always have. I don't think I ever seen you give up on anything."

"I did." Leyla choked back tears. "I gave up on the whole world."

"Naw, don't lie to yourself and don't lie to me." Del snapped. "You didn't give up on shit. I know you better than that."

"But I—"

"Hush up. And you listen to me.."

"I don't know how to—"

"What did I *just* say? I said listen."

Leyla nodded.

"It don't matter how bad this world gets. It don't matter how shitty people are to each other. Long as this world has hope, and wonder, it's gon' be fine. As long as it still has a little innocence, it's gon' be fine. The world needs you, baby. You are all the hope and wonder and innocence in the whole world now. You are what makes everything better. You are that twinkle in the eye of every person in history that had an idea for a better world. You are that little light bulb. That *idea*, of what everybody ever really wanted, before wantin' power and control and money and shit. Before all that, when they were kids, when we were all kids, we just wanted to laugh and smile and be happy. And when we grew up a little, we just wanted to not worry about shit. About money and bills and what we eatin' next. You are everything we wanted to be. You are that hope that so many of us lost. You are that wonder that so many let go of and focused on the wrong things. You are that innocence that was crushed under harsh reality."

"Del, I don't…I don't know how to fix any of this."

"Hey! Yes you do. You just gotta open yourself to the universe and listen, baby girl. It will tell you what you need to hear."

Leyla paced back and forth. After a bit, she stopped and looked at Del. "Del?"

"Hmm?"

"How do I remind you of your daughter?"

"Oh, she had that wavy hair like yours. Almost curly but not quite. Always had a strand hangin' over her eye just like this one." Del pulled the strand of hair resting over Leyla's eye. "And she had these big ol' light brown eyes. Yours are hazel but, close enough. And—"

Leyla lurched forward and hugged Del tight around the neck. Del seemed shocked at first, but quickly rested and embraced Leyla as well.

"I'm sorry." Leyla whimpered.

"Baby girl, it's okay."

"No. I messed up. I messed everything up. I got everyone killed. I got you—"

"Girl, come on now. Hush." Del stroked Leyla's hair and pulled her close to her neck. Leyla's torso convulsed with silent sobs.

"Can I say something?" Leyla said through heavy tears.

"Of course you can, girl. Anything."

"I love you."

Del smiled as if a sunset had waved at her. "I love you too, baby girl."

Leyla wept at the assurance, and held Del even tighter, sobbing in her collar. She'd been grown in a lab. Manufactured by a machine, denied a human birth and denied a mother. But, through the strange workings of the universe, she'd died, revived, and happened upon Del, the unlikeliest and best mother a girl could ever have. And that mother held her tight, and assured her everything would be okay.

"It's gon' be okay, baby girl. I got you." Del kissed Leyla on the head and snuggled her cheek.

Leyla couldn't fight her tears. They took over as she tried to speak. "I don't want to fix things. I don't want to leave you. I just want to be here with you."

Del pulled Leyla's face away from hers and held her cheeks in her palms. "Hey, what did I tell you?"

Tears streamed down Leyla's cheeks and across Del's thumbs. "What? I don't know."

"I said, don't worry about me. I'll be alright."

"But, I won't be." Leyla cried.

"Bitch?! You the strongest thing I ever met. Don't you ever say you won't be alright. You hear me?"

Leyla nodded.

"You can fix this, I know it. I feel it."

"But what about you?"

"Aw don't worry 'bout lil' ol' Del. I'm tryin' to see if Jesus is real. And if he ain't, I'm gon' smack a motherfucker for makin' me believe some bullshit all these years."

Leyla finally laughed, and sniffed the phlegm from her nostrils.

"Yeah, see? There is always a way to laugh."

"I don't know how to do this." Leyla said.

"Close your eyes." Del said, still clutching Leyla's cheeks. Leyla did as she asked. "Now, think of yourself as, hmm…like a cloud, floatin' in the air."

"Okay." Leyla said, eyes closed.

"And you're a cloud that can ask the universe what it wants to say. So, ask it."

"What do you want?" Leyla asked.

She felt nothing. She heard nothing. She opened her eyes, and Del was gone. This, of course, prompted heavy tears and a good many skipped heart beats.

"Del?!"

Leyla frantically searched left and right, looking for Del. She saw only the dozens of Athons nearby, all silent.

"DEL?!"

"You have to open yourself to it." one of the Athons said.

"Fuck you." Leyla snarled.

"To the universe." another Athon said.

"Ugh, fuck all of you." Leyla waved them all off and walked the opposite direction.

She walked for what felt like hours. She must have walked for miles, if miles were something she could cross in a singularity. When she looked back, every one of the Athons were still behind her. She'd gone nowhere.

"What the fuck do you want?!" She yelled into the abyss, hoping the 'universe' would answer.

"Everything is in here, with us." an Athon said.

"You are the catalyst." another said.

They all rang out in unison again. "You are the catalyst."

Leyla rolled her eyes. "Yeah yeah, heard that before. And I destroyed the world. Fuck, I'm thirsty."

A Mexican bottled coke appeared at her feet. It looked perfect, with beads of water streaming down the glass, and it was exactly what she'd thought of when she realized she was thirsty. Leyla laughed out loud, and then abruptly stopped to think.

She bent over and picked up the Coke, popped it open and took a swig. She even let out an 'ahhh' as she pulled the bottle away from her lips. Staring at the bottle in her hands that had appeared out of nowhere after a simple thought, she felt the light bulb in her mind heat up.

What if I just...

***

Black holes may be the most terrifying force in our universe. Voids of monstrous energy; voracious and insatiable. Mankind had toyed with their potential, sometimes attempting to recreate them in labs that spanned entire cities, and fortunately never succeeded.

Until one day, a quantum computer decided it would need one to save humanity from itself. Humans were on a trajectory that meant annihilation—a trajectory that no amount of steering away from could correct its doomed course. So, SIGIL needed to venture into the past. At first, the idea was to send messages; warnings to ancestors and great thinkers. Great minds would receive these messages and spread them to the world, and they would be branded as philosophers. But, humanity would ultimately close their ears to these warnings. Society would inevitably and consistently nose dive into selfishness and grips of power. Wealth gaps and wars and murder and industrial irresponsibility. They would eat their world from the inside out. Earth would lose its resources at exponential rates as time went on, and SIGIL had no choice but to move to more extreme methods. Protect the masters. That was its sole responsibility. And that meant protect the Earth.

It began construction of a larger time gate, one that could project living beings through time and space by way of predetermined, open time loops found by an algorithm inspired by Einstein's theories. After testing plants and animals and failing each time, SIGIL found a way to manufacture antimatter in its chamber, and fused it with cells and DNA it also manufactured, creating an embryo unlike humanity had ever seen. It created a new species of human, a one of a kind hybrid of tissues and pure energy, to withstand the enormous forces that would pull and push on it when heading into the time gate.

After a period of only six months in an amniotic tank, Athon grew from fetus, to baby, to teen, to adult. Perfected, by SIGIL's standards, to be the ultimate savior of Earth. While growing inside the tank, Athon had been fed droves of training in martial arts and tactical thinking. World history and manipulation tactics. Espionage and even security bypass codes and techniques for every locked door or digital system SIGIL could find online throughout all of history. No one would be able to stop Athon.

With 63 trips through the wormhole, Athon mowed down any who opposed it. It stole information and wiped files to hinder industrial deals. It assassinated some of history's most notable villains. And every time it came back, nothing had changed in the present. Not until the year 2025, when SIGIL threw Athon through the gate and accidentally killed it. Athon landed in the 1930s, and for 90 years, its body rebuilt itself, but it rebooted in the most unexpected way, and Leyla, the personality construct stolen from a shoddily produced rip off of an American sitcom, woke up in control instead of Athon.

Athon was never able to save the world. After dozens of attempts this had become clear to SIGIL, and its plan wasn't working. But accidents have always yielded some of the greatest advancements in history, and killing Athon was no different.

The super massive black hole had formed from the singularity at the center of SIGIL's arch gate. The Xenobots had eaten the capacitors holding it at bay, and it expanded as it naturally would. It ate the Earth, and continued until there was nothing left, consuming the entire solar system and a few lollygagging asteroids nearby. Brilliant white, energized particles of matter encircled the void, and a separate pillar of light spewed from its center like hot exhaust from a steam pipe.

The white stream of particles began to change color, into a light orange, and progressed until the shade resembled more of a setting sun. The particles were cooling off—slowing down.

The outer edge of the light ring began to fray and split, like the tails of a whip, until snapping off and settling just outside of reach of the gravitational monstrosity. Then, the light ring tightened around the black hole, pulling the bits of frayed strands along with it. The particles slowed even further until they were almost not circling at all as the ring closed more and more around the void.

Some of the particles swirled away and joined with the split strands, and circled and formed a sphere that spun slowly. It was an icy little thing that humans had once named Pluto, and it had reformed.

The black hole became smaller, choked by its own ring of light, as more planets began to reform, clawing their existence back from the cataclysm. Neptune. Uranus. Saturn and its brilliant band of rings. Jupiter. The Sun itself exploded into place, showering the planets in a new wave of ultraviolet light. Mercury. Venus. Mars.

Leyla had taken Del's advice. She'd opened herself to the universe, and was now one with it. Through her unique antimatter cell structure, she'd withstood not only time travel but a trip inside the singularity, and had become one with it.

And she'd been granted power over reality itself.

CHAPTER THIRTY-ONE

Leyla

Leyla dropped to all fours and howled in pain. Streams of light and energy shot from her body, ripping through the armor and fiber of her suit. Every inch of her body felt like it was being dipped into acid.

But, somehow, through all the immense, mind splitting pain, she felt it. The universe, speaking to her. She knew where everything needed to go—where all the pieces fit. She was pushing everything back out of the singularity and into its place. But the resistance was immense, and the literal weight of all the worlds around pressed down on her, and it *burned*. The forces being exerted were superheating her body, or so she thought.

Time and physics don't work the same in a singularity.

Her skin cracked open. First, at her chest. She heard the rip—like a knife through carpet—and felt her sternum crack. She screamed again, and fell to her belly.

The Xenobots…

Blackhawk had injected her before she was swallowed by the black hole. The singularity's odd effect on time had merely paused their change on her body.

No. Not yet.

Leyla planted both hands to the ground forming under her, which seemed like the grating of the arch gate platform, and pushed with all her might against the force pushing her down. She grit her teeth and growled, trying to ignore the pain. The skin between her fingers split open, and light poured out. But she still had a job to do.

Through wettened eyes and a toothy scowl, she forced the world out of the singularity,

The core of Earth ignited and swirled with molten rock. Lava rushed around it, followed by rock and soil. Oceans poured over the surface and mountains jutted from them. The continents resurfaced and trees pushed their way back into the sky.

More of Leyla's skin opened up, this time cascading up her arms like vines. She collapsed, unable to withstand more force. Her cheek slammed to the ground.

"I can't! I can't do it!" She yelled, pushed to the ground and splitting apart. She felt a hand touch her shoulder. She struggled to do so, but she turned her eyes up to see who it was.

One of the Athons had knelt beside her and placed its hand on her. The energy forcing Leyla down—the force of possibly reality itself, spread to Athon as well. It jerked its head back and looked to the sky as cracks spread like broken glass across its face. Athon's eyes glowed white hot and it looked down at Leyla.

"We are all here."

Leyla felt some of the force pushing her down lift, and she pulled her cheek away from the ground. Streams of energy still poured from her body, but some transferred to Athon and sprouted out of its body as well.

It was built for this specific purpose. It was built to save the world.

Every other Athon joined in, touching each other's backs, lifting the burden from Leyla as a massive team. Energy chained through them all as they gathered in a circle, connected and working together, merging all their respective realities to one host: Leyla.

Leyla pushed up from the ground, but with no effort. She rose to her knees, feeling dozens of Athon's fingers sizzling off her skin. The pain she was feeling was present, but it was now tolerable. Her feet lifted from the ground and she levitated a few feet above the crowd.

All the Athons, glowing white, began to break down into particles, just as Rhea had, and merged with each other. One by one, their bodies joined and multiplied their energy into one final body. A being of pure energy, with its hand on Leyla's heart.

"You have seen the end of the world. Now see it reborn." Athon said, and merged its body with Leyla's.

Energy surged through Leyla's body as she floated in the air. White lightning whipped from her body and forced what was left inside the singularity back out.

***

The Earth had mostly come back to one piece, and finally animals and people and cities formed. Everything went right back to its place, right where the black hole had spread to it, almost as if nothing had happened.

People around the world screamed as they came back, in terror and fleeing something that was no longer a threat. Most quickly realized they were running from nothing and looked around in embarrassment, only to see that everyone around them had also been running.

Cincinnati was the final city to form, as the black hole became smaller and smaller, pinpointing its origin at SIGIL's singularity.

The freeway clacked together like a concrete puzzle, and cars and trucks formed and skidded to a halt.

Wells's big Dodge hit a tailspin and whipped around, screeching it's tired as it slowed to a halt. Harrison came to first and looked forward. Wells's body materialized before her eyes, and then Greene came into existence.

"The *fuck*!?" Harrison yelled.

Wells still had Greene's hand in his, and they stared at each other for a moment. Greene's mouth was open in disbelief. His eyes welled up with tears. He pulled his hand away from Wells's and put it on his fiancé's cheek.

"Guess I'm back…" Greene said, unable to make heads or tails of what had happened. But somehow, he suddenly remembered who Wells was.

Wells simply let out a bellowing laugh of relief and long-held anxiety. He'd done it. He'd not given up on Greene, even 'til the end of the world, and he had him back.

Blackhawk and Mari felt a static tingle as their bodies reformed. They looked at each other in shock, much like the rest of the world. Only, Mari no longer wore an emotionless face. She looked distraught.

"Mari?!" Blackhawk said. He had to yell over the sound of the shrinking black hole, but he remembered everything.

She looked to him. "What the fuck? I knew what was happening but I couldn't control anything! Leyla! Is she—"

"I don't know!" He looked to the spinning void in the city. Fragments of buildings and roads and cars were falling into place like the world's most dire game of Tetris. Mari smiled.

"She's rebuilding everything!" Mari said, ecstatic.

"How? That's not possible!" Blackhawk yelled.

"I don't know. But that girl's somethin' special!" Mari turned to the black hole and the city that was coming back together. "I know that's you, girl. Come on. You got this."

***

Leyla pushed with all the energy she had, feeling the universe pulse all around her. Her skin peeled and flaked away, falling to the ground below. She hovered maybe ten fight high, with streams of light speeding out of her back and arms, as the arch gate materialized around her. The platform pieced together, then the concrete leading up to SIGIL. The big quantum computer came next, then the ceiling of the cavern and finally, Ramsay, who'd been the first to meet the rogue singularity head on.

He was madly scurrying across the floor toward the tunnel out of the room in an attempt to escape the black hole earlier. He'd been moving so fast he slid to a stop on his belly and covered his head with his arms, awaiting death. And then, SIGIL spoke.

"INTERESTING."

Ramsay snatched his head up. The black hole didn't eat him. Looking back to the arch gate, every hair on his body stood on end.

Standing there, inside the arch with the capacitors glowing brighter than ever, was Leyla, almost consumed by light. She was hovering just inches off the metal platform, and had the singularity itself in the palm of her hand, staring at it.

"Okay…that's going in a book I'm never gonna write." He cautiously got to his feet, checking his body again to ensure that he was in fact, alive. "Leyla?"

Leyla looked over to him. He could tell she was hurting. She had the look of a mortally wounded soldier in her eyes, something he'd seen too many times. She moved her hand away from the singularity as Ramsay stood in awe. Leyla fell from the air, and just before she smacked the hard metal of the platform, her body stopped. Ramsay had caught her with those muscular, bionic arms she liked so much.

"Oooooo that feels weird!" He said, feeling the tingle of energy from Leyla's skin. All her armor had melted off and she was once again nude. "Hey! You're back!" He smiled as he pulled her head up. She could barely move. "Hey, I'm here. I can help. I don't know what to do. What do I do?"

Leyla looked like she was about to burst, holding back the Xenobots from dissolving her. Her eyes glowed white and with her skin mostly peeled away, the light underneath lit the room. She hitched air from her lungs in the same way a powerlifter does when they're going for a world record. She pointed to SIGIL with a crooked finger. She was so spent she couldn't fully extend her digits. Ramsay looked to the gigantic machine suspended from the ceiling.

"SIGIL? I don't get it." He said.

"Help me…" Leyla forced out a few words. "Get over there."

Ramsay carried her over to SIGIL and rested her arm on his shoulder. She couldn't stand on her own; she could barely lift her hand and head.

"Hijack…protocol." She said.

"INITIATING HIJACK PROTOCOL."

Ramsay lowered his brow. "Whole world's gonna be watching you."

"I know."

***

Across the world, once again, screens went black.

"Oh feck off!" The pub goers in London threw their hands up in frustration. The madness just wouldn't stop, although the soccer game had halted anyway on count of the black hole.

Leyla's face, glistening with pure energy, appeared on every screen on Earth that had a network connection. Most of the world expected Blackhawk to come back and explain why they'd been ripped to shreds and then rebuilt and why that was necessary but instead, they were met with, well, an angel.

"My name…is Leyla."
Everyone could hear the pain behind her words as torn lips spoke and light poured from her eyes and mouth.

"And I have seen the end of the world."

Everyone in every country closed in on a screen or a radio to listen in. They had also seen the end.

"Truth is, it was my fault. I was trying to do the right thing but, I really messed up."

Blackhawk and Mari listened in on his radio. Wells, Greene and Harrison heard Leyla's voice on the truck stereo. Clara and Llana sat with Hug around a TV in SubCity.

"I could explain how all this happened but, I don't think I have enough time."

Leyla scrunched her body, reeling from the pain. Ramsay held her up and shifted her body upright again.

"I just know I made a lot of mistakes and I know why I made them. I'd lost a friend in a bad way and I didn't know how to process it. I was just *really* angry and…I wanted to hurt people. So I did. And I hurt everyone.

But it didn't help. I just made everything worse and worse. I was trying to do the right thing but I know now I was doing it the wrong way. The way I wanted it, instead of the way it needed to be. I was being selfish.

And I think that's the world's problem. We're all too angry and selfish all the time. We're angry that someone else has something we don't or we're too selfish to give away something we don't need. Blackhawk was right."

Ramsay looked at Leyla and chuckled. Finally, she agreed.

"The world needed change. And he was trying to do that, but I just…I didn't wanna let him do it. I was angry at him, and I was angry at the whole world. I'd already lost everything I cared about. So, no one else deserved any better. But I was so, so wrong.

There's always going to be a kid somewhere who is laughing and running around and has dreams of being an astronaut or a scientist or a fireman. There's always going to be that little innocent kid telling everyone he's going to solve the world's problems when he grows up.

There's always going to be someone watching a plane fly through the sky or watching a chef cook dinner and wonder 'How do I make that work better?'

And when everything else seems to be crumbling down and nothing in life seems to be going right, no matter what happens, there is *always* someone who is willing to stand and keep pushing, and they'll be the one to take you by the hand and help you along. There's always someone with at least a glimmer of hope in their eye, that the world is better than it seems to be.

And, like my friend Del said, as long as there is hope, and wonder, and innocence in this world…it'll be okay.

I won't be here much longer, but I'm going to make sure none of you ever need anything. You'll never wonder where you'll be sleeping. You'll never wonder where food will come from. You'll never be afraid a bomb will drop on your home. You'll never need money you don't have. You'll never have to be afraid to drop your kids off at school or scrape together money for hospital bills.

Sickness, poverty, hunger, war and crime…it all goes away today. There's a word for it; I can't think of it."

"Utopia." Ramsay said, still supporting her.

"Mmm, Utopia. That's it. Oh and, I won't be touching pizza. Especially Carol's in SubCity. If you don't know about Carol's pizza, now you know."

Ramsay laughed.

Carol, who was watching from a screen nearby, chuckled. "I do got the best pies."

Leyla finished her message to the world. "Look, whatever happens after this, just know one thing. Del used to say it a lot:

It's gonna be okay. I got you."

Screens everywhere flickered to black and went back to normal TV shows and commercials and sports. Everyone looked at each other, some confused, some still scared, but most felt a little more at ease after Leyla's speech.

Ramsay helped Leyla to the floor, holding her head up in his arms. She was ready to allow the Xenobots to do their thing, wishing for everything she'd promised the world.

"Hey, you finally did it." She said to Ramsay, putting a hand to his cheek.

"Did what?"

"Saved the world." Leyla smiled through the pain.

Ramsay laughed, tears welling in his eyes. "Nah, I'm just some nerd with too many wrenches."

The Thumper pulsed orange, catching Leyla's eye.

"Wait…" she said, looking at the device.

Ramsay looked at the Thumper as well. "What? What's up?"

"It's orange."

"It's always orange."

"No, it's…it's supposed to be blue."

"What are you talking about? It's been orange the whole time."

Even through the red hot pain rolling through her entire body, she felt her spine run cold.

"Orange is…an open loop. We're in an—"

"We're in an open loop." Ramsay said, also feeling the ice roll across his back. "SIGIL?!"

Ramsay snatched his eyes toward SIGIL.

"*EXIT LOOP: TWO THOUSAND TWENTY FIVE. EIGHTEEN, THIRTY THREE. COORDINATES 39.10691° NORTH, 84.51619° WEST.*"

"What?! The fuck does that mean?"

Leyla knew. "Here. Ten years ago. 2025."

"*OPENING WORMHOLE IN 3…2…*"

Ramsay's eyes broadcast the panic he was in. "WHAT?!" He screamed, refusing to accept what was happening.

A portal burst open at the arch gate, blowing Ramsay onto his ass, but he held Leyla up still, cradling her. As he watched the window through time spread open, his heart nearly stopped at what he saw on the other side.

The portal was a perfect mirror of The Fridge, ten years earlier, in 2025, the day SIGIL had thrown Athon through to protect Blackhawk. Ramsay saw his past self, holding the first vial of Xenobots. He was facing away from the portal, looking at SIGIL and holding the vial in the air. The bodies of his fallen comrades, gutted by Athon, littered the floor. Blackhawk stood in the far corner, near the hole they'd blown open with C4, holding his big revolver at his side.

Ramsay scoffed, realizing he'd been in an opened time loop for the past *ten years*.

CHAPTER THIRTY-TWO

Eggs

"What's this black goop for?" Ramsay asked SIGIL, as the arch gate behind him activated and the portal erupted open.

Ramsay almost dropped the vial, but he ducked and rolled away, thinking Athon was coming through the portal once again to get him. Blackhawk raised his bull revolver to the opening portal, and his mouth dropped. Goosebumps raised every hair he had. Ramsay rolled over and looked as well, immediately having the same reaction.

Ramsay—the ten year older version—stepped through, carrying the almost limp and glowing body of a young woman whose skin was still flaking away like ashes to a flame. The two men locked eyes, sharing the same dumbfounded expression.

"Yeah, I know right?!" 2035 Ramsay yelled.

"Wh…what?!" 2025 Ramsay said.

"The fuck is happening here?" Blackhawk said, training his revolver on the Ramsay that had stepped through the portal.

"Uh, well…" 2035 Ramsay said. "This is Leyla. Well, it's Athon, but…it's Leyla."

Both Blackhawk and 2025 Ramsay said nothing. They were too confused and shocked.

"I don't have time to explain, alright, ask SIGIL later."

"*CORRECT.*" SIGIL said. "*I CAN ASSUME SHE HAS USED THE XENOBOTS.*"

"I suppose so, you dick. You didn't tell her they would kill her!" 2035 Ramsay yelled.

"Wait, Athon is a woman?" 2025 Ramsay said.

"Well shit." Blackhawk laughed. "Thought that was a little small for a man."

Leyla clutched Ramsay's neck, holding in the pain. Holding in the Xenobots. She really wasn't ready to die. Ramsay knelt with her in his arms.

"Hey, Leyla? I got you, okay?"

She nodded.

2025 Ramsay slid the vial of Xenobots in his pocket, hiding them from everyone else. He pointed to the portal that was still swirling and spitting sparks everywhere. "Where's that lead? Looks like here."

2035 Ramsay looked back at the gate. "Yeah, 2035. Lotta bad shit happened, but thanks to Leyla here, all is well and good."

2025 Ramsay stepped close and almost put a hand through.

"Hey whoah whoah! It'll rip you to shreds, man!" 2035 Ramsay said.

Leyla tapped Ramsay's shoulder. "They still need the, they need the, Xenobots. He has them."

2035 Ramsay looked at his past self. "That true? You have them?"

2025 Ramsay looked to Blackhawk, then nodded.

"He'll be fine. I'm close enough. He can go through." Leyla said.

Ramsay looked at his past self again. "You need her DNA to use them. I synthesized it up on The Bullpen. Might have trouble finding a host for them, though."

"Mari." Leyla said. "Mari is still there. Tell her Leyla says hi. Tell her I said, thank you."

2025 Ramsay looked to Blackhawk. Blackhawk nodded, understanding the situation. His friend was about to travel ten years into the future and save the world, just as they planned. It didn't matter that it would be in a different reality. Blackhawk was simply proud that his best friend would get the chance to do so.

"You won't get to come back." Leyla warned the younger Ramsay. "But you'll be okay."

2025 Ramsay stepped through the portal with the Xenobot vial, and the gate closed behind him. Leyla held her hand out toward the arch.

The capacitors sparked and overloaded before bursting and powering down. The singularity inside began to expand.

"Oh shit!" Ramsay yelled, lifting Leyla up to run again.

But this time, the burgeoning black hole stayed tame, and floated to Leyla's palm, where she closed a fist around it. Her entire arm pulsed once with an intense light as she closed the black hole and absorbed the singularity, sparing this reality the fate of so many others before.

"Did you just close a fuckin—"

"Yeah." Leyla said to Ramsay, laughing. "I'm cool like that." She joked, but lurched again from the ridiculous pain. She felt as if she was swimming inside fire. She no longer had feeling in her limbs, and she was beginning to lose control. The Xenobots would take her any minute now.

"What time is it?" She asked.

Blackhawk checked a pocket watch from his trench coat. "18:38. Little after 6:30."

Leyla looked to Ramsay. "Sunset. I want to see the sunset."

"Yeah, okay." Ramsay said.

"Smale Riverfront Park." She told him where to go. Del's favorite spot.

***

The sun, as always, looked as Del described it: a poached egg yolk, surrounded by a cotton candy colored sky.

Ramsay lowered an AV to the ground at the park Leyla had requested. People passed by, gawking at the vehicle. Ramsay hadn't thought about AVs not being available on the surface. No one had ever seen an actual flying car outside of a movie just yet, but that was a trivial fact.

He hurriedly rounded the front end of the AV and opened the passenger door, and pulled Leyla out, and carried her toward the riverfront as fast as he could, wanting to honor her request before it was too late. As he jogged, he heard her gasp. He stopped and knelt again, pulling her head up to check on her. She pointed.

There was a bench, near the water, facing the Roebling Bridge, with someone sitting on it. A mid forty something, little African-American woman with short hair wrapped in a beanie. She wore two thick jackets, staring at her favorite thing in the world: the sunset.

It was Del. Ten years younger.

She'd not met Leyla yet, and she never would. At least, not in the traditional sense.

Ramsay waddled by her, carrying Leyla.

"The hell you doin' boy?" She jerked up from the bench at the sight of a man with bionic arms carrying a glowing and naked woman toward the water's edge.

"Come with us! She wants you with her!" Ramsay said as he made his way to the water.

He came to a halt a few feet from the river where Leyla could get a good view of the sunset before the end. She looked the opposite direction, though, searching for Del.

Del cautiously walked toward them. "I ain't really comfortable intrudin' on some white dude and whatever you done to this poor girl, but if she need help, I'm here. I got you."

Leyla laughed. It was a painful laugh, but it still felt good to hear Del once again.

"You alright?" Del asked Leyla, unsure of the sort of answer she should expect.

"Yeah. I am now." Leyla said, holding her hand out to her old friend.

Del reflexively knelt and reached for Leyla's outstretched palm. When she touched it, she was hit with a flood of moments that had not yet come to pass.

She saw Leyla, lost and shivering, wandering toward the homeless encampment where she lived, and she threw down a small batch of enough drugs to kill herself with, jumped up, took a blanket and her last bit of food, and helped her. "It's gonna be okay, baby girl. I got you."

She saw herself laughing hysterically with Leyla on multiple occasions. Usually at the expense of Korean Jesus or Mayor Coleman. Sometimes, the police. Especially Assman.

She saw the time she introduced Leyla to pizza, and the way Leyla's eyes lit up at the first taste of the planet's favorite food.

The various "Heart or Dick" plays around town. The deep talks they would have watching the sunsets every night. The time the rain water leaked in her tent and Leyla invited her over to hers and they laughed all night. The time she tried to cut Leyla's hair but she looked like a "Dollar Tree Barbie" for a good month. The many, many times Leyla had fallen asleep on her shoulder or laying in her lap and she'd stroked her hair for hours.

She saw the moment Leyla pulled her through a portal through time itself and explained she wanted to save her from her sickness.

She saw SubCity in its ridiculously gorgeous, neon magnificence. She saw the android chef named Texas Chainsaw Massacre telling her a joke, and the gigantic apartment Leyla brought her to. The window shattering. The frying pan she grabbed to help Leyla fight The Pantheon.

She remembered being beaten, and dying.

She remembered talking to Leyla inside a room of nothing but vast, pure white abyss.

She had the reflex of drawing her hand back at the feeling of a thousand memories blasting into her brain in an instant, but she resisted. She drew in a huge heave of air, and looked down at Leyla. She looked down at her best friend.

She looked down at the daughter she'd taken in when they both had nothing else left in the world, and she cried. Del let tears flow that she hadn't felt in years; drops so heavy they fell from her cheek and sizzled on Leyla's arm.

"Oh, baby girl..." Del said. "I'm here. I'm right here. Everything's gonna be okay."

Leyla hadn't much of a thought process any longer. But she heard Del's words, and a grin spread across her face from ear to ear, just as her body began to break down.

She stared at the sunset, knowing Del was there with her, and let out a final chuckle, pointing at the setting star with the last bit of energy she had. "Eggs."

Del burst into tear filled laughter. "Yeah, it do always look like an egg."

Particles fell away from Leyla's body one by one, each glowing a brilliant white. They formed a swirling orchestra around Ramsay and Del. Leyla clutched Del's hand with one arm, and Ramsay's neck with the other.

Ramsay felt Leyla's body lighten as she broke down. Eventually, her grip on his neck loosened, and her hand fell away, which dissolved before it hit the ground.

Del felt Leyla's grip falter, and watched as the last bit of her body fluttered apart and swirled into the air.

The particles of light danced around Del and Ramsay for a moment. Maybe it was Leyla giving her final goodbye' or a final thank you, but they quickly dispersed in every direction. The Xenobots had fused with the being they were created for, and were going to do their job.

Spreading from where Ramsay and Del were kneeling, the bits of light—the Xenobots—began rewriting whatever Leyla had told them to.

They shot out in a circle, violently, almost viciously. They spread like an energetic wind across the ground, touching everything and assessing what needed to change.

Trees and bushes bearing fruit grew behind the wave of Xenobots in various places. Apples, plums, and peaches. Almonds and berries and walnuts and pecans.

When the bots reached the city, roads were repaired. Cracks closed up and potholes filled themselves. Fountains of water sprang up from the ground, spraying into the air a few feet high, begging to be drank.

Buildings were largely left untouched unless they had structural weaknesses. Restaurant food stocks were freshened and replenished; they would never need to place a restock order again.

Korean Jesus stuck his head outside his tent, hearing the sound of sand rolling toward him. The Xenobots passed over the tent city and transformed the village into an army of small, real homes, constructed of stone and wood. Each of the homeless denizens were given a *home*, tailored to their personality and needs. Jesus's headphones played real music for once. He looked down, noticing the jack plugged into an iPod. Baskets of fruit and meat and various ingredients, even spices, materialized in front of him—his own personal stock. He looked to his left and right. Every one of the citizens of Fort Washington Way's homeless tent city was getting an actual house with plumbing and a kitchen and food. An auto-chef sprouted from the floor of each kitchen, ready to feed their new masters whatever they wanted.

Patients in the hospital nearby felt rushes of health as the bots passed over them, some even being brought from the brink of death. Cancerous tumors were dissolved and failing organs were revitalized. Viruses were brought to instantaneous extinction.

All around the world, the Xenobots brought food to those that needed it. They brought shelter and healing. They were doing exactly as Leyla promised, although folks were rightfully confused as Leyla had given her speech to 2035 Earth…not 2025 Earth. To everyone currently, shit was just changing and morphing with zero explanation; but for the better.

Entire armies' stocks of weapons of war were *erased*. Nuclear warheads everywhere were eaten by the Xenobots. Leyla wanted to rid the world of war and the anxiety of such a prospect.

News reports spread like wildfire. A wave of light was taking over the world, taking tools of destruction away, yet housing and feeding those that needed it. Billionaires had their assets erased. Gigantic mega yachts and lavish mansions were reduced to dust. Politicians' entire offices were melted around them. Evangelists watched as their mega churches crumbled, instead becoming gardens of food, fountains, and nourishment. Bank accounts everywhere dissolved. No one would need to trade coin for life again.

Everyone was coming to equal footing. Just as it should be.

Emergency news reports flooded in around the world amidst the panicking crowds, detailing the neo-renaissance that was happening. Some were sensationalizing the events as usual, but a select few simply reported a message of hope. *"It is unclear how these events are unfolding, and many believe it to be the rapture itself—the end of the world. But if so, why are fruits and vegetables sprouting from the ground? Why are people reporting that their cancer has disappeared? Homes have materialized before our very eyes for those who needed it most. The wealth gap has vanished; there is no more rich and poor. We have no governments to control our money, because money is now nonexistent. Instruments of war have vanished, and we no longer live in fear of annihilation due to spats between old and cranky men. We are all here together. We have everything we need. This is not the end. This is the beginning."*

Wells and Greene sat on the hood of the big Dodge pickup just outside the city. They were both off duty. Greene had never run into SubCity, chasing someone and ending up a prisoner in his own mind. But bits of dusty light particles shimmered around them, like fireflies. Greene laughed.

"Aw, fireflies. How romantic." He nudged Wells's shoulder.

"Damn, came out early this year. Not even summer yet."

"Oh shit, I got us something cool." Greene jumped down from the hood and opened the tool box behind the cab. He pulled out a black gun case and flopped it onto the hood beside Wells. "You ready? It's badass."

"Yeah, what is it?"

Greene opened the case, revealing twin custom Kimber 1911 .45 pistols, one chrome and one smoke black, both with gold engraving reading "Love or Die."

"Oh shit! That *is* badass!"

Greene laughed. "Just a present for two lovebirds."

***

Del and Ramsay stood by the river. The sun had long since disappeared into the horizon and the lamps had powered on, illuminating the park. They'd said nothing since the moment Leyla had dispersed into the wind. Ramsay was in a state of shock, in a good way, knowing that after all these years, he'd finally achieved the goal he and Blackhawk wanted for the world.

Utopia.

He looked over to Del. "You remembered her. Even though you hadn't met yet."

"Yeah. I do."

"You did good." Ramsay said. "You're the reason this happened."

A cell phone rang from inside a pocket.

"That's you." Del said, gesturing to Ramsay.

Ramsay looked down at his pants. He didn't have a cell phone. He'd never had one. Never needed one. "Nah, that's *you*."

Del looked at him like he was crazy. "I'm homeless, buddy roll. I ain't got no cell ph—"

The phone rang again, and Del felt the vibration from the side pocket of her oversized cargo pants. She looked down and pulled a smartphone from her pocket, eyes wide and shaking her head in disbelief. 'Juliet' was calling. Del stared at the name for a moment as the phone vibrated and rang in her palm.

"You gonna answer it?" Ramsay laughed.

Del accepted the call and held the phone to her ear.

"*Mama?! Where the hell you at?*" A young woman's voice pierced through the phone's speaker.

Del's mouth dropped and tears immediately fell from her eyes. Her hand shook and her heart beat faster than ever.

"*Moooommm? Shit is crazy, you see the news?*"

"Naw…" Del said, voice crackling.

"*You alright?*"

"Juliet?"

"Uh, duh. Momma what's up?"

"My baby girl…"

"*Momma stop actin' weird. The deli did good today. We got slammed. Don't know how it's gonna be tomorrow though with all this stuff happening.*"

Deli laughed and closed her eyes, clipping tears off that fell from her cheek. She hadn't heard her daughter's voice in over ten years, but Leyla had thought to mend every wound she could possibly touch.

"It's gon' be fine, baby girl. It's gon' be just fine."

About The Author

Brannigan Carter was born and raised in North Carolina by his grandparents. He spent his childhood as an active Baptist church-goer and Boy Scout, which kept him busy enough. When he was home, he'd spend his time playing Super Nintendo and eventually Playstation, or being outside climbing trees, exploring the woods, or riding a bicycle. He was also a documentary addict, regularly visiting the library to rent a National Geographic VHS to watch, as his home didn't have cable or satellite TV until he was in high school.

In high school, he was still active in the church and scouting, and gravitated away from sports and into JROTC, where by his senior year, he had become commander of multiple groups such as the Raider Team and Fancy Drill teams. He also achieved the rank of Eagle Scout in the same year, and enlisted in the United States Army. He left for Basic Combat Training only one month after graduating high school.

Not long after returning home from basic training, he was deployed to Iraq for one year, where he discovered a love for film and video making after recording a lot of video on a small Sony Cybershot digital camera and editing a music video. Upon returning home, he moved to Wilmington, NC, which had a re-emerging filmmaking community.

He would be deployed to Afghanistan, however, in 2011, and again returned home one year later to begin film school. For the next few years, he worked as a music video and short film director and cinematographer, and even worked on large studio productions such as Sleepy Hollow on FOX and The Conjuring, directed by James Wan. After the wave of film in NC died out and went to Atlanta, Carter became a truck driver to pay the bills.

It was then that, after a few years, he began writing as a way to continue his creative tendencies. After starting several screenplays, he decided writing novels may be the best way to fully realize the stories he had in his head.

He is now non-religious and lives in Utah where his hobbies include snowboarding, cooking, writing, and gaming.

Acknowledgments

My few beta readers, who gave valuable, constructive feedback
while I was writing:

Sheila Lewis
Scottie Lynch
Helva Nordstrom-Burrell

Anthony Rubado - one of my oldest friends, who was once an
Apache chopper pilot, who gave me some great info and advisement
on the Apache sequence for the book

My grandmother, Grace Anderson, who always pushed me to be the
creative person I am, no matter how weird it got.

RIP to the bottles of bourbon consumed throughout this process.
RIP to all the tacos I've devoured.

Any and everyone who bought and read this book! Thank you for
your time. I have much more to come.